Blood of Briar

E.M. DOWNEY

Spellcast
Books

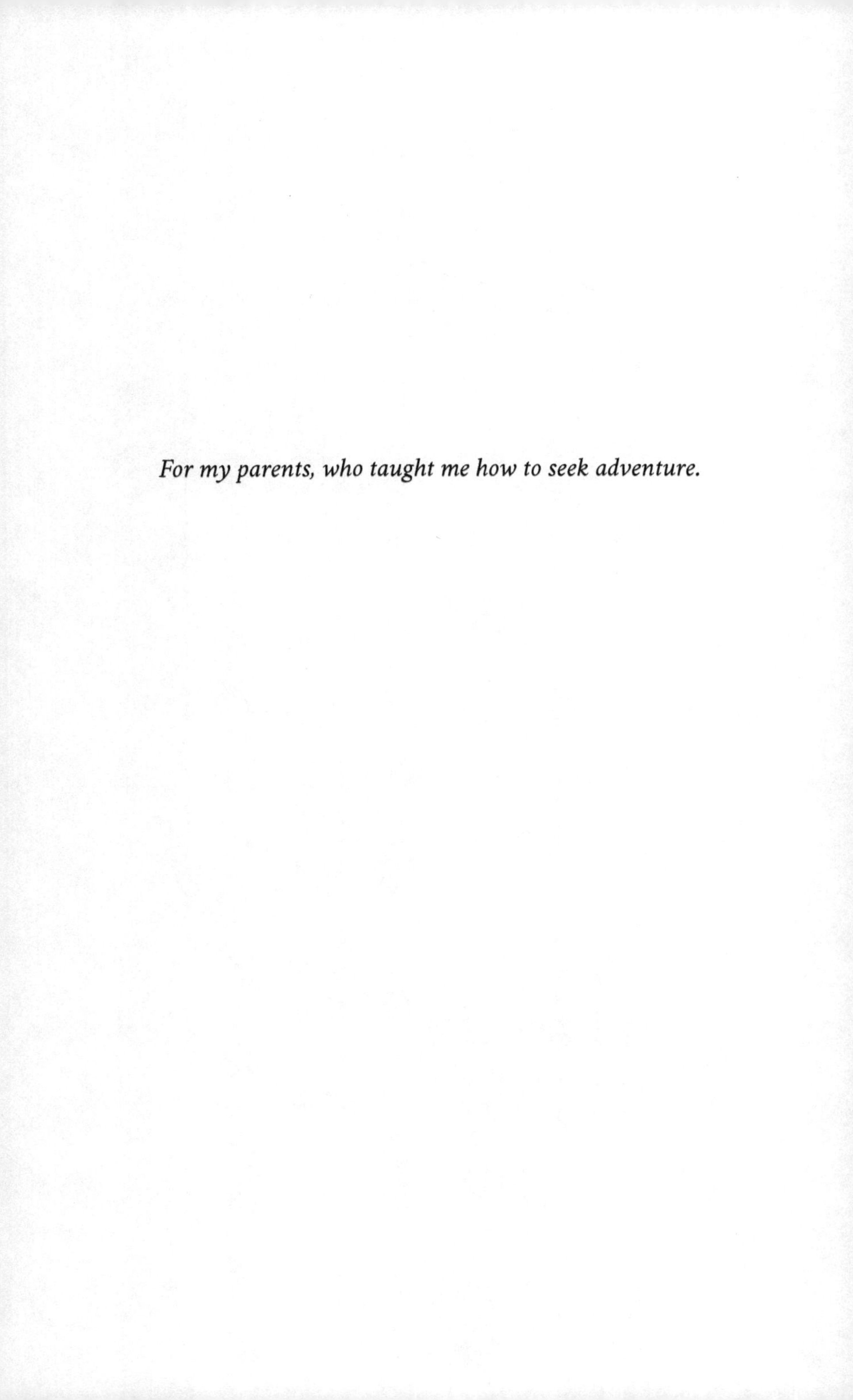

For my parents, who taught me how to seek adventure.

Contents

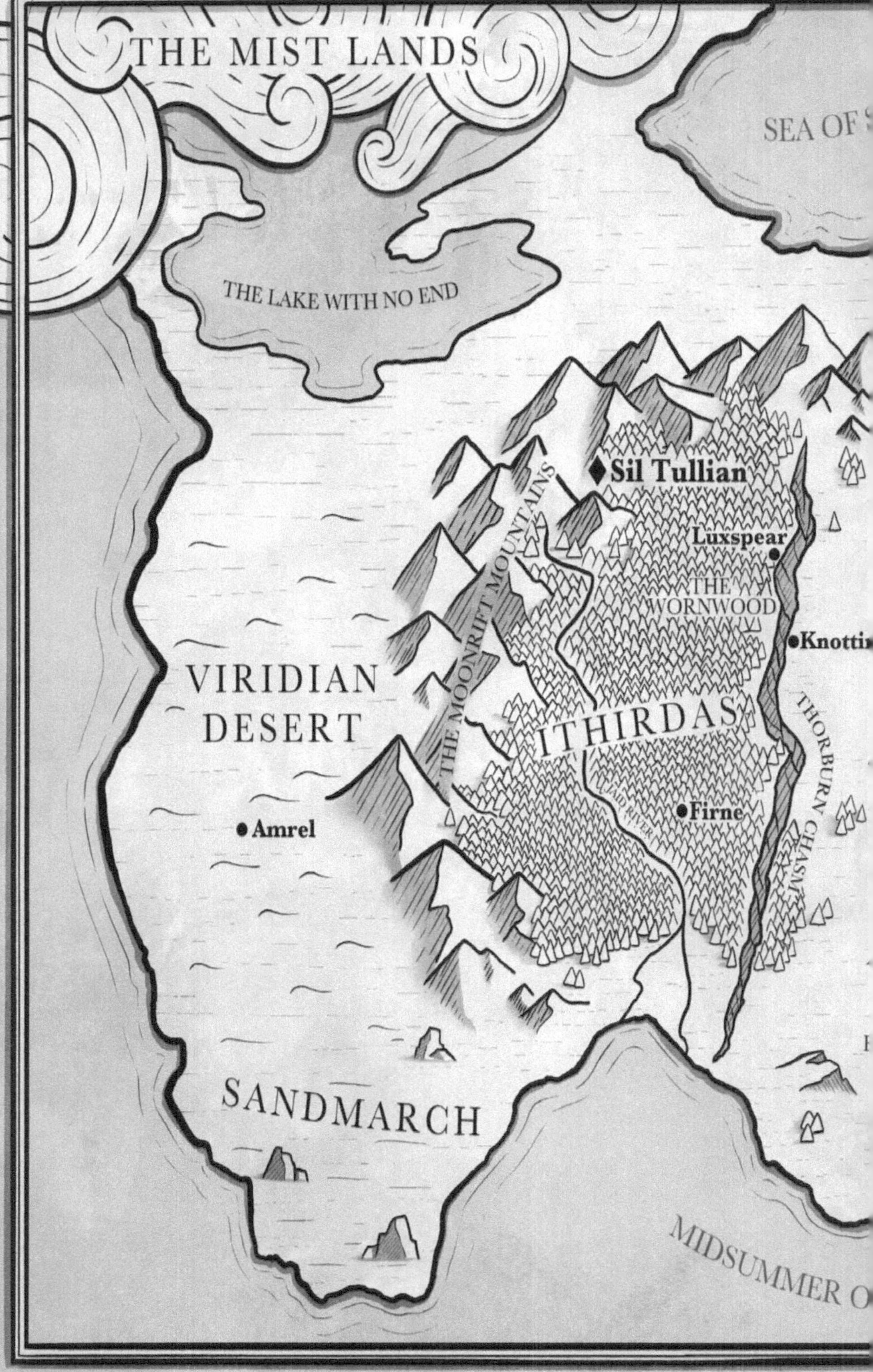

THE MIST LANDS
SEA OF S
THE LAKE WITH NO END
Sil Tullian
Luxspear
THE WORNWOOD
Knotti
VIRIDIAN DESERT
THE MOONRIFT MOUNTAINS
ITHIRDAS
THORBURN CHASM
LAID RIVER
Firne
Amrel
SANDMARCH
MIDSUMMER O

The Kingdoms of
SOARDEN
FELLNAROK
THE TALONS
GREY ISLES
NIDARIA
THE VALEWOOD
Hearth
LOR RIVER
STOANE RIVER
Fort
Milanthos
EASTERN SEA
GLASTR
THE HORNS
BRIMHOLD
LARIMAR LAKE
Delm
NDS
Briar
SKAILRIDGE
Midport

Prologue

The slaughter began as night fell on the great city of Delm.

The night's watch stood vigil in front of the large, iron gates that led to the castle. Dusk fell quickly as fog rose into the air, broken only by the feeble flickering of the occasional torch. The two soldiers on duty stood shivering in their armor, looking out upon the lower city. Their breath hung in the air as the temperature dropped with the sinking sun. An uneasy silence descended. The soldiers adjusted their positions, settling in for a long, frigid night.

Soon after, through the fog and darkness, came the sound of boots on the stone road. A loud click, followed by a pause, over and over as someone made their way steadily towards the castle gate. The soldiers exchanged a look.

"Identify yourself!" One of the guards called out, his voice piercing the night. The other soldier, a broad man with a long red beard, moved his spear forward. "Step into the light and state your intent."

From the shadows came a hunched figure in a worn, gray cloak that dragged its way across the road. The figure raised its head, revealing an elderly woman with sharp eyes and a crooked nose. She smiled slightly at the guards, who relaxed their tense positions.

"I seek an audience with the king." The woman's voice held a surprising strength. She moved subtly closer to the gate.

"The king has retired for the night. I suggest you come back tomorrow."

"Oh no," the woman replied slowly, tilting her wrinkled face up at the soldier. "I'm afraid this matter cannot wait."

In an instant, there was a blade in the woman's hand. She drove the weapon swiftly into the guard's heart. Blood spilled from the wound as the man fell, dead before he hit the ground. The second soldier barely had time to react before the woman pounced on him, slashing her dagger, her eyes wide and crazed like a wild animal. The blade found the man's throat, and his body soon lay next to the first. The night fell into silence once more, the smell of blood staining the air. The woman stood looking down at her victims for a moment, her face thoughtful. She bent over, plucking the helmet from the first soldier and the dark violet cloak off the second. With her prizes under her arm, she walked calmly to the gate, pulling it open with a strength greater than her size allowed. She slipped through the opening and entered the gloom that led up to the castle.

Inside the fortress, a soldier paced back and forth across the entryway. He stifled a yawn, his gaze wandering over the elegant portraits and banners that hung around him. The night was young, yet he already grew weary of the boredom that the night's watch brought. The minutes inched by, and the guard had almost risked sitting on the staircase when a loud knock sounded at the castle door. The soldier froze. No one came to the castle at this time of night. The guard moved to the entrance and cautiously slid open a panel in the wooden door. He peered through the hole, breathing a sigh of relief as he caught sight of the mysterious visitor. The guard unlatched the door and pulled it inward, admitting an icy patch of air.

"Nigel, you great oaf, you scared me half to death." The soldier moved aside, waving the newcomer through the door. Nigel slipped inside, his red beard damp from the fog, and his helmet clasped beneath his arm. The door slammed closed behind him.

"What are you doing up here? Is something happening at the gate?" the entry guard asked, eager for a bit of excitement.

"Everything's quiet, just needed to step in out of the cold," Nigel replied rather stiffly. He moved deeper into the castle. The entry guard followed, a frown forming on his face.

"I know you're new, Nigel, but you're really not meant to leave your post—" The guard was cut off as Nigel surged towards him. There was a sickening snap, and the soldier fell to the castle floor. His head lay at an odd angle, eyes wide and staring.

The sound of warning bells echoed through the castle, and the cries of soldiers floated up from the castle gate. The man called Nigel sighed under his breath. He moved further into the castle, stealing through the dark corridors. He could hear soldiers running towards the entrance hall, the sound of the bells snapping the sleeping castle to attention. Nigel slipped around a corner, pausing by a tapestry of the royal family. He stared up at it with narrowed eyes. As the sound of soldiers drew nearer, Nigel began to change. It was gradual at first, slowly and carefully creeping over him. Then, in the span of a heartbeat, he shifted. Nigel was replaced by a tall, young elf maiden. Her hair was bright like fire, cascading down her back in waves. She turned to face the oncoming soldiers, bloody dagger drawn. An eerie smile flickered across her beautiful face.

The elf made her way meticulously through the castle, killing most of the guards she faced. A few she left alive, though unconscious, collapsed among the bodies of their fallen comrades. Blood ran through the corridors. Battle cries were replaced with screams, and the thrill of battle soon fell away to the terror of a massacre.

Across the castle, the princess sat on her bed, the queen pacing nearby. Occasionally, a shout or scream would pierce the night, and the queen would pause, her head whipping towards the door. After a moment of rigid silence, she would relax, continuing her march around the room.

"Mum," the princess called from her perch on the bed.

"Yes, Camillea?" the queen looked once more towards the door.

"I don't understand what's happening," Camillea replied. "Where's Dad?"

"Your father is helping fight the intruders."

"But who are they? Why are they—" Camillea's questions were cut off by a bellowing voice that shook the princess to her core.

"The king is dead!" the voice called, over and over, loud with panic. "The king is dead!"

Camillea cried out as the echoing voice transformed into a scream. The queen dashed to Camillea's side, placing a warm hand on her face.

"I want you to stay here, my sweet. Whatever you hear, do not leave this room." The queen stared down at her daughter for a long moment before rushing from the room, a sword in hand.

"Mother, don't!" Camillea screamed after her, body frozen with fear. Outside the room, metal clashed on metal, the sound of slashing weapons ripping through the air. There was a final grunt and a thud as something large fell to the floor. Then, for the first time in a long while, complete silence fell across the castle. Camillea did not, could not breathe. Someone stood on the other side of her door. Someone who was not her mother.

The door let out a low groan as it creaked inwards, and Camillea scrambled farther back onto her bed. Her hands shook with fear. A strange woman entered the room. She had beautiful scarlet hair that hung past her shoulders, with pointed ears that peeked through the long strands. Camillea would have found her quite striking were it not for the blood that covered every inch of her body. The elf walked serenely towards the princess, pausing at the foot of the bed. A dagger swung in her hand. Camillea could only stare up at the elf in shock. Her breathing came in hysterical gasps.

"Just leave me alone," Camillea pleaded. "Please, just leave me alone."

"Don't be afraid, Princess," the elf said softly. Her eyes were unreadable. "You just have something I need."

"I don't have anything! What could you want from me?" Camillea asked, eyeing the door desperately.

The Red Elf smiled.

I

Part One: Light

In mountains old and oceans dead,
In minds and hearts,
And veins of red.
Through twisting wind and river's bend,
Shines a Light to never end.

1

A Sacrifice

Sydney was eleven when the soldiers came.

The queen's men barreled into town, the hooves of their horses pounding the earth, a cloud of dust billowing up behind them. Townspeople stood warily in their doorways, while children abandoned their games and fled home to their mothers.

Sydney was down by the docks, as usual. She loved to watch the mermaids barter with the local merchants. Sometimes, if she was lucky, one of them would give her a shell from a far off shore or a broken trinket that no vendor would buy. Today, Sydney watched a young mermaid trade a basket full of fish for a few shining coins. But as the soldiers rode past, the mermaid ducked beneath the waves, her scarlet tail disappearing into the dark water. The dock master turned to Sydney with a furrowed brow.

"You better run home, lass."

Sydney took off across the small town, jumping fences and jutting through back alleys, the streets of Briar a familiar map beneath her bare feet. She slid in the dirt as she rounded the final corner. Soldiers shouted from a street over as she crashed into her father's store.

Sydney's father was a tall man, with broad shoulders and warm, brown eyes. He was talking cordially with the butcher's wife, but at the sight of his daughter, the smile slipped from his face.

"What is it, dear, what's wrong?" Daniel stepped out from behind the counter, placing a comforting hand on Sydney's shoulder.

"Soldiers… down the street," Sydney panted. Her breath came in shallow gasps.

Daniel's eyes widened. "The store is closed, everyone out."

Sydney had rarely heard her father speak with such harshness. The store's few customers shuffled through the front door, muttering to themselves. Daniel hastily latched the door behind them.

"Where's Abigail?" Sydney asked.

"Upstairs resting." Daniel cast an anxious glance out the window.

"Maybe they're just passing through?" Even as she spoke, Sydney knew it was a false hope. Her father looked down at her sadly. Before he could respond, there was a pounding on the door.

"Her Majesty's royal army! Open up!" The booming voice caused both Sydney and her father to jump. With a deep frown, Daniel opened the door.

Two soldiers stood on the doorstep, their silver armor gleaming in the sunlight. Behind them, Sydney could see the rest of the unit visiting houses up and down the street.

"How can I help you, gentlemen?" Sydney's father asked stiffly. She felt his hand once again find her shoulder.

"Her Royal Majesty, Queen Camillea Cortellin of Brimhold has issued another recruitment order for the war effort." The soldier spoke with the drawl of a man who had repeated the same words too many times.

"As I told the last recruiters, I have no child old enough to fuel *Her Majesty's* war."

The soldier scowled at the shopkeeper's tone, placing a large, gloved hand on the hilt of his sword. The hand on Sydney's shoulder tightened.

"Her Majesty has lowered the recruitment age. The oldest child over the age of thirteen from each family is to report to the capital for training," the soldier sneered, his eyes lingering on Sydney.

Daniel took a small step backwards, pushing Sydney gently behind him.

"The queen is sending little girls out to fight her battles now, is she?"

Sydney cringed as the soldier slid his sword from its sheath. He took a threatening step towards Daniel with the other soldier close behind.

"Careful there." The soldier lowered the point of his sword to the shopkeeper's chest. "You are on the verge of treason. Another ill word about your queen, and I'll be taking a lot more than your daughter."

For a moment, Sydney saw something rise up inside her father. Something she did not recognize. His chest heaved with fury, and his hand clenched into a shaking fist. She knew that any second he would lunge at the soldiers. She saw the long, silver sword slicing through him. She saw his blood in the air. But after a moment of tense silence, Daniel deflated, his shoulders resigned. Sydney felt her lungs begin to work again. The soldier lowered his sword, and his face broke into a smug smile.

"That's better. Now, how many children are in the household?"

"Two," Daniel muttered.

"And the oldest?"

Sydney's father glanced down at her. She saw desperation reflected in his eyes. They both knew if he offered up his eldest daughter, she was as good as dead.

Meanwhile, Sydney imagined the life her sister would gain. She would see the great city of Delm, the Horns of Stoane looming behind it, the rest of Brimhold, the rest of the world. All while Sydney stayed in Briar, selling flour to the butcher and searching for what little adventure she could find at the docks.

When Daniel and Sydney's eyes met again, they had traveled different journeys but reached the same conclusion.

Sydney squared her shoulders and stepped forward.

"I'm the oldest," Sydney said, her voice as firm as she could manage. "I turned thirteen just last month."

"Is that so?" the soldier asked doubtfully through narrowed eyes. Even for her actual age, Sydney was a small girl.

"Come off it, Rodgins," the second soldier spoke up for the first time. "We're supposed to check if they say they're underage, not over. What does it matter as long as we reach our quota?"

The first soldier paused for a moment, considering Sydney. Finally, he nodded, moving towards the open door.

"You have until mid-day to gather your things. One bag only. Don't make us come looking for you."

The soldiers left, letting the door swing closed behind them. As soon as they were out of earshot, Daniel turned to his daughter, his faced creased with concern.

"Sydney, you can't—"

"Papa, I have to," Sydney insisted.

"You're so young, you're going to get yourself killed…"

"And what if Abi has one of her fits in a battle? She'll be killed for sure," Sydney reasoned. "Please. I have to do this. Let me go."

A few seconds passed, and Sydney was sure her father was going to argue again. But instead, he knelt down and wrapped her in a tight hug.

"We better get your bag packed," Daniel said gruffly.

The pair hurried up a set of long, wooden stairs to their home above the shop. It was a small, two-bedroom loft, with worn furniture and the vague smell of flour and cinnamon wafting up from the shop below. Three oak chairs sat by the tiny fireplace, which lay barren. The loft wasn't lavish by any means, but it was warm in the winter, and soft light filtered in through the windows when the day was clear. It was home, the only one Sydney had ever known, and the sight of it now nearly broke her resolve.

Sydney entered the bedroom she shared with her sister, readying herself for the lies formulated in hushed whispers on the stairs below. Abigail sat in her bed, her hands busy with a pair of knitting needles. Despite being older, Abigail was smaller than her sister, her skin stretched over sharp, fragile bones. Her dark brown hair, like Sydney's, hung in long waves around her shoulders. But she had her father's chocolate eyes, while Sydney's were a steely gray. Everything about Abigail seemed shrunken, as if the life had been drained from her. At Sydney's entrance, the girl lifted her head, her bright smile clashing oddly with her feeble body.

"Syd! You've been gone for ages. Anything interesting down at the docks?" Abigail asked cheerfully. Sydney mumbled an incoherent response. She crossed over to her side of the room and began stuffing her few possessions into a leather satchel. Abigail sat down her knitting.

"What are you doing? Are we going somewhere?"

"I'm going to visit a family friend in Delm." Sydney swallowed hard. She avoided meeting her sister's eye.

"What?" Abigail sat up straighter, but she did not get out of bed. "Am I going too?"

"No."

"But of course I am. Why should you get to go and I don't?" Abigail demanded. Still, Sydney would not look at her.

"Abi…"

"This is ridiculous. If you get to visit the capital, I want to go too,"

Abigail continued angrily.

Before Sydney could respond, their father entered the room, a small pouch clasped in his hand. Abigail quickly refocused her anger.

"Papa, what is this about Sydney going to Delm? Surely she's lying."

"Your sister is staying with a friend of mine for a while. A neighbor is headed up that way and has offered to take her," Daniel lied smoothly.

"But I'm older! If anyone gets to go, it should be me," Abigail protested, glaring up at her father.

"You know why you can't go, Abi. You're sick. What if you have one of your episodes on the road?" Abigail opened her mouth to reply, but Daniel held up his hand. "That's enough. My decision is final."

Abigail sat in a seething silence as Sydney finished packing. Daniel rambled on about various things. Eventually, the sun reached its peak, and they could stall no longer. Sydney shouldered her satchel and walked over to her sister. She was met with crossed arms.

"Abigail, say goodbye to your sister," Daniel admonished from the doorway.

"Goodbye," Abigail said coolly, making no move to embrace Sydney. Sydney felt her throat close up as tears threatened to overwhelm her. She could not leave like this.

"Abi, please," she pleaded. "I'm leaving. Give me a hug."

At her tone, Abigail relaxed. She reached up and wrapped her arms around her little sister. The two clung to each other for a moment. Sydney took a deep breath, letting her sister's warmth spread over her. Then she pulled away and left the room before she could change her mind. Daniel and Sydney headed back downstairs into the shop. Every step felt to Sydney as if she was walking to her execution. At the doorway, Daniel placed a hand on his daughter's shoulder, turning her to face him. He pressed the small brown pouch into her hand. She opened it to find a considerable stash of coins.

"Papa, I can't take this. It has to be all of the savings." Sydney tried to return the bag to her father, but Daniel shook his head.

"Don't you worry about that. We will get by just fine."

Sydney wanted to refuse, but something in her father's face stopped her. She stowed the pouch in her bag. Daniel got down on his knees so that he was eye level with his daughter. Words began to pour from him in an endless stream.

"Listen to me, Syd. The first few months of this will be the hardest. Your training will be rough, and they won't go easy on you because of your age. You have to stay sharp, stay focused. Don't bring attention to yourself. Keep your head down. We will write you as often as we can. We will try to visit, but with your sister the way she is…" Daniel hesitated. "We'll try. Do as you're told, and you'll get along fine. With any luck, the war will be over before your training is even finished. You might not even have to fight."

Sydney nodded along to her father's words, but she didn't believe them. The war was on its twelfth year with no sign of subsiding. Sydney knew, like her father, that new recruits rarely returned home. And those that did were not the same. Mad-men, haunted by the ghosts and terrors of war.

Outside, soldiers began calling for the draftees to form ranks in the street. Sydney's heart pounded in her ears, hands shaking at her sides. Her father's face tightened as he pulled her into a final hug. For many years after, Sydney would recall that moment. The rough fabric of her father's shirt. His warm, musky smell. And she would think about how she wished that moment had gone differently. She wished her father had fought harder for her. Wished more than anything that he had forced her to stay. Wished that he had never let her go. But this was her choice, wasn't it? This was what she wanted.

Too soon, the hug ended. Daniel rose to his feet and, together, father and daughter left the shop. Outside, families were huddled up and down the street. Mothers cried over their departing children. Younger siblings watched the spectacle in stunned silence. One by one, the new recruits headed towards the cluster of soldiers that stood by a handful of wagons.

In that instant, Sydney found she could not look at her father. In fact, she couldn't bear to stand there a moment longer. Swallowing hard, she shouldered her satchel and marched forcefully towards the band of soldiers and new recruits.

"Sydney!" Daniel's voice called out behind her, but she did not turn around. She would not look at him. She *could* not look at him.

"State your name and age," one of the soldiers droned at Sydney, not bothering to look up from his parchment.

"Sydney Krane, thirteen."

The soldier scribbled lazily on the scroll, motioning towards the wagon behind him. Sydney pulled herself up onto the wooden platform and sat down hastily on one of two long benches. She fumbled with her satchel before placing it at her feet. She stared down at her hands, not watching as the wagon filled up around her.

Soon the soldiers were ready to depart. Most mounted their horses, and a few climbed into the fronts of the wagons. Sydney heard the crack of a whip, followed by a surging sensation as the wagon began to bounce and roll forward. It was only then, as the wagons began to move out of town, that Sydney allowed herself to look up. Down the street, she could just make out her father in front of the shop. He wasn't waving, like many of the families, and his shoulders were hunched forward and stiff. Sydney could not see his expression, but he had never looked to her so small and far away. She turned. For the first time, tears began to race down her face.

"Soldiers aren't supposed to cry," an older boy across from Sydney sneered. She hastily tried to wipe the tears away.

"He's right," a second boy remarked. His face scrunched in a permanent sneer. "If you can't handle this, the elves will make quick work of you. Maybe you should just jump in front of the horses and save them the trouble?" The other kids in the wagon laughed. All except for the boy sitting next to Sydney.

"Leave her alone, Garrick," said the boy beside her. His voice was low and sharp. The group fell into silence.

"What's it to you?" Garrick snarled back.

"I just think it's strange that you would mock someone for crying, Garrick. As I recall, your eyes were red for a week straight when you got to the orphanage." The boy's tone was conversational, but the edge remained. Garrick narrowed his eyes. For a moment, the two boys stared at each other, their eyes locked in a silent duel. Finally, Garrick turned away, muttering under his breath. The silence fell away, and conversations broke out among the other children.

The boy next to Sydney leaned back against the bench, and she looked at him closely for the first time. He seemed to be a few years older than her, with a tangle of long limbs and floppy brown hair. He turned to her with caramel eyes set in a square face. The boy said nothing for a moment. Instead, he dug through the bag at his feet, emerging with a worn handkerchief. He held it out to Sydney.

"I'm fine," she said stiffly.

"Liar," the boy replied with an easy smile. She took the gift reluctantly.

"You didn't have to do that," Sydney muttered, her voice thick with tears. "I can take care of myself."

"I know," the boy said simply. He held out a hand. "My name is Brandon Lockes. What's yours?"

"Sydney." She shook the boy's hand. "Sydney Krane."

"Well, Sydney," Brandon said easily. "If we can handle a bunch of gits like these our first day out, I don't think those elves will know what hit them."

Sydney smiled despite herself as the wagon rolled out of Briar, down the dusty road to Delm.

2

Swords and Stories

9 Years Later

"Come on, Brandon, I don't have all day!" Sydney sneered at her opponent. She whipped her dual blades casually through the air, the silver glinting in the sunlight. Across the small grass field, Brandon scowled, raising a shield and sword of his own. A dozen soldiers lined the makeshift arena, goading the fighters on.

Brandon lunged first. Sydney grinned as she dodged his strike, parrying with one sword and striking with the other. Back and forth they went, circling each other in an intricate dance. They were too well matched, predicting each other's every move. Sydney knew Brandon would never leave himself open long enough for her to land a blow. He was too skilled for that. As usual, she would have to resort to deception. She lowered her left arm slightly, leaving her side vulnerable. Brandon took the bait immediately and aimed a swing to knock her off balance. But Sydney was faster. She dashed past his guard, smashing into his chest with her shoulder. Brandon hit the ground hard. Before he could recover, the point of her sword lay at his heart.

The spectators cheered, applauding Brandon's defeat. Sydney laughed as she pulled her friend to his feet.

"Alright, alright, get back to training!" Brandon barked at the onlookers. Then, to Sydney, he said, "I'll best you one of these days, Krane."

"Oh, really? Is that the same day the war ends and pigs fly?" Sydney teased.

"No need to get smart," Brandon remarked with a smile.

The pair wandered off the training field. Below them, the city of Delm stretched out in intricate rings of homes, shops, and stables. The lower rings were bordered by the city walls on three sides and a great gleaming lake on the fourth. Beyond the lake rose twin mountains, straddling the mighty Stoane River. From their position just outside the castle gates, the view was simply breathtaking.

Brandon turned from the scenery, and Sydney joined him in watching the other soldiers parry back and forth.

"See anyone you think is Honor Guard material?" Brandon asked. Sydney snorted in response.

"Hardly. But it makes no difference. I've told you, we don't need new recruits."

"We could always use good fighters. You're just being stubborn, as usual."

Brandon yelped as Sydney punched him squarely in the arm.

"It takes more than a strong arm to make it in this guard. You know that. And none of this lot has it." Sydney waved her arm at the troops. "Besides, being co-captains means you have to listen to my opinions."

Brandon sighed. "Yes, but it doesn't mean I have to like them."

Sydney looked up at her friend, whose brow was set in a deep furrow over his brown eyes. For nine years, they had trained and fought together through a seemingly endless war. She knew him backwards and forwards, like the worn pages of a well-loved book. And though much had changed through their time together, Sydney could always tell when he was hiding something from her.

"What's wrong, Brandon? You're not this passionate about expanding the guard."

"I am, actually."

"Liar," Sydney fired back relentlessly. "You know you'll tell me eventually, so can we skip the goading?"

Brandon sighed again. "I'm… restless. We've been in the capital too long. I need to be out there, I need to be doing *something*…"

Sydney understood this Brandon well. To him, the war with the elves was personal. Brandon's father had been killed during an elf attack when he was ten years old. His mother had died shortly after, and with no family left, he was sent to live at the orphanage. So, unlike the other children in Briar, when the soldiers came recruiting, Brandon was glad to go.

"We *have* been doing something. Training new soldiers is important." Sydney's words sounded forced even to herself. Brandon threw back his head and laughed.

"So, you're just as eager to leave Delm as I am."

"Maybe," Sydney admitted. "But there's nothing we can do about it at the moment."

"No, I guess not."

The friends stood in silence, continuing to watch the students battle in the warm afternoon sun. Sydney glanced up at the castle that towered above them. She wondered if the queen had a new assignment for them or if they were doomed to another week of stagnant boredom. She longed to ride out of Delm. Every day she stayed within the city walls felt like a day of her life wasted.

Across the training field, a girl called out to Sydney and Brandon as she picked her way around the fighters. Julia Caraway, another member of the Honor Guard, was a petite girl with a bob of jet black hair and an easy smile. She had a quick wit that Sydney admired and a spear just as deadly.

Julia came to a stop next to Brandon. She was breathing heavy, like she'd just run up from the barracks.

"Sydney, Brandon, how are things? Any promising trainees?" Julia asked.

Sydney made a noncommittal grunt. Julia chuckled.

"That good, eh? Well, perhaps this will cheer you up. A horse just rode in with letters from home. This one's for you." Julia handed Sydney a carefully folded piece of parchment with her name written in a tight, neat script. Something in Sydney's chest clenched.

"Thank you," Sydney managed. She could feel Brandon's scrutinizing gaze as she slid the letter into her belt.

"No problem," Julia replied, oblivious. She smiled brightly and turned her attention to Brandon. "Are we still on for that skirmish tomorrow?"

"Of course, I wouldn't miss it," said Brandon.

"Great. Well, I better finish mail duty," Julia waved as she took off again. Brandon's eyes followed her as she left. This did not go unnoticed by Sydney, who rolled her eyes.

"Would you please ask her to drinks already? This is getting ridiculous."

Brandon turned to her, startled. "What do you mean?"

"The two of you have been eyeing each other for months now," Sydney replied. "I know you like her. So what's the problem?"

"Nothing." A blush spread its way across Brandon's face. "It just hasn't been the right time."

"When is the right time?" Sydney persisted.

"I don't know. When the war is over?"

"You can't wait until the war is over to live your life."

"That's interesting, coming from you," Brandon muttered.

"What do you mean by that?" Sydney protested, crossing her arms with a huff.

"When do you plan on reading that letter from Briar?" Brandon asked with a nod towards the parchment in Sydney's belt. She opened her mouth, mumbled something incoherent, and snapped it shut again. Brandon knew the letter would end up with all the others. In a box, under her bed, with the seal intact.

"You know I… I can't…" Sydney stuttered.

"Can't or won't?"

Sydney struggled to respond when a great horn sounded from the city below. The friends froze and exchanged a glance, their conversation forgotten. They both grinned.

"Gilliad's back," Sydney exclaimed.

"I'll inform the queen," Brandon said excitedly, turning towards the castle. "Don't bother Gilliad, he's only just got home. *Sydney!*"

Sydney ignored him and ran off in the opposite direction.

Throughout the lower rings of the city, the streets were filled with the sounds of reuniting families. Parents hugged their children, wives their husbands. At a glance, it was a happy scene. But as Sydney pelted past, she noticed smaller details. Tears slid down a woman's face as she spoke with a solemn soldier. Hopeful children searched for their father or mother only to return home crestfallen. A man gripped a burnt soldier's uniform. All these scenes, along with the realization that the returning group of troops was a great deal smaller than the force that had set out, left a feeling of dread in the pit of Sydney's stomach.

She slid to a stop beside a small house in one of the nicer portions of the city. She stared up at the home for a moment, heart racing in her chest, before pounding on the bright red door. She peaked anxiously in the windows for any sign of life. After a moment, the door creaked open to reveal an older man of average height, whose features were dominated by a well-trimmed, gray beard.

"For god's sake, Sydney, I just got home. Could you not have waited…" Gilliad's grumbling was cut off as Sydney surged through the doorway, wrapping him in an embrace. He sighed, patting her on the back.

"I wanted to make sure you were okay," Sydney said, releasing him.

"You want to know what happened at the battle," the general replied shortly.

"Maybe."

"You know you'll hear everything at the council later."

"Come on, Gilliad, it's been weeks! Please?"

Gilliad sighed again, waving her inside and shutting the door behind him. They stood in a modest kitchen, a wood burning stove crackling beside them. Gilliad sat down at the table, and Sydney followed suit.

"Our borders are secure once more, but at a terrible cost," he began, staring down at his hands. "The elves were indeed making a move on Knotting, just as our scouts reported. By the time our troops arrived, they had a considerable force mustered. A thousand at least."

"A thousand?" Sydney asked. "You should have outnumbered them easily."

"We did. But we were fighting too close to the chasm. One of the elves had earth magic and…" Gilliad buried his face into his hands.

"They fell?" Sydney whispered, her eyes wide.

Gilliad nodded, barely looking up.

"It wasn't your fault," Sydney insisted quickly. "You couldn't have known."

"That's not all," Gilliad continued. "After we drove the elves back, I sent some soldiers to do a quick sweep of Knotting. The citizens did not welcome our presence, and they tried to keep my men from searching the town. A few of them were hiding warriors from Ithirdas in their homes."

"What?" Sydney shouted, pounding a fist on the table. The sound echoed throughout the tiny home, and Gilliad cringed.

"Now you've done it."

"Sydney!" an ear splitting screech sounded from the doorway. Gilliad's two daughters, Hazel and Tess, came crashing into the room. They tackled Sydney, squealing with excitement and rattling on at an astonishing rate.

"We haven't seen you in ages. Look at these pendants Papa brought us. Mine is bigger than Hazel's."

"Where's Brandon? Did he fight in the battle? Do you have any new stories? Tell us a story!"

"Oh yes, tell us a story, Sydney!"

"Please!"

Sydney looked up from the two shrieking girls to see Gilliad sneaking from the room, probably going to check on his wife, Susan, who was pregnant with the couple's third child. Gilliad glanced at Sydney as he rounded the corner, his eyes pleading for a reprieve. *We can talk later*, he mouthed. With a sigh, Sydney resigned herself to the role of storyteller.

"Alright, alright, I have a story for you. But you have to be very quiet, so we don't bother your mom." The girls fell into silence and sat in front of Sydney eagerly, their eyes wide and waiting. She thought for a moment.

"Have I told you about the beginning of Soarden and the start of the Shadow War?"

Hazel shook her head, her light hair whipping back and forth. Sydney cleared her throat and began.

"Long ago, when the world was new and the great trees of the Valewood were still in their youth, four races were given dominion over Soarden. The race of men, mortal beings of honor and strength, were given the land and the fields. The elves, long-lived creatures filled with magic, were given the mountains and woodlands. The great seas and rivers were bestowed upon the merfolk. While lacking in true magic, the merfolk have long been a race of kindness and beauty. And finally, the skies belonged to the dragons, the greatest of all the races. The dragons were immortal, and they possessed a power so immense that even they didn't know its full potential. Together, these beings made up the Light Races.

But for every bit of light in the world, there must also be a balance of dark. A fifth race was made, creatures of shadow and the dark places, known as the Sháedin. These monsters felt no love for the world and sought only its destruction. Their magic gave them power over the shadow-borne, beasts of nightmare, which they used to terrorize those that lived in the light.

Centuries passed. The world grew. For many years and many lifetimes, the Light Races lived in a state of peace. The Sháedin were struck down again and again, and they rarely strayed from the cracks and crevices they called home. But a day came when the Sháedin gained something they had never had before. A leader by the name of Malith. He moved through his people, uniting them for a singular purpose. The Shadow King they called him, the one that would bring an end to the light."

Sydney paused. Hazel's eyes were now wide with terror, and Tess peaked out from behind tiny fingers. The moment she stopped speaking, the girls begged her to continue. Sydney smiled and began again.

"Evil swept over the land like a plague. Shadow-borne hid around every corner, and the Sháedin, led by Malith, killed as they pleased. The mermaids fled to the sea, the dragons the sky. Men and elves locked themselves away. These were dark times, and for many years there were more burials than births. None of the Light Races had the strength to defeat the Sháedin and end their reign of terror.

But, when hope had all but drained from the world, four heroes stepped forward. Leona Nightslayer, a bold elf warrior from the west. Asper Allantus, a ruler of the merfolk renowned for his strength and wisdom. Yoric Thorburn, known as Yoric the Great, a white dragon from the north. And lastly, Elizabeth Cortellin, the queen of what would one day become the kingdom of Brimhold."

"That's Queen Camillea's ancestor," Hazel told Tess wisely. As the oldest, Hazel always took it upon herself to educate her baby sister.

"These leaders joined the races of Light to form one great army, the likes of which the world had never seen before. Together, they marched on the Sháedin. Countless lives were lost but, bit by bit, the Light Races beat the Sháedin back. At last, the mighty heroes cornered the Sháedin in the caves of Kieheld, where they made their final stand against Malith. Using their combined strength and powers, the Light races defeated Malith and his followers. And though they could not destroy the Sháedin completely, the leaders of the Light used ancient magic to seal them away deep beneath the earth. Neither the Sháedin nor shadow-borne have been seen since," Sydney concluded dramatically.

Tess stared at Sydney in an awed silence before bursting into applause, as she always did at the end of Sydney's tales. Hazel, on the other hand, had a pensive look about her.

"Sydney," Hazel started. "What happened to the Light Races after the Shadow War?"

"They formed the kingdoms we know today and entered an era of peace," Sydney replied.

"But the elves… they were our friends?"

"Well, yes," Sydney said with hesitation. She did not like where this conversation was headed.

"But you, Brandon, and Papa fight the elves."

"It's complicated, Hazel," Sydney explained. "The Shadow War was a long, long time ago. The world has changed since then. Ithirdas betrayed our friendship when they began attacking our villages. They invaded the castle and killed Queen Camillea's parents."

Hazel thought for a moment. "But maybe not all of the elves are bad. Maybe just a few of them did those things."

"That's not how it works Hazel," Sydney said gently. "The elves protect the murderer of the royal family. The king of Ithirdas sends soldiers to fight against us and they obey. If any of the elves are not the monsters we fight, I have yet to meet them."

Hazel hung her head but made no further comment. Sydney wished there was something more she could say.

Before she could change the subject, someone knocked on the front door of the home. Sydney could hear low voices followed by a thud as the door closed once more. Gilliad entered the room, his face weary.

"It's time to go, Sydney," Gilliad said as he hugged his daughters goodbye. "The queen has called for a war council."

3

The Council of Brimhold

Sydney was among the first to arrive in the great hall. At Gilliad's announcement, she rushed to the barracks to wipe the dust from her face and run a brush through her knotted hair. She hurriedly pinned the Honor Guard emblem to her chest, a silver badge of two crossed swords. Then, grabbing her favorite cloak, though the summer heat hardly warranted it, she sped up to the castle gates. The evening sun was just setting below the castle turrets as she made her entrance.

The hall was outfitted for the council meeting with a long wooden table placed at its center. Candlelight cast long shadows upon the stone walls like the fingers of a giant. The air hung moist and thick with the leftover scent of pipe smoke and the stagnant heat of a summer evening. As Sydney passed through the hall, servants bustled about, trading the court's daily gossip among themselves. At the far end of the room, the queen's throne loomed in the dim light. Behind it hung a large banner featuring the royal standard of Brimhold, twin black mountains bordered by dual swords. Above the mountains blazed three white stars on a field of deep violet. Each star represented the principles upon which Brimhold was founded:

Integrity, Courage, and Justice. It was by these principles that Sydney had sworn to when she first joined the queen's army all those years ago.

Over the next hour, the hall filled up slowly as lords and important officers trickled in for the meeting. Sydney found herself restless, pacing the room before retiring to her chair near the end of the table. She then took to tapping her boot against the hard floor. Her impatience went unnoticed, and the rest of the guests formed friendly clusters around the room as they awaited the arrival of their queen. Just as Sydney was contemplating sneaking down to the kitchen for a quick snack, Brandon entered the room looking fresh and composed. She hurried to meet him, practically shoving aside a handful of disgruntled dignitaries.

"What did the queen say?" Sydney inquired as she reached her friend.

"She didn't say much of anything," Brandon replied. "As soon as she learned of Gilliad's return, she called for the council. She sent me to round up a few of the officers. How is Gilliad?"

"Alive. Many weren't so lucky." Sydney pulled him aside, ducking behind a stone column for some privacy. She quietly filled him in on the details of the battle. By the end of her story, Brandon's eyes were wide with disbelief.

"The townspeople were sheltering elves? The same elves our soldiers are fighting and dying to protect them from?" Brandon's voice was calm but sharp. His hand gripped the hilt of his sword, his knuckles white. Sydney looked up at him with concern.

"Brandon…" Sydney wanted to reassure him, but the words never came. What could she say? She shared his anger. How could they protect their kingdom when entire townships were aiding their enemies?

A rhythmic pounding saved Sydney from responding. Heads

turned towards the far end of the room where a guard called the crowd to attention. Sydney and Brandon moved to stand behind their chairs at the center table.

"Presenting Her Royal Majesty, Queen Camillea Cortellin of Brimhold and her honored guest, General Gilliad Norwell!"

The oak doors opened, and the queen herself swept into the room. Sydney was struck as usual by the queen's beauty, her neck long and her chin proud. She sported high cheekbones with long locks of golden hair. Her eyes were a pale blue, complimented by the stunning sapphire dress that spread out behind her in cascading folds of blue and silver. The royal crown sat daintily on her head. Slightly behind Camillea, strode Gilliad. The general wore a respectful expression, and he was dressed in his finest silver armor. Only Sydney noticed how uncomfortable her friend looked, with beads of sweat running down his forehead. Camillea and Gilliad reached the table, Camillea at the head and Gilliad to her right.

"You may sit." The queen spoke softly, but her voice carried. The standing lords and knights took their seats. Looking around, Sydney noticed a man on the queen's left that she had never seen before. She pulled her gaze away, but it was difficult not to stare. The man's face was dominated by a long, ragged scar.

"Lords, ladies, warriors, and honored guests," Camillea said with a small smile. "Thank you for meeting on such short notice. The duties of war cannot wait, and we have much to discuss. First and foremost, I would like to welcome home General Norwell and congratulate him on a successful battle. He valiantly led our troops to victory, and thanks to his bravery, the town of Knotting continues to fly under the Brimhold banner."

The room filled with the celebratory pounding of drinks against the table. Sydney rushed to join in. Gilliad gave a small nod.

"You are too kind, my queen," Gilliad replied. He squirmed in his seat. "My soldiers deserve all the credit."

"Your humility is your greatest gift, Gilliad." Camillea spoke with amusement. "Now, before General Norwell recounts the battle for us, we have a few other matters to attend to. I would like to introduce the new training commander, Sir Malcolm Moor. He hails from Midport but graciously came to the capital upon my request."

The queen motioned to the scarred man on her left. Sir Moor raised his hand in greeting but otherwise said nothing. Confused whispers floated around the table, and Sydney realized she was not the only one that did not recognize the new leader. Previously, Gilliad held the position of training commander for nearly twenty years. He received a promotion to general just a few months before; since then, the position had remained vacant. The soldiers expected an experienced captain would be chosen to take Gilliad's place. Not a foreign knight.

"I expect everyone to make Sir Moor feel welcome," Camillea said, an edge to her voice. The whispers died off.

"Secondly, as the next round of troops finishes their training, it is nearly time to divide them into their permanent guards and divisions. Captain Krane, Captain Lockes, do you have any recommendations for Honor Guard placement?"

"Yes, your Majesty," Brandon announced before Sydney could respond. She glared at him reproachfully. "We would like to assess two or three of the trainees before we make any final decisions, but we have high hopes for them."

"With all due respect, your Majesty," Sydney spoke up, ignoring Brandon's swift kicks at her beneath the table. "It is not more soldiers we need but more assignments. The Honor Guard is growing weary of training. We are ready for action."

Silence filled the chamber. The gathered lords and ladies froze. The queen stared at Sydney calmly.

"While I appreciate your honesty Captain Krane, it is not your place to decide where the Honor Guard is sent. Your guard is vital to the war effort, and I have not forgotten your success in the past. But right now, I need you in Delm."

"But your Majesty…"

"That's enough." The queen's voice was like ice. Her mouth lay in a flat line. Sydney sank back into her chair, embarrassed.

"Now then," Camillea continued. Some of the sharpness fell from her tone, and her pale eyes swept the chamber. "I would like to hear General Norwell's account of the battle. Gilliad?"

The general sat straight in his chair and scratched his beard absently, his face weary. The attention in the room shifted, and Gilliad began his tale, starting with the army's march to Knotting and ending with the defeat of the elves. At the news that half the fighting force had fallen into the Thorburn Chasm, gasps of shock and outrage erupted around the room. Camillea folded her delicate hands on the table in front of her, head bowed.

"This is a great tragedy," she said solemnly. "Once again, the elves and their cursed magic have taken countless innocent lives in their pursuit of power. We will not forget the lives that were lost. And the victory at Knotting will go a long way in avenging them."

The queen turned her head, as if the matter was finished, but Gilliad raised his hand solemnly. "With respect your Majesty, there is more to report."

Gilliad grudgingly told the room of the traitors in Knotting. This time there were no cries of anger. Just shocked and furious silence. The queen's mouth reformed its flat line.

"This is unacceptable," a portly lord from the north called from down the table. A few men grumbled in agreement. "Housing our enemies? The nerve of it! Those peasants should be hung for treason."

"I would have to agree with Lord Halithe," another dignitary said coolly. Her eyes were sharp as steel. "This type of behavior must be discouraged at all costs. We cannot fight a war on two fronts."

Voices rang out across the hall, all calling for the execution of the accused. Sydney watched the exchange with apprehension, her eyes darting from Brandon to Gilliad to the queen. Brandon was silent but seething, while Gilliad looked as if he had swallowed something sour. Meanwhile, the queen's expression was unreadable. The shouting had reached a dangerous level before Camillea raised her hand.

"Silence. I hear your concerns. This type of behavior from our citizens cannot be tolerated. However..." The queen eyed plump Lord Halithe who was looking smug. "I will not be issuing mass executions. Our people are afraid and desperate, especially those along the border. We will find out why these townspeople housed elves among them, and we will put an end to it. But we will show our people mercy. I will not allow us to sink to the level of our enemies."

"And what if these citizens continue to have *personal* relations with the elves? The last thing we need is a bunch of greyblood half-breeds running around on top of everything else," Lord Halithe growled. Camillea's frown deepened further.

"I will listen to rational opinions, but I will not tolerate such outbursts in this council. Is that understood, Lord Halithe?"

The man lowered his eyes. "Of course, your Majesty."

"That being said, I doubt your fears are warranted. Greybloods were rare even before the Scour wiped them out. They are not a concern. Now, does anyone else have something *productive* to say on this matter?"

The chamber filled with the sound of disgruntled muttering, but no one else dared defy the queen a second time. Sydney felt a great sense of relief at Camillea's words. She was furious that citizens of Brimhold would aid their enemies, but she knew executions were not the solution. And they certainly had nothing to fear from potential half-elf children. A quick glance at Brandon's face, however, sent a chill down Sydney's spine. His eyes bore the fury of an oncoming storm.

When the queen spoke again, her voice was calm and careful. The words were clearly rehearsed with a great deal of thought. "I know times are hard. The war continues with no clear end, and the news of betrayal among us only makes matters worse. But now is the time to be vigilant. We must secure our borders. We must push back against our enemy. For ourselves, for our families. For our children. We cannot allow this war to continue for another twenty years. With that in mind, I will be issuing a new recruitment order, effective immediately. The oldest child of each family, eleven and older, are to be drafted. They will report to Delm for training."

Sydney froze. Her throat closed in on itself. Looking around, she saw the same shock written on the faces around the table.

"Your Majesty," Gilliad floundered, sweat dripping from his forehead. "The recruitment age has lessened over the years, but it has never been that young. And the last recruitment was only two years ago."

"I am aware, General," Camillea replied smoothly.

"We cannot keep sending more and more of our children to die," said a local nobleman. His voice shook with emotion. "At this rate, we will have no citizens left to defend."

"Tell me, Lord Mortan, how safe are Brimhold's children in their own homes? With elves from Ithirdas pouring over the border, raiding and killing as they please? Would our children not be safer here in the capital?" The queen raised her chin, neck long and pale as a swan. She looked down at the nobleman as she spoke. "If anything, this act is a protective measure. With my upcoming visit to Nidaria, I hope to initiate a plan to end this war once and for all. With any luck, these recruits will never see a battle. But we must be prepared if our plan fails, and we must protect our children from the reach of the elves."

Sydney barely heard Camillea's words. She was eleven years old again. She saw her father's face as the wagons pulled out of Briar. She felt the dust and tears on her skin. She heard parents crying in the streets as their babies were dragged off to war.

"Now," the queen continued in the heavy silence. "With that in mind…"

The doors to the hall flew open as a man came crashing into the room. Guards were at his side in an instant with their swords drawn. Camillea rose to her feet, eyes flashing.

"What is the meaning of this? We are in the middle of a private war council—"

"Your Majesty." The man gasped for air as he struggled against the guards. Sweat poured down his grimy face, as if he'd sprinted across Brimhold itself. "Apologies, your Majesty… I have news…. news from the south."

"Out with it then!" the queen snapped as the man wheezed.

"The town of Briar… is under attack."

4

A Desperate Plan

Sydney was on her feet in an instant, and only Brandon's calming hand kept her from flying at the messenger, demanding more information. The room sat in silence aside from the pounding of Sydney's heart in her ears.

"Explain," Camillea barked at the messenger.

The man took an agonizingly long moment to slow his breathing. Sydney almost strangled him.

"I've been stationed in Sabell for a fortnight, your Majesty, just across the river." The man squirmed as he spoke, and his eyes darted around the hall. "This morning, a scout rode in from the coast. Run ragged. Said a band of elves was spotted moving toward Briar. He thinks they mean to burn it. Burn it right to the ground, just like they did Morinth."

Sydney gripped the table until her knuckles turned white. Morinth was a small farming village not far from the Thorburn Chasm, which acted as a border between Ithirdas and Brimhold. The town had been set ablaze not three months ago. The elves gave no warning, no motive. Hundreds of innocent lives had been lost. And Morinth was not the first.

"I rode out as soon as I got the news, your Majesty, as fast as my horse could carry me," the messenger continued. "But I fear that by the time your help reaches them… it will be too late."

Images of Briar flashed across Sydney's vision. She pictured her family's store burnt to ash. Worse, her father and sister, buried beneath it. She couldn't let it happen.

"My queen," Sydney said, amazed she could find her voice. "I ask that you let me take my guard to Briar. We will wipe out these… these…" Monsters. Murderers. She could not find a word strong enough for her anger.

Camillea's eyes held such pity, Sydney was forced to look away. "Captain Krane, I know what Briar means to you, but you know the odds," the queen said gently. "You will never reach them in time."

Them.

"Your Majesty, please. Briar is my home, my family is there. I can't abandon it. Would you not do anything to save your family?" Sydney continued quickly, afraid she had once again overstepped her bounds. "If there is even the slightest chance we can save innocent people, we have to try."

Camillea did not speak for a long time. She stared, her cold blue eyes boring into Sydney's gray ones. Sydney could still feel Brandon's hand locked on her wrist like a shackle, and she yearned to know his reaction to Briar's fate, but she dared not look away from the queen. At last, Camillea leaned back in her chair with a sigh. Sydney tasted victory.

"Alright," Camillea conceded. "You may take a few members of the Honor Guard to Briar. A small company that can ride fast and discreet. Perhaps then you may stand a chance of arriving in time. But Sydney, you are not to engage the Ithirdi if you are outnumbered. Your only mission is to evacuate and assist the people of Briar. Do not take unnecessary risks. That is an order."

Sydney would have preferred to storm Briar with a thousand soldiers at her back, but she knew better than to push the issue. "Yes, your Majesty. We will leave at once."

Camillea's mouth had settled into its flat line, her eyes serious and sharp. "Good luck. And may the strength of Brimhold be with you." Looking around the room, Sydney could see the sentiment echoed in the eyes of her comrades. Carrying their determination with her, Sydney rushed from the room, desperate to be on the move. She knew without looking that Brandon was not far behind.

"Find Julia and Thomas, I want them with us," Sydney barked at Brandon as she rushed down the stone steps of the castle. "And one other, I don't care who. A fast rider."

"Sydney, wait…"

"I'll need to head back to the barracks to gather my things. Have everyone meet at the stables when they're ready. And make it fast, we need to ride out within the hour…"

"*Syd.*" Brandon caught hold of her elbow and spun her to face him. She saw the same pity in her friend's face that she had seen in the queen's. She hated it. "I'm sorry about Briar. Are you okay?"

Sydney pulled her arm free. "Now's not the time. Get ready to leave." She strode off towards the barracks before Brandon's comforting voice could break her.

The night air had done little to chase away the summer heat as Sydney made her way across the castle grounds. The warmth smothered her, filling her lungs with the dust and bugs that hung around in clouds. Covered in sweat, she finally reached her room, yanking the door open and closing it behind her. Alone, Sydney felt her dwindling courage leave her in a rush, like breath knocked from her lungs. She slid slowly to the floor with the door at her back.

How strange her room looked. Calm and undisturbed by the night's events. Her small bed was pushed against the wall next to a rickety table. A large, wooden chest sat at the end of the bed, Sydney's dual swords balanced across the top. Various belongings lay scattered about the room, a cloak across the bed, parchment and candles on the table, an unused shield propped up in the corner. The room was hardly more than a cupboard, but it had been Sydney's home since she left Briar all those years ago. She found it soothing.

One piece of Sydney's room did not bring her comfort. In fact, her eyes darted past it, as if the small box beneath her bed would vanish if she didn't focus on it for too long. Every letter she had ever received from home lay neatly packed away in the confines of that box. Unopened. Unread. Shame washed over her as her eyes settled upon it. *What if I see my family when we reach Briar?* Sydney thought. *What will they say to the daughter lost to the war? To the sister who never wrote home? Even worse, what if I never have the chance to make it right?*

A knock on the door startled Sydney out of her rumination. Who was bothering her now? "Brandon, if that's you, I don't want to talk." Sydney's words faded as she stood and opened the door to reveal Gilliad. He still wore his fine armor, and sweat poured down his blotchy face. He scratched at his beard absently.

"I didn't mean to bother you, I just thought I'd come..." Gilliad paused, his voice gruff. "Come see you off."

Ignoring the general's bulky armor, Sydney surged forward and pulled her mentor into a tight hug. She fought back a sob quickly building in her chest.

"Gilliad, I'm too close to this. I can't lose Briar. Maybe you and Brandon should go instead." The words fell out of Sydney's mouth before she could stop them. She pulled away from Gilliad to look at his face.

"That doesn't sound like the Sydney I know, and it certainly isn't the soldier I trained," Gilliad replied, not unkindly. "Ignoring this fight won't make it any less real."

Sydney sighed, turning to begin her packing. "I know that. But what if it's too late? What then?"

"You continue to fight and protect Brimhold," Gilliad said simply. The general had always been a stone in a sea of uncertainty. His resolve was absolute, his morals unwavering. It was something Sydney had admired in him even as a little girl. But right now, Sydney did not want words of perseverance. She wanted anger and passion and fury. At the very least, she wanted lies that Briar would live to see another day.

"That's not what you wanted to hear, I take it?" Gilliad leaned against the door frame. He seemed large and out of place in the tiny room.

"Not particularly."

"I will not lie to you, Sydney. You know the chances as much as I do. But your home needs you now, for better or for worse. You must be strong for your family. Be brave for that little girl I trained all those years ago. The girl who sacrificed everything so that her sister might live."

Yes, Gilliad knew her secret. Brandon as well. She wasn't supposed to be in this war. This was never her fight. But while her friends knew she had volunteered for recruitment to protect her sister, they did not know the other piece of her story. The piece Sydney often denied herself. Deep down, she had always longed to leave Briar behind.

"You're right of course," Sydney said, swallowing hard. She strapped her swords to her back. "How does it feel to always be right, Gilliad?"

The general chuckled. "Less satisfying then one would think."

Sydney rolled her eyes as she crammed the last of her belongings into a leather bag. She brought very little, wanting nothing to slow her down on the desperate flight to Briar. Giving her room a final glance, she followed Gilliad out into the warm summer night.

*****

The other members of the Honor Guard had already saddled their horses by the time Sydney and Gilliad reached the stables. Brandon had chosen Phillip Salander, along with Julia and Thomas Grindle, to join them on their mission. A good choice, as he was the best scout in the Honor Guard and a skilled horseman. He was also an archer, but Sydney tried not to hold that against him. As Sydney and Gilliad drew near, the small band of soldiers lapsed into silence. Sydney looked to Thomas, whose long face was always an easy read. He looked down quickly.

"Talking about me?" Sydney asked as she mounted her horse. She shot Brandon a pointed stare.

"Of course not," Brandon protested loudly with eyes that were just a hint too wide.

"Liar," she fired back. "Is everyone prepared to leave?"

The friends replied with a series of a determined nods. Gilliad pulled Brandon aside and began speaking to him with a quiet urgency. Suspicious of the exchange, Sydney tried to catch the words that passed between them, but she was distracted by Julia.

"I'm sorry about Briar, Sydney." The girl's dark hair cast a long shadow across her face. "We are prepared to do whatever we can."

"Thank you," Sydney said with a sad attempt to hide her annoyance. She was already weary of her friends' pity. "But I'm okay."

"Liar." Brandon rejoined them, clambering onto his own steed. Ignoring the daggers shooting from Sydney's eyes, the captain turned to address the soldiers. "You all know our task. We are to aid the town of Briar and evacuate civilians if needed. This is a rescue mission, not a battle. We will avoid combat unless absolutely necessary.

Understood?"

A chorus of agreement came from the group. "Good. Then let's be off. Ride as if your life depends on it. And may luck be on our side." Brandon spurred his horse and set off towards the city gates, the others right behind. He cast a final wave at Gilliad who stood nearby with his arms folded stiffly across his chest. Worry lay plastered on his red face. Before Sydney could follow her guard, the general grabbed hold of her reigns.

"What is it, Gilliad?" Sydney asked with surprise.

"I just wanted to say…" His eyes struggled to meet Sydney's. And when they did, they said something she did not understand. "Whatever happens… do what you must."

Sydney stared at her friend. She reached down to grab his hand. His fingers were rough and calloused from years of wielding a sword. They stood there, hand in hand, listening to the crickets chirp in the summer breeze and watching the flickering lights of Delm spread out before them. When she finally released Gilliad's hand, Sydney found that the words she needed would not come. So she merely nodded, squared her shoulders, and rode off into the night. But if you had asked her, Sydney could not have said if home lay ahead of her or behind.

5

Burnt Hope

It was a long night. The soldiers rode at a swift pace towards the southern coast. The lower Stoane River glimmered in the moonlight, acting as their guide across rocky terrain. The lights of Delm faded into the distance, and the wilderness swallowed them up like a great hungry beast. Though invisible in the darkness, the presence of the Brimholdian highlands loomed in the distance, and Sydney was thankful that their path led them away from those towering cliffs and plateaus. The soldiers stopped briefly to give the horses a moment of rest, but Sydney was eager to be on the move, farther, faster, forward into the night.

Just as Sydney was able to taste salt in the air, Brandon called for the group to stop. Sydney opened her mouth to protest, but her friend was quick to silence her.

"We have to rest, Syd." His voice was gentle. "We will be no use to Briar with half-dead horses and soldiers falling from their saddles."

A quick glance at her friends told Sydney he was right. Thomas' eyelids drooped, and Julia's mouth was stuck in a constant yawn as she guided her horse forward.

"Fine," Sydney conceded reluctantly. "But just until dawn." The captain led her team to an outcropping by the river that lay sheltered from the road. She took the first watch as the others slept, but when Philip came to relieve her, she waved him away. She would not sleep while Briar's fate hung in the balance.

Thoughts of her family tormented her. *What are they doing now? Are they fleeing the Ithirdi attack? Or do they lay peacefully in their beds, unaware of what's coming for them?* Worse than the musings on her family's imminent danger was the guilt. She remembered her father's voice calling after her as she left with the soldiers. Her sister's indignation and cold goodbye. They were nothing more than pale memories now, dulled by years of death and blood. But would those be the last memories she had of them? And if they were, could she really blame the elves? That fear clutched at Sydney's heart, hard and sharp like talons in her chest. *You could have seen them. But you kept yourself away.*

Relief washed over her as the first rays of daybreak peaked over the hills. She woke the others, rushing them through a quick breakfast and getting them on the road again. Brandon kept glancing in her direction, and Sydney knew her sleepless night was evident in the bags under her eyes. But when her friend moved to talk with her, she was quick to avoid his gaze and spur her horse forward. Words would not help her now.

They rode through tired farmland, small fields of wheat, potatoes, and barley. The land was lush and green from the recent summer rains, and oxen grazed lazily under the rising sun. Occasionally, they would pass a farmer with a loaded cart or a tinker selling his wares to travelers on the road. The locals would eye the solders suspiciously as they galloped past, staring pointedly at their groomed horses and polished weapons. It was clear they thought very little of the warriors paid to protect them. The idea bothered Sydney, but she pushed it down, focused on the mission at hand. At last, the friends came over the crest of a hill, and the sea spread out before them, waves rippling in the breeze. Eagerly, Sydney pulled at her reigns and directed the team to the west. They were making excellent time. A short ride along the coast and they would be on the final stretch to Briar. *Perhaps we can make it in time after all,* Sydney thought. For the first time since the beginning of this nightmare, she felt something like hope.

*****

It was late afternoon when they saw the smoke. Billowing black and gray clouds, obscuring the horizon. No one spoke.

At last, Julia whispered, "Is that…"

"Let's go," Sydney interrupted. A cold calm had settled over her. She motioned for her team to follow.

Some of Briar was still burning when the soldiers arrived, but most of the town lay in charred heaps, smoke tendrils curling out from beneath crumbled homes and stores. The entire village was silent. *The silence is the worst part,* Sydney thought to herself as they led the horses down the main road. But that wasn't true. The smell was worse, though the friends tried their best to ignore it. The smell of burnt skin and hair.

"Search for survivors," Sydney heard Brandon bark. His voice seemed far away. Julia, Thomas, and Philip quickly vanished between two collapsed buildings. But Sydney's co-captain stayed by her side, and together they made their way deeper into what was left of Briar.

She took in everything. Every smoldering cart. A townsperson's untouched laundry. The smell of burnt meat wafting from the destroyed butcher's shop. A villager laying in the street, arrows sticking from his breast. All of these things Sydney imprinted on her heart like a brand. She would never forget.

When she finally came upon her family's shop, Sydney's courage almost failed her. She climbed down clumsily from her horse, her legs shaking as she hit the ground. Brandon's hand touched her shoulder hesitantly, but she shook it off. She moved forward, reaching out to stroke the blackened beams of the doorway. That smoking mound… that was the counter where Sydney's father had sold his wares while his daughters played hide and seek in the storage room. Those broken steps… the steps that led to the loft, where Sydney had spent night after night telling her family about her daily adventures. Where her father had sung them to sleep at the end of a hard day. Dust and ash, that was all that was left.

Sydney imagined herself digging through the rubble, not stopping until she found her father and sister buried beneath. And then she ran. She heard Brandon yell her name, but she did not stop. She ran, out of town, her feet following a well-worn path from her childhood. Her boots pounded against the packed earth as she fled into the small patch of woods that bordered Briar. The grove was not big enough for a proper name, but as a girl Sydney had called it the Lost Wood. It was a quiet, solemn place. Tall oaks and alders rimmed the woods, isolating the interior from the rest of the world. Sydney used to pretend the Lost Wood had been cursed by an ancient being, doomed to sit in eternal silence. And only she, Sydney of Briar, could restore what had been lost. At one time, it was Sydney's favorite place. She had only let Abigail join her there on special occasions, when her games required two adventurers instead of one.

Sydney found her way to a fallen tree that lay across the forest floor. She sat down heavily. Her mind was numb. She had hoped putting distance between herself and Briar would wash away the horrors she had seen. But the images remained, seared into her memory, waiting every time she closed her eyes.

Something prodded against Sydney's side as she shifted her

position. A folded paper stuffed in her belt. Sydney stared at it. The letter from Briar, forgotten since Julia had given it to her yesterday. Could it have been only yesterday? It felt as if a hundred years had passed. With trembling hands, Sydney unfolded the parchment, forcing herself to read the words.

Dear Sydney,

I don't know if you're reading this. Honestly, I'm not sure you even get my letters anymore. But I've been writing them for so long, I can't seem to stop.

Papa is getting worse. The past few weeks he has mentioned you often. "Where's Sydney?" he wonders. I stopped telling him the truth after the first three times he asked. It's easier to say you are down at the docks or off in the woods or buying a fish for supper. He forgets within an hour anyway. Clara says he will only get worse now that fighting has cut off shipments of his medicine. There is only so much she can do for him without it.

But there are good days. Some days, Papa's mind is clear, and I can even get him to come down and help me around the shop. He always sneaks a bit of chocolate from the store room like he used to. Do you remember? Yesterday was a particularly good day, so we closed up the shop early and went to the docks to watch the sun set. I don't think we've done that since the first year after you left.

Business is poor, but we are getting by. It is hard now that I must run the shop on my own. Sometimes James from down the road will help me unload new shipments. I think he fancies me, but I know you would not approve. You always thought he was quite full of himself. Still, it is nice to have someone to talk to other than Papa.

I hope this letter finds you well. While I would do anything for a reply, I know that as long as the letters are not returned to me, at least you are alive somewhere. Stay safe and write me if you can. Please.

Yours,
  Abigail

The last words were smudged by the tears that now fell freely from Sydney's eyes. How could she have been so stupid? She had ignored her family for years. Years, while her father grew ill, while her unhealthy sister held them both afloat. Years of unopened letters. And for what? Pride? Fear? Yes, it was fear. Fear that her family was better off without her. Fear that letting them in would be like leaving them all over again. Fear that they would not like the person she had become. Fear that the blood on her hands had changed their daughter beyond recognition. But wouldn't all of that have been better than what she was left with now? *You were a fool*, Sydney told herself. *And now they're dead. Do you understand? Your family is dead, and you will never see them again.* Sydney buried her head in her hands, weeping for Briar, for her family. And even for herself. The trees of the Lost Wood rustled softly in the breeze, as if they mourned too.

She wasn't sure how long she sat there before Brandon found her. She could hear his steady footsteps moving through the undergrowth, but she did not raise her head.

"Sydney." That was it? Just her name? Was that all he could say? Sydney surged to her feet, ready to scream at him, to order him to leave her alone. Any excuse to feel anger instead of this pain like a knife in her chest. But when she saw him, Sydney deflated. Brandon's face, usually calm and guarded, held an openness that he reserved only for her and Gilliad. It was the face from their first battle together. The face he wore when he spoke of his family, lost to him too soon. The face of that little boy in the back of a wagon who dried her tears and made her smile. And Sydney could not find any anger towards that boy. Without speaking, she lifted the hand that still clutched her sister's final letter. Brandon took it wordlessly. He read the words quickly, his expression becoming one of understanding. When he finished, he passed the parchment back to her and pulled her into a tight hug.

"I'm sorry," Brandon whispered. "I'm so sorry."

The sun was low in the sky by the time Sydney's tears began to dry. She pulled herself from Brandon's embrace and took a deep, shuddering breath. Her body felt fragile, like an empty shell. But her heart was still beating. Her mind was clear. She heard Gilliad's voice in her head. *Your home needs you now, for better or for worse. You must be strong for your family.*

"Were there any survivors?" Sydney asked Brandon, her voice cracking.

He nodded, still watching her carefully. "One. A young girl. Her mother hid her when the town fell under attack. She's with Julia now."

"I want to speak with her," said Sydney. "She might have seen something that can make sense of this nightmare."

The friends made their way back to Briar. The sight of the ruined town was like a punch in the gut, but Sydney felt another emotion brewing. Fury.

The other soldiers stood just outside of town, huddled around a small figure. The evening was warm, but the little girl shivered beneath a bundle of blankets. Her tiny face seemed so pale in the fading light. The girl did not cry. She simply watched her saviors, eyes shifting from one soldier to another. The friends ignored Sydney's red eyes and tear stained face, for which she was grateful. She crouched down in front of the lone survivor of Briar with a heavy heart. The girl turned to her with haunted, hazel eyes.

"What's your name?" Sydney asked softly. The girl still jerked at the sound.

"Lillie."

"Could you tell me what happened here, Lillie? Anything you remember."

Lillie picked absently at the blanket around her shoulders. Her eyes looked as hollow as Sydney's chest. "We heard horses coming from the northern road. Mama thought it was the soldiers coming to recruit more of us for the war." She eyed her rescuers again. "She told me and Egor to hide. We were separated. I ran to the cellar behind the smith's shop."

"How long ago was this?"

"I don't know," Lillie murmured. "A while."

"And did you see any of the attackers? Did they have pointed ears?" Sydney questioned gently.

"I didn't see anything," Lillie whispered. "But I heard the screams. They're dead, aren't they? All of them. Egor too."

Sydney swallowed hard. She felt the girl's loss as sharply as her own. "I'm sorry, Lillie. You are the only one we've found. Briar was my home when I was your age. I've lost my family too."

Lillie did not shed a tear at the realization that her whole world was gone. Perhaps the thought was too heavy, too unreal for her mind to carry. But she reached out and grasped Sydney's arm. The grip was surprisingly firm for such a tiny hand. Those fierce hazel eyes pulled Sydney in.

"You will find them, won't you? The ones who did this?" the girl asked.

How can one so young be filled with so much hate? Sydney thought. But she knew the answer. War. War was the only thing that could age children so fast, hardening hearts that were meant to stay soft for a while longer.

"We will bring those monsters to justice," Sydney promised. She could feel Brandon's eyes on her back.

"You should kill them." Lillie's cold voice sent a shiver down Sydney's spine. "For Egor. For your family." The girl released Sydney's arm, leaning back and closing her eyes. Sydney wondered if she was listening to the screams of those they had lost.

Sydney rose and returned to the Honor Guard. Her friends were looking at her expectantly. Could they see the rage growing inside of her?

"I want the rest of you to take Lillie back to Delm," Sydney ordered using her best captain voice. She would not meet Brandon's eye. "Tell the queen what happened here. She needs to know what fresh horror the elves have wrought."

"The rest of us? What about you?" Philip asked. He was a quiet soldier, but he was observant. Sometimes too observant.

"I'm going to track the elves to be sure they are headed back to their side of the border. I will rejoin you in Delm as soon as I can." Sydney continued to ignore Brandon, but she could hear his unspoken accusation as easily as if he had said it aloud. *Liar.*

"May I speak with you for a moment?" Before she could answer, Brandon dragged Sydney away from the others. His brow wrinkled like it always did when he was upset. His fists were clenched at his side.

"We both know you're not just tracking the elves. What do you think you're going to do? Fight them all on your own? What's your plan?" Brandon spoke with his calm anger.

The truth was, Sydney didn't know what she would do if she caught up with the elves. But if she went back to Delm, she knew the fire in her chest would burn her alive.

"You're going to get yourself killed," Brandon seethed when Sydney didn't answer, running a furious hand over his short brown hair. The words echoed in Sydney's head. They were the same words her father had said when she left for the war. *Well,* Sydney thought. *I haven't died yet.*

"Whatever words you've prepared, you can save them. No matter what you say, I'm still going," Sydney replied to Brandon calmly.

"You think I don't know that?" Brandon's voice rose to a dangerous volume, and Julia glanced over at them with concern. Brandon stared at Sydney as if he could look into her head and maybe change what he found there. But after a moment, he merely sighed and turned away from her. "I'll tell the others to wait for morning before they head out. That will at least give us some extra time before the queen realizes we've disobeyed her orders."

Sydney knew her shock was written all over her face. "You're not coming with me! Camillea will be furious. There's no need for you to be dragged down with…" She trailed off when she saw the look on Brandon's face. They did not discuss the topic further.

6

The Trillium Inn

Sydney and Brandon set out just before sunset after bidding their comrades a quick farewell. With the scarlet sea at their backs, they began their search. The trail was not hard to find. Hoof prints and trodden earth led them north, towards the crags and rugged bluffs that marked the beginning of the highlands. But finding a trail was not their only obstacle. They knew so little about their target. How long had it been since the attack on Briar? How many elves were involved? And what would they do if the enemy had already reached the border? Sydney pushed the thoughts from her mind.

They followed the elves for four long days. They rode hard, stopping only to rest the horses, eat, and get a few hours of sleep. The highlands rose and fell around them, great green cliffs and outcroppings that formed long, narrow valleys. Fields of wildflowers dappled the hillsides while tiny streams tumbled over the land towards the ocean. The landscape, though beautiful, slowed their progress. The friends had to crisscross the terrain to avoid treacherous cliffs and crevices. A storm on their second night sent sweeping blankets of rain and thunder, forcing them to seek shelter for hours, much to Sydney's dismay. Every setback made the elves' trail harder to find, and eventually they resigned themselves to questioning citizens in the many tiny villages that populated the countryside. The men and women that made the highlands their home were a tough, private people. Getting any usable information was a slow process and only increased Sydney's frustration. By the time they reached the Trillium Inn on the evening of their fourth day out of Briar, the travelers were exhausted, irritable, and desperate for a hot meal.

The Trillium Inn sat on the edge of a small town. The inn itself was plain, but delicious smoke wafted from the chimney and candlelight danced in every window. Sydney and Brandon exchanged eager glances at the sight of it. Night wrapped itself like a dark blanket over the village as they stabled their horses and entered the tavern that occupied the lower floor of the inn.

The friends were greeted by a barmaid with a quick smile and emerald eyes that sparkled in the dimly lit bar. She seated them at the far side of the room near a group of rowdy locals. The server hustled about, supplying the travelers with two overflowing mugs of ale. She returned not long after with a steaming meal of tomato and onion soup, fresh bread, and baked potatoes the size of Brandon's fist. They devoured the food and listened to a bard play a rather sad looking lute in the corner. He wasn't terrible, though his rendition of *Oh Sally Silvertongue* could use some work.

"How much for a room at the inn?" Brandon asked after the friends had eaten their fill.

"Rooms are seven pykes, and drinks keep coming for a din a piece," the woman said with a wink. Sydney requested two rooms for the night, and the barmaid flitted off to attend to her other customers.

"Seven pykes," Sydney muttered in disbelief. "If this wasn't the only inn for miles, I wouldn't pay a nickel more than four."

Brandon shrugged, distracted.

"People have to make their living. Times aren't what they used to be. Besides, maybe we're paying for more than just a room." Brandon waved his mug towards the nearby patrons. Sydney gave him a knowing nod. She learned long ago that pubs were the best places to seek out information. In small towns, villagers disliked newcomers and trusted soldiers even less. Asking for help rarely produced results. But with enough luck and enough ale, even the most tight-lipped townsperson would spill their deepest secrets. All you needed was patience and a keen ear.

Sydney turned her attention to the villagers clustered around the bar. They were all listening to a loud, skinny fellow with a receding hairline and a wide grin. The townspeople exchanged humored looks among themselves as the man spoke. Sydney would have bet her entire purse that this man was the town drunk.

"I'm telling you lot, I saw a real, honest to life shadow-borne, straight from the Mist Lands. It was in my barn the other night," said the man. He leaned heavily against the bar, motioning with his hands. "It was as big as a horse, with blood red eyes and more teeth than I could count. I managed to fight it off, but the damn thing nearly killed me."

Brandon chuckled into his mug while Sydney hid her smile behind her hand.

"And that's not the only strange thing that's been happening around here. Some folk say a dragon's been spotted up north, in the Nidarian marshes." The man's voice lowered for dramatic effect. "A *black* dragon, mind you."

The old rhyme, chanted by children throughout Soarden, came to Sydney's mind:

A noble dragon, scales of white

Send the world down paths of light.
A dragon black with shadow wings
Will be the doom of ancient kings.

She rolled her eyes at the thought. The dragons flew away hundreds of years ago, disappearing over the northern mountains. They were dead, gone, lost. But every town drunk from Midport to Knotting believed they saw dragons in the sky, omens of crop failures or natural disasters or the end of days. Sydney thought it more likely that enough ale could make an eagle look a lot like a dragon.

"Black dragons always mean trouble," said the man as he downed the rest of his drink. "Brimhold's doomed if you ask me."

"Give it a rest, Dennis," another man called out from the back of the room. "Every week you've got a new theory about the end of the world."

"Tell me, Grady, how's business been lately? I see you only bought one pint tonight. Aren't your wares selling?"

The room was silent. Everyone was listening now. Dennis straightened himself, looking smug.

"Times are rough. Not a single one of you can deny that. Elves ride by almost every fortnight. Our kids are taken away to become soldiers. The roads are crowded with bandits and elves and gods only know what else. And if that's not enough, the queen's practically taxing us to death. If you ask me, our little wench here could rule Brimhold better than Queen Camillea." As he spoke, Dennis grabbed the barmaid around her waist and pulled her to his side. The young girl squirmed against him, her face uncomfortable. The surrounding men laughed among themselves.

Sydney's hand curled into a fist upon the table. Brandon eyed her warily.

"Keep your head, Syd. He's just a drunk. We're trying not to draw attention to ourselves."

"Why don't you get me some more ale, sugar?" Dennis handed the girl his mug. She gave a short nod, and he released her, taking a swat at her as she walked away.

"Deep breaths, Syd."

"Now if you ask me," the man continued. "Her Majesty has been at war too long. It's scramblin' that pretty head of hers. I bet I could show that fancy whore a good time. Really get her to ease up."

"Damn," Brandon sighed, placing his mug on the table with an air of finality.

In a second, Sydney surged across the room, a dagger in her hand. She grabbed Dennis by the shirt and flung him back against the bar. Stabbing downwards, Sydney drove her knife into the man's sleeve, pinning his arm to the wood. She pulled a second dagger from her belt and thrust it against the man's throat.

"What in the—" spluttered Dennis. The other patrons scrambled away from the commotion, their faces ranging from fear to outrage. "Who the bloody hell are you?"

"I am Sydney Krane of Briar, a Knight of Brimhold, and Captain of the queen's Honor Guard," Sydney snarled, moving her cloak to reveal the silver pin on her chest.

"Co-captain," added Brandon, appearing beside Sydney. He pulled his own badge from his pocket. The small crossed swords glimmered in the candlelight. Dennis' face changed in an instant, and Sydney noted true terror in his eyes. The Honor Guard's reputation obviously preceded them.

"My Lady… Sir…"

"State your name and trade," Sydney interrupted, her voice sharp.

"Dennis Yull, my Lady. I own a farm not two miles from here," Dennis replied quickly. The putrid smell of alcohol and tobacco poured from the man's mouth as he spoke. Sydney wrinkled her nose in disgust.

"Tell me, Dennis Yull," said Sydney gently. "Are you aware that the punishment for treasonous words against your queen is, at best, ten years in the palace dungeon, and at worst, hanging until death?"

"Please… please… I meant no disrespect, honest. Why, it was a compliment really…" Dennis was cut off as Sydney's knife dug farther into his throat. A thin line of blood slid down his neck.

"I am finding it rather hard to believe you, Dennis. I might need some convincing."

"Anything! Anything you want, my Lady." The man shook so hard that the sleeve pinned to the bar began to rip and tear.

"I need information. We're searching for a group of elves that came by this way. It wouldn't have been more than a few days ago."

Dennis opened his mouth before Sydney had finished speaking.

"Yes, yes, I saw them! Rode past my farm just last night. Came up from the south."

"How many were there?" Brandon asked.

"No more than a dozen I'd say, Sir."

"And where were they headed?"

"Couldn't say for sure. But looked like they were movin' west, towards the chasm. There's a bridge the elves use not far from here." Dennis waved his free arm in a directional manner.

Sydney glanced at Brandon, silently asking if he had anymore questions. He shook his head. Sydney nodded and leaned in towards her captive. The drunkard swallowed loudly.

"Listen to me closely, Dennis. For the information you've provided, I am prepared to let you go." Sydney spoke just above a whisper, but her voice carried throughout the bar. "You will tip the barmaid whatever measly earnings are currently in your possession, and you will leave. You will not come back. Ever. I have eyes and ears all over Brimhold, and if you so much as glance at this pub again, I will know. You have heard of us. I can tell from the look in your eyes. You know what we're capable of. Years from now, when the fear from this moment has faded and you think you are safe, remember my face. Know that all those tales you've heard of the Honor Guard, all the nightmares and ghost stories, will be nothing compared to what I have in store for you. Do we have an understanding?"

Pale faced and sweating, Dennis managed to nod. Sydney yanked her dagger from the bar and backed away. The man frantically emptied his pockets onto the counter, coins flying in all directions. Then, with one last terrified glance at Sydney, Dennis was gone, the tavern door slamming shut behind him.

Sydney strolled over to the bar and looked through the coins on the counter. She was pleasantly surprised to find three nickels, two pykes, and a gold half-brillean.

"Laying it on a little thick there, don't you think?" Brandon commented with a hint of amusement.

Sydney shrugged. She picked up the gold coin, leaving the rest for the barmaid, and turned to Brandon with a small smile.

"The man's a scumbag. Besides, it got us free drinks, didn't it?" She waved the coin and turned to address the room. "Drinks on Dennis!"

The crowded room filled with cheers, and the tense silence fell away into comfortable chatter once more. Sydney and Brandon returned to their table with the tavern's finest ale (which was "on the house" according to the now smiling barmaid). The two sat quietly for hours, enjoying the warm crackle of the nearby fire and the kind, simple laughter that only comes from a room full of neighbors and childhood friends. Later, after most of the tavern's occupants had wandered home for the evening, Brandon spoke.

"Last night," he said softly. "You know what that means."

Sydney nodded, fresh knots of anger and purpose forming in her stomach.

"Yes. We're catching up."

7

Across the Chasm

The Thorburn Chasm was a ragged gorge that ran almost the entire length of Brimhold's western border. Named after Yoric the Great, people said the ravine was created centuries ago during the last Shadow War, when the immense white dragon ripped the earth apart with his claws. He dug deep to reach the Sháedin and shadow-borne hiding in their caves, wiping out hordes of the dark creatures with his red fire. Or so the stories said. Sydney had always been skeptical of such things.

Sydney and Brandon came upon the chasm less than a day's ride from the inn. The highlands fell away, replaced by tall, old evergreen trees covered in moss. The trees went right up to the edge of the chasm, as if the forest really had been torn in two. At the sight of the plunging ravine, Sydney cursed. They had not caught up with the elves, and now they stood at the boundary of the two kingdoms. If they traveled any further, they would enter Ithirdas. Enemy territory. Brandon said nothing as Sydney led them along the gorge with the trees on their right and the cliff to their left. It wasn't long until they came to the bridge.

The bridge was old and narrow, barely wide enough for a single horse to cross. Made entirely of stone, moss hung from its sides, almost camouflaging it against the cliff face. Across the chasm, Sydney eyed a single elf sentry. The friends stayed among the trees and watched their foe from afar.

"Syd…" Brandon spoke first. Sydney watched his face. He was always so easy to read.

"I know," she rubbed her tired face. "You think we should turn back."

"We *have* to turn back." Brandon waved a hand towards the elf guard.

Sydney stared at the trees across the chasm as they swayed in the summer breeze. The ones who killed her family waited in that forest. The idea settled like a stone in her stomach. She met Brandon's eyes and hated the desperation she saw there. But in her heart, she had known her path would lead here. And she knew she had to see it through to the end.

"Syd, please. We'll go back to Delm. The queen will send soldiers. We will get justice for your father and sister, I promise. But not like this."

"What would you do," Sydney said quietly, "if you knew the elf that killed your father was in those trees? Just across that bridge. Would you listen if I asked you to quit now?" He didn't reply, but Sydney knew the answer. She swallowed hard.

"Brandon, you have been a brother to me all these years. You've saved my life countless times, and I cannot thank you enough for coming with me this far. But I can't ask you to go any farther. I know what I'm doing is beyond reason. But if I return to Delm now, I will never forgive myself."

Brandon sat very straight in his saddle as he gazed out across the ravine. Sydney could not believe how different he looked from that small, mop-haired boy she had met in the back of a wagon. When had that scrawny boy become a regal knight with a square jaw and a pensive stare? At last he looked at her, and she was glad that his eyes at least were the same.

"Do you remember the day you ordered Gilliad to make us *both* captains of the Honor Guard?" Brandon asked. Sydney blinked, the question startling her.

"*Ordered* is a little strong…"

"Do you remember what you said?"

Sydney smiled at the memory. "I said 'Gilliad Norwell, you will make Brandon and I *co-captains* of the Honor Guard. Brandon is a great leader. But sometimes he's an idiot, and he needs me to keep him out of trouble.'"

"You were right," Brandon laughed quietly. "But only by half. You need me too. I can be short-sighted, but you are the most impulsive person I've ever met." Sydney opened her mouth to protest, but he raised his hand. "What I mean to say is, we hold each other accountable. We keep each other alive. I would not be a good friend or a worthy co-captain if I left you now. We go together or not at all, Syd. Just like we always have."

"Perhaps we should add stubbornness to your list of character flaws," Sydney grumbled, hiding the tears in her voice. Brandon laughed again.

"Well, Captain Krane, what's your plan? How are we going to get past that sentry and into the belly of the beast?"

Sydney grinned maniacally, and Brandon groaned.

"I'm regretting this already."

*****

Brandon broke from the trees and stumbled towards the stone bridge. He limped heavily on one leg, his shirt ripped and his face covered in dirt.

"Please!" Brandon shouted, voice dripping with desperation. "Please, help me! My friend is injured!"

The elf across the bridge jumped at the noise. He raised a long bow and aimed an arrow across the chasm. "Stop right there!" Brandon slid to a stop a few feet from the bridge. He lifted his hands helplessly.

"Please, sir." Sydney could not see Brandon from where she lay in the grass, but she could tell he was selling their charade. "We were attacked by bandits, and my friend collapsed. I'm unarmed, see? Please, will you not help us?"

For a long moment, as she listened with a pounding heart, Sydney heard nothing. But then a rustling in the grass told her Brandon was moving in her direction. The elf took their bait.

"She's just over here." Brandon's voice was right above her now. A second set of footsteps followed behind him. A boot lightly kicked Sydney's shoulder. At the signal, Sydney flew to her feet. Together, she and Brandon grabbed the elf by either arm, forcing him against a nearby tree. The elf tried to yell, but Brandon clamped a large hand over his mouth.

"We need information," Sydney began. The elf looked at her through wide eyes that seemed oddly young. Sweat beaded on his high forehead.

"A group of elves crossed this bridge less than a day ago." Brandon spoke with the low voice he used when addressing elves. The sound always sent chills down Sydney's spine. "Which way were they headed?"

Some of the fear faded from the elf's eyes, replaced by a fierce determination. He flicked his pinned hand, and the earth beneath them seemed to shift. The ground pulled, trying to tug them off balance. Sydney yanked her boots from the hungry earth and pulled a knife on their captive. She dug the point into his gut until the soil stilled once more.

"None of that," Sydney warned. She could see that threats would only harden the elf's resolve. Deciding to take a different approach, she said, "Look. This can go one of two ways. You can keep quiet, and we kill you. Or, you can tell us what we need, and we let you live. Use that elvish wit. What real threat are two humans in your kingdom? Chances are we won't last the day. Is a minor slip in loyalty really worth your life?"

The elf stared at her. After a moment's hesitation, he nodded. Brandon slowly removed his hand from the sentry's mouth.

"The ones you're looking for went due west from the bridge, towards the mountains." Venom dripped from every word the elf spoke. "That's all I know."

"Thanks."

Sydney smashed the elf's face with the hilt of her dagger. Unconscious, his head rolled forward. Sydney and Brandon carefully lowered their enemy to the ground.

"I can't believe you made me rip my favorite shirt," Brandon complained. Sydney laughed as she moved to reclaim their belongings from the nearby trees. As she turned away, Brandon asked, "We're really going to let him live?"

"He's just a guard, Brandon," Sydney said with surprise. Her friend didn't argue, but he looked down at the elf with disgust. Sydney watched him warily. Sometimes it was easy to forget how much hatred Brandon carried for the elves. Sydney's anger was hot, fast, direct. Quick to rise and equally quick to fall. But Brandon's fury was slow and festering, masked by a steely calm. And some days it scared even Sydney.

The friends cut their horses loose, not wanting to make unnecessary tracks through the enemy forest. The steeds set off towards the east, and Sydney hoped they would find their way back to Delm or at least to a nearby village. Shouldering their bags, Sydney and Brandon crossed the stone bridge and were quickly consumed by the looming trees beyond.

The Wornwood Forest, or so men had long ago dubbed the never-ending expanse of woodland, covered almost all of Ithirdas. Towering spruce, maple, and hemlock trees filled the sky overhead, casting the forest into shadow. Sheets of moss coated the massive trunks, and ferns dappled the forest floor with different shades of green. The wood seemed to groan in the summer air. This forest was alive. The leaves trembled, the branches spoke. Sydney felt as if she was stepping into a different world.

They traveled deeper and deeper into the Wornwood, every step bringing them farther from home and closer to their prey. Eventually, the sun sank too low in the sky, and they were forced to stop for the night. They stumbled across a small, rocky hollow set in a cliff side. The perfect hiding place. Sydney nibbled on a cold dinner of bread and salted pork while Brandon set a hunting trap not far from their makeshift camp. They made no fire so as not to draw attention to themselves among the dark trees. Later, the friends sat in silence, listening to the foreign forest around them. A wolf howled in the distance.

"Brandon," Sydney said quietly. "Do you think I'm doing the right thing?"

He looked at her. "You've seemed so certain up until now."

"I know." She picked a stick off the ground and broke it into tiny fragments. "I've just been thinking of my family. Is this what they would want from me? Running off on a suicide mission?"

It was hard to make out Brandon's eyes in the darkness. When he finally spoke, his voice was subdued. "I've always been so sure my family would be proud of what I've done in the Honor Guard. I remember so little of my father, but he must have hated the elves too.

He volunteered to fight them. They killed him in the end."

Sydney stayed silent as he continued. Brandon rarely discussed his family.

"I do remember my mother, though. I would like to pretend that I carry her fury with me into battle. But that would be a lie. My mother was never angry. Not at the elves. Not at my father for leaving us. Not at anyone." Brandon met her eyes again, and this time Sydney was sure she could see fire in them. "We have to be angry for them, Syd. Evil wipes away the soft hearts of this world. If we don't fight for them, darkness prevails."

"I'm not so sure," Sydney said with a sigh, pushing a strand of dark hair behind her ear. But who was she to say what her family would want? She hadn't truly known them for years.

"Uncertainty is a sign of wisdom. For only fools believe they have all the answers," Brandon recited the words as if reading them from a book. Sydney laughed.

"Gilliad is reusing advice again. The old man needs new material," Sydney said lovingly.

They both smiled, lost for a moment in fond memories and a simpler time. But Brandon quickly pulled them back to reality.

"I understand your hesitation, Syd. If I remember correctly, I've tried to make you turn back multiple times now. As always, you're stubborn as a mule. But you have good instincts, and I will follow you wherever they take us." He leaned back against a tree, closing his eyes. "Besides, I understand better than anyone the need for revenge. I will never get mine. But I can help you get yours."

Sydney's voice drifted into the quiet night, hushed and unsure among the shadowed trees. "I don't want revenge. I want justice."

"Well, aren't they the same thing?"

8

A Boy in the Woods

The next morning brought a cool breeze that hinted at summer's end. The trees overhead were filled with the songs of strange birds, and sunlight trickled down through the mossy branches. Sydney had to admit that, despite its inhabitants, she found the forest enchanting.

As Brandon fetched water from a nearby stream, Sydney went to check the trap he had set the night before. Her stomach growled for something to eat other than stale bread. But as she rounded the final tree, she froze. She silently pulled a sword from its sheath.

An elf boy crouched on the forest floor, his hands making quick work of Brandon's trap. The child had a slender frame with an oval face and short, sandy hair that stuck out in every direction. He whispered gently to the small creature that had sprung the trap, lifting his grimy hands in triumph a moment later. A rabbit leapt from the coiled rope and took off into the undergrowth. It was only then that the boy looked up, noticing Sydney and her drawn sword for the first time. He had large eyes, a lighter green than the trees overhead.

"Taldell ethe?" the boy asked in Elvish. His voice chirped like a bird,

high and clear.

Sydney said nothing but took a few steps forward. The elf glanced from her sword to her ears, and his eyes grew wide.

"Oh. I see." The Elvish fell away, replaced with perfect Soardic. "Who are you?"

Sydney continued to move closer to the boy. There was no fear in his eyes. He wiped one of his small hands across his forehead, leaving a smudge of dirt behind.

"Was that your trap? Traps scare the animals. And they hurt." The boy spoke simply, as if teaching a young child.

Another step. Sword raised.

The boy smiled. Then he ran, dashing away like the rabbit before him. Cursing, Sydney bolted after him. He was fast, but luck was on her side. As the boy tried to vanish between the trees, he smashed straight into Brandon, bouncing off of him, a bird against a glass window. Brandon seized the boy and lifted him from the ground. The elf struggled against his captor, but Brandon was far too strong. He eventually hung limp in the soldier's arms. Sydney caught up with them and locked eyes with the elf. Childlike innocence glowed in their green depths. His light hair stuck up in a state of eternal surprise, but the boy still seemed unafraid.

"What are you doing out here alone?" Sydney asked hesitantly. She was not used to interrogating children.

"I'm never alone." The boy still spoke to Sydney as if she was a simpleton. Brandon tightened his hold on the child who squirmed uncomfortably.

"How many are with you?" Brandon glanced at the forest around them, looking for enemies among the shadows.

"Oh, you mean elves?" The boy paused. "Ten, I think. Eleven including me."

Sydney and Brandon exchanged a glance. She remembered the

words of the drunk at the Trillium Inn. *No more than a dozen I'd say.* Had they found their targets at last? Did Ithirdi soldiers always bring children with them to their massacres?

"Did you and your… *friends* cross the border? Were you on Brimhold's side of the chasm?"

Something changed in the boy's eyes. The general friendliness that hung on his face seemed to crack. "You shouldn't be here. You should go."

That was as good as a confession.

"We aren't going anywhere," Sydney said, excitement bubbling inside her. Her mission had been failed from the start. An outright attack on the enemy soldiers would never work. But a prisoner? A child for that matter. Sydney could work with that. For the first time, she felt as if the justice she sought might be attainable.

"Let's take him back to camp," Sydney said. Brandon nodded, slinging the boy easily over his shoulder. Together, they made their way back through the trees.

The boy would not stop chattering. "You're making a mistake. We didn't do anything to you. Why won't you just leave? Go home while you can. They'll come for me if I'm not back soon."

"What's your name, kid?" Sydney was walking behind Brandon, so she could keep an eye on the boy.

"Raiden."

"Well, Raiden, your friends coming after you is exactly what I'm counting on."

Her words silenced him.

When they reached their makeshift camp, Brandon tied the boy to a tree, making sure his nimble hands were secure. Raiden watched them carefully.

"Are all humans this foolish?" the elf asked. He seemed to be genuinely curious.

Brandon glared at the boy and pulled Sydney aside so that they were out of earshot.

"What's our play here?" Brandon asked, still glancing uncomfortably at Raiden.

"We wait," said Sydney. She could hear Gilliad's voice in her head. *Be patient. Let your enemy come to you.* "If we go traipsing through the forest, we're sure to be surrounded and ambushed. At least from here we should see them coming long before they see us. Besides, now we have something they want."

"And what are we going to do when they find us? Kill the boy?"

"Of course not!"

"Well, then what? I don't like this, Syd. We should ditch the kid, find them on our own, make a plan… what's that?" Brandon stopped speaking abruptly. Sydney whipped around.

A goldfinch sat on Raiden's knee, and he seemed to be whispering to the creature. The bird gave a few soft tweets before taking off, leaving behind a single yellow feather. Brandon stormed over to their captive.

"What was that? Some of your vile magic?" Brandon snapped. Sydney placed a warning hand on his shoulder.

Raiden looked up in surprise. That face. So open and innocent. "It was just a bird. I like birds."

"I've seen elf magic. You all do something. Move the earth with the flick of a hand, spark fire from nothing." Brandon took another threatening step towards the boy. Raiden looked afraid for the first time, and Sydney swiftly moved between them.

"Brandon, enough! He's a boy." Sydney held up her hands in a calming gesture. "If you're worried about his magic, we can gag him as well."

Some of the tension fell from Brandon's square shoulders. He nodded. "You're right. I'm sorry. It's just this place. It's driving me crazy. We're surrounded by enemies, and now one's sitting in our camp."

The friends fashioned a gag from Brandon's ripped shirt and wrapped it snugly around Raiden's mouth. The boy gave them a fierce frown but didn't protest. He still seemed uneasy after Brandon's outburst.

The day passed slowly. Sydney and Brandon took turns scouting the surrounding forest while the other kept a close eye on their captive. As the hours dragged by, Sydney grew more and more frustrated. She had hoped the elves would be close behind their lost child, but evening came and still the trees sat silent and waiting. All the while, Raiden stared at her, as if he could see straight into her head.

The friends ate a quiet supper that night. As Sydney finished her meal, she glanced over and saw the boy eyeing their food. With a sigh, she dug some stale bread and an apple from her bag.

"What are you doing?" Brandon asked as she crouched beside Raiden.

"Giving him something to eat. Or are we in the habit of starving children now?" Brandon said nothing as Sydney loosened the elf's bonds and gag.

"Here." Sydney placed the food in Raiden's grimy hands. He stared at the gift, making no move to eat it.

"Look, I'm not trying to poison you, kid," Sydney said. "I just thought you might be hungry."

Raiden peered up at her with that penetrating stare of his.

"Thank you, Lady." The boy dipped his head at her before starting on his meager meal.

"It's Sydney."

"Sydney." Raiden pondered the word as he chewed. "How did you earn that name?"

"I didn't earn it," said Sydney, puzzled by the question. "It was given to me by my father when I was born."

"Oh," the elf said simply. He took a large bite of his apple.

"Sydney?"

"Yes?"

"You asked me earlier if my friends had entered Brimhold. Why do you want to know?"

Sydney searched Raiden's small face for signs of deception. Elvish manipulation. But all she could see was a little boy, full to the brim with unbridled curiosity. Why lie to him?

"A few days ago, my entire village was burned to the ground. My father and sister were among the dead." Sydney could taste tears in her throat.

"I'm sorry." Raiden eyes were wide with pity. He reached to touch her wrist with a comforting hand. Sydney recoiled instinctively, and the hand fell away.

"You think my friends did that to your people." The boy's voice was soft. His hand wrapped around a small carving that hung from his neck. A bear maybe? "That's why you're here. But what will you do if you catch them?"

"*When* we catch them," Sydney said evenly, "I will get justice for those who were taken from me."

Raiden said nothing for a while. He finished his meal, then held out his hands to be bound once more. When he looked at her again, his eyes held the weight of a much older soul.

"I hope you get your justice, Sydney," Raiden assured her. "But I don't think you'll find it here."

Later, once their prisoner slept and Brandon snored gently beside her, Sydney sat alone with her thoughts. She felt the child's words settling over her. Denial. Doubt. Fear. Had she let her anger carry her too far? Perhaps this road ended in regret instead of closure. *No,*

Sydney thought as Brandon relieved her from guard duty and she settled down to sleep. *My family led me here. My heart, my instinct. I will not let an enemy distract me from that.* But through the night, when Sydney dreamed, it was of green eyes, a small, oval face, and her own bloody hands.

9

The Archer

Sydney awoke suddenly with adrenaline pumping through her veins. Something was wrong. Every muscle in her body urged her to jump to her feet. Only her training kept her still and quiet on the ground, eyes tightly closed.

She tried to breathe normally as she sensed what she could of her surroundings. Warm, morning light glowed behind her sealed eyelids. A light breeze brushed through the branches overhead, rattling pine needles to the forest floor. Sydney could smell the remains of the fire they had dared to light the day before, all smoke and ash. A seemingly normal morning. Sydney increased her focus. She noted the absence of Brandon's heaving breathing as he paced the camp. The small, subtle footsteps of someone that did not want to be heard. Cautiously, Sydney opened her eyes a minuscule amount, no more than slits. She lay facing the elf boy, Raiden, still tied against the tree. Through her squinted eyes, Sydney could just make out the boy's face. He seemed to be looking over her at something in the trees. Sydney eyed her swords where they lay near her face, hands twitching towards them.

In a single motion, Sydney leapt towards her prisoner, plucking the swords from the ground as she soared over them. She landed in a crouch, one sword out towards Raiden, the other pointed towards her assailant.

Ten paces away, an elf warrior froze, his bow drawn and ready to fire. *Great,* Sydney thought. *An archer.* The approaching elf was lean and angular, with a tuft of windblown brown hair. His face carried the sharp angles and features characteristic of the elves, and he looked to be in his early twenties, though with elves it was impossible to know for certain. He wore light leather armor and a long green cloak attached at the shoulders. The silver fox of Ithirdas was stitched in careful detail at its center with a matching silver trim. He moved slowly towards Sydney as he kept his arrow pointed directly at her chest.

A lump formed in Sydney's throat. Brandon lay unmoving on the other side of the camp.

"Back!" Sydney hissed, moving beside Raiden. Her blade hung in front of the boy's throat.

The elf stopped again and took a half-step backwards. He was close enough now that Sydney could make out his eyes. Fierce forest green, just a shade darker than Raiden's. Realization hit Sydney as she noticed the similarity between the two elves.

"Is this your brother?" Sydney guessed with a nod at her prisoner. The warrior did not respond, but his jaw gave a tiny twitch. Sydney smiled. "I thought so. If you care for your brother, I suggest you stay where you are and lower your weapon."

Eyes flashing, the warrior lowered his bow slightly. The elf's gaze shifted from Sydney to Raiden. His expression softened.

"Lanethe nell?" the elf spoke for the first time, his words only for Raiden. Sydney cursed herself for not speaking Elvish. Raiden nodded and some of the tension fell from the elf's shoulders. He looked back at Sydney.

"Who are you?" the elf asked in Soardic. His words were smooth, no hint of an accent in his voice. "What do you want with my brother?"

"You're not in a position to be asking questions." Sydney smiled and wiggled her blade meaningfully. "What have you done to my companion?"

"Your friend is fine," the elf replied, irritation coloring his tone. He moved subtly closer to Sydney. "He'll have a sore head when he wakes up but no lasting damage."

Well, that was some relief.

"If you take one more step," Sydney said, her voice low, "your brother dies."

The elf stared at Sydney for a long moment. His eyes swept over her, sizing her up. After a heavy silence, the elf broke into a crooked grin, and he lifted his bow once more.

"I don't believe you. You're not going to kill him. We both know that."

Sydney rose from her crouch, slightly weary. She hadn't expected the elf to call her bluff so soon. Raising her swords, she said, "Let's get on with it then."

The first arrow came so fast that Sydney barely managed to deflect it in time. The elf warrior let loose one shaft after another, moving sideways across the campsite. Sydney brought her blades up in wide arcs as she sliced the arrows from the air. She followed the elf's movement, keeping herself between her attacker and her captive. Lunging forward, Sydney dodged past the arrows and made a swipe at the elf. He sprung away, keeping just out of reach. He was good. And fast. His arrows flew with deadly accuracy. But he was also distracted. Those sharp eyes kept flitting over to Raiden, still bound and vulnerable. Sydney moved closer to the boy in an attempt to take advantage of this weakness. The elf warrior gritted his teeth in anger. He aimed another arrow, but Sydney could tell by the angle that the archer was finally off his mark. She grinned, sensing her opening.

Then something changed. One moment a gentle breeze floated through the forest, barely strong enough to stir the trees overhead. The next second brought a wind so powerful that it rocked Sydney back on her heals. It took her a split second to realize what was happening. A split second too long. *Magic.* The archer loosed his arrow. Impossibly, the arrow curved through the air, guided by the gale at its back, and lodged itself into Sydney's shoulder.

Sydney let out a sharp cry of pain as she fell to her knees, losing hold of one of her swords in the process. Cursing at her mistake, she tried to swing her other weapon in a weak defense, but the motion tugged painfully at her wound. The second sword landed softly in the grass. With an arrow in her shoulder and another pointed at her face, Sydney knew she was beaten.

The elf stood panting in front of her, another arrow nocked. He planned to kill her. Sydney could see it in his eyes, cold and unforgiving. His arrow hovered in front of her eye, and Sydney imagined it sliding into her. Sharp, unimaginable pain and then nothing. For the first time, the fear of death washed over her. True, nauseating fear that settled in the stomach. It was over. Sydney closed her eyes, not wanting to see the end when it came, not wanting to see the pain before she felt it.

"Lukaris, wait!"

The shout pulled Sydney from her fear like a bucket of cold water. Her eyes flickered open in disbelief. The scene was the same. The elf warrior stood over Sydney with his weapon poised. But his focus was now on Raiden. The boy looked stricken, his eyes wide and his face pale.

"Don't hurt her, please! It's not her fault. Please, Luka," Raiden pleaded. Sydney was shocked to see tears in the boy's eyes.

"Raiden," said Lukaris gently. "She's a Brim soldier."

"Is that all it takes to make us murderers?"

The wind died. The leaves stilled. The entire forest held its breath. Lukaris looked at Sydney. Really looked at her, straight through, so deep that she wanted to look away but couldn't. After a moment that lasted a lifetime, the breeze picked up again, and the elf lowered his bow. Air rushed from Sydney's lungs, and she realized she had been holding her breath too.

"Stay where you are." There was no anger in Lukaris' tone, just an unspoken threat. Sydney obeyed. She was in no condition to go anywhere. With a dagger from his belt, the elf cut away the ropes binding Raiden and freed him at last. The brothers fell into a tight embrace, whispered Elvish passing between them. When they pulled away, Raiden wasn't the only one with tears in his eyes.

"Never do that again," said Lukaris gruffly. He smacked Raiden on the back of the head, but his mouth twisted into that half smile.

"I didn't *mean* to get captured," Raiden replied with a grin of his own. "It just sort of happened."

Rolling his eyes, Lukaris ruffled his brother's hair, somehow making it messier than it was before. He passed the boy a single yellow feather. The goldfinch. So Brandon had been right. The boy had used the bird to call for help. *You were a fool, Sydney,* she thought. *A damn fool.*

The elf warrior turned his attention back to her. His expression was unreadable.

"What's your name?" Lukaris asked. "And don't bother lying."

"Sydney."

"Your full name."

Sydney glared, gritting her teeth against the pain in her shoulder. "Sydney Krane… of Briar."

"And tell me Sydney of Briar, Captain of the Honor Guard," the elf shot a pointed look at the silver pin on Sydney's chest. She cursed her stupidity, glad at least that Brandon had removed his own emblem when baiting the chasm guard. "What are you doing in Ithirdas? Kidnapping my little brother for that matter."

At this point, Sydney saw no real advantage in lying. She would either die from blood loss or from a second arrow once the elves got the information they desired.

"Elves burned down my home and killed my family a week ago in the town of Briar. I have come seeking justice." Sydney looked up at Lukaris defiantly. Black spots danced across her vision.

"Your queen sent you alone into enemy territory to get revenge for the killing of your family?" Lukaris asked skeptically.

"The queen knows nothing of this. I acted alone."

Lukaris gave her a hard stare. She met his eyes without a flicker of deceit. Finally, he nodded. "I believe you."

"What a great relief," spat Sydney, her head spinning as more blood welled up from her wound. The pain only sharpened her temper.

"I don't know who destroyed your village," Lukaris said evenly. "But I can assure you that Ithirdi soldiers were not responsible. My brother and I were *certainly* not responsible."

"Forgive me if I don't trust the word of an elf," Sydney said. "You're lying to protect your friends or lying to protect yourself. Either way, you're still a liar."

Lukaris squatted down so that he was eye level with Sydney, still on her knees in the dewy grass. His eyes changed in the light. They were now the dark green of an old forest in the early morning. Calm and solemn, full of secrets that only gather during the blackest parts of the night.

"I swear to you. By the sun and the moon. On my names and my honor. By the great Light that runs through us all. Whatever tragedy befell your family was not the work of the elves." Lukaris spoke with such sincerity that Sydney was forced to look away. She felt tears forming in her eyes though she didn't know why.

"It's true," Raiden added, his voice startling. So soft and innocent among the talk of death and the smell of blood.

"I have been tracking the murderers all the way from Briar." Sydney's voice was choked. "If the Ithirdi did not destroy my village, then who did? And why did their tracks lead straight to you?"

"I don't know," said Lukaris simply.

They lapsed into silence. The elves exchanged a glance full of hidden meaning. Sydney watched them, trying to read their expressions through her pain addled state. After a moment, Lukaris sighed.

"Well, with misunderstandings out of the way, we are left with a wounded Brim soldier and her unconscious partner miles into my kingdom. I can't kill you. I can't let you leave. So what am I to do with you?"

Fear closed around Sydney's throat. She could not let Brandon pay for her mistakes. "Do what you will with me. Take me prisoner if you must. But leave my companion. He's just a sword for hire I picked up in Layton. He's no soldier, just a man trying to earn some money to care for his family. Please. Let him go. Take me."

Lukaris looked at her, the now infuriating smile on his face. He didn't believe her. Sydney could tell. She opened her mouth, ready to pile on another lie, when something rustled in the undergrowth. The smile fell off Lukaris' face as he swung to face the new threat, his bow poised and ready. He moved to stand protectively in front of Raiden.

A third elf came crashing into the hollow at a sprint. He looked to be the same age as Lukaris with short, curly brown hair. His features were softer than most elves, dominated by a round face and round hazel eyes. Even his large, pointed ears seemed rounder than normal. He wore the same soldier uniform as Lukaris, leather armor and a green cloak.

The intruder froze at the sight of Sydney, wounded and bleeding on the forest floor. His eyes flitted from Sydney to Raiden to Lukaris' bow to the arrow in Sydney's shoulder. Somehow his round eyes grew even rounder. Lukaris relaxed and lowered his bow once more.

"Flindir!" the eldest brother said with relief. He clapped the new arrival heartily on the back. Flindir's eyes remained a bit wide around the edges. He opened his mouth, but no sound came out.

"Ah, yes," Lukaris said meekly. "We had a bit of a situation. But Raiden's unharmed. He's safe."

The words broke some kind of tension that hung in the air. Flindir's shoulders relaxed as Raiden ran to him, and they fell into a familiar embrace. Flindir whispered Elvish to the boy, his voice soft and warm. When they pulled away, both elves were grinning ear to ear. Lukaris rolled his eyes at whatever words had passed between them. Meanwhile, Sydney tried her best to stay conscious. She looked over at where Brandon still lay in the grass on his stomach. A trickle of dried blood stained his forehead, but otherwise he could be sleeping. Sydney stared at him with a sickening dread pooling in her stomach.

"Not that this isn't touching," Sydney spoke up, her voice dripping with venom. "But if you were planning on letting me bleed to death while you chatter away, I would prefer you just kill me outright. Not that I expect any mercy from an honorless elf."

Sydney had hoped to anger Lukaris into a quick decision. The longer they mulled about, the less likely Brandon would be allowed to leave. Particularly if he woke up and tried to kill her captors. But much to Sydney's dismay, Lukaris did not appear angry. He looked at her thoughtfully. After a long moment, the elf lifted his chin as if a decision had been made. He turned to Flindir.

"Do you have your things?" Lukaris asked his friend. Flindir nodded, shrugging the sack slung across his back.

"Good." Lukaris motioned to Sydney. "Our captive needs medical attention."

Flindir looked at Lukaris quizzically, as if wondering why they weren't leaving Sydney to die, but he didn't argue. He crouched in front of her, taking his bag from his shoulder. The elf reached out slowly to explore Sydney's wound. Flindir had a nervous energy about him, but his hands were calm and steady as he pulled gently at the arrow shaft. He prodded at the skin around the wound and nodded as Sydney winced.

"This is a clean shot," Flindir said in Soardic. He spoke in the same kind, soft tone he had used with Raiden. "The arrow just missed the muscles in your shoulder. If we can get it out and stop the bleeding, you should make a full recovery."

"How lucky for me my attacker missed his mark," Sydney said through gritted teeth.

Flindir looked up, startled, meeting Sydney's eyes for the first time. His irises were a golden honey in the flickering sunlight. Warm yet serious.

"If the arrow hit you in this spot it's because that's where Lukaris intended," Flindir said simply. There was no doubt in his voice. He held Sydney's eyes for another moment before returning to his work. He pulled a small glass vial from his bag, filled with a thick orange liquid, and a large number of crumpled, but clean, bandages.

"Raiden, I need you to go and find me some stellaria. You remember I showed it to you the other day?" The young elf nodded eagerly. Flindir closed his eyes, his left hand to the ground and his head tilted as if he was listening. Sydney felt something stir. To say the wind shifted would be wrong. The breeze did not change, and Sydney felt no sensation on her skin. Nor did something move in the clearing, like a rodent foraging or a bird taking flight. It was not something Sydney could see or hear. Instead it was a feeling deep in Sydney's stomach, a small twist in the air. Sydney shivered as she recognized the use of magic, though she wasn't quite sure what kind. Flindir opened his eyes and pointed north. "There should be some along that way. Hurry." Raiden sped off into the trees.

The curly-headed elf busied himself once more, pulling rags, a small flask, and a worn leather water skin from his sack. Flindir opened the flask and passed it to Sydney without speaking. She took it gingerly, careful not to pull at her injury, and sniffed the contents suspiciously. Her gray eyes narrowed.

"This is ale."

"And?" Flindir responded dryly. He arched an eyebrow.

"Oh." Sydney blinked, understanding. She upended the flask, drinking until her throat burned. As she passed the bottle back to Flindir, he took a large swig of his own.

"That's not the kind of behavior I would expect from a healer," Sydney remarked.

"Who ever said I was a healer?" the elf replied with a grin. Sydney paled and grabbed the flask for another drink. While she was distracted, Flindir snapped the head from the arrow sticking through her shoulder and set it aside. He waved Lukaris over.

"I need you to brace her shoulders as I pull out the arrow. I need to do it as cleanly as possible, which will be more difficult if she's squirming all over the place," Flindir said, his voice wavering more than Sydney would have liked. Lukaris moved to stand behind her, his hands hard and unyielding on her arms, yet soft as a summer breeze. Flindir placed one hand around the arrow, the other braced against Sydney's shoulder.

"This is going to hurt." Flindir maintained his gentle tone, but his eyes were fearful. Sydney's eyelids flitted closed to hide her own anxieties. A deep breath in. A deep breath out. Then, she nodded.

"Just do it."

Sydney cried out as Flindir dragged the arrow from her shoulder, but the pain could have been worse. She opened her eyes to see fresh blood flowing from the now gaping wound. Her head swam at the sight of it. Flindir worked quickly, pressing rags against the injury in an attempt to stop the bleeding. Sydney winced as he applied pressure, and she swayed dangerously. Only Lukaris' hands kept her from toppling to the ground.

Raiden came sprinting back into the camp, his hand clutching a bouquet of small white flowers, roots and all. The boy hurried over to Flindir, placing the bundle beside him. At the sight of Sydney's wound, his small face paled.

"Is she… is she going to be ok?" Sydney was surprised by the fear in the young elf's voice.

"She'll be fine, *osan*." Lukaris moved to block his brother's view. He stared down at Sydney as if daring her to prove him wrong.

Flindir whipped together a strange mixture of flowers and orange liquid while Lukaris worked to stop the bleeding from Sydney's shoulder. Once Flindir applied the salve and wrapped the wound in fresh bandages, Sydney felt some of her dizziness fall away. The flask of ale didn't hurt either. Lukaris finally released Sydney's shoulders, and she was pleased to find that she could sit up on her own. Flindir looked relieved.

"The shoulder should heal fine, but we should get her back to Ettee just in case. She'll know better than me. That is…" Flindir paused. "We *are* taking her back with us?"

Lukaris nodded and watched his friend for some sort of response. Flindir wrung his hands nervously but didn't fight the matter. Sydney almost wished he would have. Satisfied, Lukaris walked over to Sydney's belongings, rifling through them curiously as he filled up her bag. He glanced down at her swords that still lay abandoned in the grass, uncertainty clouding his features. After a moment, the elf plucked them up, wrapping them snugly in her cloak before adding them to his bundle. Lukaris slung the sack over his shoulder before moving to stand beside his prisoner.

"Can you walk?" the elf asked. Sydney's shoulder ached miserably, but it was manageable. She nodded shortly. "Good. Then listen and hear me. I have no plan to bind you. You may walk on your own. But if you try to run or hurt my family, I will kill you before you can reach the nearest tree. Do you understand?"

Anger boiled in Sydney's stomach, but she nodded again. Lukaris pulled Sydney gently to her feet and began to lead her from the clearing.

"What about him?" Flindir asked, nodding down at Brandon's motionless form.

"Leave him," Lukaris said without turning around. "He'll find his way back where he belongs, or the forest will claim him." Sydney breathed a sigh of relief. Flindir and Raiden followed behind them, clearly eager to be on their way. Sydney spared one final glance at Brandon. His expression was peaceful, the years of fighting washed from his face as he slept. Sydney turned away quickly, swallowing hard. Her situation was bad, there was no denying that. Injured, captured, and soon to be alone in Ithirdi territory. But she was alive. When Brandon awoke, he would go get help. Either that, or Sydney would just have to rescue herself.

10

The Wornwood

"Are we there yet?" Sydney asked for the tenth time, pausing between two lofty hemlocks. She glanced back at Lukaris who had followed silently behind her for nearly an hour, a slender shadow, as the party headed deeper into the Wornwood. His jaw twitched with irritation, and Sydney suppressed a smile. Her shoulder ached and the severity of the situation weighed heavily on her mind, but she refused to let anything break her spirit.

"No," Lukaris said, forcing a smile. The lopsided grin Sydney had already grown to loathe. The elf gave her a firm shove in the back. "Keep walking. I will let you know when we arrive, since your eyesight has clearly failed you."

So, they kept walking. Despite herself, Sydney continued to marvel at the forest around her. Moss covered branches stretched in every direction, a patchwork of green. The shade felt cool and fresh like an eternal autumn, and the breeze carried the smell of sweet pine and damp soil. They passed down into a valley, where an icy stream fed down from the mountains, so clear Sydney could see the trout swimming by. Raiden ran to plunge his grimy hands into the tumbling water, waving at the fish as they passed. He clambered back up the riverbank, grinning, the smudge of dirt still streaked across his face. The boy had not stopped smiling since they set out, and he bounded through the woods without a care in the world. Sydney couldn't remember ever feeling that free.

Raiden stopped beside Sydney often throughout their journey, mainly to pester her with questions. Did her shoulder hurt? Was she tired? Do humans need to rest more than elves? On and on he went. Sydney answered the boy honestly. He still puzzled her, so curious and open. The child made her wonder if the elves she hated, the elves she often killed, had all been that innocent once. The idea made her uncomfortable. She pushed it from her thoughts.

Sydney could feel Lukaris' eyes on them every time she spoke to his brother. The elf warrior baffled her too. He always seemed to be thinking, his eyes watching and pensive. Often he would move to speak with his friend, Flindir, in quiet voices. Sydney tried to catch their words, but they always spoke in Elvish. She wondered what they planned to do with her. Why hadn't they let her die in the woods? The answer couldn't be good.

You know the answer, a quiet voice inside her whispered. *They want information. You're an enemy captain. You could help them bring Brimhold to its knees. They only have to pull the words from you.*

The dark thoughts haunted Sydney through the trees.

They followed the stream through the valley, the rippling of the water a comforting sound in the quiet wood. The ground began to slope up, and the river grew along with the incline, until rushing rapids flowed beside them. The elves moved with a graceful certainty, surefooted on the uneven ground, their footsteps silent and unnerving. Beside them, Sydney felt like a fumbling child. She tripped over roots, her boots clung to puddles of mud, and branches tugged at her long hair. Lukaris guided her gently, a hand under her elbow whenever she hesitated beside a rocky cliff or a patch of loose earth. For this, she found him all the more irritating. Eventually, the trees opened up to reveal an immense waterfall that plunged over a fern covered cliff and onto the rocks below. Sydney stopped, starring in wonder. The highlands and fields of Brimhold were beautiful, but this was something else entirely. The echo of the pounding water vibrated in her chest like a drum. She closed her eyes, breathing deeply, letting the mist drift across her face. When she opened them a moment later, she found Lukaris watching her. Uncomfortable and angry, Sydney hurried along, feeling as if she had shared a private moment with an enemy.

The path ahead twisted into a shallow cavern, scooped out of stone beside the falls. The elves paused at the entrance, and with a nod from his brother, Raiden cupped both hands around his mouth and let loose a perfect bird call. It echoed through the small cave several times before fading away in the dim light. They waited. Raiden turned to the others with a worried frown. Lukaris and Flindir exchanged a look. The boy raised his hands, preparing to signal again, when two distinct shadows loomed from the trees beside them. Sydney spun in alarm, reaching for a sword that wasn't there and losing her balance as her feet twisted on pieces of shale. Only Lukaris' hands kept her from slipping off the cliff and into the churning waters below. Sydney did not scream, though her heart caught in her throat at the sight before her.

A fourth elf stepped forward. Her clothes were different from the others, loose linen garments of scarlet and cream, but she was still a warrior. Two long throwing knives spun menacingly in her hands, and her elvish face was equally fierce. She had dark brown skin, full lips, and black hair tucked beneath a tightly wrapped head scarf. Sydney felt a twinge of surprise to see a Viridian elf here in Ithirdas, acting as a soldier, but she was too startled by the second shadow to dwell on the idea. A bear lumbered from the trees. *A damn bear,*

Sydney inwardly cursed. The creature swung it's enormous golden head in her direction, snuffling, like a dog seeking a treat. Sydney suspected she was the treat.

Raiden called out happily to the new arrivals. "Itari! Honey!" The boy ran straight for the bear, and Sydney reached out an instinctive hand to stop him.

"Don't worry," Flindir told her in his calming voice. "Honey's a friend."

The bear grunted as Raiden threw his scrawny arms around her, his tiny form all but buried in the animal's coat. Sydney watched in bewilderment. As the elf spoke in quiet tones, the bear seemed to hear him. To understand. When Honey sat back on her haunches at the boy's request, Sydney was finally hit by the scope of Raiden's magic. She remembered the goldfinch and the rabbit he released from its trap. The boy could understand them. Or at the very least, they could understand him.

The Viridian elf hadn't moved a muscle since revealing herself. Her sharp eyes bore into Sydney, suspicious and threatening. Sydney was not one to be intimidated. She returned the stare with a glare of her own.

Lukaris spoke first. "Itari, *nas lon. Noth des sahen tahellin ethe.*"

Reluctantly, Itari lowered her throwing knives, but she did not take her eyes off Sydney.

"Explain yourselves." Itari's voice snapped like a whip. Unlike the other elves, her voice carried a heavy accent.

Lukaris and Flindir spoke quickly, slipping in and out of Elvish as they told her of Raiden's capture and rescue. The boys acted almost fearful of the Viridian, especially the anxious Flindir, who wrung his hands every few seconds. Raiden scaled the side of his bear and watched the conversation curiously from the creature's back. Meanwhile, Sydney and Itari stayed locked in their silent duel. It wasn't until Lukaris finished speaking that Itari finally looked away. Her mouth lay flat and disapproving as she sheathed her knives.

"This is foolish," the Viridian said. "She is *nahalis.* The others will not approve."

"I'm not asking for their approval," Lukaris replied evenly. Sydney noted the authority in his tone.

"And what of me? I am your *Dualin.* I could deny you."

"Will you?"

For a moment, the only sound came from the rhythmic pounding of the nearby falls. Sydney held her breath, aware that her fate hung in the balance. Finally, Itari shook her head.

"Curse you, *Valen,*" Itari sighed. "Why must you always complicate things?"

"Because no one else will," the archer said with an easy smile. He turned to Sydney. "This is Itari of the Viridian Province, my second in command."

"Pleasure." Sydney's voice dripped with sarcasm.

Itari narrowed her eyes, but before she could respond, Flindir stepped between them. "Where is everyone?"

"I sent them ahead to Firne," the Viridian replied. "They were growing restless."

"Good." Lukaris motioned towards the forest beyond. "It will be easier to explain to everyone at once."

Itari shook her head once more, but made no further protests. She lead the way into the shadows, her footsteps light on the packed earth, followed closely by Flindir and Lukaris. Sydney came next, with Honey the bear bringing up the rear. Raiden smiled at her from the back of the beast as they continued their trek through the forest.

*****

Sydney had never set eyes on an Ithirdi village.

Every piece of Firne, the buildings, the streets, even the people, seemed to melt into the forest, as if they had grown from the ground along with the trees. Quaint homes sat scattered and tucked in the landscape, shaped from a variety of wood and stone. All green and gray and brown, like stone mushrooms with moss strewn caps. Tents formed from woven canvas and sheets of hanging moss hugged against massive tree trunks, while carefully carved wooden steps led up to the lowest branches where more homes sat perched on the great boughs. Over a bustling market, hundreds of round lanterns, magically lit of course, cast a warm glow across the town and over a tiny silver stream that ran down between the buildings. Elves of all kinds could be seen bustling from one place to another, laughing and smiling as they carried about their daily routine. Despite the activity, a type of hush hung over Firne. A serenity. As if the village lived and breathed at the mercy of the Wornwood, and no one wished to disturb it.

Sydney observed all of this with dumbstruck wonder as her captives led her passed a pair of guards and down into the town. They moved quickly through the busy marketplace, vendors calling out their wares from beneath pointed, moss-covered tents. Sizzling meats wrapped in leaves, strange red and violet fruits, handcrafted leather goods, and odd trinkets that reeked of magic. No one paid Honey the bear a passing glance, but eyes inevitably fell upon Sydney. Though she walked unbound, the elves were quick to identify her as foreign. *Other.* Whispers struck up around them, and Sydney saw a little girl point to her ears before an older elf whisked her away. Heat rose to Sydney's face, and she found herself wishing for the protective hood of her cloak.

At last, the party reached the far side of the village and trekked up a small hill. Here, the structures seemed more temporary, less sewn into the earth. Tents lined a clearing, set in neat rows of green tarp. A soldier camp. Two elves parried on a battlefield of grass, their swords ringing as they clashed. The warriors were well matched. The shorter of the two, a dark-skinned elf with short black hair, darted in and out of her opponent's guard, graceful and deadly. What the second elf lacked in finesse, he made up for in brute strength. Tall and lean, with a half shaved head and a sharp nose, each slash of his sword bore the force of an avalanche. Perfectly balanced, they stepped around each other in an elaborate dance, neither giving an inch, neither showing signs of fatigue. A strike. A parry. Both fighters retreating for a moment. Chunks of rock ripped from the earth, attempting to trip the shorter elf. Her eyes widened, but she rolled at the last second. A pool of water appeared beneath her opponent, his feet sinking into the now muddy ground. Grunting, he pulled himself from the muck as the woman got to her feet. The elves recovered in the same instant, and their swords crossed once more.

"Ettee!" Lukaris called out, raising a hand. The warriors lowered their weapons.

The shorter elf, Ettee, scowled as she walked over. She was even smaller up close, barely reaching Sydney's shoulder. "Why the interruption, *Valen*? I had Sarcys right where I wanted him."

The other warrior, Sarcys presumably, rolled his eyes. "*Na heseth.*"

Ettee's frown deepened as she took a challenging step towards her opponent, the action made less intimidating by her petite stature.

"Enough. Ettee, I need you to see to an injury," the leader interjected before the fight could resume. He nodded pointedly in Sydney's direction.

Two new enemies fixed their eyes on Sydney. She raised her chin. Sarcys stared her down with eyes like coal, anger boiling on his face.

"What's this? A Brim?" The elf glanced at her hands, his own curling into fists. "Why isn't it bound?"

"She," Sydney practically spat, "has ears. And she could kick your ass, bound or otherwise."

The elf gave a cruel smile. Beneath her feet, the earth stirred, and Sydney stumbled as Sarcys slid a sword from its sheath. She almost wished he would do it. Better to be struck down here than left to rot in an Ithirdi prison. Besides, she was pretty sure she could smash the smile off the bastard's face before she died. Unfortunately, before her adversary could lift his weapon, Lukaris surged between them, Flindir to his left and Itari to the right. With a twist of his hand, Flindir silenced the rolling earth, a thousand small roots forming a net to lock the rocks in place. Wind whipped through the camp at Lukaris' command, tearing at the flaps of nearby tents and pushing Sarcys back a few feet. In the same instant, Itari snapped her fingers and electricity rippled up the threatening sword. Sarcys dropped the weapon with a yelp. Raiden merely grinned down at the exchange from his perch atop Honey.

The defense happened in a matter of seconds. Quick, synchronized, efficient. Sydney had to admit, she was impressed. The trio made a striking team.

"I don't have the energy for your foolishness today, Sarcys," Lukaris snapped. "Captain Krane is not your concern. Everything will be explained later, but until then, leave us be."

Sarcys glowered at his leader, but he didn't protest. The elf spun away, storming off into the growing evening shadows.

"Hmph," Ettee grunted, frown still etched on her face. "That was dramatic. Let's see to this wound, shall we?"

The tiny elf led the group across camp, stopping before a tent of brown canvas stretched delicately between two robust pines trees. If Sydney had blinked, she might have missed the tiny structure, so perfectly camouflaged within the forest. Ettee turned to face them.

"No bears," she ordered, wagging a finger at Raiden. The boy stuck out a lip.

"But, Ettee—"

"You heard me, *osan*."

The pout deepened. "Fine. We'll go get something to eat." Raiden patted Honey's neck, then waved. "Bye, Sydney! Feel better."

Sydney could only watch, baffled, as the bear lumbered away. *What a strange kid.*

Inside the healing tent, the air smelled of fresh lavender and sage. Plants grew in every corner, and small bottles of elixir lined a modest table. Ettee pushed Sydney down into a chair.

"Alright, let's see what we're dealing with." The elf peeked at Sydney's shoulder, causing her to wince. Ettee gave a little *tsk* and cast a disapproving look in Flindir's direction. "Did Honey bandage this wound? It looks like a wild animal applied the salve."

"That's a perfectly good dressing, you old bat," Flindir huffed. Sydney raised an eyebrow at the tone, surprised Flindir's soft voice was capable of such sharpness.

"Yes, I suppose it's just fine... if you're a child playing a physician."

"Well, the pupil is merely a reflection of his teacher."

The pair continued their squabbling as Ettee redressed Sydney's shoulder. Lukaris spared her a smile as he prepared to leave the tent. "Don't worry. They're always like this."

Sydney didn't reply. Was he trying to comfort her?

"Flindir, fill Ettee in while I'm gone. I must speak with the rest of the camp. And the village for that matter," Lukaris sighed, muttering in Elvish. He cast Sydney a final thoughtful glance. "Don't try anything. Please."

"Of course not," said Sydney with a smile so sharp it could slice through bone.

With another sigh, the elf departed, Itari in his wake.

In fact, Sydney had formulated three escape plans since entering the tent, but she'd quickly dismissed them all. Even if she could reach the knife balanced on a nearby table, she would never manage to dispatch the two elves in her current condition. Not without drawing unwanted attention. She considered faking an illness, but what good would that do? She was already in the healer's tent. And finally, her last plan, barely a plan at all. To use the dagger on herself. A scheme born from pure fear, choosing death over captivity. But, no. If nothing else, Sydney Krane was a survivor. She had to find another way.

Flindir and Ettee paid Sydney little attention as their conversation slipped into Elvish. She didn't mind. It gave her time to think. She wondered, not for the first time, what Lukaris had planned for her. Was he out there, right now, telling his soldiers about their new captive? But telling them what, exactly? Was she to be tortured? Imprisoned? Lukaris had stopped Sarcys from attacking her, but he might be waiting for the right time to interrogate her. Perhaps he thought kindness could charm her into giving up Brimhold's secrets. If that were the case, the elf would be sorely disappointed.

Time passed slowly. Eventually, the elves lapsed into silence, casting Sydney uneasy glances. She tried her best to ignore then. When Lukaris finally returned, they all breathed a sigh of relief. The *Valen* gave the tent a quick survey.

"Leave us," Lukaris told his friends. "I need to speak with our guest alone."

11

A Bargain

Sydney searched her captor's face. Lukaris looked younger now that they were alone. Less a commanding officer and more a boy playing a part.

"Well," Sydney started, since Lukaris made no move to speak, "I take it the rest of your soldiers are delighted to have me here?"

"They think I should kill you," he replied, voice flat.

"I can't say I blame them," Sydney said. She fought to keep her voice steady. "But what do *you* think?"

"I think that I'm tired of killing." The elf leaned back in his chair, surveying her in turn.

"So, what then? I'm not keen on being an Ithirdi pet. And if it's torture you have in mind…" Sydney's eyes fell on the dagger. Lukaris followed her gaze. Slowly, deliberately, the elf captain wrapped a hand around the weapon. Then, to Sydney's shock, he offered it to her.

"You can try," he said. "But you won't make it out of this camp."

What was he playing at? Sydney met the elf's emerald eyes.

"I wasn't planning to use it on *you*."

The words achieved their desired effect. Lukaris blinked, surprise and understanding plain on his face. "You would do that?"

"I entered this forest knowing it would likely be the last thing I ever did. I had only hoped to get justice for my family first." Tears sprung to Sydney's eyes. She stared hard into the sharp light of a nearby lantern, forcing the weakness away.

"By justice, you mean the death of those responsible."

"What else?"

"That sounds more like vengeance to me," Lukaris replied, pointedly.

Sydney shrugged. "What difference does it make to you, seeing as you claim to be innocent?"

The elf did not rise to her bait. He spun the knife casually in his hand, considering her.

"I did not bring you here to kill you, nor do I plan on torturing you for information. That is not our way, whatever you might believe." Lukaris' expression held so many shadows, the harsh light accenting the sharp angles of his face, the fierce point of his ears. But his voice was soft, gentle and persuasive. Sydney didn't trust it. "I brought you here to offer you a deal."

"A deal," she repeated, skeptical.

The elf paused for a moment, gathering his words. Then, he said, "Our kingdoms have been at war for a long time. Too long. I want to stop the pointless fighting. The wasteful loss of life. But I can't do it alone. I could use your help."

"What could I possibly do to help?" asked Sydney. "Besides, I think Brimhold has every right to see this conflict through. Your people continue to shelter the Red Elf that slaughtered our king and queen. You ignore our borders. You burn down innocent villages. Why should I do anything to help a kingdom full of murderers?"

Lukaris took a deep breath, releasing it in a loud rush of air. "Ithirdas has never taken responsibility for these assaults. Both sides deny the accusations of the other. Doesn't that seem strange to you? Something is *wrong.* What do the elves have to gain from starting a war? What do the humans? The truth is, both sides are suffering over carefully placed lies and ruthless attacks placed in the cover of darkness. I don't know who, but someone is playing us. And I don't know about you, but I'm tired of being a piece in their game."

Sydney could only stare at him, incredulous. "You sound mad."

To her surprise, the elf flashed her his crooked smile. "The line between madness and genius is a thin one."

"Fine." Sydney crossed her arms in a huff. The action pulled at her injured shoulder, and in her mind she saw an arrow flying towards her, piercing her skin. Lukaris stood over her, another shaft aimed at her face. For all the talk of peace, she still knew where her enemy sat. "Say I believe you. How can the two of us stop a conflict that's been growing for twenty years? And how can we hope to beat this clever mastermind that managed to pit two entire races against each other?"

"We stop playing the game." Lukaris gave his knife a final twirl before stabbing the blade into the tabletop. "We try and understand each other again. I want you to stay here, in this camp, not as a prisoner, but as a… tentative guest. Let me show you that elves aren't the monsters you were trained to see. And in turn, show my people that Brims aren't all small-minded and arrogant." Sydney's eyes narrowed at the insult, but Lukaris pressed on. "I know it seems pointless. I know, in the grand scheme of things, you're just one person. But if I can change *your* mind about us, a Brim captain with a personal grudge… maybe it's not so hopeless after all."

She stared at him. Were all elves this convincing? She had spent so little time with them that didn't involve clashing blades and the potential for bloodshed. But Sydney had never trusted words, of elves or otherwise. Words could be spun, twisted and changed to fit the needs of their master.

"Why?" Sydney asked, after a moment.

"Excuse me?"

"Why is this so important to you? What do you gain?"

"Is peace between two kingdoms not enough?"

Sydney gave a sharp smile. "Too selfless. People rarely want something simply for the greater good. And those that do tend not to survive very long."

"You have a grim view of the world," Lukaris remarked. Sydney stared, waiting. Then, with a sigh, he said, "I don't want this life for my brother."

"If that's true, then why is he here?"

"It wasn't my decision, trust me," he replied darkly. "But some Ithirdi parents send their children to learn in soldier encampments. Similar to an apprenticeship, to see if they're cut out for life as a warrior. But I know this is not Raiden's place. Right now he's so… hopeful. Innocent. I don't want that corrupted, certainly not due to a pointless war. If he must fight, I want it to be for *something*."

Not the worst motive, thought Sydney. But the elf had not finished. His eyes changed. One minute he was there, inside the tent, and the next his gaze was far away, focused on something Sydney could not see. He looked… scared.

"There's something else. I've noticed it lately, out there, in the woods." Lukaris' voice fell, and Sydney thought she could hear the breathing of the great trees surrounding them. The labored groan of the ancient branches. "A presence is stirring. There are dark places where the forest feels… wrong. I'm afraid something terrible is coming. And if I don't stop… if *we* don't stop this war, the shadow might consume us all while our backs are turned."

He's mad, Sydney thought, not for the first time. But something sat in his tone, a seriousness that sent chills up her spine. Whatever the truth, he truly believed in this coming darkness.

"Six weeks," Lukaris continued when Sydney made no move to speak. "Give me six weeks, and after that, regardless of how you feel about the Ithirdi, you can leave. I'll escort you across the chasm myself."

Raising an eyebrow, Sydney asked, "You'll just let me go?"

"Yes."

"Just like that?"

"Just like that."

She scoffed. "Nothing comes without a price. So what's the catch?"

Lukaris smirked again. Sydney was really starting to hate that.

"The catch is, Captain Krane, you will actually have to try. Try to learn. Try to understand. And teach me about yourself and your people in return."

The deal seemed too good to be true. An easy out to a fatal mistake. Sydney could play a part for six weeks. Give Lukaris what he wanted, tell the elves what they wanted to hear. Maybe she could even learn something valuable as a peace offering to bring back to an angry queen. It could work. If Lukaris was true to his word.

But then, Sydney thought of her sister's smile. The crinkles that formed at the corner of her father's eyes when he laughed. Seeing them for the last time. A shop and home burned to ash. Bodies in the street. The smell of burnt hair.

No deal for her own salvation would bring them back. Would get her any closer to closure. Her family was still dead, and she didn't even know why.

"No." Sydney's voice cut through the small tent. Lukaris' smile fell away. "I didn't come here to make deals or build friendships with my enemies. I came here because someone killed my family. My home. You say it wasn't the elves, and hell, I might even believe you. But you know *something*. I've seen it cross your face a dozen times since we met. So no, I won't play your game for nothing in return but my own freedom. My family is worth more to me than that."

His mouth opened, closed, then settled in a flat line. Then, with a sigh, he said, "You're right. I do know something."

The words hit Sydney like a punch to the gut, taking her breath away. She wanted to yell, to scream, to push that dagger to his neck. Instead, she waited.

"New deal." The elf leaned forward with his hands clasped before him, elbows on his knees. She still saw the hidden truth in those forest eyes, but this time he held it up for ransom. "Give me the six weeks. After that, I'll let you return home. *And* I will tell you everything I know about the destruction of Briar."

Interesting. Eyes narrowed, Sydney said, "I have your word?"

"On my names and my honor," Lukaris replied solemnly, both hands moving to his heart as he repeated the same oath he'd made to her back in the woods.

She didn't like it. But then, what other choice did she have?

"Deal?" Lukaris extended a hand.

Sydney reached out hesitantly, her hand grasping the elf's forearm. "Deal."

12

New Beginnings

Sydney slept little her first night in Firne.

The elves gave her a small, gray tent, slung between a tight grove of trees in the middle of camp. A cocoon-like hammock acted as her bed. It was better than sleeping on the ground, she had to admit, but the rocking sensation pulled at her injured shoulder and did little to ease her anxieties. Outside the tent, an elf guard stood silent and omnipresent. Nothing about her surroundings would let her forget her imprisonment.

So, instead of sleeping, Sydney thought. She thought of Brandon, mostly. Where was he now? Hopefully her friend was far away, safe from the elves and not trying anything stupid to get her back. But then, when had Brandon ever been sensible when it came to elves? The thought of him alone in the Wornwood, trying to save her from a problem she had caused, set her stomach into knots. With a huff, Sydney rose from the hammock, pacing back and forth in the tiny space. She wondered what Brandon would think of her deal with Lukaris. Would he trust the Ithirdi, if he were in her place? Sydney snorted at the thought. No. No, Brandon would have already attempted to escape long ago, even if it cost him his life. And yet,

98

Sydney felt rooted to this place. She couldn't throw away the chance to find out about her family. She didn't have to trust the elves, she only had to use them. Brandon would understand that, wouldn't he?

In wasn't until the deepest hours of the morning, with a sky so black the stars dimmed under its weight, that Sydney finally drifted off to sleep. Even then, her dreams were restless and dark, and she woke too early with heavy-lidded eyes.

Lukaris appeared at the tent entrance just as Sydney dragged herself to her feet, an audible groan slipping from her lips. The elf gave her a quick once over and cleared his throat.

"Good morning, Captain Krane. You'll probably want to… freshen up."

Sleep deprived, bitter, and covered in blood and dust, Sydney cast a withering look. "You don't say?"

Lukaris merely smiled and held open the tent flap as an invitation. With a sigh, Sydney stepped out into the soft morning light.

The elf led her up the hillside away from camp. The trees stood close together, allowing only sharp, thin streaks of sunlight through to the forest floor. Sydney stepped carefully from packed earth, to a moss covered rock, to a crooked root that had burst forth from the dirt, following Lukaris as he weaved around towering trunks and boulders. Soon, the trees thinned to reveal a small hollow. Natural springs trickled into three distinct pools. A brunette elf stood by the closest pool, waving flattened hands over the surface of the crystal water. With each pass of her hand, fresh steam rose from the spring. After a few minutes, the elf turned away from the water, looking satisfied with her work. She clasped both hands to her chest and gave Lukaris a respectful nod before disappearing into the woods.

"There's soap and fresh linens by the baths," Lukaris said after an awkward silence. "You'll have complete privacy. But I must emphasize that if you try to escape…"

"You'll kill me. I get it," Sydney interrupted. "You don't have to keep saying that, you know. I said I would stay. I gave you my word."

Lukaris stared at her, demeanor thoughtful. "Very well. I'll leave you, then. Give a shout when you're finished."

In the time it took to draw a breath, he was gone.

Despite the elf's promise of solitude, Sydney could not shake the feeling of eyes watching her from the trees. With a distrustful glance around, she carefully began to remove her worn clothing. She placed her boots and trousers at the pool side, taking special care as she pealed off her shirt. The fabric clung to her wounded shoulder, and she sucked in a painful breath as it finally tugged free. At last, she stood in her undergarments, goosebumps racing up her arms as they embraced the cool morning air.

Sydney crouched next to the nearest bath, ripples running out across the surface as she tested the water with her hand. When the current finally settled, her own face stared back at her from the smooth water. The face she recognized well, oval and pale, with dark brows and stern lips. But something sat in her eyes, a foreign hollowness. The cold gray of a rainstorm, dull and sad. With a swallow, she passed her hand through the pool once more, disrupting the image. She did not spare her reflection a second glance.

She scrubbed herself clean with berry scented soap, careful to avoid her shoulder and its bandaging. With a good deal of grumbling and cursing, she yanked knots and dirt from the depths of her dark hair before braiding the troublesome strands out of her face. After the bath, she reluctantly re-dressed in her soiled garments, the cloth stiff and itching against her skin. *Well, this is as good as it's going to get,* Sydney mused as she looked down at herself with disdain. When she called out to Lukaris, the elf appeared from among the trees.

The *Valen* held a small pile of Ithirdi clothes in his arms. He tried to pass them to her, an offering. "Here."

"Absolutely not."

"They're just *clothes*, Captain Krane…"

"What I'm wearing is fine," Sydney interrupted.

"Your shirt is covered in blood. Not to mention it has a giant hole."

"Yes, well, whose fault is that?"

Eventually, Lukaris convinced Sydney to take the fresh clothes after he agreed to return her favorite cloak. She still felt traitorous in the foreign garments, but at least the cape hid some of her shame behind its familiar gray folds.

The pair returned to camp just in time for breakfast. The smell of fresh bread and cooking sausage sent a sharp pain through Sydney's empty stomach. They wandered over to a small eating area on the hill overlooking Firne. A few elves stoked a fire amid a ring of tables, passing out food to the others. Lukaris grabbed two heaping plates and led Sydney to the farthest table where Raiden and Honey sat waiting. As they walked, Sydney could feel the stares of the other elves hot on her neck. Sarcys, the dark-headed elf from the day before, scowled as she passed his table. But Sydney kept her chin high, forcefully meeting each glare, one by one. No one maintained eye contact for long.

Raiden looked up from his plate as Lukaris plopped their food down across from him. He broke out in a toothy grin at the sight of Sydney. Somehow the boy already had a fresh smudge of dirt on his nose.

"*Allon*, Sydney!" Raiden exclaimed. "Did you sleep well? How's your shoulder?"

"I'm fine," Sydney grunted in response to both questions.

"*Osan*, I have to step away for a minute. Would you mind keeping Captain Krane company until I return?" Lukaris asked.

"Sure," Raiden mumbled around a mouthful of bread. Lukaris laughed, ruffling the boy's hair as he turned away.

"Wait, you're just going to leave me here?" Sydney demanded, the hostile glances around her seeming to heighten.

"Relax, I'll be right back. No one will bother you." The *Valen* melted away into the crowd, leaving Sydney to stare at the elf kid and his giant pet bear.

Raiden shoveled a pile of food into his mouth and cast Sydney another smile with two bulging cheeks. Looking down at her own plate, her stomach rumbled. Some of the food was foreign to her, strange meat wrapped in crisp leaves and purple fruit with an odd fuzzy coating, but most of the haul looked familiar and inviting. She munched cautiously on a handful of blueberries. They reminded her of warm summers in Briar, picking wild fruits in the Lost Wood with her sister. The memory sent a small pain through her chest.

When she looked up, Raiden was staring at her with wide eyes.

"What?" Sydney demanded around her mouthful of food.

"It's just... do all humans eat berries like that?" The boy's voice dripped with disgust.

"How else are you supposed to eat them?"

With a sigh, Raiden plucked two berries from her plate. He held them up for her to see, as if teaching a child. Then, he shoved both berries into his nose.

Sydney looked at him, mouth open, uncertain. Raiden could only hold her eyes for a few seconds before he let out a joyous snort. The berries flew from his nostrils, rolling off the table. Honey scrambled for the treats in the grass as Raiden howled with laughter.

"You should have seen your face!" the boy giggled. He popped a fresh berry into his mouth, clearly satisfied with his prank.

"You're a weird kid, you know that?" Sydney said once she recovered, shaking her head.

Raiden cast her a puzzled look. *"Weird?"*

"You know, weird?" He continued to stare, uncomprehending. "It means odd or… different. Not like everyone else."

"Oh." The boy thought about this for a moment, chewing thoughtfully. Then, he decided, "It sounds like a good thing to be."

Sydney smiled, despite herself. "Yeah, I guess it is, kid."

They ate in a comfortable silence, though Honey's presence still set Sydney on edge. She used the quiet to collect herself, preparing, planning, though for what she wasn't sure. This was all uncharted territory. Was she a lax prisoner, a questionable guest, or something in between? Whatever she was, she wasn't sure how to act. But she would have to learn to play her part until she got the information she needed.

A shadow passed across their table, blocking out the growing warmth of the morning sun. Sydney ignored the looming presence. She took a bite of her breakfast, waiting.

"Oh, hello *avun*," Raiden said brightly. Only then did Sydney spare the intruder a glance.

Behind her stood the largest elf Sydney had ever seen. If most elves were slender aspen, this man was an oak. Two meaty arms crossed an equally dense chest, and his face sported a dark beard on a square chin. His head was entirely shaved, with intricate tattoos crisscrossing his skull and disappearing behind severely pointed ears. Even Sydney's ego had to admit, the elf was intimidating.

"So," the elf began, his voice surprisingly light, "this is our human… guest."

Guess he doesn't know what I am either, Sydney mused.

"This is Sydney," Raiden replied. He waved a tiny hand to the new arrival. "Sydney, this is my *avun*, Ordell."

"*Avun?*"

"My father's brother," the boy explained.

"Uncle. Got it." Sydney gave the man a once over. "I gotta say, I don't see the resemblance."

Ordell raised an eyebrow. "Is she always this bold, *osan?*"

"Pretty much," said Raiden, sounding almost proud of her.

"I'm sitting right here," Sydney interjected. "If you have a problem with me, you can say it outright."

Leaning on the table until it groaned under his weight, Ordell barked out a laugh. There was no humor in it.

"I would find your impertinence amusing, Captain Krane, were in not for the fact that only yesterday you kidnapped one of my nephews and tried to kill the other."

"To be fair, he tried to kill me too," Sydney said with a sharp smile, motioning to her injured shoulder. "And the kidnapping was an honest mistake. Right, kid?"

"It's okay, *avun,* really" Raiden insisted. "Sydney thought we hurt her family. She's here to see that the elves aren't bad."

Ordell's face softened at the boy's voice. "I know, Raiden. And I trust your brother's instincts. Still, it does not mean I will lower my guard to potential threats."

He said the last part to Sydney, a warning. Unsure how to respond, she held his eyes.

"Am I interrupting something?" Lukaris appeared suddenly at his uncle's elbow. Ordell returned to his full height.

"Just meeting our new guest, young *Valen,*" he replied evenly. "I'd keep a watchful eye on her if I were you. She's bound to ruffle a few feathers."

With a respectful nod, the towering elf departed. Lukaris watched him go, a worried frown on his sharp face.

"You still think this is a good idea?" Sydney asked in the silence.

The concern washed from the elf's face, replaced with a wide smile. "Good ideas aren't always easy ones, Captain Krane."

Sydney rolled her eyes. She took a tentative bite of foreign meat. It wasn't bad. A little stringy.

Lukaris dug into his own plate. "I've cleared my day so I can show you around camp. Flindir and Itari have agreed to assist in your…" He paused, chewing thoughtfully. "Cultural education."

"How kind of them," Sydney retorted. "And the rest of your soldiers?"

The *Valen* winced. "They'll come around eventually."

"Right."

"Can I come with you, Luka?" Raiden begged. "I want to help with Sydney."

"Don't you have a lesson with Ettee, today?" Lukaris eyed his brother over a mug of cider. "She's supposed to teach you about the healing properties of Light magic."

"But Ettee is so *serious* and healing is so *boring,*" the boy groaned. "She'll just go on and on about salves and tonics and sour stomach remedies."

"You're going."

"But *Luka…*"

"End of discussion, *osan.*" Lukaris motioned with his fork. Glowering, Raiden sunk back in his seat. They finished their meal in a layered silence, part unease and part sullen.

After breakfast, Raiden gave Sydney a quick wave, stuck out a pointed tongue in his brother's direction, and sulked away, animal shadow in tow. Lukaris shook his head as he rose from the table.

"Little brothers are a rare and terrible breed," the *Valen* said quietly, almost to himself. Then, louder, "Ready to go, Captain Krane?"

"Do I have a choice?" Sydney grumbled.

Lukaris did a good job pretending not to hear her.

13

Questions and Answers

The sun rose high and warm above the treetops as Sydney and Lukaris strolled through the soldiers' camp. Sydney walked at her guide's shoulder, still unsure of her place. They stopped at the camp's border, overlooking the village below. In the fresh daylight, Ithirdi homes of stone and moss were easier to spot, though they still blended into the landscape.

"As you might have noticed, our camp is a temporary edition to the town of Firne. We are a *tatell*. The closest Soardic translation is *guard*, though our purpose differs greatly from your Brimholdian interpretation. *Tatells* are stationed at villages throughout Ithirdas. We serve as protectors and guardians to the citizens here; however, we can be called to battle at a moment's notice if needed, to join a larger fighting force." The words spilled from Lukaris so smoothly, it caught Sydney off guard. She hadn't expected such valuable information to be offered up without any type of coercion.

Curious despite herself, Sydney asked, "How many elves make up these… *tatells*?" She spoke the word hesitantly.

Lukaris nodded his encouragement. "The number varies, but its usually a few dozen at least. I have thirty warriors here."

"So many to protect a single village?"

"We branch off into smaller groups from time to time." Lukaris picked up a stick from the ground, using it to point at a large rock. He tapped it lightly. "Firne acts as our base. From here we can protect smaller towns and outlier dwellings in the surrounding Wornwood." With the stick, he traced a dirt circle around the rock.

Sydney squat down next to the rock, making a show of examining the circle. She traced the shape with her finger. "Interesting. I don't see Briar within the boundaries of your protection, *Valen*."

Lukaris' jaw twitched an almost imperceptible amount. "Captain Krane—"

"Relax." Sydney stood, rolling her eyes. "I'm just reminding you of the answers you've promised me at the end of this charade."

"I haven't forgotten. And it's only a charade if you make it one," he retorted.

They moved deeper into the camp. Lukaris introduced her to elves they passed along the way. Petras, Yunara, Numir. The names soon ran together. They all greeted her with various degrees of disdain, though none dared give her anything worse than a curt nod in the *Valen's* presence. Lukaris, to his credit, stayed upbeat and chipper through the introductions, though Sydney could see the strain building in his tight smile.

"All these warriors answer to you?" Sydney asked as they turned past the final group of tents.

"More or less. I am the *Valen*, first in command. Itari acts as my *Dualin*. She takes command of the *tatell* in my absence and can challenge my orders. Luckily, that doesn't happen often, though she likes to make the threat." Lukaris gave a mischievous grin.

"Right. And are there any other important leaders I should know about?" Sydney wondered, thinking of Ordell. As Lukaris' uncle, Sydney figured the elf must have some role in the hierarchy.

Lukaris pondered this for a moment. "Leaders, no. Though everyone has a part to play. You've met Ettee, who acts as our healer—"

Nearby, a small explosion cut off the *Valen*'s words. White smoke billowed from the far side of camp. Lukaris laughed. "And that'll be Flindir."

They hurried to a lone tent on the outskirts of camp. The shelter appeared intentionally isolated, and it wasn't hard to see why. The unusual tent boasted countless burns, holes, and mysterious stains. Currently, a steady stream of smoke and cursing poured from the opening. Coughing, Lukaris pulled open the flap.

"Flin? Are you alright?" Lukaris called out. A round, curly head appeared among the haze.

"Yes, fine, so sorry, really thought I had the right mixture this time," Flindir wheezed, waving two hands frantically through the air. "Would you mind?"

Lukaris lifted his hands, palms down, fingers pointed towards the smoke. Eyes focused, he dragged both hands skyward. Sydney sucked in a sharp breath as wind ripped through the tent. The breeze quickly pulled the smoke up and away. With the haze gone, Sydney got her first good look at Flindir's... laboratory? Garden? The space was hard to define.

The tent was the largest in the camp by far with canvas draped two stories high, precariously wrapped around a giant redwood. Plants covered every inch. Ferns in clay pots, wildflowers littering the ground beneath tables and stools, trillium and dragon's breath, honeysuckles and daisies. Tight vines wrapped around the tree itself, anchoring a small loft to the trunk. It created a balcony of sorts. Beakers and parchment sprawled across the tabletops in the few spots left free of greenery. Sydney noted meticulously written notes on some of the papers. She tried to eye a few, but the words were in

Elvish.

Flindir leaned sadly over a broken flask. A few wisps of smoke still drifted from the wreckage.

"It must have been the proportions," Flindir muttered to himself. He made a careful mark on a nearby scroll. "Maybe more foxwood? I suppose the runes could've been off. No, but that wouldn't account for the combustion…"

Lukaris cleared his throat.

"Right, sorry!" The round-eyed elf broke away from his musings. He clapped Lukaris heartily on the shoulder, all smiles and sunshine. "How's the tour coming?"

"You're our last stop." Sydney noted how comfortable the elves seemed around each other. They easily fell into each other's company, like two sides of a coin.

"Well, Captain Krane, welcome to my humble workshop." Flindir spread his arms proudly, flashing a soft smile. "Can I interest you in some tea?"

The elf waved a hand over a nearby seedling. The plant twitched and began to grow, tea leaves sprouting from fresh sprouts. The use of such casual magic, while fascinating, still sent Sydney's stomach into knots. She had only ever seen such things on the battlefield.

"No, thank you," Sydney quipped as politely as she could muster. Some of Flindir's smile slipped away.

Lukaris picked up the the threads of the conversation before it could unravel. "Flindir is something of an inventor. He creates useful remedies for the *tatell* and the citizens of Firne. He even helps Ettee with her healing work from time to time."

"When the old witch doesn't bite my head off, that is," Flindir replied, plucking a few tea leaves with unnecessary force. Sydney raised an eyebrow.

"Anyway," Lukaris continued before his friend could elaborate further. "Flindir has agreed to teach you some Ithirdi customs and histories while you're here with us."

Flindir nodded. "I give lessons to Raiden anyway, and I'm sure he wouldn't mind the company."

"Great," Sydney said dryly. She couldn't muster up the enthusiasm the two elves shared. Her shoulder ached something terrible, and she was struggling to see how any of this brought her closer to her family's killers. Maybe she made a mistake accepting Lukaris' deal. Maybe she should have snuck away in the dead of night rather than traipsing through an enemy camp, pretending to be something that she wasn't.

The elves continued to chat about small things while Flindir fussed over his drink. Sydney tuned them out. The smell of green tea permeated through the small space. As Sydney breathed in the familiar aroma, bitter nostalgia latched on to her heart. For a moment, she was transported back, long ago, to a winter morning in Briar. Frost coated the window panes. Outside, the street was quiet, too cold for leisure and too early for errands. The small apartment above her family's shop was warm from the strong fire in the hearth, and her sister poured them three generous cups of freshly brewed tea. Abi laughed at some story their father was telling, and Sydney smiled as she cradled her hot mug against her chest.

Flashing forward. A home crumbled to ash. The smell of burning flesh. A childhood buried and gone.

Back in Ithirdas, deep in the Wornwood, the memories sent Sydney spinning. Her throat collapsed in on itself. The urge to run filled her so completely, she fled the tent without a word.

Outside, the sun poured down hot and blinding. Sydney blinked, trying to calm her racing mind.

Lukaris appeared at her side, a worried crease between his brows. "Are you alright?"

"I'm sorry, I can't do this." Sydney sucked in gulps of air, letting the smell of fresh pine cleanse her lungs.

"Do what?"

"*This.*" She gestured to herself, to Lukaris, to the surrounding camp. "Whatever it is you expect me to do here. It was a mistake. I can't do it."

"You gave me your word." The *Valen*'s frown hardened his face. It made him look older. "You said you would try."

"I did try. But everywhere I look I see enemies and the pain they've caused me."

"What, did you think it would be easy?" Lukaris snapped, a sudden wind whipping at his hair. "Did you think by the second day you'd be best friends with every elf in Ithirdas? That years of distrust and anger would evaporate over night?"

"Well no, but…"

"But, nothing. If resolving the tension between elves and humanity was easy, we wouldn't be twenty years into this war. Thousands of innocents would be alive and well right now instead of rotting in early graves." Lukaris sucked in a sharp breath through his nose. "Hatred is easy. It pours naturally from the heart. Understanding is harder, love even more so. But it is the only true path to peace. So tell me, Captain Krane. Are you, like so many others, going to take the easy way out?"

Oh, he was good. Appealing to her pride. And deep down, she knew he was right. *You started this mess. Now, the only way out is through.*

"Fine," Sydney sighed after a long moment. "But no more parading me around your camp. Stop pretending I'm just an ordinary guest. If you want to teach me about the elves, then teach me. No more games."

Lukaris looked at her, forest eyes thoughtful. "Very well. Perhaps

I'm going about this wrong."

Sydney let out a long breath. "So, what do we do now?"

"We continue with our agreement, but this time with a little more honesty. Instead of feeding you whatever information comes to mind, you can ask me anything you like, about Ithirdas, myself, the *tatell*. I will do my best to answer. But only if you answer my questions in return. Don't forget, the point of all this is to learn from each other."

"A question for a question," Sydney mused.

Lukaris nodded.

"Alright. I'll go first then." Sydney locked eyes with the *Valen*. "If Raiden hadn't intervened yesterday, would you have killed me?"

"I don't know." His voice came so quick and even, Sydney was forced to believe him.

"My turn. The rumors about the Honor Guard, about the things you've done. Are they true?" Lukaris looked away as he spoke, watching two soldiers train in the distance. Interesting. Would her answer change his opinion of her?

"Most of the rumors I started myself. Sometimes your reputation can be your strongest weapon." Sydney chose her words carefully. "But I won't lie to you and say none of them are true. I've done things necessary to defend my people and my kingdom. Would you have done any less?"

Lukaris' mouth turned up at the end. "Is that your next question?"

"Is that yours?" Sydney shot back.

The *Valen's* smile broke into a full grin.

"Oh, this is going to be fun, Captain Krane."

14

Lost

"Idiot!" Brandon muttered. "Stupid, blind bastard."

The captain had been cursing himself for days as he desperately searched the Wornwood for any sign of Sydney. But the elves were either excellent at covering their tracks, or they made no path at all through the dense forest. The cries of ravens and the moaning of the ancient trees seemed to mock him while he hunted in circles.

How could he have let this happen? Brandon was the one on watch. He should have seen the elf soldier creeping up behind him. He should have warned Sydney. He should have been taken instead.

"Damn!" Brandon cursed as, in his haste, he misplaced his foot on the uneven earth, his ankle twisting. For the next few miles, he walked with a noticeable limp.

The day passed slowly. Brandon watched as the sun set beneath the trees, casting the forest into shadow. He had followed sets of footprints for most of the afternoon, only to find a small house tucked in the woods, home only to a family of elves. Brandon watched the civilians from the shelter of a towering trunk, seething, blaming even the innocents for the loss of his friend. For in Brandon's eyes, they

113

were all the same. Murderers and vermin. He would burn this forest to the ground if that's what it took to wipe them from the world and find Sydney.

But it was that night, huddled alone in the dark, expansive forest, that Brandon decided to give up his search. He could not find her. Gilliad's parting words haunted him, murmured in secret. *She needs you, Brandon. Take care of her. Wherever she leads you.*

"I failed, Gilliad. I failed her. I'm sorry," Brandon found himself whispering. The sound drifted through the trees like the wind. The soldier buried his head in shaking hands, silent tears streaming down his face. He sat there for hours until he was stiff and weary, feeling the weight of it all. Brandon wished more than anything that he had kept Sydney from coming here. But remembering the look on her face, the fierce determination in her steel eyes, he knew that not even the gods could have stopped her. As he drifted to sleep, Brandon prayed to the same gods that at the very least, out there, somewhere, his friend was still alive.

*****

"What do you think you're doing?" Brandon asked Sydney. He had found his new friend alone in the sparring yard, swinging a wooden sword wildly though the air. The weapon looked bigger than she was.

"I'm practicing," Sydney huffed. The sword fell to her side.

"Is that what you call it? Looks more like you're chopping invisible wood."

"Shut up!" she snapped, shooting him a piercing glare. Brandon lapsed into silence. He noticed her lower lip was quivering and quickly regretted his jab. "What are you doing here anyway?"

"I was looking for you. You didn't show up to dinner, and Gilliad was worried." Brandon was worried too. It had been three months since the new recruits had arrived in Delm, and while most of the children had begun to settle into their new lives, Sydney continued to struggle. She was the slowest in sparring practice, she barely ate, barely slept, barely spoke to the other soldiers. Brandon wondered if she would make it through another month of training, let alone the many years to come.

"Gilliad frets like a mother hen," Sydney replied. She tied her hair back in a tight knot, revealing a high forehead and pale face. It made her look older. She then resumed the frantic slicing of her sword. "I'm fine. You can go back to your dinner."

Brandon had had enough. Surging forward, the boy grabbed the weapon as it whipped through the air. Sydney's eyes widened as the flat of the blade slapped hard against Brandon's hand. Then the weapon was wretched from her grasp, sent skidding sideways into the dirt.

"Well, that was rude," the young girl said dryly as she moved to retrieve her sword. Brandon stood in her way, an unyielding wall.

"What's gotten into that oafish brain of yours?" Sydney grumbled. She crossed her scrawny arms and scowled up at him.

"Tell me what's going on." Brandon kept his voice low and even.

"What does it matter to you?"

"You're my friend. Or at least, I thought you were."

"You barely know me." The fire had fallen out of the Sydney's voice, and she refused to meet Brandon's eyes. She stared off towards the docks, where tiny fishing boats floated under the blue, evening sky.

"I know enough. I know you're strong and resourceful and clever. And I know you have a good heart, no matter how much you snap at the other recruits. But you're letting something hold you back." Brandon shook his head. "I don't get it. Do you want to be sent back to Briar?"

Sydney's head whipped towards him, her wide gray eyes filled with such fear that Brandon almost took a step back. "They wouldn't do that. They won't. Take it back!"

"Okay, okay, I didn't mean it," Brandon replied quickly, placing calming hands on the girl's shoulders. Her whole body shook.

"I can't go back to Briar. I can't."

"It's okay, nobody is sending you anywhere."

"They might take her instead. She'll die if they take her." Sydney spoke so quickly, Brandon could barely catch her words.

"Die? Who will die?"

"Abigail," Sydney muttered after a moment.

"Abigail? Your sister?" he said, confusion clouding his voice. "I don't understand. They wouldn't take her unless…" Brandon cut off abruptly, understanding hitting him like a sword to the gut. Sydney's small stature, her distrust of others, the fear that seemed to follow her like a shadow. "You took her place. Your sister should have been recruited, not you."

"Yes," Sydney said softly, taking a small step away from him.

"Why? Why take her place?"

"Abi… She's sick. She's *always* been sick. Her whole body shakes, she can't move or speak. If that happened in a battle…"

"She would be killed," Brandon finished. He stared down at his friend, seeing her in a new light. "By the gods, it's a brave thing you did."

"Bravery had nothing to do with it," Sydney said, her face guarded. An expression Brandon had grown used to over the past few months. She lifted a pointed chin, eyes flashing. "Now that you know, who are you going to tell?"

"Tell? Nobody."

"You're not going to turn me in?" she asked suspiciously.

"Of course not. And I'll start helping you train. Tonight. You don't have to worry about being sent home anymore. No one will suspect you."

"I don't understand." Sydney looked at him as if she was really seeing him for the first time. "Why do you want to help me?"

"Friends?" Brandon held out a hand, forming the word as a question. Sydney stared at him, her face thoughtful. She wrapped a small hand around his forearm, her grip firm.

"Friends."

Brandon grabbed a second practice sword, and the newly forged friends squared off against each other, setting to work. Sydney attacked first with a reckless swing of her weapon. Brandon disarmed her easily, and she landed with a thud in the dirt.

As Brandon pulled her to her feet, he said, "That was a good first try."

Sydney grinned. It was the first time he'd seen her smile in a long time. Maybe ever. The expression changed her face, made her dark features seem lighter.

"You're a rotten liar, Lockes."

*****

Brandon awoke with a smile on his face, the sound of Sydney's teasing voice still echoing in his ears. He hadn't had that dream in months. It had become so familiar, Brandon wasn't sure which parts were memory and which were imaginary. He supposed it didn't matter. Sparring with Sydney, the sounds of laughter and clattering swords echoing through the evening air… it was the first moment in a long time that Brandon felt he wasn't alone.

And as the dream left him, Brandon made a decision.

He'd lost his father to war.

He'd lost his mother to grief.

He'd be damned if he lost Sydney too.

Brandon quickly packed up his meager belongings and began the long journey through the ancient trees. Morning dew blanketed the forest floor, and the birds chirped happily from their branches, making the previous night, all dark and lonely and bitter, seem like a distant nightmare. Brandon headed due east, straight for the chasm. Yesterday, returning to Brimhold had felt like giving up, like abandoning his friend. But with the morning light came a renewed purpose. He would ride back to Delm as fast as a horse could carry him. He would return to the Wornwood with an army at his back. He would save Sydney. And to hell with the elf that stood in his way.

15

Among the Elves

In the days that followed, Sydney fell into an odd sort of routine. She would awaken to Lukaris at her tent entrance, ready to lead her to breakfast. They would eat together, sometimes with Raiden or Flindir or maybe even Itari. They were the only elves that didn't give her venomous glares as she ate. After, the questions would begin.

Sydney quickly realized that there was so much she didn't know. About the elves, their day to day lives, their history. As a soldier of Brimhold, it had always been easier to think of her enemies as merely that. Enemies. The less she knew about them, the simpler it was to do her job. But now that the information lay in front of her, free for the taking, Sydney was curious to know more.

Lukaris on the other hand, used his questions quite differently. He focused persistently on Sydney herself. How was her childhood? What was her family like? What did young Sydney dream about? These were touchy subjects, and Sydney did her best to avoid them or give away as little as possible. Why Lukaris cared about such things was beyond her.

Around midday, they would eat again. After, Lukaris usually

handed Sydney off to one of the few elves that would tolerate her. She spent a great deal of time in Flindir's strange tent. He gave Raiden lessons on botany and history, among other things. Sydney joined these sessions, along with Honey the bear of course, though she mostly listened quietly while Raiden pestered his teacher. Flindir took everything in stride. He had a steady patience, a warm laugh, and an eagerness to spread knowledge. Little by little, he even dragged Sydney into the conversations.

When Flindir was busy, Itari or Ettee took charge of their human "guest." They were less relaxed than Flindir, but they were respectful at least. Itari would take her around the camp while she did her *Dualir* duties, mostly monitoring the training of the *tatell*. Sydney even got to watch a few elvish scrimmages. They were full of magic and swords and lightning fast footwork. Her days with Ettee were less exciting. Raiden was right. If Sydney had to hear about one more healing salve, she might die of boredom.

By nightfall, it was time for a quick supper, and then Sydney was hurried back to her tent for the evening. A soldier would hang around the entrance, trying to appear casual, but Sydney knew a guard when she saw one. The elves would stay up a while longer, ringed around a campfire. Sydney could hear them laughing and singing from her isolation. She often took to pacing her small space, thinking and grumbling until she finally collapsed into her hammock for the night.

When she woke, the whole process would begin again.

Slowly, gradually, and against her will, Sydney grew used to Lukaris' company. Something about his insistent peppering of questions made her forget she was talking to an elf, an enemy. The feeling was brief, and Sydney was quick to mentally berate herself. *Focus. He is not your ally. He holds answers you need. That's it.*

A few days after her arrival in Firne, Sydney walked through camp with Lukaris. The day was bright and cool, the sun beaming down on them from above. The excitement from Sydney's arrival had dimmed somewhat, and she now received only brief glares from passing elves.

"Tell me about your family," Lukaris insisted, abruptly. Sydney scowled.

"That's not a question."

"Come on, Captain Krane. It's not as if I'm asking for Brimhold's deepest secrets."

She sighed. "Fine. But there's not much to tell. My mother died during childbirth, so I never knew her. My father raised me and my sister, Abigail. Now they're gone too."

"I'm sorry." He sounded like he meant it. "Do you have any *viscir?*"

"*Viscir?*"

"Oh, right. *Viscir* are… friends. Friends that are as close as blood. Chosen family," Lukaris explained.

"Well," Sydney mused. "I suppose my co-captain, Brandon. He is as much a brother to me as a friend. And Gilliad. He has always been a father in the absence of my own."

"Gilliad Norwell? The general?" Lukaris asked, surprised. "I've heard he is an honorable soldier. A good man."

"He is. The very best." The praise of her mentor, even by an enemy, warmed her heart. Sydney cleared her throat before tears could form in her eyes.

"What about you? Besides Raiden, what's your family like?"

Lukaris blinked, no doubt surprised that Sydney was asking a personal question. "Raiden is my only sibling, but both my parents are alive, thank the Light. They live in Sil Tullian."

"Growing up in the Silver City must have been exciting," she noted, daydreaming of the fabled mountain fortress with its cascading waterfalls and spiraled towers.

Lukaris' face darkened. It was subtle, a passing shadow at the corner of her eye, but unmistakable. "Exciting, sure. But I much prefer it out here, in the Wornwood. More green and less cold stone."

The elf's mood flipped in an instant. He spun on a heel to face Sydney, eyes bright.

"So!" Lukaris began. A sharp breeze rushed past them, raising the elf's porcupine hair. "What does Captain Krane of Briar do for fun?"

Sydney stared at him. "Fun?"

"Yes, fun. Or is that kind of thing not allowed in Brimhold?"

"Well, I guess… I always enjoy a pint and a game of bait at The Steel Anchor," she said, fumbling for an answer.

The *Valen* rolled his eyes. "Drinking isn't a hobby, Captain Krane."

"It is the way I do it," Sydney replied with a wicked grin.

"I'm serious," he insisted. "Name something you enjoy that isn't fighting or training or gambling."

"You just ruled out half my personality," Sydney joked. But in reality, she was stalling. Lukaris' question bothered her. Why couldn't she think of a single thing she found fun? A single thing she loved?

What had she enjoyed as a child? Most of her time had been spent running around Briar. Or praying to be anywhere else.

"I guess I like exploring new places." It was the best answer to a complicated emotion. "If nothing else, the war gave me the chance to do that. I used to stare out from the docks in Briar, wishing a ship would take me away. Now, every Honor Guard assignment takes me somewhere new. I can't get enough of it. Even if sometimes I end up with an arrow to the shoulder," Sydney finished with a smirk.

Lukaris had been watching her, eyes thoughtful. Suddenly, he lit up, smile as wide and bright as the sun reflecting off the treetops.

"I've got an idea! Wait here, don't move a muscle, I'll be back before you can say *hoth*."

And the elf was gone. Sydney stood alone at the center of camp, feeling the hostile stares around her intensify without the protection of her *Valen* shield.

By the time Lukaris returned, Sydney had said *hoth* at least a hundred times —whatever that meant — and she was convinced the elves two tents down were plotting her murder. The *Valen* slung a stuffed leather bag over his shoulder, green eyes glittering.

"Ready?"

"Ready for what?" Sydney grumbled, shifting from one foot to another.

Lukaris grinned. "To see something new."

He led her west, up the hill, and out of camp. Sydney asked no further questions. She was just happy to escape the confines of Firne for a little while, her boots landing on fresh, untrodden earth. Lukaris practically vibrated with excitement as he guided them through tight glades of ancient trees. The breeze followed them up into the forest, bringing with it the smell of damp grass and pine. Their trail steepened as they climbed higher into the foothills, and Sydney found her lungs struggling in the thin mountain air. Yet for some reason, she couldn't wipe the smile from her face.

They hiked in silence for a long time, but it was a comfortable silence, one built from momentary freedom and the promise of adventure. Eventually, the trees opened up to reveal a roaring river, the source that fed Firne's small creek. They followed the rapids up and up, so far that Sydney worried her heavy human feet might not carry her back down the mountain. Eventually, they crossed over the final ridge. Sydney let out an audible gasp, and Lukaris turned with a grin.

A great stone statue towered out of the water, twenty times the size of an average man at least, the largest sculpture Sydney had ever seen. Etched in agonizing detail was the elf goddess, Alur. Silver hair fell in long waves past her shoulders, pushed back to reveal both perfect pointed ears and four eyes carved carefully into the rock. Each eye managed to capture a different emotion. Anger, fear, happiness, love. The goddess wore a sweeping robe, the skirts pulled gracefully over one arm. The folds of her gown acted as perfect conduits for the river, which cascaded over her outstretched arm into the waters below. Mist stirred up from the pounding waterfall and drifted downstream with the wind.

And then, behind the statue, like great snow-capped wings spread across the horizon, rose the Moonrift Mountains. Sydney had never seen the peaks so close before. From Brimhold, the mountains were little more than distant accents to the skyline. She hadn't realized how giant and eerie and *solid* they were.

Lukaris continued to stare at her, so Sydney fumbled for a response. "I… this is… I've never… wow."

The elf laughed, and the sound echoed among the rushing water.

"My thoughts exactly, Captain Krane."

She picked her way across boulders to the base of Alur, neck straining as she stared up at the statue.

"Who built this?" she asked in awe.

"Some say it was dragon forged, long before Ithirdis even existed. Others think it was the last work of the elf stone worker, Tillas. Who can say?" Lukaris called from his place on the riverbank. "Whoever made it, I'm grateful to them."

Me too. Sydney spent the remainder of the morning exploring. The sun rose to its summit, and sunlight bounced off the water, the statue, and the surrounding mountain tops. Lukaris settled himself across the river, while Sydney skipped stones in the calm parts of the stream, the way Abigail taught her as a child. The elf pulled something from his satchel and began fiddling with it in his nimble hands.

"What are you doing?" Sydney called as another rock *splooshed* into the crystalline water.

Lukaris waved a small knife and a half-carved chunk of wood.

"Whittling."

"Whittling? What are you, an old man?"

He chuckled, smiling down at his hands, paper ribbons pooling by his feet. "It relaxes me."

"Whatever, grandpa."

"Well, why are you throwing rocks?"

Sydney shrugged. "It's fun."

Eventually, Sydney's stomach began to growl almost as loud as the waterfall, and Lukaris pulled a second surprise from his bag. A tiny feast. Soft brie and fresh bread rolls, strawberries and cinnamon pastries. He even brought a tiny bottle of Rumstar Ale, much to Sydney's delight. By the time they finished eating, both their faces were tinged pink.

Lukaris picked up his whittling again while Sydney lounged lazily in the grass.

"What are you making anyway?" she asked after a while.

"I'm not sure yet."

"How can you not know?"

"Sometimes I don't know where I'm headed until I'm halfway there," the elf replied easily.

Sydney watched him for a while longer, but the silence had grown heavy, and she couldn't let it hover.

"Isn't this difficult for you at all?"

His hands stopped. He looked at her. "Isn't what difficult?"

"Being here. With me."

"Why would it be?"

Sydney rolled her eyes. "We're enemies. We fight on opposite sides of a war. Doesn't that mean anything to you?"

"I've told you. I think both our kingdoms have been played. It doesn't bother me to spend time with a human, because we never should've been enemies in the first place," Lukaris insisted. She didn't believe him. And she hated being lied to.

In a burst of inspiration, Sydney plunged a hand into her cloak like she was reaching for a weapon and shifted her body in Lukaris' direction.

The elf's eyes went wide. His hand gripped the whittling knife before Sydney could blink. In the same moment, the wind shifted so fast and so drastically, it pulled at Sydney's breath. She gasped, choking as her lungs emptied without warning.

The air returned just as quickly, and Sydney could breathe again. Lukaris' hand shook as he lowered his weapon.

"I'm so sorry, Captain Krane. Are you alright?" the *Valen* asked, voice dripping with remorse.

"I'm fine," she wheezed. She couldn't hold back a small smile. "But I proved my point. I make you nervous after all."

The sympathy dropped from his face like a hammer's fall, his sharp jaw twitching. "What game are you playing at? You've proven nothing. Any soldier would react the same way to a perceived attack. By the Light, if Sarcys came at me like that, I'd think he meant to stab me too!"

Sydney felt a bit embarrassed. Why was she trying to make things harder than they needed to be?

"You're right. I shouldn't have said anything."

Lukaris stared, forest eyes boring into her. "Is elvish company really that difficult for you, Captain Krane? Have we made no progress at all?"

We have. It's easier every day. That's the problem.

But she wasn't about to tell him that.

"We better get going," Sydney muttered, trying to change the subject. "I'm sure your brother won't know what to do with himself if he can't pester me at supper."

The elf still carried a frown, but he didn't press the issue. Any warmth or excitement the day held had passed like a cloud across the sun. They packed up their few belongings in silence and started the long trek back to camp. As they reached the first river bend, Sydney turned back for one last glance at Alur's statue. She looked lonely there, where the trees began to falter at the mountains' edge. An end and a beginning. And for a brief moment, in the bright light of the afternoon sun, water droplets appeared as tears racing down the goddess' stone face.

16

The Cursed Place

Walking back to Firne felt like the walk to a prison cell. Sydney sighed, wishing she hadn't ruined the afternoon with useless mind games. Lukaris was quiet on the path ahead of her, shoulders hunched. He didn't seem overly excited to return to camp either. Every step seemed to add another weight upon his back.

Clouds coated the sky in swaths of gray and white. A chill prickled at Sydney's spine as the wind stirred up fresh air from the north. A day full of light turned sullen.

Lukaris stopped so abruptly, Sydney nearly crashed into him.

"Hey! Watch where you're—"

The elf held up a hand, cutting her off. His pointed ears twitched slightly.

"We're being followed," he breathed.

Sydney usually had a good instinct for such things, so at first she thought the *Valen* was acting paranoid. But then she felt it. The heavy weight of watchful eyes upon her skin.

"Bandits?" Sydney murmured, eyeing the trees. Lukaris' head shake was little more than a quiver.

"I don't think…"

A low growl stirred the undergrowth behind them. They turned in unison, Lukaris with two daggers drawn, Sydney wielding useless fists.

A monster stalked out from beneath the ferns. Or at least, it looked like a monster. The creature was smaller than a wolf, fox-like and graceful, with matted fur the color of stone. Twin rows of salivating, white fangs filled a gaping mouth. Sydney took a reluctant step towards Lukaris as the monster's yellow slit eyes fell upon her.

"What in Kon's name is that?" she hissed. Her hands clutched for weapons that weren't there.

"A riphound," Lukaris said, tone laden with dread. "And if there's one, there's more."

On cue, another hound slithered out from Sydney's left. And her right. And behind her. And in the branches above.

"Shadowed hell," Sydney cursed. She found herself back to back with the elf as they tried to keep each creature in view. "I thought riphounds live high in the mountains. What are they doing here?"

"They must be hungry."

"Oh, *that's* helpful."

One of the hounds made an experimental lunge for Lukaris. He swiped with his blade, and the creature retreated quickly out of range. The riphounds circled their prey, fervent. Waiting.

"These things are fast, and if they get ahold of you, they won't let go. Don't make any sudden movements," Lukaris instructed.

"How exactly do you expect us to escape then?" Sydney demanded.

The *Valen's* anxious silence was answer enough.

"Pass me a knife, will you?" she said, her resolve hardening.

Lukaris didn't move. Sydney could feel the indecision rolling off of him even if she couldn't see his face.

"Are you serious?" Sydney huffed. "If I was going to try and kill you, I would have done it days ago. But I'll be damned if I let a bunch of hounds rip me to shreds without fighting back. *Now, give me a blade, you feather-brained dolt.*"

"Alright. Okay. I'm trusting you." Sydney felt a hilt press into her hand. Her fingers wrapped around the familiar grip.

I'm not asking for your trust, she wanted to say. But her gaze was already fixed on the enemy.

"If we run are they going to chase us?" Sydney asked. The riphound in front of her licked its lips suggestively.

"Definitely."

"Can you… throw some wind at them or something?"

"I doubt that will accomplish much besides making them mad."

Okay, think Sydney, think.

"How far are we from camp?" She took another step, forcing their backs firmly against each other.

"Too far. But…"

"If you've got an idea, now's the time to share it."

"There's a steep ridge up ahead," said Lukaris. "If we can get down it, they might give us up for easier food."

"Which way?"

"Straight ahead of me."

"Alright then, lead the way, ace," Sydney decided. Despite the danger, her blood surged in an exciting way. It felt good to have a blade in her hand. "Give them everything you have and run."

"Are you sure—"

"One," Sydney counted, bending her knees.

"Captain Krane—"

"Two."

"Are you even listening—"

"Three." Sydney shoved Lukaris in the back. She dove to the left, slashing at the first riphound in reach. Her blade sliced through the beast's shoulder, blood bright red among the green. It gave an ear splitting howl. Another hound leapt from a nearby tree and onto Sydney's back. She pushed it off, desperate to ward off its gnashing teeth.

Then, Lukaris was there.

The wind rushed through the trees like a riptide through the sea. The hound in front of Sydney staggered, pointed ears flattened against its skull. Lukaris appeared at her shoulder. He spun, weapon raised, face tight and fierce, and dispatched the beast still blocking their path. It snarled before finding stillness in the dirt, yellow eyes wide.

"Let's go," Lukaris urged. Sydney sprinted after him through the trees.

All around, they could hear the sound of panting breath and claws scraping the earth as the beasts pursued them through the forest. Sydney's boots pounded in the dirt on beat with her drumming heart. Despite her best efforts, Lukaris outpaced her. She lagged behind, the unfamiliar woods dragging at her with misplaced branches and tangled roots. The elf must have sensed something was amiss, because he turned just in time to shout. "Look out!"

Sydney raised her dagger just as a riphound crashed into her side. The blade sat sideways in the creature's mouth, the only barrier between Sydney's throat and a double row of fangs. She stumbled backwards, and her feet struck a soft patch of earth. She grunted, pushing her weapon deeper into the hound's jaw. The creature fell to the ground, dead, and the cliff side gave way. Lukaris had rushed back, and he reached out, catching at her arm. But Sydney was already slipping, and she dragged the elf down with her.

They half rolled, half fell down the ridge. Sydney felt every bump like a fresh arrow to her shoulder. After what felt like an eternity, they tumbled to a stop upon level ground. Lukaris groaned. Sydney cursed. High above, the riphounds paced furiously at the cliff's edge, but they did not attempt the decent, and after a few final snarls, the beasts fled.

Minutes passed. Peace returned to the woods. Sydney lay listening to birds chirping in the distance until the black spots left her vision. Eventually, she pushed herself up with a moan and looked over to where Lukaris sat. Twigs and grass stuck out of his disheveled hair, and dirt streaked every angle of his face. He looked ridiculous, and a snicker slipped out of Sydney's mouth before she could stop it. And once she was laughing, she couldn't stop. Her sides heaved. Tears slipped down her face. Lukaris looked at her as if she'd lost her mind, which only seemed to make her laugh harder. After a moment, the elf began laughing too. Soon they were both chortling so loud, Sydney was sure a new beast would find them.

It felt good. Really good. She couldn't remember the last time she'd laughed.

When she finally regained her composure, Sydney drew a deep, shuddering breath, and took in their surroundings. They'd fallen into a large hollow. Packed trees circled the clearing on all sides, cutting it off from the rest of the forest. It was quiet. The birds and the wind and the river felt a world away. Hairs stood up on Sydney's arms and the back of her neck.

At the center of the hollow stood a house, though that was being generous. It was little more than a shack. The dwelling blended so well with the encompassing woods that Sydney overlooked it at first. The hovel lay barren, walls caving in on themselves, the moss strewn roof barely clinging to a nearby tree. As Sydney's feet drew her closer, she saw the remnants of ash and soot streaking the wooden doorway.

Lukaris' hand caught at her arm, making her jump.

"We should leave," the *Valen* said in a hushed voice. All of the laughter had left his face. His eyes darted to the house.

"Why?" Sydney asked, curiosity sparked. She pulled away.

"This is a cursed place," he muttered urgently. "Please, let's go."

But Sydney wasn't listening. She rounded the crumbling structure. Drawings, either in blood or a dark red paint, stained the nearest wall. There was a sentence of writing in Elvish, but most of the wall was dominated by a large symbol. A raven's skull atop the outline of a rising sun. Sydney laid a hand on the symbol. Something about it was familiar. Like a faded memory.

"What does this say?"

Lukaris hesitated. She turned to face him, hands to her hips. "I'm not leaving until you tell me."

The *Valen* sighed. He wrapped both arms around himself, like they could protect him from the raven's empty eyes.

"*Scoured and found, cleansed and burned,*" he read. Sydney's stomach rolled at the words, and she took a step back. She realized where she'd seen the drawing before. It littered history books about the Greyblood Scour.

Before Lukaris could stop her, Sydney stepped through a hole in the rotting wall. She knew what she would find, but she needed to see for herself. And beneath the rumble, under a broken table, she found it. A tiny skull, the remains of a child. A young boy or girl, killed for their blood. For the mere potential of evil. War was one thing, but this? Who could do this? Another part of her wondered if she stood in the ruins of Briar a hundred years from now. Sickened, she scrambled back out to the fresh air, bringing the skull with her.

Lukaris stared, eyes watchful and waiting. Sydney shook the ash from her boots.

"This place should be destroyed," she declared. "The Scour was a tragedy. A disgrace. Those who died here deserve a proper end."

The *Valen* didn't respond. He just looked to the red writing, eyes sad.

"Did you hear me?" Sydney demanded.

"I did," Lukaris replied at last. "But destroying this place will not erase the history. Some will say it should stay, as a reminder."

Sydney had a snappy retort prepared, but something in Lukaris' face stopped her. She had a sudden thought.

"Were you alive, when it happened? The Scour?"

"No," the elf said with a small shake of his head. He found a boulder sticking from the grass and took a weary seat. "But my parents were. We've spoken about it in length."

"And?" Sydney had never seen Lukaris so reluctant to share something with her. "By your reaction, I'm guessing they supported those monsters?"

"Of course not," Lukaris snapped. Sydney raised an eyebrow at the reaction. The *Valen* sighed again. "I apologize, Captain Krane. It is a sore subject. My parents never supported the Scour, but they never denounced it either, which is almost as bad."

"You can disagree with your family and still love them," Sydney told him. He gave her a small smile in response, thankful. She turned back to the ill-fated home. "I never understood how the Scour reached such strength. Magic runs in elves too, and yet they helped kill children and families because of it."

Lukaris looked at her. "How much do you know of magic?"

She shrugged, slightly embarrassed. "Elves have it, humans and merfolk don't. The dragons had the strongest magic of all, but they're long gone. What else is there to know?"

"That barely scratches the surface," he told her gently.

"Alright. Explain it to me then."

"Our magic..." Lukaris paused, gathering his thoughts and beginning again. "Light is a force that flows through everything. You, me, the sky, the earth. When we die, the Light that is in us returns to its source. The Light is then born again through another.

Elves are able to tap into their own personal Light and the Light in the world around them. I can *feel* the wind, Captain Krane, like it's a part of me. Humans and merfolk still carry Light within them, but it is dim and hard for them to reach. And then there are the dragons, who were so full of Light that magic came as easy as breathing.

But this is not the only type of magic. Shadow magic acts as the balance to the Light. The Sháedin were the only creatures ever able to wield its power. As you know, they created such chaos in the world, our ancestors worked to lock them away.

Light and Shadow magic are natural. They are two dueling forces in the universe. But still, they are not the only types of magic. Humans, and merfolk to an extent, have created a kind of cheat. Blood magic. It pulls from the small bit of Light that exists within their blood."

"I'm guessing you don't approve of such power?" Sydney asked. She'd seen Blood magic used in Delm for simple charms and enhanced weapons, among other things. It was a rare and dangerous craft and far from the same level as Light magic. Still, it helped even the odds.

"You will find few elves that do," Lukaris replied tersely.

Sydney decided to keep her thoughts on the subject to herself. "So where does greyblood magic stand? Light, Shadow, or Blood?"

The elf shrugged, at a loss. "That's the age-old question. If you mix two creatures of Light, an elf and a human, surely the resulting greyblood is also of the Light? And yet, their magic is different. They don't merely shape the wind. Greybloods are able to manipulate minds or change what the eyes perceive. They could convince a man to kill himself with only a word. Even the darkest Shadow magic cannot do that. I know of greybloods that went on to do terrible, terrible things."

"I suppose I see where some of the fear comes from," Sydney

admitted. "But that's all it is: fear. Elves, humans, merfolk. They all do horrible things. It's no excuse for *this*." She brandished the skull between them.

Lukaris looked away. "You're right. As I said, this is a cursed place. It's a reminder of what unbridled fear is capable of."

They remained in the clearing for a while longer. Sydney gave the skull a proper burial, away from the ruined home, at the roots of an oak tree. She wondered what magic the greyblood child possessed that could've led to such evil. She wondered too, if the murderers had ever suffered for their crimes. Would Briar's destruction go unpunished too?

Lukaris hung back. Sydney could not guess what the elf was thinking. But whatever moment they shared earlier lay buried beneath ash and bone.

As the sky began to darken, Sydney turned away from the Scour ruin. She did not care to be anywhere near that place when nightfall came. Lukaris rose to his feet, eager.

"Let's go," Sydney said. She spared a final glance at the overturned earth beneath the oak tree. "I've had enough adventure for one day."

17

Deaf Ears

"Open the gate!"

Two guards stepped forward onto the road, spears partially lowered, violet cloaks snapping in the breeze. They tensed as a sole rider barreled towards them up the hillside, as if he meant to storm the castle all on his own.

"Stop!" one of the soldiers called out shrilly. "Halt and state your business here."

At last, the rider slowed. He pulled his steed to a stop before the lowered weapons, hooves clattering on stone. The horse's sides heaved with exertion while the man dismounted, his own legs shaking as his boots struck the road. Eyeing the pointed weapons with something close to disgust, the rider moved forward, square jaw twitching with annoyance. The first guard swallowed hard, hands tightening around her spear.

"Sir—"

From a pocket, the stranger pulled a small pin, holding it up for the guards to see. Two crossed silver swords. The symbol of the Honor Guard.

"I said," Brandon began, his voice low and hard, "open the damn

137

gate."

The iron gate swung outward, and Brandon ran, leaving his horse behind. Sweat ran down his forehead and into his eyes. He wiped the beads away angrily. *I have to find Gilliad. The queen. Someone.* Every second felt like an eternity as he raced through the castle grounds. He'd taken too long reaching Delm. How many days had he left his friend to the mercy of the elves? Sydney needed help *now*, and by the gods *where was everyone?*

In his haste, Brandon nearly collided with Julia. She swayed, grabbing at his arm to regain her balance.

"Brandon?" Julia's grip on his arm tightened, her eyes lighting up with realization. "We were so worried. What happened? Where's Sydney?"

The captain deflated, the strength falling from his limbs. Julia must have read the answer in his expression, her face paling. "Oh no."

"She's in trouble," Brandon forced the words. *She's not dead.* Julia brushed back her dark hair, face determined.

"Then let's get help."

They found Gilliad first. The general sat overlooking the training fields. His eyes were glazed, staring but not seeing. At Brandon's arrival, the man snapped to attention, rising quickly to his feet. He scratched at his gray beard as the soldiers approached, eyes flitting over Julia, before settling on Brandon. The captain had rarely seen his mentor so troubled.

"Is she…?"

"She's alive," Brandon assured him. The general let out a deep breath, pinching the bridge of his nose. He stayed that way as Brandon rushed through his story, beginning with the destruction of Briar and ending with his desperate search through the Wornwood. "We have to mount a rescue. We'll take the entire Honor Guard if we have to."

"Brandon, I'm not sure that's a good idea." Gilliad's voice was gentle, but Brandon wasn't listening. He spotted a flash of blonde hair over the general's shoulder, headed towards the royal stables. Queen Camillea.

"I have to talk to the queen," Brandon insisted as he pushed past his friends.

"Brandon, wait—"

"Maybe you shouldn't bother her!" Julia called after him. The captain pretended not to hear her.

"Your Majesty," Brandon called, giving a quick bow as he approached the queen of Brimhold. Camillea, surrounded by a small legion of soldiers, paused at the call. The queen was dressed for travel, sporting gray riding pants with matching boots and a muted scarlet top. She still looked commanding despite her commonplace attire. Her authority was found not in her clothes, but in the tilt of her head and the weight in her eyes.

Those eyes turned now to Brandon, flashing through a mixture of emotions. Surprise. Relief. And finally, anger.

"Captain Lockes," Camillea said slowly, voice low and brittle. "You're alive then."

"Yes, your Majesty."

"And Captain Krane…"

"She's alive too, but…" Brandon felt Gilliad and Julia come up behind him, listening quietly to the exchange.

The queen stared, cool eyes boring into him, and then sighed. "Brandon, what have the two of you done?"

He explained, once again, the actions that had led him here. The captain found he could not meet the queen's gaze.

"We have to save her. Sydney is out there at the mercy of the elves. Please, allow me to lead a rescue mission." Brandon tried to sound firm, but desperation leaked through the words. He looked to

Camillea, searching for an ounce of sympathy in her face.

He found none.

"Let me make sure I have this straight, Captain Lockes," the queen said. "You and Captain Krane blatantly defied my orders, crossed into enemy territory without permission, and proceeded to get one of my high ranking officers captured. Now, you expect me to risk not only the lives of my soldiers, but Brimhold's entire war effort, just to clean up the mess you made. Does that about cover it?"

Brandon swallowed. "Yes, your Majesty."

"And tell me, when you and Captain Krane committed your act of treason, did you do so with the expectation that my army would come to your rescue if you failed?" Each word was a slap to the face. Brandon stared at the ground.

"No, your Majesty."

"So, what makes you think I will help you now?"

Brandon had never been good at politics. He knew how to break bones and swing a sword. But he didn't know how to convince others to join his cause, didn't know the right thing to say and when to say it. That had always been Sydney's job. She always got her way if she set her mind to the task. *Everyone has a weakness,* she would say. *Find their trigger, their fear, their love. Always make your opponent use their heart instead of their head.*

"I hope that you will help me, because you understand. You know why Sydney pursued the elves. She witnessed the destruction of her home, her family, just like you did all those years ago." The queen's jaw clenched, but Brandon soldiered on. "Captain Krane made a mistake. We both did. I'm not denying that. But, her actions came from a place of love, not disobedience. She doesn't deserve to die seeking the same justice you've been searching for the past twenty years."

The gathered soldiers held a collective breath. While Camillea's frigid gaze held Brandon in place, the captain prayed. He prayed to the gods and to the Light and to anyone else that would listen. *Please.* At last, the queen spoke.

"Do you have any idea where the Ithirdi might have taken her?" Camillea asked, the sharp edges of her voice beginning to melt. Brandon's heart soared.

"I don't have an exact location, your Majesty, but…" Brandon explained the area as best he could, the bridge they took across the chasm, the surrounding Wornwood, any detail that could lead them to his friend.

Camillea nodded as he spoke. "I know of an elf village not far from where you were attacked. It's possible that's where they took Sydney. I've had a mole stationed there for a few months, gathering information for a future attack. I planned to discuss all of this at the next council… but I suppose, given the circumstances, we might be able to move up the invasion. But Brandon, I don't want you to get your hopes up. There's no guarantee the elves took her there, or even that she's still—"

"It's alright, my queen." Brandon cut her off, not wanting to hear the word. He had a goal now, something to fight towards. He would worry about the rest later. "I know the chances. When can we leave?"

"If all goes well, perhaps we could leave with the next full moon."

The captain's throat closed in on itself. "A month?" He choked.

"Is there a problem?"

"It's just—" Brandon worked to calm his breathing. *Steady.* "Why the delay?

As if to answer, a young stable hand led a large, white steed over to the troop. The queen grasped the reins in one hand, patting the horse with her other. The two made a striking pair, both pale and regal. She cast Brandon another icy glance.

"I've agreed to help you find Captain Krane, but I will not derail the rest of Brimhold's war effort in the process. This trip to Nidaria is important. If I'm successful, it could pave our path to peace. If Sydney is still alive, she will have to manage until I return."

"Allow me to lead the mission in your stead," Brandon pleaded, scrambling. "We could accomplish both goals at once."

"My spy in the Ithirdi camp will collaborate with me, and me alone. And without my agent's help, we cannot hope to make it to the village undetected. No, you will wait for my return, however long that may be. Do we have an understanding, Captain Lockes?" Camillea asked as she swung up onto her horse. The height only made the queen more intimidating.

Brandon did not understand. He did not want to sit for weeks while Sydney's life hung in the balance. But he knew he could not save her alone. Swallowing his complaints, Brandon nodded.

"Good," said Camillea. As the ruler turned to leave, she spared Brandon a final glance. A small smile crossed her face. "For the record, Captain Lockes, I *am* glad you are alive."

Dust rose in the air as the company departed, trotting down to the castle gates. Brandon watched them go with fresh knots twisting in his stomach. *Hurry*, he wanted to call after the queen. *Please hurry.* A steady hand fell upon his shoulder.

"She'll be alright, son," Gilliad promised. Julia offered him a comforting smile.

"How can you be so sure?"

"Because it's Sydney," the general said simply. Brandon's heart clenched to match his stomach.

They stood there for a while, together, watching the queen and her soldiers fade into the east. But eventually, the general had other duties to attend to, and Julia departed as well, giving Brandon a light peck on the cheek as she left. Heat rose to his face, and he gazed after her, uncertain. He could almost hear Sydney's teasing voice in his head. If she were there, she would tell him to act, that there was no time like the present. But his mind was not in the present. He thought of the past, the family he couldn't save, the best friend he couldn't protect. And of the future, reunion or loss, relief or heartbreak. No, he didn't have time for joy amidst his fear.

Brandon stood on the hillside for a long time. The sun set beyond the mountains, red and sharp and terrible.

And as another day ended, Brandon's vigil began.

18

Different Hearts

One calm morning in late summer, the elves of Firne received a war summons. It came as a harsh reminder to Sydney that the fighting still raged on, whether she participated or not. The Ithirdi still fought and killed her people. No amount of civility between her and her captors could erase that.

Lukaris did not share the contents of the message, and Sydney knew better than to ask. All she could do was watch as soldiers strapped weapons to their waists, their backs, their horses, donning leather armor and green cloaks etched with the silver fox of Ithirdas. They were preparing for a fight.

Not all of the elves were leaving Firne. In total, only half of Lukaris' warriors. And to Sydney's surprise, Itari would lead the mission while the *Valen* stayed behind. She wondered if the decision had anything to do with her.

The fighting force was ready to leave by afternoon's end. The entire *tatell* met at the camp's edge to see them off. Sydney stood near Lukaris and Raiden atop Honey. The young boy's face was unusually somber as he patted the neck of his bear.

"When will they be back, Luka?" Raiden asked with a frown.

"I don't know for certain, *osan*," Lukaris said. He cast a sidelong glance at Sydney. "Hopefully a few days."

Flindir rushed from between two tents, a parcel clutched to his chest. Sydney watched as he passed the package up to Itari where she already sat high on her horse. The *Dualin* unwrapped the gift, a small smile on her lips. She bent down, pulling Flindir into a deep kiss. He had to stand on his toes to reach her.

Sydney blinked in surprise. "Those two are... together?"

Raiden smiled at her. *Silly, simple Sydney,* it seemed to say. "Itari and Flindir are *promised.*"

"Promised?"

"To be married," Lukaris explained.

"Married?" Sydney repeated, incredulous. The two elves seemed as different as ice and fire.

Before Lukaris could respond, Itari pulled her horse alongside them.

"I will leave by your word, *Valen,*" she said. She looked severe in her battle gear, throwing knives striking against her Viridian reds.

"Safe travels, *Dualin,*" Lukaris said formally. "*Silvas.*"

"*Silvas,*" she replied with a nod.

The Viridian turned and raised a fist. The departing elves looked to her, a dozen pairs of determined eyes.

"With me!" Itari called. A chorus of shouts echoed through the small camp. The *Dualin* gave a final wave before leading her warriors east, beneath the shelter of the trees. Sydney watched them go with a growing dread in her stomach.

*****

"And what caused the dragons to leave Soarden?" Flindir asked his pupil. Unfortunately, Itari's departure was not enough to postpone

145

Raiden's history lesson, and somehow they had roped Sydney into the discussion. The group sat on lush pillows in Flindir's tent, sipping on a sweet, lavender tea. Honey snoozed lazily, her giant golden head sticking in through a slit in the canvas wall. The afternoon warmth wrapped around them like a cocoon, and Sydney struggled to keep her eyes open.

"Uh, the War of Hearts?" Raiden guessed, only half listening. A lizard had found its way into the tent, and the young elf's eyes followed it as it paced through the dirt. Honey let loose a wide yawn, teeth flashing.

"Yes, but what started the War of Hearts?" Flindir prompted. Raiden didn't answer. He stuck out a hand towards the lizard, and the creature wiggled towards the boy's outstretched fingers.

"*Osan.*"

Raiden glanced up, and the lizard disappeared among a stack of old books. He cast a sheepish smile. "Hm?"

Flindir sighed. "If you're not going to pay attention, at least do a better job pretending."

"I'm listening!"

"Then what did I just ask you?"

"Um… something about dragons?"

While the elves squabbled, Sydney's eyes wandered around the cluttered mysteries of Flindir's tent. Strange blossoms. Ancient scrolls. Her focus finally landed on the closest tower of books. Near the top of the stack, a small leather volume caught her eye. The title was in Elvish, but underneath in a black script, read the words "*Soardic Translations*".

Sydney thought of words spat at her in passing, of foreign sentences sneered in her face. Not being able to fight back with Elvish the way she could fight back with her swords. And before she knew what she was doing, Sydney had slipped the book from its stack.

"Captain Krane," Flindir said, just as Sydney hid the tome in the folds of her cloak. "Perhaps you could help our young Raiden?"

"I'm not your student," Sydney scoffed.

"Everyone is a student," Flindir replied easily. His steady tone had a way of easing any rising tension. "Please, just humor me."

Raiden grinned over at her, clearly pleased to share his teacher's attention. Sydney rolled her eyes.

"The dragons left because the other Light races were using their magic to gain power."

Flindir nodded. "That's right. The dragons never cared for kingdoms or politics. They saw themselves as citizens of Soarden, and their magic as something to better the world. When their Hearts were twisted into weapons, they saw it as the ultimate betrayal."

"Hearts? Like our hearts?" Raiden asked, placing a small hand to his chest.

Flindir chuckled. "Not quite. A lot of the knowledge has been lost, but dragon Hearts were the source of their Light magic, and somehow they could be wielded by others. The holder of the dragon's Heart had access to incredible power, not to mention control of the dragon itself."

Raiden's eyes were now wide with wonder. Sydney was less intrigued. She had never understood the point in studying ancient history. Blood from the War of Hearts had long since dried and turned to dust. What good did it do to dwell on the past? She was much more interested in the hearts that still beat and bled.

"Speaking of hearts," Sydney interjected, hoping to breach a more fascinating topic. "I saw you with Itari before she left this morning. I didn't know the two of you were *involved*."

Scarlet blossomed on Flindir's round cheeks. "Is there a question in there somewhere, Captain Krane?"

"I guess I'm just wondering how the two of you— how you and

her—" Sydney hesitated.

"You think Itari is too good for me," Flindir interrupted with a laugh.

"No, no, that's not it—"

Flindir smiled, his eyes warm. "Don't worry, Captain Krane. I ask myself every day what she sees in me."

"I didn't mean it like that," Sydney insisted, almost apologetic. Raiden had lost interest again, digging through Flindir's controlled chaos in search of his lizard friend.

"You just seem like such different people. From different worlds, almost."

"Oh, we are," the elf agreed. "But I often think the parts that make us different are the parts worth loving the most."

"It seems like it would make things… harder."

He shrugged. "Love is never easy, Captain Krane."

Sydney wasn't sure she understood. She'd only seen love in glimpses, between battles of hate and rage. She had never seen her parents together, never known what their love looked like. Only secret midnight meetings between soldiers in the barracks or the embrace of two lovers in the dark corner of a tavern. The look in Gilliad's eyes when they fell upon his wife. But she'd never thought differences could pull two people together. Too easily the disparities grow, the gap widens, growing to distrust and ending in fear.

Later that evening, Sydney settled into her tent and pulled the stolen book from her cloak. She flipped through the pages, eager for something to do besides pace the grass floor or dream up new schemes in her head.

The volume was written in a messy, cramped Elvish, that would have been difficult to read even if she knew the language. Sydney had no idea if the book was a diary or a record or something else entirely. A few of the passages had bits of Soardic scribbled underneath, but they were far from the direct translations Sydney had been hoping for. Instead, they seemed to be extra musings or rough summaries of the previous text. One such section read:

Where does this discovery lead us? Good or bad, Light or Shadow? I almost wish it hadn't fallen to us. The responsibility is too great.

And another:

More progress made, but maybe in the wrong direction.

Sydney tried to compare the Soardic to the Elvish, make comparisons between the words. She gave up after a long, frustrating hour. *Useless.* If she was hoping to pick up a new language, this wasn't the way. With a grunt, Sydney tossed the book onto her hammock. The fabric spun widely back and forth.

She would just have to accept that the elves could trade secrets right in front of her face. The words were too strange, too foreign. Differences too great to overcome.

Surprisingly, Flindir's words echoed through her head.

The parts that make us different are the parts worth loving the most.

Sydney snorted. It sounded like a load of troll shit.

19

A Day With An Enemy

The morning was bright and clear. Sydney's demeanor was not.

"No," she growled, crossing her arms. "Absolutely not."

"It's just for one day, Captain Krane—"

"You said I wouldn't be tortured by the elves, and yet here you are, breaking your promise."

"Don't be so dramatic," Lukaris grinned. "What's the worst that could happen?"

"We could kill each other, to start."

Before Lukaris could reply, Sarcys sauntered from between a pair of tents. Sydney had seen little of the dark-headed elf since her first night in camp, for which she was grateful. He was everything she had expected the elves to be. And twice the ass.

"*Allon, Valen.*" Sarcys stopped before Lukaris, both hands across his heart. He ignored Sydney entirely. "Why have you asked me here?"

"I have a few things I need to attend to this morning," Lukaris began. "I would like you to show Captain Krane around Firne. She's seen plenty of camp, and I think touring an Ithirdi town might give her a fresh perspective."

Sarcys stiffened. A single vein twitched in his high forehead. "I don't think… surely there is someone *else…*"

"This isn't up for debate, Sarcys." Lukaris' voice held an edge like glass.

"I just… Yes, *Valen.*" The soldier resigned after a glare from his captain.

Lukaris brightened. "Excellent. I will meet up with you later."

"Wait," Sydney hissed at the departing elf, but he was gone before she could blink.

The enemies were left alone. After a moment of heavy silence, Sydney cleared her throat. Sarcys finally spared her a glance.

"I will take you into Firne as my *Valen* demands, but don't think this changes anything between us, Krane."

Sydney put on an innocent face, eyes wide and blinking.

"I'm sorry, have we met? What was your name again? Sack of…?" Sydney grinned as Sarcys stomped away. Maybe it wouldn't be such a bad day after all.

She followed her reluctant guide into Firne. The elf village bustled with activity. It was a market day, and the banks of the riverbed were laced with dozens of tents and vendors. Tinkers, hunters, and craftsman, among others. They called out their wares as Sydney and Sarcys weaved through the booths. Music washed through the crowd, upbeat melodies plucked from harp and lute strings. Sydney was surprised to find she recognized a few of the tunes.

Sarcys paid Sydney little attention. He walked at a brisk pace, as if he thought the faster they made it through town, the faster he could lose his human shadow.

"Hey, aren't you supposed to be teaching me or something?" Sydney demanded, struggling to keep up with the elf's long stride. She narrowly dodged a woman carrying a basket full of trout.

Sarcys cast a withering look over his shoulder. "What, you've never seen a market before, mortal? People trade, they barter, the end. Lesson over."

"So, what, you're just going to ignore me all day?"

"That's the idea."

"I can't imagine Lukaris will be happy with that arrangement," Sydney noted.

Sarcys slid to a halt. He turned slowly to glare at her.

"The *Valen*," the dark-haired elf emphasized the word as he towered over her, "is not who I thought he was if he insists I spend my valuable time humoring a rotten Brim."

Sydney smile was brittle. "I'm sure the *Valen* will be happy to hear you're questioning his judgment."

"Listen, you nasty little *mahil*—"

"Careful now," Sydney laughed. "Wouldn't want to cause a scene."

All around them, elves gaped openly at the exchange. A blush crept it's way up Sarcys' pale neck.

"Enough," he hissed under his breath. "Follow me and keep quiet. I won't tolerate any more of your insolence."

Sydney did not like being told what to do. And she particularly did not like being told what to do by gits like Sarcys. There's a reason she had worked her way up to captain so quickly. And so, as the elf moved away, Sydney slipped into the crowd, disappearing between two nearby booths. She could see the town without a chaperone. Besides, she couldn't wait for Lukaris to discover Sarcys had lost track of her.

The next row of tents was quiet compared to the hustle and bustle she'd just passed through. Most had closed flaps, shuttered against the elements and casual passerby. Music drifted in faintly, an afterthought, and the smell of food was a distant promise on the wind. A few figures passed from tent to tent without urgency. Curious, Sydney pulled up her hood, hiding her human features, and entered the nearest booth.

Woah. If Sydney could summarize the space in one word it would be *magical.* Trinkets and oddities covered every surface, every inch. Dozens of glass orbs hung from the tent posts, shining in a rainbow of colors. To Sydney's left, a table housed bottles, potions, remedies. Each was carefully labeled with ingredients and instructions. Most were in Elvish, but a few had translations into Soardic. The closest said: *Burn Salve. Crafted by Flindir of Sil Tullian. Aloe mixture, Light Magic grown. Particularly concentrated. Apply twice daily.* Another bottle filled with metal shavings read: *Spark Start. Use with caution. Shards of flint, infused with Light Magic, rune bound. Will ignite upon opening.* Sydney paused halfway through uncorking the bottle. She returned the item carefully to its place.

Before Sydney could explore the tent further, an elf stepped from behind a case of strange looking keys. She had chestnut hair chopped short, even with the severe line of her jaw. The elf dressed plainly, but she carried herself like a lady. While her face held no lines, Sydney got the feeling she was older, what might be considered middle age to a human.

"Allon," the elf said. *"Das ra halethe?"* Her voice held the careful consideration of a merchant looking to make a sale.

"Allon." Sydney returned the greeting with a nervous swallow. "Your wares are very interesting."

"Melánethe. Everything comes from local artisans and rune workers." She slipped easily into Soardic. "You may call me Quinell."

"I'm Sy—" Sydney stopped, realizing a human name would expose her instantly. "Sydi."

Quinell's eyes narrowed a fraction. "An unusual name. What is its meaning?"

"It's more of a nickname really." Warning bells rang in Sydney's head, but she tried to remain relaxed.

"I see. Well, Sydi, I have a strict policy in my shop. No hoods or helms. It helps keep out customers of a sinister variety. I'm sure you understand. If you wouldn't mind lowering your hood."

Sydney scrambled for an excuse. "Actually, I would rather keep it on. Bad hair day and all—"

"I'm afraid I must insist." The glowing orbs surged with a sharp, almost painful light. Sydney sighed. As Lukaris had said, what's the worst that could happen? Reluctantly, Sydney removed her hood.

Quinell sucked in a sudden breath. Anger flared in her expression so quickly that Sydney took an instinctual step backwards.

"Look, I have permission to be here. I'm Sydney Krane of Briar—"

"I know exactly who you are." Quinell's voice shook as she reached for something on a nearby shelf. "I just never thought I'd see you. Never thought I'd have the chance."

Sydney took another step towards the tent entrance. "The chance to what?"

"I've heard quite the story about your Honor Guard. Two years ago, you kidnapped a young elf guard along the Thorburn Chasm," the elf said, ignoring her question. "Do you deny it?"

When she didn't answer, the lights surged to such a degree that Sydney was forced to squint.

"Alright, alright, it sounds vaguely familiar. I might have taken an elf prisoner for questioning."

"Questioning?" The elf's voice rose, high and shrill. "Torture you mean. And what happened to that elf, after?"

Realization chilled Sydney to the bone. She remembered. She and Brandon were freshly anointed Captains. The queen had received word of elves stationed on Brimhold's side of the chasm, preparing for a raid. She sent the Honor Guard to investigate. Julia found an Ithirdi soldier, alone. They'd taken the elf back to camp and interrogated him, trying to nail down the details of the attack. When he refused to answer, Brandon insisted they push further. Eventually, the elf burned through his bonds and made a break for it. If he made it back to Ithirdis, the Honor Guard would lose the element of surprise, and the details of the raid would change. They would be right back where they started. Sydney was the first one to catch up to the escaped prisoner. She remembered her sword slicing across his back. She remembered the way his body lay where she left it in the woods.

"Your guard killed my son." Tears streamed down Quinell's face. "Do you deny it?"

Something heavy settled in Sydney's stomach. "No."

The elf squeezed her eyes shut, nodding. "When they found him… when they returned him to me… I'd never seen such cruelty. Such evil. He must have felt such pain." Quinell's eyes fluttered open as she slid a cooking knife from the shelf. It shook in her grasp. "Was it you? Was it by your hand?"

Sydney should have lied. She should have run. She should have kept her eyes fixed on the weapon. But she couldn't take her eyes off the elf's haunted face.

"Yes." The whispered word hung in the air between them.

"You're honest at least," Quinell said. Neither her voice nor her hands wavered any longer. "I'll give you that."

The elf lunged across the tent, the knife slicing in a path meant for Sydney's throat. She tumbled backwards at the last second, and the blade embedded itself in a tent post. Sydney crashed into the table full of potions, upending dozens of bottles and flasks. One shattered as it struck the earth, and the booth filled with a slow-moving cloud of scarlet gas. It smelled distinctly of raspberries. Holding her breath, Sydney made a scramble for the exit. Behind her, Quinell tried to pry her weapon from its wooden prison, shouting angrily in Elvish. As Sydney whipped the tent flap aside, light blazed out behind her, followed by a sharp crack. The glass orbs surged and burst into a thousand flying shards. Only Sydney's thick cloak protected her from the projectiles as she burst out into the sunlight.

Elves turned towards the commotion as Sydney stood gasping for air. An elf girl, about Raiden's age, poked her head out of a nearby booth. She marveled at the scene, gaze falling on something behind Sydney. The girl's eyes widened, and she slipped abruptly back into the safe folds of her tent.

Sydney spun around. Quinell staggered from the ruined booth, skin laced in tiny cuts from the shattered orbs. The knife swung in her grip once more.

"Face me, coward!" the elf cried. Her eyes were wild around the edges.

"Look, lady, I don't want to hurt you," Sydney said, holding up her hands. She backed slowly down a narrow alleyway in what she hoped was the direction of camp.

The elf barked a laugh. "That wish died two years ago when I buried my son."

Quinell moved forward as Sydney weighed her options. Fighting seemed unwise. Pleading to the other elves seemed unproductive. So, she made the only logical choice.

She turned and fled.

Sydney could feel Quinell breathing down her neck as she raced through the tight maze of tents. She dodged a tall, disgruntled elf, slid past a booth laden with sweets, and dove through a narrow opening between two wooden carts. Left, right, left again. Sydney hoped she was still moving in the direction of camp, but to be honest, she had lost her bearings. As she rounded another corner, she slid to a halt. *Damn it all.* A wall of green canvas blocked her path. She was trapped.

Quinell closed the gap between them in the time it took Sydney to draw a breath. The elf crashed into her, knife slashing. The blade passed so close to Sydney's cheek, she felt the air stir as it flew past. The weapon ripped a jagged hole in the closest tent. Sydney scrambled for the opening, giving Quinell a swift kick as she crawled into the booth.

The tent they emerged into lay open to the surrounding market. Glass lights swelled and shattered as Quinell got to her feet, blood-stained and half mad. Elves screamed and scattered. In the chaos, Sydney saw a familiar tuft of dark hair in the crowd. Sarcys. Their eyes met briefly, his gaze black and unreadable. Then, he was gone.

Bastard. Sydney wasn't surprised by Sarcys' abandonment, but it sparked a fresh knot of hatred in her chest. As much as Lukaris liked to pretend, she was not wanted here.

Sydney backed away from Quinell, placing a table between herself and her adversary. If she couldn't fight, couldn't flee, then she would stall.

"Your son," Sydney said, bringing the advancing elf to a halt. "What was his name?"

The knife lowered slightly. "What?"

"Your son's name. What was it?"

"His name… Jantis." The elf's voice wavered. Her mouth tasted the name gently, as if the word had not passed her lips in a long time.

"Jantis," Sydney repeated. "I'm sorry I didn't know it. To me, he was a nameless soldier. A soldier in *my* kingdom. A soldier who, if allowed to live, would have killed my people, easy as breathing. Who would have killed me instead, if given the chance. What was I supposed to do in the face of that? Your son and his allies meant to attack Brimhold. Can I be called a monster for defending my home?"

A hardness fell back upon Quinell's face. Her mouth worked up into a snarl.

"Lies from a human rat! My son and his *tatell* were escorting elves to the Valewood. It's a dangerous journey through your barbarian kingdom," Quinell sniffed. "You call any elf an invader. You kill for the sake of it. That sounds like a monster to me."

Sydney's stomach churned at the words. "That's not true. The raid... our scouts told us..."

Quinell laughed, the sound high and brittle. "More excuses. Admit that you didn't care about the reason. You saw a chance to murder, and you took it."

"No." Sydney backed away, this time out of denial more than a desire to escape. "Everything I've done has been to protect my people. I don't kill innocents."

"And yet," Quinell said with a sad shake of her head, "my son is dead. Because of you."

Sydney's head swam, heart pounding. She was so caught up in her thoughts that she didn't see Quinell's attack until it was too late.

The elf slammed into her, shoving her back against a tent post. A wave of pain radiated from her still healing shoulder. She barely managed to catch the elf's arm as the knife rose to her throat. The blade shook in the air between them as it was pushed and pulled by two opposing forces.

Quinell was not a warrior, but she wielded a mother's rage. Sydney could feel the weapon inching closer to her neck. Pushing with all her might, she desperately searched for an out, an escape, and found none. Would she die here, alone among enemies? Her thoughts were only of regret as the sharpened edge kissed her skin.

"Stop! Please!" The words flew from Sydney's mouth in a moment of desperation, though she knew it was futile.

Then, to her surprise, Quinell's force lessened. The knife halted in its shaking path towards her neck. In the elf's hesitation, Sydney dove beneath the blade, slipping passed her opponent's guard. She grasped Quinell's arm and drove it into the tent post at the elbow.

There was a snap and a scream, followed by metal striking the ground. The knife was in Sydney's hand before the surrounding crowd could blink.

Quinell backed away from the weapon as it hovered between them once more. She held her injured arm to her chest, eyes darting back and forth like a wounded animal. In that instant, it would have been easy enough for Sydney to kill her. Maybe Quinell's actions even warranted it. But Sydney had only ever killed from a place of duty, of rage and necessity. And when she searched for anger towards the woman, she found none. She cast the knife back into the dirt.

The elf clearly had no such qualms about killing Sydney. She took a step forward, as if meaning to grab the weapon again. But her gaze locked on to something beyond Sydney's shoulder, and the elf recoiled, eyes wide. An angry wind whipped through the tent. Sydney turned, knowing the sight that awaited her. Lukaris moved through the crowd, brow uncharacteristically furrowed. The elves parted before him. Sarcys walked at his side. His expression was shadowed and unreadable.

"What is going on here?" The *Valen* demanded, voice low. He stepped between Sydney and her assailant.

Quinell rattled off a quick explanation in Elvish. She alternated between wringing her hands and making furious gestures in Sydney's direction. Lukaris listened, frown etched onto his face. When Quinell finished, he spoke to her in quick, concise sentences. She lowered her head, and Sydney saw tears swell in her eyes. The gathered elves watched the exchange in a tense silence. Sarcys stared pointedly at the ground.

"Yes, *Dynas*," Quinell said, at last. She gave a quick bow, backing into the crowd. She cast a final glare at Sydney. Then, she was gone.

"Come," said the *Valen*, voice heavy. Sydney didn't argue. She let Lukaris and Sarcys lead her through the circle of hostile faces and away from the market. In the distance, music picked up once more, though it seemed sadder this time.

"Leave us." Lukaris spoke once they reached the outskirts of camp. "I will find you later, Sarcys."

The dark elf nodded, refusing to meet her eye as he departed. Did he regret fetching his leader? How easy it would have been to leave Sydney to her fate.

They continued to her tent, silence deep and deafening. Sydney took a swinging seat on her hammock. Her chest felt like lead. Lukaris stood by the entrance, arms crossed.

"Captain Krane," the elf sighed. He rubbed a hand across his face. "I know it's difficult, but I must ask that you don't wander on your own. It's not safe. Not yet. For you or the people of Firne."

Sydney stared at her hands as they tangled in the fabric of her cloak. "I understand. I'm sorry."

She saw Lukaris start out of the corner of her eye. "That's it? No argument?"

"Do you want me to argue?"

"No, I just..." Lukaris paused. "Are you alright?"

Sydney looked up, hands curling into fists. "I'm guessing she told you. Quinell. She told you what I did to her son."

He stared at her for a moment. "Yes."

"So, is it true? That attack, two years ago. Were the Ithirdi just traveling to Nidaria? Is it true they never planned a raid into Brimhold?" Sydney almost didn't want to know the answer. Almost.

Understanding flickered across Lukaris' forest eyes. "Yes. To my knowledge, it's true."

She had expected the answer, but it still felt like a fist plowing into her gut. She closed her eyes and took a shaking breath.

"So, I'm a monster too. We're all just killers in the end."

"You didn't know," Lukaris said gently. "You were trying to protect your kingdom."

"But how many times have we killed because of a lie? When does it stop?" Sydney could feel her mind spiraling, but the words kept coming. "I still look around this camp and see enemies. How can you look at me and see anything else?"

Lukaris didn't answer at first. Sydney watched as he gathered his words, choosing them carefully. "I used to see things like you. Right and wrong, light and dark. I used to be so angry at the humans. All I could see were the terrors they caused. Then Raiden was born, and I knew I didn't want him to grow into a world of war and hate. For the world to change, we must stop seeing the humans or the elves as *other*. It's the greatest lie the war has told us. There is evil on both sides, but there is also good. I don't think you are a monster, Captain Krane, for I have seen the same mistakes made by every participant in this fight. Including myself."

"If that's true, it's a nice way to see things," Sydney said softly. "But do you really think we can change? Even after all we've done?"

"I have to," Lukaris replied. He seemed young then, like a boy who'd been carrying a terrible weight on his own. "If not, then what's the point?"

With that, he made his exit, leaving Sydney to a heart full of heavy thoughts. She couldn't erase the feeling that the elves were responsible for the destruction of her village. Her murdered family. Years of fighting an enemy could not merely wash away. But now she wondered, how easily would she kill innocents, just like the killers of Briar? With the right orders, who's to say what she wouldn't do? Were you still evil if you did a terrible thing for a good reason? Her time in the Honor Guard had been filled with tough choices, but she had never questioned them until today.

Or were the elves manipulating her? Making her doubt herself, her actions, her kingdom. It would fall in line with everything she'd been taught about the Ithirdi since she was a child. She knew, with utmost certainty, that if Brandon had been in her place today, he would have killed Quinell without hesitation.

Pull it together, Sydney, she thought with a sigh. She shook the nagging worries from her mind. *You're an officer of Brimhold. All you've ever done has been for the good of your people.*

Right?

20

Trust

Sydney awoke the next morning feeling significantly less conflicted. A fresh day and fresh eyes helped push down any lingering guilt.

Outside her tent, the normal guard was gone, but an unusual visitor waited. Ordell hovered, his bulky form blocking what little sunlight filtered through the trees. Sydney drew up short at the sight of him. Her few interactions with Lukaris and Raiden's uncle had been brief and vaguely threatening at best. Had he finally come to run her off?

"Captain Krane," Ordell began with a nod. His dark eyes raked over her. "Walk with me."

It was not a suggestion. He turned without another word. Sydney had no choice but to follow, though she kept a watchful eye on the back of the elf's tattooed head.

Ordell led her to the edge of camp and into the first line of trees. Sydney's unease grew with each step. It was the perfect place for an ambush. A sloping hillside, ample underbrush, and out of earshot from the other elves. At least, from any elf that would willingly come to her aide. By the time Ordell came to a stop, Sydney's hands were curled into tight fists.

They stood beneath a towering oak tree. A trio of birds flitted in the branches above, their voices loud in the morning air. Sydney only saw them from the edge of her vision. Her focus was on Ordell and the carefully placed hand on his sword.

"Do you know the best type of messenger bird, Captain Krane?"

Sydney frowned. What game is he playing? "Ravens? Pigeons? How should I know? Though if you ask me, the best way to deliver a message is an honest man and a good horse."

The elf smiled a little at that. "Perhaps. The correct answer, however, is the bird you can trust."

Ordell brought two fingers to his lips and gave a loud, short whistle. In a flurry of shrieks and flapping wings, the birds took flight. Two, a sparrow and a raven, perched on the elf's shoulders. The third, the largest crow Sydney had ever seen, landed at his feet. Its beady eyes fixed on her as it let out a single *caw*.

"I have to admit, I don't particularly trust *that* bird," Sydney said as she edged away from the crow.

"The feeling is mutual, I'm sure. You see, I've trained these birds since they were very young. They trust and obey only me. They will speak to no other elf, not even Raiden, so they can carry messages of the utmost secrecy without the risk of interception." The elf stroked the sparrow fondly.

"Not that this isn't fascinating," Sydney cut in dryly. "But why have you brought me here?"

Ordell looked down his nose at her. "I heard what happened yesterday in Firne. With the elf that wished you dead."

Sydney mouth went dry. "Oh."

"You seem upset."

"Look I—" She sucked in a steadying breath. "My soldiers were misinformed. I killed that elf's son based on lies, and I regret it. If I could take it back, I would."

"You misunderstand me, Captain Krane," said Ordell. "When I heard how you handled the situation I was… pleasantly surprised."

"Really? I know I destroyed at least two high quality tents," she remarked in an attempt to hide her shock.

Her words pulled a laugh from the elf, the sound light and airy like wind through high grass. "True, but that seems preferable to the alternative. You could have killed Quinell. She attacked you, and I'm sure the *Valen* would have protected you from the resulting consequences. But you didn't do it."

Ordell whispered something, and the birds took flight. They sailed up and away, the silhouettes of their black wings tracing lines in the sky.

"My eldest nephew lives with stars in his eyes. He doesn't always see things for what they are, and I fear his hopeful heart will be his ruin one day. When he brought you to Firne, I was sure that day had finally come. But I think, perhaps, that I was wrong about you. I wouldn't use the word trust," the elf noted. "Still, I know few people, elves or humans, that would have shown mercy in your position."

Something about the elf's approval made her chest tighten. One less hostile face in camp couldn't be a bad thing, right? And yet, she couldn't help but think that if she was liked by her enemy, it meant she was doing something wrong.

"Can I ask you something?" Sydney said, mostly to change the subject.

Ordell raised a dark eyebrow. "I suppose."

"The tattoos, on your head." Sydney eyed the ribbons of ink that crisscrossed his skull. "What do they mean?"

He stared at her for a moment, as if weighing her interest. Finally, he sighed.

"There is an old elvish custom, practiced now only in the Viridian province. When someone close to you dies, you paint your body in symbols of mourning. With each passing day, you are meant to erase one of the markings, and when the last bit of paint is removed, the time for grief has passed."

"But that's not paint on your skin," Sydney prompted.

"No. I needed something more permanent."

"So you would always remember the one you lost?"

"Because the time for grieving never ended," Ordell replied, voice heavy. "Because healing is only possible with closure, and that is something I never had."

Sydney yearned to know more, her curiosity sparked. But before she could word a response, Ordell turned his back to her.

"You had better return to camp, Captain Krane. Wouldn't want to keep my nephew waiting."

The dismissal in his voice was clear. Sydney sighed, disappointed, but she left the towering elf to his birds.

Back outside her tent, she was surprised to find no Lukaris and no Raiden. Had they forgotten about her, or did they finally trust her to find her own way? Uneasy, she picked her way through the camp in search of breakfast.

When she passed Flindir's tent, hushed voices drifted from inside. Familiar voices. Her boots dragged to a stop. She knew she should keep moving, but the intrigue of whispered secrets drew her in. She slipped between two tents, close enough to listen, but not so close to arouse suspicion.

"… and you're sure there's no lasting side effects?" Lukaris' voice asked, sounding excited.

"None," Flindir confirmed. "I took the warroot last night, and this morning, my magic is back to full strength."

Warroot? What was that, some kind of herb? Sydney took a few tentative steps forward.

"Think of all we could do with this discovery, Flin," Lukaris continued. "Bandits and prisoners will be so much easier to deal with if we can temporarily mute their magic."

Sydney froze. A plant to prevent Light magic? She needed a closer look. Picking around the corner of the tent, she neared the opening flap. A breeze tugged at the fabric, giving her a brief glimpse inside.

Lukaris and Flindir stood across from each other. Between them sat a small, clay pot, an unfamiliar blossom growing from the soil, all vibrant and yellow. Warroot, Sydney guessed. Flindir glanced over at Lukaris, eyes nervous, before the tent flap fell back into place, obscuring Sydney's view.

"Are you sure about this?" Flindir asked. "I see the benefits, but if this ability got into the wrong hands… I can't imagine. It's not too late to destroy all the warroot we've gathered. Maybe this experiment is better left unexplored."

"You worry too much, Flin," Lukaris soothed. Sydney could see their shadows moving behind the canvas. "Let's not get ahead of ourselves. We're still in the trial phases after all. But, I still think the benefits outweigh the risks. We just need to be careful."

"If you're sure…"

Sydney stopped listening, head spinning. A flower that could tamper with magic. What Queen Camillea wouldn't give for this information. It could change everything. It could change the course of the war. Sydney could almost hear Brandon's excitement.

So, why did the knowledge fill her with dread?

The hairs stood up on Sydney's arms, snapping her back to reality. She could no longer hear the elves' voices. *Shit.* Sydney scrambled back onto the main pathway, trying and failing to act casual. She practically plowed into Flindir.

"Woah! Are you… Sydney?" The curly-headed elf blinked in surprise. Behind him, Lukaris stumbled to a stop.

"What are you doing here, Captain Krane?" The *Valen* asked. His eyes narrowed, flicking from her to the tent entrance. His thoughts were clear. How much did she hear?

"I got impatient waiting for you at my tent like a toddler," she replied smoothly.

"Right," he said, searching her face. Luckily, Sydney was a skilled liar when she needed to be. She kept her expression smooth and unconcerned.

The *Valen* relaxed slightly. "Well, now that you're here, let's get something to eat. Coming, Flin?"

The other elf was not as adept at controlling his emotions. He wrung his hands anxiously. "What? Oh, right. Food. Sounds good."

Lukaris led them away, Sydney trailing behind. Flindir cast a nervous glance at her over his shoulder.

More secrets. More problems she never asked for.

21

A Shift

Sydney stood on an abandoned street in Briar.

Not burned. Not destroyed. Just empty.

No sound came from the houses, and no wind rushed across the dirt road. Through a crack between two crooked homes, Sydney could just make out the choppy waves of the Midsummer Ocean. The water crashed silently against the shore, and the smell of salt was distinctly absent.

What's going on? Where is everyone?

"Syd?"

Sydney's heart leapt to her throat as she spun towards the voice.

"Abigail!"

Her sister stood in the middle of the street. Sydney blinked. It wasn't her sister as she should be now. A young woman. Instead, it was the girl from Sydney's childhood, all sharp edges and sunken cheeks. Thin, chestnut hair hung around her like a cloud.

"How are you here?" Sydney asked, voice hoarse.

Abigail cocked her head.

"Why did you leave us?" The girl's voice seemed to echo across Briar, a whisper on still air.

Sydney's breath caught. "I had to, Abi. I left to protect you."

"That's a lie!" The girl snapped, and suddenly she didn't sound like a child at all. "You wanted to leave. You always wanted to leave."

"That's not true," Sydney whispered. *Liar.* Tears fought their way down her cheeks. "Abi, please…"

Sydney reached out a hand, meaning to cradle her sister's face. But when her fingers touched skin, the girl screamed. Her face flaked away, crumbling to ash.

"It's your fault!" Abigail's haunted voice cried. The air filled with the stench of burning flesh. Sydney backed away in horror as the girl disintegrated. All around, the homes of Briar collapsed.

"Abi! Gods. No. Please," Sydney pleaded. Dust filled her lungs, stinging her eyes. She fell to her knees and landed in something wet.

Freshly fallen snow. She knelt in a cluster of trees. In the distance, the outline of a village hugged the horizon. Sydney shuddered, realizing where she was. The site of her first battle. The first death by her hands.

Across from her, Brandon crouched next to a body. Blood stained the ground, a blinding scarlet against the white.

"Lockes," Sydney croaked. His eyes lifted. They held an anger he'd only ever directed towards the elves.

"Why did you leave me?" Brandon demanded. He stood, towering over her. "Why are you always running away?"

The last of Sydney's strength seemed to leach from her body. "I don't know. I'm sorry."

"Sorry?" Brandon barked a laugh, cold and brittle as the winter air. "You only ever think of yourself. Always looking for something better. Abandoning those that need you. And all you can say is sorry? *This is all your fault.*"

He stepped aside, and Sydney finally saw the body he'd been blocking. Lukaris. The elf's eyes were wide and staring, sandy brown hair matted with blood. Behind him, more corpses littered the landscape. Somehow, Sydney knew they were the bodies of every elf she'd ever killed.

This can't be real.

Sydney clutched at her elbows. Her chest felt like it might rip open.

"Brandon, please. Why are you doing this?"

"Because it's what you deserve."

Sydney was almost glad when he stepped forward and plunged a dagger into her heart.

"Sydney? Are you awake?"

Sydney bolted upright with a gasp, the hammock bed swinging wildly as she tried to regain her bearings. Two wide, green eyes stared at her over the folds of fabric.

"Oh, sorry," Raiden said cheerfully. "Were you dreaming?"

Sydney leaned her head back, nightmare still clinging to her mind like cobwebs. "Gods, kid. You nearly stopped my heart."

"Sorry," the boy said again, sounding anything but apologetic.

"What are you doing here so early?"

"Itari and the others are back. I thought you'd want to know."

Sydney's bare feet struck the earth. "They're back? Lead with that next time, kid."

"Hurry!" Raiden urged over his shoulder as he slipped from the tent. Sydney sighed, slipping on her boots and pausing by the water basin. Her reflection rippled across the surface as she scooped water into her cupped hands. For a moment, the face staring back was her sister's, from her dream, all ash and dust. Sydney's breath caught. With a shiver, she splashed her face and followed Raiden out into the morning air.

A crowd had gathered at the forest's edge. Raised voices and laughter echoed down the hillside as the returning elves dismounted their horses, embracing their comrades and recounting the journey.

Sydney peeked past heads and shoulders. She didn't notice any missing elves or tearful faces. Was that a good sign or a bad one? At last, she spotted Lukaris and Itari, heads bent, speaking urgently. A lump worked its way up Sydney's throat as she picked her way through the throng of elves.

"—like nothing I've seen." Sydney caught the last of Itari's words as she shoved between two irritated elves. Her throat clenched impossibly tighter.

"What happened?" Sydney demanded. She hadn't asked for any details when the soldiers rode out of Firne. She hadn't pestered Lukaris in the days that followed. But now she needed to know if the war had advanced without her. She *had* to know.

Itari's eyes narrowed, and she opened her mouth to answer, but Lukaris spoke first. "A few Ithirdi families were found dead near the chasm. Our scouts thought a Brimhold guard might have crossed the border…"

"… but it was a false alarm," Itari finished.

The air rushed from Sydney's lungs so fast it made her dizzy. "Thank the gods."

Lukaris said nothing, but his eyes were soft, face unreadable.

"So what attacked those families?" Sydney asked, now that her fears had been quelled. "Bandits? Riphounds?"

"Neither," Itari answered, her expression darkening. She looked to Lukaris, as if asking for permission. He nodded, and she continued. "We reached the cluster of homes where the families lived. There were no signs of looting, no destruction, no prints in the dirt. Just dead bodies with not a wound or drop of blood among them."

A warm breeze drifted through the camp, but Sydney found herself shivering. "Maybe a sickness?"

"Perhaps," Itari murmured. Lukaris stared toward the shadowed trees, fingers bone white where they wrapped around his elbows.

"Were there any witnesses?" Sydney continued, mostly to counter Lukaris' heavy silence.

Itari's sharp eyes flicked to the *Valen's* face and back again. "Only our scouts. They saw none but the dead."

The air around them stilled as Lukaris finally spoke. "Something is not right. I have said it for months. Our woods are stalked by an unknown enemy."

"*Valen,* we've seen no sign—"

"Are innocent deaths not enough, *Dualin?*" Lukaris snapped, his voice unusually cruel. But after a moment, the elf sighed, pinching the bridge of his nose. "Forgive me, Itari. I'm just frustrated by our lack of knowledge."

Itari's eyes held a spark of concern. She looked like she wanted to discuss the matter further, but just then, two scrawny arms wrapped themselves around her waist.

"You're back, you're back!" Raiden chanted gleefully. He grinned up at the Viridian. "What did you bring me?"

Itari smiled down at him. "A strand of moonbeam from the chasm's edge."

Raiden's owl-like eyes widened. "*Woah.* Did Luka get one too—Luka?"

Sydney turned to find Lukaris vanished, nothing more than a boot heal around the nearest test. The *Valen* was taking these villagers' deaths to heart. In a way, that made Sydney respect him even more. *Damn these elves.*

She turned back to Raiden's confusion with a forced smile. "Your brother has something to attend to. Let's go eat some breakfast. I'm sure he'll join us later."

Sydney led the boy away, Itari's calculating gaze on her back.

*****

The day passed quickly. The returning elves fell back into the rhythm of camp as if they'd never left. But Sydney noted a strange tension to the air. Whatever they'd seen on their mission had left its mark.

Lukaris did not leave his tent for the remainder of the day. Sydney spent the afternoon entertaining Raiden, keeping him distracted from his brother's absence. The tiny elf dragged her through Firne, showing her a hive of bees at the town's edge, a nest of robin eggs, an abandoned fox den. She was thoroughly exhausted by the time she made her way back to her tent, hoping for a quick nap before dinner. She pushed aside the tent flap with a sigh.

Sydney froze.

Itari sat on the hammock bed, Flindir's stolen book across her lap.

"Um… hello," Sydney said after a long pause.

"*Allon*, Captain Krane," the *Dualin* replied smoothly. Her fingers tapped on the book's worn cover. "It would seem you have something that does not belong to you."

Sydney didn't try to deny it. "How did you know?"

"My promised mentioned a missing volume after one of your lessons," Itari said. "He did not think it was worth troubling over. I disagree."

Sydney shrugged. "It's just a book."

"Yes." Itari continued to move her fingers, white lightning sparking with each strike. "So why take it?"

"I—" Sydney considered lying. But she didn't see the point. "I wanted to learn some Elvish. I thought the book might help, but I couldn't make any sense of it."

The elf tilted her head like a bird. "Why would you want to learn Elvish?"

"Language is always used as a weapon against me," Sydney answered honestly. "Now more than ever. If others wish to talk about me, they could at least do it out of earshot or in a tongue

I understand."

Itari stared at Sydney with eyes of brown and bronze, impossibly deep. Viridians had this way about them that Sydney often admired. A presence. She supposed you had to be solid when you came from a land of shifting sands.

The elf rose to her feet. She gave Sydney another thoughtful once-over.

"Very well. With the *Valen*'s permission, I will begin your instruction today."

"My instruction," Sydney repeated dumbly.

Itari frowned. "In Elvish. You will need to keep up, Captain Krane, if you wish to make any progress before your time with us is over. Meet me before sunset at the Clearing of the Fallen. The *Valen* can tell you the way."

The *Dualin* departed, book beneath her elbow, leaving Sydney dumbstruck in her wake.

*****

Sydney dragged her feet on the way to her first lesson. She had a bad feeling about learning from Itari. Lukaris, on the other hand, had been so excited by the prospect it managed to drag him out of his day long brooding session.

"What a splendid idea!" Lukaris said with a grin when Sydney explained the *Dualin's* proposal. "I can think of no better teacher."

Sydney stared at him. "And you're fine with this? Me studying Elvish?"

Lukaris blinked. "Why wouldn't I be?"

Because you're giving your enemy another advantage, Sydney thought, exasperated. But she kept the words to herself.

Now, Sydney picked her way through the forest in the direction

Lukaris had indicated. The sun fell fast behind the trees, streaking the sky with pink and lavender.

The Clearing of the Fallen turned out to be a small field full of old tree stumps and rotting trunks. Itari sat cross-legged on a large stump, hands on her knees, eyes closed. At Sydney's approach, the Viridian's eyelids flickered open. Her lips tilted up in a small smile as she motioned to the stump across from her.

"Captain Krane. Sit, please."

Sydney hesitated, but only for a moment. She clamored onto the base of an ancient redwood, trying to mimic Itari's neat shape, and failing miserably.

Itari's smile widened. "I take it the *Valen* saw no issue with these lessons?"

Sydney shook her head.

"Good. Then here is the arrangement. We will meet in this clearing daily, at the same time. You will not be late. I am your teacher, so you shall call me *loran*. Likewise, as my student, you will be *scolas*. We will work at the pace I set. No faster. Is that understood?"

Sydney nodded, wondering what she'd gotten herself into.

They began immediately. To Sydney's frustration, most of the evening contained little to no Elvish at all. Instead, Itari instructed Sydney on the etiquette of Ithirdi greetings. Apparently, just a simple "hello" wasn't enough.

"When meeting another for the first time, it is important to acknowledge their position in relation to yours," Itari instructed. The Viridian stood now, pacing in front of Sydney's stump. "The wrong gesture could be extremely insulting in some circles. In others, it could result in a battle for respect."

Sydney could think of few encounters she had with elves that *didn't* lead to fighting, but she kept her mouth shut.

"If the person before you is a lower rank, say, a soldier in your

Honor Guard," Itari continued. "In that case you would clasp a single fist to your chest."

Itari placed a fist over her heart.

"Someone of equal rank would deserve a flat palm," the elf's hand flattened. "And one ranked above you would deserve a salute of both hands." Itari's second palm covered the first.

"So, since we are both leaders," Sydney asked, "I would greet you with a flat palm?"

Itari shook her head. "Before today, perhaps. But teachers hold a position of great importance. As my student, you would show respect with the use of both hands."

Sydney didn't take kindly to her rank being lowered, but she bit back her irritation. She mimicked the elf's motion.

"Good. Now, after the greeting, it is important to use the correct name when addressing an elf."

"Like their title? *Valen* or *Dualin?*"

Itari shook her head. "Not necessarily. Elves have many names. A few given, many earned. Most elves never use the name they received at birth. It is important to address the elf before you with the proper name at that point in time."

"And how do you know which is the correct name to use?"

"Most elves will give you their preferred name at introduction. If they have earned another name through great feats, you may use that as well. Of course, this only covers initial meetings. If it is someone you know well…"

Sydney's head spun as Itari launched into another round of rules.

They continued like that until night had fallen, and Sydney's eyes strained to make out Itari's silhouette among the shadowed trees. Finally, the Viridian rose to her feet and gave a satisfied nod.

"I believe that is enough for today. I will see you here tomorrow, *scolas.*"

"Wait!" Sydney crawled off the tree stump, her cramped legs groaning in protest. "We didn't cover a single word of Elvish."

Itari shook her head. "You wish to leap before you stand. *Pachel, scolas.*"

"What does that mean?"

Itari smiled. "Patience."

Sydney sighed. "Fine. But can I ask you something?"

"Of course."

"Why are you teaching me at all? Not that I'm ungrateful," Sydney added quickly. "But I wasn't sure you even approved of my being here."

Itari gave her a long look. The elf seemed to be weighing her words.

"When I first came to Ithirdas, years ago, things were not easy for me. Though the Viridian Provence is part of Ithirdas, many elves here do not consider us equals. They see me as foreign. My people as *uncivilized.* I did not learn Soardic until I joined the war effort." Itari took a deep breath. Her bronze eyes were distant. "Other warriors were cruel. They would use the common tongue to taunt me."

A lump formed in Sydney's throat. Itari was so unwavering, so steady. It felt strange to see her shaken.

"I'm sorry."

"*Melánethe, scolas.* I do not let the past define me." Itari locked eyes with her, and for the first time, Sydney felt something like understanding pass between them. "But I will not let my history repeat itself in you. If you wish to defend yourself with words, then I shall be your armorer."

22

Bows and Blades

In a few short weeks, Sydney's injured shoulder had almost completely healed. It was a remarkable recovery, and Sydney had her suspicions a dappling of Light magic sped up the healing process. Could Ettee's water abilities somehow knit together flesh and blood? The thought made Sydney shiver. Still, she was grateful for the full use of her arm.

"You'll want to stretch the muscles every day," Ettee ordered. The tiny elf removed Sydney's final bandage with a satisfied nod. "If it starts to ache, you can chew some ginger."

"So, is she free to train?" Lukaris piped up from his place in the corner. Sydney raised an eyebrow at the question.

Ettee scowled. "I suppose. But don't overdo it, *Dynas*."

"I wouldn't dream of it," Lukaris replied easily. He gave the healer a loving pat on the shoulder. "*Melánethe*, Ettee. You're a Light send. Come on then, Captain Krane. I have a surprise for you."

"Your last surprise ended with a riphound attack," Sydney reminded him as Ettee shooed them out of her tent. Lukaris grinned.

"I hope this one will be just as exciting, if not as dangerous."

He led her to the portion of camp designated for battle training.

Sydney's heart began to race. Was he really going to let her fight? And if so, against who? Sydney had a sudden daydream of swinging a sword at Sarcys' head. But her excitement dwindled as they came to a halt.

In front of the archery targets.

Lukaris waved an arm towards the designated trees, their trunks beaten and battered from the piercing of a hundred arrows. He turned to her with such unbridled enthusiasm, it almost hurt Sydney to crush it. Almost.

"You're joking, right?" she asked bluntly. The elf's smile wavered.

"It's a good way to test your shoulder. I thought you'd be excited to have a weapon in your hands again."

"Yes, but archery?"

He looked truly offended. "What's wrong with archery?"

It was about time they had this conversation. "It's a coward's weapon. If you're going to kill someone, you should have the decency to look them in the eye when you do it."

Lukaris stared at her, mouth agape. Had she finally cracked through that bubbly facade of his? But then, the corner of his mouth lifted.

"I think I know what this is about."

"Is that so?" Sydney replied, crossing her arms.

"There's no shame in being less than skilled in archery, Captain Krane. We all have our talents."

Now it was Sydney's turn to take offense. Her face blossomed red.

"*Excuse me*, just because I'm not a fan of littering trees with arrows, doesn't mean I *can't*."

"Right," he said, now openly struggling to hide a grin.

Arrogant, pointy-eared... Sydney stomped over to a nearby weapon rack and plucked a long bow from its stand. Grabbing an arrow from Lukaris' quiver, she notched the foreign weapon, the shape bulky and unnatural in her grip. Drawing a deep breath, she placed herself a reasonable distance from the targets while Lukaris watched in an amused silence. She quickly regretted her overconfidence. Gods, when was the last time she even held a bow? But it was too late to quit now. She drew back her elbow, the effort straining her arm, her shoulder, her chest. Her breath went out in a rush as her fingers released their hold.

To be fair, she hit the tree. A full horse length below the target.

"Alright, so it's been a while," Sydney huffed. "But that doesn't make archers any less despicable."

The *Valen's* lips pressed together so tightly, she could almost see the laugh trapped between them. "Of course. I'm a terrible monster with a cowardly weapon. Still, shouldn't a captain of Brimhold be able to hit a standing target? If only to prove to others that she hates the skill for the right reasons."

"Careful, bowman," Sydney growled. "I'm the one that's armed."

"And I've never feared for my life more," Lukaris laughed, the glee finally breaking across his face like an ocean wave against the shore.

Sydney's fist itched to smack the smug look away. Instead, she sighed. "Fine. Show me what I did wrong. If you're not too scared I'll beat you at your own trade."

There was little chance of that. Sydney quickly learned that Lukaris knew the bow the way she knew a sword. Even without his magic, the elf never missed a shot. Sydney might have been impressed if she wasn't so focused on her own failings. Brimhold's warriors picked a weapon and stuck with it, so her archery had been left behind somewhere around the age of thirteen. Lukaris rehashed the basics, guiding her through proper form, how to breath, and how to aim.

"You look like a chicken," Lukaris noted, his hand reaching to lower her elbow. Sydney recoiled instinctively at the contact, her arrow ricocheting into the bushes. Sydney's stomach knotted at the look that crossed over her teacher's face.

"My apologies," the Valen murmured, not meeting her eye. A part of her wanted to apologize, but she wasn't sure how or what for. So instead she powered past it, pulling back a new arrow.

"Like this?"

The training didn't last long after that, but Sydney improved enough to satisfy her pride. As she replaced the borrowed bow in its rack, her eyes lingered longingly on the skirmish field.

"I think I deserve a reward for allowing you to force me into archery," said Sydney.

Lukaris laughed. "Is that so? What did you have in mind?"

"*Real* training. With a sword and an opponent."

"Competition isn't the only way to learn, Captain Krane," the *Valen* sighed. "But very well. Come with me."

They found Flindir and Itari sparring at the edge of camp. A ring carved into the dirt acted as their boundary. In truth, it was more of a dance than a fight. Itari planted a kiss on Flindir's cheek as she spun past his guard. He laughed, making bellflowers sprout where her feet grazed the earth.

"*Allon!*" Lukaris called, pulling the couple from their game. "Our guest is looking for a duel. Will either of you answer her challenge?"

Itari pushed a wayward strand of hair back into her head scarf, expression thoughtful. "And what are the rules for this challenge?"

"Uh…" Sydney floundered. Rules? In Delm, you just fought until someone fell. "Swords only. No magic."

Itari studied her carefully, eyes gleaming. "Very well. I accept. But don't expect me to go easy on you, *scolas*."

Sydney grinned. "I wouldn't dream of it."

They retreated to opposite sides of the sparring ring while Flindir joined Lukaris at a safe viewing distance. Sydney picked up two practice swords, and Itari selected the same. The blades felt good in Sydney's grip. Fighting had been a staple in her life for so long that she felt lost without it. Across from her, Itari bowed gracefully, stomach parallel to the earth. Sydney repeated the gesture, a little late and with far less finesse. The warriors raised their weapons and began to pace around the circle. Bronze and gray eyes locked.

Sydney had only fought elves on the battlefield, where thoughts of survival overshadowed all others. This was different. She could study her opponent. Strategize. Itari didn't give her much time. The Viridian plunged across the space that divided them, swords swinging at Sydney's side. She brought both blades up to block the blow, and Itari dashed backwards, light on her toes. This repeated a few more times, the elf striking and retreating. Testing Sydney's defenses.

But Sydney was learning too. She noted the attacks, while fast, weren't particularly strong. Elves were like arrows, light and swift and deadly. But human's were axes. Sturdy. Powerful. And with the right timing, an axe could split an arrow in two.

Sydney relaxed her stance. Itari, sensing an opening, lunged forward, her sword aimed at Sydney's gut. But Sydney was ready. She dodged the blade and brought a hilt down on the elf's outstretched hand. Itari yelped as the weapon fell from her grip. Still moving, Sydney swung two swords at the elf's remaining one. She smashed through the guard. Before Itari could recover, her blades leveled at the elf's throat.

The *Dualin's* lips twitched into a smile.

Sydney grinned and lowered her swords.

"Not bad, *scolas*."

"Not bad, yourself."

"What's going on here?" A third voice entered the fray. Sydney's stomach twisted into irritated knots as Sarcys approached the sparring circle, his dark features set in a scowl. Ordell trailed at his shoulder. The large elf was unreadable. He crossed his arms as the two elves came to a halt at Lukaris' side.

"Just a bit of training," the *Valen* replied easily. An edge of warning rang in his voice.

"With *her*?" Sarcys demanded. Sydney supposed it was an improvement to being called *it*. Ordell remained silent, but his face gave the impression he didn't disagree.

"Care to join?" she asked, excitement bubbling at the thought of landing a blow on Sarcys' arrogant face.

"Absolutely not," Lukaris said.

"You're on," Sarcys hissed at the same time.

Lukaris shook his head. "Not happening. I promised Ettee we would take it easy, and I'm not sending her any broken bones."

"You're no fun," Sydney quipped. "Who's next then? Flindir?"

"I think I'll sit this one out," the curly-haired elf replied, hands raised in a type of surrender.

"What's the matter?" Sydney asked. Her grin sharpened into glass. "Scared?"

"Absolutely," he laughed, unashamed.

"Alright, I guess that leaves you, ace," Sydney said, turning to Lukaris. "Care for a rematch? I'll bet my entire purse you won't win this time around."

Lukaris' eyebrow raised. "You mean the purse that's with your other belongings in my tent?"

Sydney frowned. She'd forgotten about that. And she didn't care to reveal the hidden coins at the bottom of her boot.

"A different wager then. I win, and I get my stuff back."

"Even your swords?"

"*Especially* my swords."

"And what do I get if I win, Captain Krane?" Lukaris asked, amusement clouding his tone.

"You can't be seriously considering this," Sarcys scoffed from the sidelines. "The last thing we need is an armed enemy strolling through camp."

"Do you have so little faith in your *Valen*, Sarcys?" Lukaris asked, voice brittle. The dark elf blanched. His eyes met the ground. Satisfied, Lukaris refocused on Sydney. "Well?"

"What do you want?"

The elf studied her for a moment. "A secret."

"What kind of secret?" Sydney asked warily.

"I haven't decided yet," Lukaris answered with a grin.

Normally, Sydney would have rejected such a bargain, but she was feeling confident from her previous victory, and the practice blades in her hands hungered for more. Besides, she'd shared so much with the elf already. What was one little secret?

"Deal," Sydney said, extending a hand. Lukaris gripped her forearm.

"Deal."

The two squared off. Lukaris grabbed a sword of his own, looking irritatingly at ease. Sydney grit her teeth. She'd be damned if she was going to let him best her a second time.

They began the age old dance, pacing in a circle just outside of each other's defenses, waiting for the other to make a move. Lukaris stepped lightly, his feet seeming to float across the earth.

Sydney struck first. Her blades sliced out, fast as snakes, one aimed at Lukaris' head, the other his gut. The elf ducked and parried, moving easily out of the way. Sydney did not relent. She crashed into him, delivering one blow after another, forcing Lukaris on the defense. He looked less calm now, his brow furrowed in concentration as he countered each strike.

They broke apart, both breathing heavy. Sydney took a grim satisfaction from the sheen of sweat on the elf's forehead.

Time to finish it.

Sydney lunged forward, feinting to the left before slashing at Lukaris' opposite side. It was a tricky move to pull off, but Sydney had used it in a hundred fights and it never failed her.

Until now.

It was as if Lukaris had read her mind. He didn't fall for the ruse. Instead, he used Sydney's ploy against her, moving forward to force her off balance. She stumbled backwards, trying to avoid his blade in her face. It was too late. The elf knocked her swords from her hands as she landed in the dirt.

The watching elves cheered. Sarcys laughed in a way that sent Sydney's blood boiling.

"Good match, Captain Krane. I will claim my secret at a later date." Lukaris smiled as he offered a hand to help her up.

Sydney rose on her own, brushing the dust from her pants.

"Again," she growled.

Lukaris raised an eyebrow.

"I'm not sure that's such a good idea. Your shoulder…"

"*Again.*"

The elf sighed. "Very well."

They battled twice more, Sydney giving everything she had. Both fights ended the same. Sydney sprawled in the dirt with Lukaris above her.

"How?" Sydney demanded as she pulled herself off the ground for the third time. "How are you doing that?"

Nearby, Sarcys rolled his eyes. "Maybe you aren't as good as you think you are, Brim."

"There is no shame in loss to a worthy opponent," Ordell added.

With much restraint, Sydney ignored them both. She stepped closer to Lukaris who had a strange, almost sheepish look on his face.

"You are always one step ahead of me, no matter what strategy I use. It doesn't make sense. How?"

Lukaris sighed. "Fine. But don't be angry. Before you make your final move… well, you hold your breath. It's slight, but it's rather telling."

Sydney stared at him, dumbfounded. "You're a cheat!"

"Now hold on…"

"You're using magic! That's against the rules!"

"I can't just turn it off, Captain Krane," Lukaris said. "Besides, it's obvious once you know to look for it. The magic made no difference in the outcome."

Sydney turned to the watching elves. "I'm guessing the rest of you agree?"

She was met with a chorus of shrugs and adverted eyes. Sydney squared her shoulders.

"Very well, *Valen*. I'll give you your counterfeit victories. But next time, you won't be able to hide behind your magic tricks."

"Is that a threat, *mahil?*" Sarcys snapped as Sydney turned away from them.

Sydney flashed a sweet smile over her shoulder.

"It certainly is."

23

The Dance of the Dying Sun

As summer drew to a quick end, Sydney watched the elves prepare themselves for a mysterious celebration. The villagers down in Firne worked tirelessly for two full days, toiling sun up to sun down. They wove colored ribbons of gold and scarlet in branches along the riverbank, each strand accented with small orbs of warm light. The spheres were crafted with simple Light magic and flickered like candlelight in the dark trees. Hunters amassed a feast fit for royalty, while others set up rows of tables in a clearing on the hillside. Even the soldiers ventured down into town to help prepare for the coming event.

Lukaris appeared at Sydney's tent one evening, a bundle of fabric in his arms. The *Valen* hadn't shared what the elves were planning, and likewise Sydney didn't asked. She assumed the gathering was not meant for humans. That is, until Lukaris entered her tent with a mischievous glint in his eyes.

"What's going on?" she asked warily.

The elf laid the pile of clothing on her hammock, seating himself next to it. He swung his legs back and forth like a child.

"Tonight is a very important night in Ithirdas. We call it *Sil a*

Tokiyas or Dance of the Dying Sun, in Soardic. It marks the last day of summer, the beginning of a new season. We celebrate the time that has passed and encourage prosperity in the months ahead." Lukaris smiled. "I was hoping you would come."

"Hoping? Do I have a choice?"

The smile slipped. The hammock halted mid swing. "Of course you do, Captain Krane. As I've said many times, you are not a prisoner."

"Fine. But if this festival is as significant as you say, maybe I shouldn't go." Sydney toyed with the folded fabric. "I may be an enemy soldier, but I don't want to make a mockery of your customs."

Lukaris' expression softened. "You wouldn't be. The dance is just another piece of the elves that I wish to show you. Think about it. It won't kill you to have some fun every once in a while."

The accusation sounded so much like Brandon's nagging that for a moment, Sydney was at a loss for words. Just for a moment.

"The elves wouldn't know fun if it bit them in their collective ass," she replied with a cross of her arms.

"Is that so?" That infuriating, impish grin on his face, Lukaris lifted the tent's entrance flap. "I guess you'll have to verify that for yourself then. See you tonight!" He called the last part over his shoulder as he departed.

Sydney sighed. She put on the garment Lukaris had left her and stared down at the strangest dress she'd ever seen. The bodice was gold, light as honey, with exposed shoulders and flowing silk sleeves. Cinched at the waist, the skirts of the dress were composed of hundreds of small leaves, sewn together in rippling waves of green. Each leaf held a different shade, a different shape, and yet they all fit together seamlessly. The hemline ended below her knees, but short enough to expose her worn boots beneath the folds. It was a dress meant for a woodland goddess, an elf princess. Certainly not a human warrior of Brimhold.

Sydney removed the dress, casting it onto her hammock. She couldn't go. *But maybe just one more look.* Gown on. Off. And on again. For the next hour, she deliberated.

"Damn it," Sydney muttered to herself, as curiosity won out. She ran a quick hand through her hair, deciding to leave the long strands free, and splashed some water on her face. Then she strode from the tent, a storm of hair and leaves.

Raiden slouched against a nearby tree not far from the tent. He looked bored, eyes wandering around for something to occupy him. At Sydney's appearance, he brightened, straightening up and running over to her. The boy wore a tunic vest, composed of interlaced leaves, with a golden shirt beneath. The outfit matched Sydney's gown exactly. The same could not be said for the rest of the boy's appearance. Somehow his face was already dirty, and his hair stuck up in its usual disarray.

Skidding to a stop in front of her, Raiden dropped into a low bow. "My lady," he proclaimed dramatically. "My brother requested I escort you to the dance."

"Dear gods." Sydney rolled her eyes. "Let's just get this over with, kid."

With a grin, he led her out of camp and through the outskirts of Firne. They joined a steady stream of elves, all heading for the same clearing, all wearing the same ensemble of golden silk and stitched green leaves. The sun began to set beyond the mountains as they reached their destination. Orange streaked the cloudless sky, and the light orbs danced like stars in the treetops.

"*Allon*, Sydney." Itari appeared at her elbow, looking stunning in her festival attire. Normal head scarf gone, her dark hair was twisted in a magnificent braid, leaves woven into the folds. Flindir stood at her side, beaming, eyes only for his betrothed.

"*Allon*," Sydney replied with a nod. "Where's our esteemed *Valen*?"

"Preparing for his speech, I'd imagine. He'll be opening the festival," Flindir explained. He offered Itari his arm, and the pair moved towards the festivities. "Let's eat before the dancing starts. I have a lot of magic to work later."

"*Ka!*" Itari scolded, swatting Flindir's arm. She gestured in Sydney's direction.

"Ow! What?" He exclaimed. Then his eyes followed her motion, realization dawning. "Oh, um, I mean…"

Sydney said nothing, graciously pretending not to hear. Whatever they meant to surprise her with, she was more than happy to ignore. The troop wandered in search of dinner, and it didn't take long to find it. Half a dozen tables were overloaded with food, enough to feed the village twice over. They filled their plates with smoked venison, freshly baked bread, and strawberries the size of Raiden's fist. As Sydney neared the end of the buffet, she noted a table filled with tall, slender bottles. The colors, red and gold and green, sparkled in the evening light.

"What are these?" Sydney asked.

"They're elvish spirits, but I don't know if you should…" Flindir looked to Itari for backup.

The Viridian shrugged. "I see no harm. Captain Krane seems to be a woman who can handle her drink."

"You're correct," Sydney boasted. She picked up a gold bottle, giving it a small whiff followed by a tentative sip. Then a bigger gulp. It was cool and bubbly, with the sweet taste of pear. In short, it was delicious.

"What is this, some kind of wine?" she questioned, her tone doubtful.

Itari's gave a small, secretive smile. "Not quite."

Sydney shrugged, placing another bottle under her arm. If she was going to join the party, she planned to do it right.

The wooden benches that circled the clearing were remarkably full, so the group found a comfortable seat in the grass. They ate their meal and spoke of easy things. No war, no politics. Just sweet evening air and the joy of good company.

Soon, soft music rose from nearby lute and harp strings. A flute rose to join them. The melodies began low, sweet background musings, before growing quick and greedy. It was a song meant for dancing, for pounding feet. Elves leapt from their seats, twirling in time with the music, weaving back and forth. Dozens of leaf laden skirts rustled in the breeze.

Itari was quick to pull Flindir to his feet. The curly-haired elf groaned around a mouthful of bread, but Itari laughed off his protest. The couple moved in delicate circles, growing nearer to each other in ever shrinking arcs. The tempo rose, reaching its peak, the dancers' feet a flurry of movement. At last, the song collapsed, and Flindir grinned as Itari's hands finally found his own. Sydney watched as they settled into the folds of each others arms. Her heart twisted, though she couldn't say why. She downed the rest of her bottle.

A new song began, this time an easy ballad. Flindir and Itari swayed back and forth. Raiden leapt around the edge of the circle, spinning in a dance that was all his own. Sydney opened her second spirit. This one tasted of strawberries.

The sun had all but gone, the last tips of red kissing the treetops, when Lukaris made his entrance. The *Valen's* outfit was much the same as all the others. Shirt of silk, with a vest of twisting leaves. But, a crown of painted gold upon his brow set him apart. It mimicked the setting sun, a yellow base with streaks of scarlet and orange reaching towards his hairline.

The elf hesitated at the edge of the celebration, eyes sweeping over the dancing soldiers and citizens. Sydney watched a strange expression filter across his face. Fear? Sadness? Whatever it was passed in a blink as the *Valen* stepped from the shelter of the trees. The song reached its end, and the elves' feet settled as they turned to face their leader.

"Allon!" Lukaris called out with a wide smile. His voice carried on the breeze. "Friends and welcomed guests." Green eyes met Sydney's for an instant. *"Sil a Tokiyas* is upon us, and we gather, as we do each year, to celebrate. Another summer has passed, and autumn begins with the setting sun. Tonight, we give thanks to the ever-changing Light, as it begins to wane for the winter. We honor the days ahead and the days behind. We ask that our inner Lights shine bright and clear for the dark nights to come. But most importantly…" The *Valen* grabbed a spirit, raising it high into the air. "We drink! *Tokiyas!"*

"Tokiyas!" The gathered elves chimed, tipping back their own bottles. Sydney raised her drink late, but recovered quickly. When she brought down her second empty bottle, the edges of her vision held a soft glow.

The dancing began again in earnest. Lukaris picked his way over to sit beside her.

"Well," he began. "What do you think so far?"

Sydney shrugged, putting on an indifferent mask. "I'll admit, the spirits aren't half bad."

The elf eyed her. "I would go easy on those if I were you. They hit differently than those brown drinks you Brims are so fond of. Especially for a human."

"Your concern is duly noted," Sydney retorted. She made a silent vow to out drink every elf in the Wornwood.

They sat in an easy silence as the elves twirled past them. Eventually, Lukaris rose to offer her a hand.

"Care to dance?" The invitation was calm and gracious, but Sydney's heart hammered awake in her chest.

"Not on your life," she replied, voice even. Lukaris sighed, but didn't push the matter. He drifted off, leaving her alone. She slipped another spirit from the nearby table.

And so, the evening passed. The elves danced in mesmerizing patterns, moving seamlessly from one song to the next. Lukaris partnered with Ettee, and the solemn elf was surprisingly light on her feet. Meanwhile, Sydney watched, trying and failing to drown the feeling of solitude with bottles of sweet tasting liquor.

As a new song began, Sydney looked up to find Raiden grinning down at her. He gave her another dramatic bow, extending a small hand.

"Lady, would you do me the great honor of this dance?" He squirmed from one foot to the other, and Sydney noted the boy's boots had disappeared sometime during the evening.

"Look, kid, I don't really dance," she said.

Raiden frowned. "Humans don't dance?"

"*Humans* do. *Sydney* doesn't."

The boy considered this for a moment. Then, in a surge, his hands found Sydney's, pulling her to her feet with surprising strength. "Maybe you've just never been to a proper dance, is all. You can't *watch Sil a Tokiyas!*"

Before Sydney could protest, they were dancing. In every way, the elves danced in perfect harmony, movements as old and timeless as Soarden itself. Raiden, however, broke the mold. He moved in time with the music, but erratically. It was the dance of a child, lost to the music, not caring who was watching. He led Sydney around the clearing, hands tight, laughing and reveling in each misstep. Somehow, the imperfection was perfect. The dance was their own, unique and free and gone before they could tame it. Sydney found a grin forming on her lips.

They danced for a few more songs, ignoring those around them. Then, the music shifted. Sydney could feel the change in her chest.

Raiden looked at something behind her, eyes twinkling, almost mischievous. As she turned, two new hands found hers. Strong and slender. She raised her head to see Lukaris smiling shyly. Raiden danced away with a laugh.

Sydney's entire body stiffened, and she tried to step back, but Lukaris held her tight.

"Please, Captain Krane. Just one dance. This one is important," the *Valen* pleaded.

The eyes that bore into hers looked too much like Raiden's. With a sigh, Sydney let herself relax.

"I don't… I don't know how to dance," she muttered, gaze downcast.

Lukaris' wry smile resembled the soft lights that swayed in the trees. "Don't worry. I'll lead."

The pair moved further into the circle of elves. They stepped once, Lukaris surefooted, Sydney uncertain. As she raised her foot again, she felt a misstep coming. Except it didn't. As she went to place her heel, a strong, directed wind pushed her in the right direction. She narrowed her eyes at the *Valen*, but he merely grinned in response.

And so, they danced. The song rose to meet them. The Dance of the Dying Sun. Sydney followed Lukaris' lead, and when the right move wouldn't come, the wind was there, guiding her.

Then, at the center of the clearing, Flindir stopped. Itari placed herself at his side. She began to sing, and Flindir closed his eyes, hands cast out.

The song was in Elvish, but Sydney felt its meaning. It spoke of endings and beginnings, the passing of seasons. It was old and ancient and eerie. The hairs rose on her arms, and the elves danced faster and faster as the tempo grew. Itari's voice lifted. Sydney felt Lukaris' hands slipping from her own.

"Spin," he whispered. The breeze caught at her skirt, and she had no choice but to obey. All around the clearing, the elf maidens spun in graceful circles. Sydney turned, pines needles stirring at her feet in the center of her own personal storm.

Sydney felt the pulse of Light magic in the air. It tugged at her, and she looked down with a gasp. The leaves on her skirt began to change. One moment they were the bold greens of summer, dark and strong. But autumn caught at their edges, bleeding out the life, until every leaf held the orange and scarlet hues of fall. Sydney stared around the clearing in wonder as every leaf on every skirt completed its transformation. The music reached a crisp end, and the elf men bowed to their partners. With the motion, their own vests became a quilt of amber leaves. Flindir lowered his hands, eyes tired yet proud.

"Well?" Lukaris asked.

Sydney opened her mouth, then closed it. She was not usually one to be left speechless.

The *Valen* laughed at her expression. "I understand, Captain Krane. *Sil a Tokiyas* affects us all that way, the first time."

He coaxed her into another dance, and then another. And so, the evening passed. Sometimes Sydney joined the festivities, and sometimes she watched, sipping on yet another spirit. If you had asked her, she wouldn't claim to be drunk. But her head grew light and airy, as if it meant to float off and join the stars that seemed to grow larger in the night sky. The edges of her vision were a soft and peaceful blur.

Elves took turns singing at the center of the circle. The others would settle in the grass, eyes turned upwards, listening. It was deep into the night when Flindir and Itari took the stage once more. This time they both sang, hand in hand.

When a cold winter blows
The feeling so rare
A wing beats all hollow

Mountain caverns left bare.

The wind whips as water
   Through deep rooted tree
   Alas, alas
   Next summer we'll see.

Another moon passing
   Crisp leaves to the ground
   All small creatures hiding
   Fresh snow to be found.

With each darkened hour
   Your soul carries me
   Alas, alas
   A new summer we'll see.

The current is standing
   A river runs cold
   Two hearts are stilling
   No stories untold.

I hope you remember
   The days we were free
   Alas, alas
   The last summer we'll see.

Their voices spun around each other, Flindir's smooth and steady as river rock, while Itari was the stream itself, always moving, flowing, taking shape around the stone. Together they formed a story of sorrow and loss, hope and remembering. When their words died away, the surrounding elves wiped tears from their eyes. Sydney reached up to hide the wetness on her own cheeks.

After, the celebration began to die off. Elves drifted away in pairs or small groups, swaying on their feet as they departed. Some lingered behind, unwilling or unable to let the party end without one more dance. Sydney stayed long after the bulk of the elves had gone, soaking in the freedom, the last breath of summer, the elvish spirits that helped ease a troubled soul.

*****

"I think you better turn in, Captain Krane," Lukaris said to Sydney finally. A single sad lute and a few elves swaying in time with the music were all that was left of *Sil a Tokiyas*. Itari and Flindir, Raiden asleep and slung across his shoulder, had long since departed. Sydney sighed, accepting the evening's end. She waved off the *Valen's* extended hand, climbing unsteadily to her feet. She lifted her chin when she managed to stand on her own.

The pair began the arduous trek back to camp. A crisp, fall chill hung in the air. Sydney hardly felt it around the warmth in her chest. Her mind was clear, but buoyant and careless, the ground a fuzzy maze beneath her feet. She was secretly grateful for Lukaris' firm hand at her elbow.

They made it halfway up the hillside when Sydney stumbled and crashed to the earth. Her curses might have been heard as far away as Nidaria.

"Perhaps we should take a break?" Lukaris suggested, struggling to hide the laughter in his voice. He settled himself in the grass next to her.

Above them, the night sky stretched out in a blanket of shadow, highlighted with shining silver pinpoints. A sliver of moon peaked out between the tree branches. Sydney turned her head towards Lukaris. His eyes were fixed above him, focused and pensive. Sydney could almost see the wheels turning inside his mind, a million thoughts forming all at once.

"What are you thinking about?" Sydney asked. The question always seemed to sit at the front of her mind when she looked at him.

"The stars, mostly. How old they must be, and the things they must have seen. It's humbling to realize there are parts of the universe so old that we've shared them with everyone that ever lived."

"Oh."

"Why, what were you thinking about?" He turned to meet her eyes. They looked almost black in the low light.

"Just that my burps taste like strawberries."

Lukaris laughed, the sound a soft breeze. "Is that all?"

"No," she admitted. "I was also wondering how your head manages to never stop spinning."

He blinked at her, surprised. "I didn't realize it was so obvious."

"I *am* unnaturally observant and clever," Sydney boasted with a wry smile. "Most of the time, you're a hard read. But when you get quiet, and you think no one is watching, that's when you let your guard down. Behind your eyes… it's like you're trying to solve all of life's puzzles in one sitting."

What am I saying? Some deep part of Sydney recoiled in embarrassment at the words spilling from her mouth.

Lukaris seemed equally shocked by her observations. He took a deep breath, glancing away. "You're not wrong. Sometimes I find it hard to clear my thoughts. There's too much to worry over. My soldiers, my kingdom, Raiden… even you."

Sydney chose to ignore that last part. "I wouldn't fret over your brother too much. He's a good kid. For an elf."

"He is. But he's so young. I wish he was still at home, safe to be a child for a while longer."

Sydney lowered herself farther into the grass, resting her head on an outstretched arm.

"At least here your brother isn't fighting, just learning. I wasn't much older than Raiden when the queen's soldiers drafted me."

"I still think it's barbaric, the way your kingdom forces its people into war," Lukaris sniffed. He gave her a sidelong glance. "How old were you, exactly?"

"Eleven."

The elf nearly choked. "Eleven? By the Light. It's a wonder Brimhold has any children left."

"In fairness, the recruitment age was thirteen."

Lukaris rolled up onto an elbow with narrowed eyes. The question hung between them in the evening air.

And Sydney answered. She wasn't sure why. Maybe it was the soft sound of laughter and music in the distance. Maybe the strange spirits were muddling her wits. Or maybe it was just nice to tell the truth for once.

"When the soldiers came to Briar, they should've left with my sister, Abigail. She was thirteen at the time, the eldest." Sydney swallowed hard, eyes fixed on the branches swaying above her. "But Abi was sick. So, I lied. I went to Delm in her place."

Sydney didn't turn, but she could feel Lukaris' gaze.

"I…" The elf cleared his throat. "I had no idea. That must have taken a great deal of bravery."

The words sparked a familiar anger.

"You don't understand!" Sydney meant to shout, but the words came out slurred. Sloppily, she rose to her feet, glaring down at him.

Lukaris seemed shocked by her reaction. He lifted his hands in a calming gesture. "Alright. Explain it to me, then."

"I didn't volunteer to save my sister." As the words left her, Sydney felt a weight nine years old lift from her shoulders. "That's what I told myself. That's what I told my family, Brandon, everyone. But it was just an excuse."

"An excuse for what?"

"To leave. To leave Briar. I wanted more. Something beyond a tiny fishing village at the edge of nowhere." Sydney returned to the grass, head in her hands. The truth felt good until guilt replaced it.

"I'm not brave. I've never been that. I was just a selfish child that abandoned my family."

Lukaris stared at her for a long time. She could feel his gaze down to her bones, her skin crawling from the weight of it. She felt vulnerable, exposed. Only the dazing effects of the alcohol kept her from punching him, fleeing, or both.

"Can I tell you a secret?" The elf asked at last. "It's only fair, after the things you've shared with me."

Not trusting her words, Sydney nodded.

"When I said I wished Raiden was back in Sil Tullian... that was the truth. But I don't want it just for him. In a larger part, I want it for myself." Lukaris glanced away, ashamed. "I begged my father not to send him here. I never wanted the added responsibility. It's bad enough having the fate of the entire *tatell* resting on my shoulders. But now I'm my brother's protector as well. It's selfish and foolish and unfair to Raiden. But it's the truth."

Sydney blinked, head swimming. "Why are you telling me this?"

"Because I know what it's like to feel guilty for wanting something for yourself." The *Valen* looked to her again, eyes bright in the dark forest. "But it shouldn't be that way. You are a creature of the Light. You have depth and complexity. Your heart is a spider's web, ever branching. You are not bound to one motivation or one desire, and it's unfair to think you must follow a single path. Tell me, Captain Krane, did you want your sister dragged away to die as a soldier?"

Sydney swallowed the tears that hung in her throat. "Of course not."

"And did you know that by volunteering for the queen's army, you would save your sister from that fate?"

"Well yes, but…"

"And did you make your sacrifice with that knowledge in mind?"

"But it doesn't matter!" Sydney huffed. "I wanted to leave Briar long before the soldiers came."

"So, you accomplished two goals with one action. That hardly seems worth berating yourself over. Life is messy. Our actions are not always pure and simple like the heroes from old tales. But that doesn't make them bad. You saved your sister that day. That's what matters. And it *was* brave for a young girl of eleven to leave everything she's ever known." Lukaris smiled. "Even if the woman she became is too stubborn to see it."

Though the words spoke to her, Sydney felt no great weight lifted from her shoulders. No epiphany of wrongly placed guilt. Maybe she would carry that burden with her forever, given that her family had died despite everything. Still, somewhere deep in her gut, a tight knot began to unravel.

"You might be right," Sydney murmured. "But my heart and my head sing two different songs."

The *Valen* sighed. "I know that struggle too well."

They sat in a soft silence for a while. The stars swam above them in circles. Or at least, they did to Sydney's tipsy eyes. She watched as one fell from its home in the dark folds of the night sky.

"For the record," said Sydney, at last. "You're not a bad brother for wanting your own life. You still love him. You still want what's best for him. That's what matters."

She thought she saw tears form in the elf's eyes, but it could have been the shadows playing tricks on her.

"*Melánethe,* Captain Krane," Lukaris replied. "I hope you can apply the same understanding to yourself."

"Sydney." She spoke so softly, she almost hoped he wouldn't hear.

"What was that?"

"Sydney. Call me Sydney."

Lukaris grinned, teasing smile wide and bright. "It would be an honor. I suppose you can continue to call me whatever suites you that particular day."

"You got it, air head." They laughed, the sound drifting down the hillside to join the festivities below.

For what might have been hours or minutes, Sydney and Lukaris lay there, backs to the grass, eyes on the stars. They spoke of many things. Things that might have never passed between them had they not been full of music and drink and deep nighttime musings. And as the evening slipped into memory, Sydney couldn't help but feel that the world had changed in some small way.

II

Part Two: Shadow

Lies and truth,
Light and dark,
Shadows run from fire's spark.
But who can save the troubled kin,
That tamed the beast and let it in?

24

The Merfolk

The shining towers of Milanthos glimmered above Koraline as she swam along the rocky coast. The mermaid was eager to reach her destination, her powerful golden tail propelling her through the gentle waves. The sun was just beginning to set, and the final silk rays of light bounced off the surface of the sea.

Koraline was worried. She had promised to meet the traders at midday, but her father had trapped her in long talks of court etiquette in preparation for their guest's arrival that evening. And King Triak of Nidaria was not one to rush through such important discussions. Koraline's father lived in constant fear of angering the Brimholdian men to the south or the Ithirdi elves to the west or any other powerful force that might try to wipe out the merfolk if the urge came upon them. As such, Koraline spent her days in the Crystal Keep, reading scroll after scroll of political strategy while the world flowed on around her.

What if they left? Koraline worried as she neared the meeting spot. *What if they didn't wait for me?* An outcropping of rock jut from the cliff face, like a gnarled hand reaching out to the sea. Just beyond the rock, the Lor River met the ocean waves. Every fortnight, traders would swim down from the Valewood to barter with the citizens of Milanthos. But it had taken months for Koraline to establish this trade, and she feared missing her meeting might cost her the item she so fiercely desired.

As she worked her way along the shoreline, Koraline spotted them. Two figures lay on the rock, sunning themselves in the last few strands of daylight. The twins, Aelana and Jaelyn, were nearly identical, with emerald green fins and long chestnut hair that reached well past their waists. But Koraline had no trouble telling the two apart. Jaelyn's brow was often furrowed, her focus always on the task at hand. Aelana had kind eyes, her voice high and wistful, as if her thoughts were far away in another land.

Koraline swam up to the sisters eagerly, calling out to them as she drew near. They lifted their heads, and while Aelana appeared at ease, Jaelyn's mouth hardened into a tight line.

"Where have you been?" Jaelyn slid from the rock, her jewelry clattering before she hit the water. The twins were, as usual, covered in embellishments. Seashells adorned their necks, crystal rings upon every finger, dyed seaweed tucked among their hair. This was the way of the Rovers, or so Koraline's father called them with derision. Vagabonds, honorless outcasts. Koraline disagreed with the king on a number of such subjects.

"Jaelyn," Aelana admonished her sister gently. She glanced at Koraline with apprehension.

"My apologies, Princess," Jaelyn said, realizing her mistake. "We just have a long swim ahead of us to stay on schedule."

"The apologies are mine," said Koraline. "I was unavoidably detained. Please accept these as payment for your time."

Koraline handed over a small pouch from her belt. It was filled with Brimhold currency and the silver scails of Nidaria. Jaelyn shook her head, attempting to return the offering.

"You know we do not trade in the king's coin."

"This is not part of our trade. It is a gift for your patience. Take it, please." Koraline held out the pouch once more.

Reluctantly, Jaelyn stowed the money in a seaweed satchel slung across her shoulder. With pleasantries out of the way, fresh excitement bubbled in Koraline's stomach.

"Well, did you get it?" she asked.

"It wasn't easy," Aelana replied in her musing voice. "Our Master was not eager to part with such a rare item…"

"… but the Sorcerer of the Valewood found your counter offer quite enticing. He has a strong love for Nidarian crystal," Jaelyn continued. "I assume you have the blade?"

From her belt, Koraline pulled a long dagger. The razor-thin blade sparkled in the light and cast small rainbows on the surrounding water. The weapon was nearly transparent and forged as thin as possible, ideal for slicing through water. Nidarian crystal was exceedingly valuable, mined from sea caverns at the bottom of the Kraken, a swath of trenches that extended deep beneath the ocean surface. The ancient blades were owned solely by the royal lines of Nidaria. Koraline could picture the look on her father's face if he discovered such a weapon in the hands of a Rover.

Aelana, eyes wide, lifted the blade gently from Koraline's grasp. She tested the weight and ran her hand over the golden hilt. Sea creatures wrapped around the weapon in intricate detail, both beautiful and deadly.

"Oh, Master will love this," Aelana breathed. "Does it have a name?"

"Seawing" Koraline said, a soft pain in her chest. Though she never wielded it, the blade had been a part of her for many years. But if it was the price for her freedom, then she would gladly pay it.

"And my request?" Koraline tried to hide her eagerness.

Hands shaking, Koraline plucked a bracelet from Jaelyn's outstretched hand. The bangle was thick, composed of three large silver scales bordered in gold. Koraline's fingers grazed her prize. *Dragon scales.* Long ago, the dragons had crafted bands such as this one, bestowing them with their own shape-shifting magic. A gift to the merfolk, the cufflets allowed them to shift to human form.

"Forgive me, Princess," Jaelyn said, her eyes watchful. "But why would you trade such a rare blade for a cufflet? Surely the royal family has plenty."

"My motives are my own, Jaelyn," Koraline stated firmly. She tucked her prize into a bag of her own. It was true, her family had a number of such bracelets. Since the War of Hearts, when the dragons fled north, the cufflets had become monopolized by the rich and powerful merfolk. Koraline's parents kept a close eye on their personal collection, and they allowed the bands to be used solely for meetings with foreign leaders or by soldiers stationed on land. But now, Koraline had a cufflet of her own to use outside the watchful gaze of her parents.

"As you wish," Jaelyn replied with obvious interest. "Well, we should be on our way."

"Before you go, tell me, how are the inland waters?" Koraline asked curiously. The traveling lives of the Rovers always intrigued her. To see other lands, to speak with new people. The princess dreamed of such things.

The twins exchanged a nervous glance.

"To be honest, Princess, times are hard," said Aelana. "The war between Ithirdas and Brimhold grows. Many flee to the Valewood, without shelter or money, and bandits roam the forest. Our home feels… lawless. Overrun."

The words angered Koraline more than she expected. The Valewood lay within Nidarian borders. The people there were *her* people. They deserved watchful rulers to keep them safe, but the king and queen had always overlooked the citizens outside of Milanthos. Her parents overlooked a great many things.

"I'm sorry. Your people are entitled to protection. I will speak to the king and queen about this, I promise you."

Despite her sincerity, Koraline could tell the traders did not believe her. And why should they? What had the Nidarian royalty ever done for them?

Koraline said farewell to the Rovers, watching as their green tails vanished beneath the waves, before turning her eyes to Milanthos. Nidaria's capital loomed regal and cold in the late dusk, moonlight bouncing off the pearl towers in rippling shades of white and silver. The princess glided through the city that teemed in the waters below the Crystal Keep, past twisting stone houses and expansive coral gardens that rose and fell with the ocean floor. Mermen tugged home fishnets full of tuna, halibut, and royal goldfins, while children swam home after an adventurous day, and mothers watched the darkening water from kelp covered windows. Koraline wished she could remain in the town among her people. Sometimes, the castle felt like a world apart.

The princess entered the Keep through one of the highest windows, so close to the surface that the rooms grazed the open air during low tide. Down empty corridors of marble and crystal, Koraline swam towards her chambers, halting as she rounded the final bend. A familiar presence hovered outside her door.

"You're late," Angler rumbled with disapproval, large muscular arms crossed his chest. Everything about Angler was large, from his sapphire fins to his dark, bearded face to the broadsword he carried at his waist. The Head of the Royal Guard wore his finest courtly attire, a golden armored tunic of overlapping scales, navy blue ridges across his shoulders, and a matching belt to secure his weapon. He tapped the metal impatiently. "We have an important meeting, if you recall."

"It's not my fault father spent the entire day discussing the delicacies of court. Honestly, as if I ever even speak at these meetings." Koraline rushed past the guard and into her bed chamber. She frantically threw off her bag, stashing her hard earned treasure before it caught Angler's watchful gaze. Grabbing a silver swath of fabric from a trunk, Koraline began wrapping the garment around her torso, spinning and twisting until it resembled a simple human dress. Holding the end of the fabric at her waist, the mermaid looked around desperately. "Pin, pin, pin...?"

Angler passed her a crystal brooch in the shape of a seahorse, and the princess smiled her thanks. With her wardrobe complete, Koraline sped from the room once more. Her guard followed close behind, his brow furrowed and brooding.

"One day your parents will learn of your little excursions, Kori," the merman warned as the pair swam up through the Crystal Keep. With his long black hair pulled back, Angler's face appeared harsh, but Koraline could always see the kindness beneath the stern exterior. "And they will not be as forgiving as me."

"I am Princess of Nidaria and heir to the throne. I can go where I please." Her words held more confidence than her voice.

"Which is why I have not stopped you in the past," said Angler. "But more and more, I fear that your kind and courageous heart will lead you through dark waters, my *cypri*."

A staircase appeared in the corridor ahead, the top steps leading up and out of the water. Koraline stopped before them and turned to her friend.

"I'm sorry I worry you." Koraline placed a gentle hand on his cheek, the bristles of his beard brushing her fingers. "But you have nothing to fear. You have taught me caution and reason. Lessons I carry with me every time I leave the castle. I am never unsafe."

Angler smiled, a rare sight, but it did not reach his eyes. "As you say, Princess."

Koraline held out a hand. "Shall we?"

It was made of scarlet scales instead of silver, but otherwise the cufflet he gave her could have been the twin to Koraline's earlier purchase. The princess slipped on the band and waited. Dragon magic, first a tingling sensation, then a strange ripping in her tail, quickly overcame her. In an instant, two human legs churned the water beneath her.

Using the narrows stairs, the mermaid turned maiden pulled herself from the water, her dress and hair dripping as she stumbled into the chamber beyond. She flexed her toes first, marveling at the sensation. *I don't think I'll ever grow used to this,* Koraline mused. Angler followed her out of the sea on legs of his own, even more unsteady on his feet.

"You look like a newborn calf," Koraline teased. The guard scowled, giving her a light shove.

"Careful now, *cypri,* or I will tell the Brims of the first time you wore those legs."

"You wouldn't," she said with narrowed eyes. In response, the merman grinned, white teeth against dark skin. Koraline laughed. "Alright, you win this round."

The upper floors of the Crystal Keep rose high above the ocean, pressed against the sheer cliff face that ran along the shoreline. Centuries ago, the mermaids and their allies had raised the castle from the sea, a beautiful testament to the friendship that existed among the Light Races. People from all kingdoms had come to share food and drink in the marble halls of Milanthos. Celebrating lives, honoring deaths. But time passed. Wars and doubt and mistrust took their toll. Now, the Keep lay an empty shell of its former glory. The royal family used the rooms to meet with important visitors from the neighboring kingdoms in tense councils concerning war and trade.

This part of the castle always made Koraline sad. It reminded her of her ancestors' failures. Of her parents' failures. The mermaids had allowed themselves to become cut off from the world. They used to be a strong people, warriors of the Light. Who were they now? Maybe the other races were right to call them cowards. But perhaps, when Koraline became queen, things could be different. She would make things different.

The hallway ahead of them was lined with small fires in copper braziers and panels of reflective glass, illuminating the passage and filling it with a dense heat. She pressed close to the nearest blaze, soaking in the warmth while squeezing the water from her hair. She ran her fingers through the straight blonde strands and fretted over her appearance in one of the many mirrors. Water streamed down her round face, passed a button nose, over the golden freckles that dappled her cheeks. Gold hair, gold eyes, gold fins. Perhaps she really was the Treasure of Milanthos, as her parents said, a golden gift from the Light. The princess smiled ruefully at the thought. Right now, she looked more like a drowned cat. From a shelf set in the wall, she grabbed her crown, a gold-set ring of pale sea shells, and placed it on her head, completing the ensemble.

Koraline and Angler did their best to dry themselves, but late as they were, they arrived in the throne room damp and dripping. The hall itself sat at the highest point in the Crystal Keep. Floor to ceiling windows wrapped the room on three sides, giving visitors a spectacular view of the surrounding ocean. Now, with the sun set, Koraline could see the moon reflected in the black waters below, alongside a speckling of stars. Guards lined the perimeter of the room in their long, armored tunics, like golden statues set in a row. Angler took his place among them. Firelight reflected on the white walls and cast dancing shadows across the long banners that held the kingdom's sigil: a gold stingray on waves of navy, with ancient Nidarian script around the edges.

Koraline's parents sat on their thrones at the end of the hall, watching as their daughter made her entrance. The queen looked kind and regal in a long satin gown that complemented her hazel eyes, though her thin lips did not hold their usual smile. The king looked equally stern. His hands clasped the arms of his chair, knuckles white, and beneath bushy gray brows, his face was one of fierce disapproval. Bare feet slapping against the cold marble floor, Koraline hurried across the room and took her rightful seat beside her parents.

"Presenting, Koraline Allantus, Princess of Nidaria and Cypri of the Eastern Sea," a guard bellowed. Koraline winced as the sound echoed throughout the chamber.

"This is becoming a bad habit, Koraline," Queen Eraldia whispered. She reached over and tucked a damp strand of hair behind her daughter's ear. "Lucky for you, the humans are late as well."

The princess muttered her apologies. King Triak grunted in response, and Koraline knew the matter was not settled. But at that moment, the great doors opened, revealing their long awaited guest.

25

Stormed Castles

Queen Camillea looked regal as always in a floor length purple gown etched with white flowers, blonde hair pinned at the nape of her long neck. Her cold eyes swept the room as she moved to stand before the royal family, guards following closely behind in their silver armor. Koraline had idolized the Brim from a young age, all sharp and proud despite her misfortunes. The mermaid hoped to be half as noble a ruler, someday.

"Presenting Her Royal Majesty, Queen Camillea Cortellin of Brimhold," the guard shouted once more. Koraline felt her head begin to ache.

"Gracious hosts." Camillea dipped her chin in greeting. "Thank you for agreeing to meet with me. I apologize for the delay, we met with some resistance on the road."

"We are pleased you made it safely, dear friend," Eraldia said with a smile. "But given the late hour, shall we dine while we talk?"

The royals descended to a large table set before the expansive glass windows, where a staggering feast awaited. Smoked crab wrapped in seaweed, fresh scallops, trays of stuffed clam shells, lobster smothered with butter, and crystal goblets filled with green-tinted voka. The merfolk had spared no expense. The royal chef had even thought to prepare a human dish for their guest, some type of land bird and a mix of cooked vegetables. Mouth watering, Koraline sat with her back to the sea, across from her mother, while King Triak and Queen Camillea placed themselves at the heads of the table.

"Everything tastes delicious," said Camillea. She took a quick swig from her glass, face twisting in response. "Ah— what is this? It has an… interesting flavor," the queen hiccuped.

"That is the finest voka in all of Nidaria, centuries old," Koraline's father announced proudly. "Fermented seaweed mixed with pearls, crushed sea slugs…" The king prattled off an impressively long list of ingredients.

Camillea's face turned the color of her drink. She placed the goblet well out of reach. "It's… truly unique."

Koraline hid a smile behind her hand.

"Princess," the human queen said, setting her pale eyes on Koraline. "You have grown so much since I last saw you. When was that, two years ago?"

"Three, your Majesty."

"So long? Well, you have certainly grown into a beautiful young lady." The mermaid's cheeks grew warm at her idol's praise. "I would be honored to have you as a guest in Delm. We could throw a grand celebration at the palace, just for you. It's been too long since we had a proper ball. How does that sound?"

For a moment, Koraline was at a loss for words. Her heart drummed in her ears as she thought of visiting Brimhold, seeing the capital city, meeting the people, dancing, eating, laughing. The cuff on her wrist hummed, as if excited at the thought of becoming a more permanent accessory. But before the princess could reply, she met her father's eye, his gaze dragging her back to reality. The look held one word. Strong, abrupt, with no room for argument.

No.

"While I greatly appreciate the offer, your Majesty, I'm afraid I have to decline." The words tasted rotten in Koraline's mouth, but she forced herself to smile. "Perhaps another time."

"Any time," the queen assured her. Koraline thought she saw a sympathetic gleam in the ruler's eyes.

"Now, what brings you to Milanthos, Camillea? I'm sure you didn't come all this way for a chat and a cup of voka," Queen Eraldia asked with caution. Given their neutral status, the Nidarians rarely received visits from their neighbors. Not since the war began.

Sure enough, Camillea's eyes flashed with a sudden hunger that only Koraline seemed to notice. "You're quite right. There is something I require. Something I can only achieve with your help."

"As you know, the war between Ithirdas and Brimhold is now in its twentieth year. Both sides have suffered unimaginable loss. The conflict cannot be allowed to continue for another twenty years. I fear our kingdom — our people — would never recover." The human queen folded two slender hands on the table in front of her.

"We certainly share your concerns," said the king, scratching at his graying beard. "Though I'm not sure what role you expect Nidaria to play. We refuse to take sides in this fight."

"And for twenty years, I have respected that choice. But my people are dying, Triak." Camillea's voice grew harder as she spoke, her eyes ice. "I have a way to end this war, once and for all. All I need is your cooperation, and Ithirdas will surrender by the year's end."

"You are asking us to betray an entire race," Eraldia protested. "The king and queen of Ithirdas, their children... the elves are our friends, just as you are."

"*Friends.*" Camillea practically spat the word. Koraline picked at her food, unease growing. "Your *friends* have commanded the burning of innocent villages. They've sent spies into my kingdom, killed my soldiers… and they continue to shelter the Red Elf that slaughtered my parents."

"So you say. But the Ithirdi deny these allegations."

"Allegations! I was there that night, or did you forget? I heard the screams as dozens of soldiers were cut down. I watched as my parents left me to face *her*. I saw their blood on the Red Elf's hands." Voice shaking, Camillea lifted her proud chin. "She planned to kill me too. Only a passing soldier saved me from certain death. Yet, you continue to defend that monster and the monsters that hold her leash."

Koraline could not meet Camillea's eyes in the silence that followed. What comfort could she possibly give? Though the princess disagreed with her parents on a number of issues, as far as the war was concerned, they were of one mind. Nidaria must remain apart. They could not risk the lives of their citizens for a war ruled by rumors and denial.

"Camillea, we cannot begin to fathom the tragedy you have endured. Your parents were good and noble rulers, and not a day goes by that we don't mourn their loss." The King's gaze darkened beneath furrowed brows. "But you are not the child you were when you started this conflict. Don't you think the time has come for you to set aside your thirst for revenge? For the good of your kingdom, if nothing else."

The young queen managed to maintain her composure, though Koraline could feel her anger grow. "It is not revenge I seek, Triak. It is justice. Justice for all those that have been hurt at the hands of the Ithirdi. You claim to have loved my parents. Surely you do not want their deaths to go unpunished? If you would at least hear my proposition, I'm sure you would see things differently. No harm would come to you or your people. I only need access to…"

"Enough," Eraldia said with a raise of her hand. "Even mentioning your plans could damage our relations with the elves."

"But if you would just listen…"

"Camillea!" King Triak's voice echoed throughout the chamber. Koraline jumped at the sound, a spoon clattering from her clenched hand. "That's quite enough. I will not hear another word of this madness." For a moment, the mermaid king and the human queen glared at each other from the heads of the table. Camillea, cold and terrible, Triak, all fire and fury. Koraline and her mother shared an anxious glance.

At last, Camillea ended the silent war, rising to her feet. "Fine," she hissed, voice thin. "I will not press the matter further. My pleas clearly fall on deaf ears. But should the merfolk find themselves weary of playing the part of cowards, know that my plan for peace still stands. Since my presence is clearly unwanted, I will depart in the morning. Thank you for the generous meal." With an almost mocking curtsy, Camillea spun from the table, angular silhouette flickering across the white walls as she made her exit.

A sigh from Eraldia shattered the tension Camillea left in her wake.

"If we aren't careful, we will find *ourselves* at war with Brimhold," the queen said.

"Such nonsense," King Triak grumbled. He took a large drink of voka, the green liquid dribbling down into his beard. "What did she expect? Time and time again she asks for Nidaria to take her side. Our answer always remains the same. One would think she would know better by now."

"She's desperate," Koraline said, still picking absently at her food.

"Excuse me?"

"Queen Camillea. She's just trying to save her kingdom. I find it admirable. It's more than we do for our own people," Koraline muttered the last bit into her chalice, but her parents still caught the words. The king's nostrils flared violently.

"And what exactly do you mean by that?" asked Eraldia, her voice brittle like broken glass.

Koraline planned her next words carefully. "I met with some of the Rovers today." The princess spoke quickly, before her father could protest the unorthodox meeting. "The effects of this war do not end at the borders of Ithirdas and Brimhold. The Valewood has become a home to bandits, deserters, and outcasts from the war. Our people are not safe in their own kingdom. Yet, we do nothing."

"*Nothing?*" Eraldia repeated, clearly taken aback. "We have soldiers stationed from the southern reaches of the Valewood to the very last village north of the marshes. I think perhaps these Rover friends of yours are exaggerating."

The princess chewed her lip, hard, trying to maintain a calm and reasonable tone. "How would either of you know what troubles the outer kingdom? When was the last time you even left the palace?"

"Koraline." Triak's voice was worse than angry. It bordered on patronizing. It told Koraline that she was too naive, too young to understand. That in this matter, her opinion was all but meaningless. She hated that voice. "Nidaria is safe, despite what those *Rovers* might claim. Just because your mother and I don't gallivant across the countryside, does not mean we are unaware of the happenings in our kingdom. When you become queen you will see—"

"When I am queen," patience snapping, the princess rose to her human feet, "I will not leave our people to fend for themselves. I will listen to our citizens, *all of them*, not just those within Milanthos that you deem worthy. I refuse to be a coward. I will not turn my back on the rest of the world. You both have become the Sirens you claim to hate."

Koraline knew she had gone too far. Her parents, usually even-tempered, shared a dangerous glance. When she met her father's shadowed eyes, she saw no love there, only fury. The Siren Uprising sat a dark stain on Nidaria's history, on her family's history. The Sirens were radicals, dangerous rebels. They thought the merfolk belonged to the open sea, not tied to the shore, bound to the troubles of the other races. And when their voices were ignored, they tried to take the throne by force, murdering anyone who did not want the same future for Nidaria. Blood-stained and broken, Milanthos became host to shark invested waters as death and civil war consumed the city. The Uprising occurred before Koraline was born, but she could still see the ghosts of battle in her father's eyes.

"Well, if this is how you behave, then I hope it is many years before you take the throne," Eraldia said, her small mouth set in a deep frown. "I had thought you were growing to be a competent young ruler, but you are clearly still a child. Lashing out at your own family in matters you cannot begin to comprehend. Daring to compare us to those *murderers*. I am ashamed of you. Leave us. Now."

Koraline felt as if she'd been slapped. Her ears rang. Her face burned. While her mother could be stern, she never spoke to Koraline with such loathing. The princess looked to her father, but if Triak felt differently, he said nothing, white knuckles gripping the stem of his glass. The King and Queen of Nidaria were nothing if not a united front. With no allies, and nothing more to say, the princess made her exit. The sound of bare feet against the marble floor echoed once again throughout the hollow chamber. Just before she reached the door, Koraline paused. She hated fighting with her parents, hated disappointing them. She wanted to fix her mistake. An apology sat ready on her lips. But she had meant what she said. Swallowing the unspoken words, she left.

Koraline felt Angler, along with her regular guards, follow her down through the Keep, quiet and solemn shadows. Angler held his tongue until they reached the steps leading to the ocean below. Then, he started, "Princess—"

The mermaid slid to a stop. "Whatever excuses you're about to make for them, don't."

"Your parents love you." Angler spoke softly. He tried to meet her eye. "They are just doing what they think is best for Nidaria."

"They ignore problems they do not wish to see."

"Sometimes, doing nothing is the right course."

"Maybe for them," Koraline insisted. "But not for our people. You've been out there, Angler. Can you honestly tell me that Nidaria is safe? That our kingdom doesn't suffer while we sit safely in this castle, drinking voka and practicing proper etiquette?"

The guard stared down into the smooth water, a frown etched upon his pensive face. "What would you have me do, *cypri*?"

Koraline sighed. "Nothing. You can't solve this problem. But I was hoping, just this once, maybe I could."

The princess passed Angler the magical cuff that granted her legs as she slid into the water. Within moments, her tail reformed, gold and glittering beneath her. The fins felt strange and alien after her time on two feet. Angler stared down at her, cufflet clutched in his outstretched hand. He looked like he wanted to say something more, but the words never came.

"I'm sorry," Koraline murmured to her friend, though she wasn't sure the apology was for him. Watchful eyes followed her as she dove beneath the surface.

That night, alone in her room, Koraline made a hasty decision. For a few hours, she wished to be anyone but herself. Not one of the merfolk, with all their cowardice and inaction. Not a princess, doomed to flourish while her people suffered. It was time to give her newly acquired freedom a trial run. The mermaid gathered up her human dress, wrapping it gently around her secret weapon, and peeked outside her bed chamber. It was easy enough, sneaking past the royal guard, if you knew their routine. Koraline did. She moved silently up through the Crystal Keep, back to the stairs, silver cuff upon her wrist. This time her legs felt different. Stronger. Born of her own desire to leave the sea behind.

After that, it was simple enough to slip past the few remaining soldiers and into one of the unused guest chambers. The room was small but lavish, and above all else, very human. *Perfect*, Koraline thought to herself as she slid beneath silk sheets, the sensation strangely pleasant against her bare legs.

The princess lay there for a long time, thinking. What was she going to do? Could she really show her face tomorrow, acting as if nothing had happened, pretending her concerns had vanished? Something needed to change. The world was broken. Why was she the only one who could see that? With a sigh, Koraline rolled over and buried her face into a pillow. Her problems could not be solved tonight. For now, she would try to sleep. Didn't Angler always say that evening brought the darkest thoughts? Perhaps tomorrow she could see the light again.

*****

Shadow hung heavy in the bedchamber when Koraline's eyes snapped open, her heart pounding. Something was wrong. It was early morning, or late into the night, and sleep should not have slipped away so soon. Outside, waves lapped gently against the castle walls, a comforting rhythm in the black room. But chills covered the princess' arms and bare human legs. Nothing stirred in the room, no sound from the hallway, not a breath nor a whisper. Moving slowly, Koraline pulled her legs from beneath the thick blankets, feet skimming the cold marble floor. She reached blindly in the dim light. At last, her hands found folds of familiar fabric, and she slipped on her dress before tiptoeing across the room. The princess pressed an ear to the closed door, listening. Still no sound. Her heart moved to her throat. She wished she still had Seawing, her dagger, though she was not trained to wield it. Any weapon would be preferable to her bare, shaking hands.

Gathering her courage, Koraline guided the door open and stuck her head into the hall. The passageway was almost as dark as the bedchamber. A single window let in a pale curtain of moonlight, giving the space a dreamlike quality. The copper braziers had been extinguished, and more worrisome, not a single guard paced the corridor. Koraline swallowed hard. Where was everyone? Shivering, the mermaid moved quietly down the hallway, legs unsure and unsteady. She considered shouting, yelling for a guard or even Angler, but decided against it. She did not want to attract the attention of anyone else who might be lurking in the castle.

As the princess rounded a corner, her foot landed in something warm and wet. Koraline bit her lip, the pain sharp, but refused to cry out. She let her gaze fall slowly to the floor. Blood, a reflective silver in the soft light, pooled out from a fallen Nidarian soldier. Koraline could not make out the man's face, but she knew he was dead. Staggering away, breath coming in ragged gasps, she continued down the hall, finding more soldiers, more blood. This was a nightmare. It couldn't be real. Koraline pinched herself, trying to wake up. But she still saw the bodies, still felt the blood on her feet.

Get to the water.

The words became a mantra. An anchor in a stormy sea. If she made it to the water, she could get help. She could find her parents. She would be safe.

Get to the water.

The sound of running, heavy boots on stone floor, manifested down the hall. Koraline ducked through a random doorway. She pressed her back to the wall, holding her hysterical breaths as best she could. Eventually the intruders moved along, their footsteps fading away.

Get to the water.

Just two more turns and then down the stairs. Koraline rounded the final bend, her spirit lifting. She was going to make it. But then, she found him.

Angler lay sprawled at the top of the staircase, his dark face peaceful. The princess screamed, landing hard on her knees next to her friend. The screech echoed down the hollow passages, multiplying as it went. Koraline didn't care. She cradled Angler's face in her small hands. His skin felt so cold, his long hair still wet from the water below. Was he breathing? She put her face close to his, but she felt nothing.

"No, no, please," she whispered. The mermaid knew she should leave, continue on and find help, but how could she leave him here? She considered moving her injured friend down the steps. Then, she heard it. A footfall in the passageway behind her.

Too late. Pain radiated from the back of her head, pulsating up through her skull. Her vision swam. As she collapsed, strong hands took hold of her arms. The last thing Koraline saw was Angler's calm expression as someone, or something, dragged the princess down the hall and away into the night.

<h1 style="text-align:center">26</h1>

<h1 style="text-align:center">The Morning After</h1>

Sydney awoke and immediately wished for death.

Gods, my head. She groaned. The tent spun at the edges of her vision. *Gods, my stomach.*

The previous night came flooding back in a nauseating rush of memories. *Sil a Tokiyas.* All of that strange elvish wine. The words she'd shared with Lukaris on the hillside beneath the stars…

I'm going to kill him, Sydney decided. *As soon as the world stops twirling, I'm going to strangle that elf.*

She rolled sideways, crashing to the earth in a heap.

"Ow," Sydney grumbled. She glared at the still swinging hammock. Before she could decide whether she should remain on the ground or attempt the climb back into bed, the contents of her stomach took an unexpected turn. Frantically, she crawled to an empty water basin.

Lukaris entered the tent just as Sydney heaved up her entire *Sil a Tokiyas* feast.

"Morning, Sydney— Oh. Are you alright?"

Sydney wiped a furious hand across her mouth. The *Valen* looked perfectly normal. Upright, chipper, and not puking his guts out.

"Bastard," she moaned. "When this wears off, I might murder you.

Or if it kills me first, I'm going to haunt your ass."

He blinked, concerned. "What did *I* do?"

"You got me drunk last night on all of those sweet, delicious, poisonous…" Sydney stopped, a new wave of queasiness threatening to overwhelm her.

Realization struck Lukaris' face. His lips twitched as he fought back a smile.

"If I remember correctly, I did try to cut you off."

"Not nearly hard enough. You wanted my guard down, so you could interrogate me."

"Interrogate?" Lukaris repeated with a laugh. "That's a bit of an exaggeration. Come on, let's get you to Ettee. There's never been a hangover she couldn't cure."

The elf dragged her up by her elbows. Sydney looked down at herself as she swayed on unsteady feet. She still wore the festival dress of woven autumn leaves. Except now the skirt looked as if it had lived on the forest floor for several months.

"Wait outside. I need to change into something that doesn't smell like a cheap Valewood tavern," Sydney ordered. Lukaris slipped away, still fighting down laughter.

When she finally emerged into the morning air, sunlight assaulted her eyes like a thousand tiny needles. She cowered behind the cover of her hands.

"I'm never drinking again," she whined.

"Don't be so dramatic," the *Valen* replied cheerfully as he led her to the healing tent. Ettee sat outside grinding herbs in a marble pestle. She eyed them as they approached.

"Someone had quite the night," the small elf remarked. Her normally solemn face showed the barest trace of amusement.

"Yes, yes. Do you have anything that will keep me from keeling over?" Sydney snapped.

Ettee dumped the contents of her pestle into a nearby cup that sat half full with a thick brown liquid. She twirled a finger, and the concoction mixed at her command. She passed the finished potion to Sydney.

"Here. You aren't the only one in need of a little help today."

"Thanks." Sydney took a tentative whiff and fought down a gag. "On second thought, no thanks."

"Come on," Lukaris urged. "It really does help."

She sighed. "Fine. Bottoms up, I guess."

Sydney downed the herbaceous sludge in a single gulp. Her regret was instantaneous. If anything had remained in her stomach, she would have lost it then.

"That's by far the worst thing I've ever tasted," Sydney informed them.

"You're welcome." Ettee grinned, teeth blinding against her dark lips. She took the cup, disappearing into her tent without so much as a goodbye.

Lukaris and Sydney wandered over to their usual place overlooking Firne. Sydney collapsed onto the grass while the *Valen* sat down like a bird alighting on a branch.

"Tell me something," Sydney said after they'd spent some time watching the village below. The ground had stopped shifting beneath her, so maybe there was something to Ettee's remedy after all. "Did I sing *Sea Salt Shanty* last night?"

Lukaris' half-smile widened to a toothy grin. "All eight verses. And a ninth I think you invented yourself."

"Gods." Sydney buried her head in her hands. "If the *tatell* didn't respect me before, they certainly won't now."

"Actually, I think they like you better now. It's harder to stay enemies with someone who's embarrassed themselves so completely."

"Great," Sydney replied dryly. Then, in a more serious tone, "Look.

About what I told you after *Sil a Tokiyas*…"

"Yes?"

"I never would have said those things…" Sydney swallowed. She couldn't meet his eyes. "I shouldn't have told you all of that."

"Do you mean about your sister?" Lukaris asked quietly.

"Among other things."

"If you're worried about being discovered, I can assure you the secret is safe with me. Who would I tell?"

"It's not that." How could she explain? How could she tell him that she'd opened herself up in ways she never did, even with Brandon? She'd allowed her walls to crack, and she hated how vulnerable it made her. Once someone knew the dark scars on your heart, they could use them to break you.

"Sentiment does not make you weak, Sydney," Lukaris said as if reading her thoughts.

Sydney. Not Captain Krane. She'd forgotten she'd given him that freedom too.

She finally turned to him. Forest eyes stared back at her, considering. Sometimes she really resented the way he looked at her. It made it so hard to hate him.

"I also shared things last night that I normally wouldn't." The elf continued when she didn't respond. "But I don't regret it. And I think, deep down, you're happy someone saw a glimpse of the real you."

"You're wrong," she muttered. But of course he was right. Always right, just like Gilliad. It was infuriating.

Lukaris opened his mouth, but before he could speak, a child-sized projectile barreled between them.

"Sydney!" Raiden cried in a voice like thunder. Sydney's head threatened to split open.

"Shadowed hell, take it down a few levels, kid," she groaned.

Raiden blinked, finally registering her disheveled appearance.

"Is Sydney sick?" He asked his brother with concern.

Lukaris glanced at her over Raiden's wild hair, eyes dancing. "In a way. *Sil a Tokiyas* can be a lot for first timers."

"Is it because she's *human*?" The boy whispered behind a hand.

Sydney rolled her eyes while the Valen laughed. "It's because she's Sydney."

He said that like he knew her. Like they were friends.

Sydney stood abruptly.

"I probably just need some breakfast," she said, though the thought of solid food made her stomach twist into knots. "Let's go, kid."

"Sydney—" Lukaris started, looking upset. She cut him off.

"Don't worry, ace. I'm feeling better. Ready for another day of our standard arrangement. And to forget about the mistakes of last night." She emphasized the last part.

The Valen passed a hand across his sharp chin. "Very well. If that's what you want."

"It is," she said firmly. Raiden watched them, bubbling with curiosity. But he didn't protest as Sydney dragged him away.

27

The Passing

"Sydney," a voice whispered.

At first, Sydney thought she imagined the hushed word, the sound a mere remnant of a fading dream. But when her eyes opened, Lukaris' shadowy figure hung at the entrance to her tent. The sky was dark behind him, the air still ripe and chill with the last threads of night.

"What's wrong?" Sydney asked, her voice thick with sleep. "What time is it?"

"It's early," Lukaris replied unhelpfully. "And nothing's wrong. There's just something I want to show you."

"Something that can't wait for daylight?" She groaned, wiping at her bleary eyes.

"Unfortunately, no. Get dressed. I'll wait outside." And with that, he was gone.

Sydney heaved herself up, sighing. Of all the torture the elves could contrive, making her wake before dawn might be the worst.

A few minutes later, she stepped out into the silent camp, cloak wrapped tight. She shivered as the autumn cold struck her skin. Lukaris stood nearby. His eyes were solemn and distant as he stared

232

off into the woods. The weight of their gaze set Sydney on edge.

"Good, you're ready. Follow me," the *Valen* said without preamble. He turned, his feet set in the direction of Firne. Sydney had no choice but to follow.

A few dim fires lit the path before them, but otherwise the camp sat still and silent as a crypt. Sydney shivered again as they weaved through the dark tents. Lukaris said nothing until they reached the edge of camp, where the hillside dipped down and led into the Ithirdi town. A member of the *tatell* stood guard near a flickering torch. Sydney recognized the warrior as Yunara, a tall, slender elf with raven hair that fell to her waist. She yawned as they approached.

"*Allon*, Yunara," Lukaris said quietly. "How goes the watch?"

"All is quiet, *Valen*," the elf replied. Her voice reminded Sydney of a flute. "What has you up so early?"

Lukaris' eyes flickered to Sydney. "We're attending a Passing."

Sydney wasn't sure what the words meant, but Yunara's eyes held a strange reverence. "Don't let me keep you," she insisted, quickly stepping aside.

They continued their journey into Firne. The town still slept, doors sealed tight against the lurking night. In the distance, an owl hooted, the sound echoing off the giant, huddled trees of the Wornwood. The silence that followed pressed in hungrily from all sides until Sydney could take it no longer.

"Are you going to tell me where we're going?" Sydney demanded. She wasn't quite bold enough to speak above a whisper.

Lukaris held a single finger to his lips. "Wait."

Eventually, the elf came to a halt next to a massive redwood tree. Wooden stairs curved up and around the trunk, and Sydney could faintly make out a home cradled in the branches above. Sydney's curiosity spiked higher as Lukaris led her up the steps to a small landing. An elf stood beside a curtained doorway, where soft candlelight filtered out beneath the heavy fabric. The elf raised his head as they approached. His face was drawn, eyes rimmed with red.

"You'll have to wait a moment. He's with another," was all the elf said. Lukaris nodded, and they stepped aside to wait.

The *Valen* leaned against a railing before finally meeting Sydney's eyes. He seemed more hesitant than usual. Sydney wondered if he regretted bringing her here.

"Sydney," Lukaris said at last. "Do you know what happens when an elf dies?"

Sydney blinked, thrown by the question. Her mind flashed to old fights, bodies on the ground, blood on her swords.

"Only from what I've seen on the battlefield," she admitted.

Lukaris nodded, as if expecting the answer. "Many elves die the same way humans do. Illness, accident, war… but what happens to an elf that survives all that? What becomes of them?"

"I guess they live forever."

"No. To humans, I'm sure it seems our lives are infinite. But only the dragons knew true immortality. Eventually, an elf's body will begin to wither. The Light inside them searches for release."

Lukaris was quiet for a moment. Thoughtful. Then, he said, "When an elf reaches their final stage of life, there are signs. Eyesight fails and limbs grow weary. They can feel the end before it comes. The process can last hours or days or weeks. We call it the Passing."

Sydney stomach twisted. "That sounds… terrible."

"What?" Surprise colored Lukaris' voice. "No, you misunderstand. The Passing of an elf is sacred. Beautiful. To live all of those years, all of those centuries, and make it to the very end… most aren't so lucky."

Sydney wasn't so sure. She'd spent enough time around death to have a healthy fear of it. To feel it coming for you like that… She stared at the covered doorway where the elf still stood, arms crossed and head bent.

"Ace, what are we doing here?"

"I received word that one of Firne's citizens has begun to Pass. It is tradition to visit the elf during this time, not only to pay your respects, but to learn from the elf's long life. You are permitted to ask them a single question. We consider it a great honor."

Sydney took a measured step backwards. "We're here to watch someone die?"

She must have looked shaken. Lukaris held up two calming hands. "It's not like that."

"Lukaris." His name tasted strange on her tongue. "I think this is taking things too far. I don't belong here."

"I already asked permission to bring you," the elf assured her. His face was sharp and strange in the dim light, but his eyes were the same comforting green. "But it's up to you. I won't force you to do anything you don't want to do."

"Besides dancing at *Sil a Tokiyas*, right?"

Lukaris smiled softly. "Is that a yes?"

How did I end up here? Sydney wondered, not for the first time. She took a shaking breath.

"Alright. If you're sure."

They waited in the heavy silence. Time ticked by, so long Sydney thought the minutes might suffocate her, until finally the curtain opened, and an elf stepped from the small home. She spoke with the elf by the door and hurried off down the stairs, her eyes pointed deliberately downward.

"You may enter now."

Lukaris peeled himself from the railing and moved towards the door. He pulled aside the curtain and motioned for Sydney to enter, smiling in a way that Sydney thought was meant to be encouraging, but instead reminded her of funerals and endings. But Sydney had braved worse. So, she squared her shoulders and marched forward into the unknown.

The room beyond was cramped, little more than a bed and table. Candles ringed the room, casting dancing shadows on the wooden walls. Sydney blinked for a moment, eyes adjusting to the dim light, before she finally noticed the elf tucked neatly into the bed's center.

Sydney had never seen an elf that looked old.

Of course she'd seen elves that *were* old. Elves that had lived centuries before her father's father was even born. But they'd always appeared young and unending, smooth-faced and vibrant. Certainly not the withered ghost who lay before her now.

The elf was thin, all bones and skin, with sunken cheeks. His ears still held their point, but they looked almost too sharp where they rose on either side of his head. Silver hair hung in thin strands past two milky eyes. They wandered the room haphazardly, unseeing. Sydney shivered, trying to imagine how it would feel to know death stalked you like a wolf, that each breath might be your last. She'd rather take a sword to the gut.

Lukaris inclined his head towards the elf, though he could not see it, and placed both hands across his heart.

"*Allon*, Caedus. We are honored that you would share your Passing with us. I have brought Sydney Krane of Briar with me, as we discussed."

"*Allon*," Sydney echoed, voice barely above a whisper. Her hands clenched uselessly at her sides.

Caedus lifted his head with a clear effort, empty eyes roaming.

"Ask your questions then, *Dynas*," the dying elf said with a wicked smile. The goosebumps on Sydney's arms grew even higher. "I'm on borrowed time, after all."

Lukaris blinked at the clipped response, but he pressed on.

"Very well. My question is this. What was it like, long before the war, when elves and men were allies?"

Sydney's gaze flickered to Lukaris. Of course. The question was for her. Words she was afraid to hear because of what they might mean for her future.

Caedus *humphed*, sounding almost disappointed. "The thing about war is that it never starts with the first battle. We might have been allies with Brimhold before, but tensions between humans and elves always ran below the surface. Peaceful as things seemed, there will always be fear for those that are different."

"Still," the old elf continued. "The world felt wider. Borders were open, men and women traveled freely from one kingdom to another. We might not have always gotten along, but Soarden was united. Until the dragons left, that is. Until that blasted elf killed the Brims in their own castle."

Lukaris and Sydney shared a look but said nothing.

"Still," the elf repeated again. "I'd say things were better. Not perfect, mind you, but better."

"Thank you, Caedus." Lukaris bowed his head again. His eyes flickered to Sydney. *Your turn*, they said.

Sydney's mind emptied. What should she say? What do you ask someone who has seen and done more than she could possibly fathom? Was there a perfect question, one that should be obvious to her?

A month ago, Sydney might have asked something that would benefit Brimhold. Some elvish secret or weakness. She would have used the question to gain advantage, to extract information. But that part of her felt distant, like a mountain on the horizon. Still there, still present, but out of reach.

In truth, there was only one question she wanted to ask. The same question she asked when standing on the hillside of Delm, staring out into the distance, restless for a mission. The same question that came to her as a little girl, watching the ships leave Briar. The question she couldn't seem to answer no matter how many kingdoms she explored or battles she fought or homes she left.

"Did you ever find what you were looking for?" Sydney's voice was so soft, she wondered if she'd even spoke aloud.

Lukaris frowned, confused.

The dying elf grinned.

"Finally. A question worth asking."

Caedus sat up straighter, the flames around the room seeming to mimic his movement. His sightless eyes roamed towards Sydney, face alight.

"Yes. It wasn't easy, and I often felt I would never find what you seek. But I did, in the end."

"How?" Sydney asked eagerly. Lukaris stiffened, and she knew she'd broken the rules. One question only. She didn't care. She had to know.

Caedus didn't seem to mind the break in tradition. He leaned forward. "I stopped looking. That's the trick. The things we need have a habit of finding us, not the other way around."

Sydney wanted to scream. She had never been one to wait, to rest, to settle. She didn't want to sit patiently while the hunger in her chest consumed her.

Suddenly, the small room felt like it was closing in, the candles hot and stifling. Sydney managed a choked, *"Melánethe,"* to Caedus before fleeing the home. She burst through the doorway, gulping in the cool morning air. There were some muttered words behind her before Lukaris appeared at her elbow.

"Sydney? Are you alright?"

"Fine," she managed. "I'm fine."

Lukaris studied her but didn't reply. He spoke softly to the elf standing guard and then led Sydney down the stairs, back the direction they had come.

For a few minutes, they walked in silence. Sydney's skin prickled at the cold air and the quiet. Somehow the world felt darker, even as dawn began to lighten the sky.

"What did you mean?" Lukaris asked suddenly.

"What?"

"What did your question mean? *Did you ever find what you were looking for?*"

The elf's mouth turned down at the edges. Sydney realized how much it bothered him, not understanding. Lukaris thrived on knowledge and rooting out problems. And Sydney had presented him with a new unknown.

But the Passing had left Sydney feeling raw and vulnerable. She didn't intend to reveal any more of herself that morning.

"You're smart, ace," Sydney said. "I'm sure you'll work it out."

Lukaris' frown deepened, but he didn't press further.

Later that morning, Sydney sat eating an early breakfast with Lukaris and the normal crew: Raiden, Itari, Flindir, and of course, Honey. They chatted as usual, but Lukaris remained withdrawn and subdued. No doubt trying to unravel the inner workings of Sydney's mind.

A gust of wind sent autumn leaves tumbling passed. Next to Sydney, Itari went rigid. Sydney looked up from her food as, one by one, the elves lapsed into a reverent silence.

"What—"

Sydney cut herself off. She felt it then, a pull in the air. The current was familiar, like the sensation when the elves used their magic. But this was different. Stronger. All at once, the fires around Firne flared to life. The torches, the candles, even the cooking fire, blazed with an intensity that forced everyone to glance away.

Just as quickly, the breeze ended. The flames steadied into their normal flickering patterns. The elves cast their eyes downward, solemn. Itari whispered a prayer.

Sydney looked to Lukaris questioningly, and he gave her a sad smile.

"Sometimes, when an elf is truly connected to the Light, their spirit sends out a final burst of magic when they die. Caedus has moved on. The Passing is complete."

Sydney looked down the hillside, searching for the old redwood in the expanse of trees. She thought of Caedus and his sightless eyes. His sly grin.

Eyes glistening, Sydney watched as the sun rose, and a new day dawned.

28

When the Queen Returns

"Come on, Brandon, just one drink," Julia pleaded. She tugged on his sleeve, a perfect pout on her lips.

"I told you, I'll be along later," said Brandon.

"That's what you've been saying for days. You know, staring at the horizon every night isn't going to make them return any faster."

She was right. And yet, Brandon couldn't seem to pull himself from the hillside. He'd fallen into a steady routine since returning to Delm. He spent the days training, hard, trying to work the worry from his bones. He surveyed new recruits, attended dull war meetings, sparred with anyone who could hold a sword. Anything to keep his mind occupied. But then the evening came, and all of Brandon's welcome distractions left him. Most soldiers returned to their barracks or went to The Steel Anchor for a few pints and a game of bait. Brandon never joined them. He couldn't. Not when Sydney should be sitting there next to him. She always did love hustling the local baiters.

So instead, he trekked up to the top of the castle wall overlooking the eastern hills. The wind whipped the Brimhold standard above his head as the sun streaked crimson and orange on its way towards the earth. In the distance, he could just make out the road that would bring Camillea back from Nidaria. And it was at that point he stared, for days on end, begging for the queen's return. Waiting was worse than any battle, he decided.

"Julia," he said, forcing his eyes to meet hers. A strand of black hair had slipped from its place behind her ear, and his hand twitched with the desire to brush it back. He didn't. "I know you're trying to help. But this is where I need to be right now."

"You're going to drive yourself mad, Lockes," she sighed. Brandon winced. It's what Sydney always called him. "I'll be at the pub, if you decide to join me."

She gave his hand a squeeze and left, her footsteps echoing down the stone steps. Brandon rubbed his forehead. *You're an idiot, Lockes.*

The sunlight slipped away, leaving behind a star filled sky. Brandon's mother used to tell him the name of every constellation, whispering their secrets into his ear as he sat in her lap, safe and secure. Most of the names and stories had long since slipped from Brandon's memory, but he still knew the shapes. He passed the time by tracing their paths in the sky with an outstretched finger.

Standing there on the castle wall, staring at the horizon, Brandon was reminded of a different night, years ago. The eve of his first battle.

Brandon and Sydney were newly graduated cadets, only sixteen and fourteen years old. Days after receiving their Honor Guard placements, they were sent to the front line. A large battalion of Ithirdi had been spotted crossing the border, and Queen Camillea feared an invasion. The Honor Guard was sent to drive them back.

It was a frigid winter. Brimhold's warriors set up camp on a snow crusted hill, giving themselves a clear view of the elves settled at the forest's edge. The plan was to attack at dawn, the rising sun at their backs. The guard hunkered down for a long, shivering night.

Brandon and Sydney were assigned first watch, and they found themselves on the western edge of the hill, staring down as fires flickered to life in the Ithirdi camp. Sydney perched on a boulder, eyes dark. She pulled her gray cloak tighter around her shoulders.

"Gods, it's cold. Have you ever been this cold?" she muttered.

"Not since the orphanage."

Sydney scowled. "Don't be so dramatic. Briar is an eternal summer compared to this place."

Brandon sat on the rock next to his friend. Looking at her, he couldn't believe how far they'd come since the day they met. From kids to soldiers. And tomorrow, they would finally join the fight.

An easy silence fell. They leaned into each other, enjoying the line of warmth where their shoulders met.

"Lockes," Sydney said softly after a while. "Are you scared?"

"A little," he admitted. He thought back to the day he'd learned of his father's death. The surge of anger. "But I'm also ready."

Sydney sighed. "I don't know… I don't know if I can do it. Training is one thing. But to take a life? What if I freeze when the time comes?"

"You won't," Brandon said fiercely. "And if you do, I'll be there. I have your back. Always."

"Promise?" Sydney looked up at him. Her hands shook where they clutched at her cloak.

"Promise."

They spent the rest of their watch with eyes on the stars, sharing the constellations they knew from childhood.

Back in Delm, a new star appeared on the horizon, shaking Brandon out of the past. No, not a star. Torchlight? He sprinted across the rampart until he reached a guard.

"Give me your spyglass, quick!" Brandon demanded. The soldier frowned but didn't protest. Brandon eagerly pointed the telescope towards the eastern road.

Yes! At least a dozen horses trotted towards Delm, and at their head, a great white steed. Brandon practically flew down the steps to meet them at the castle gates.

He slid to a halt when he caught sight of the queen and her soldiers. Their heads hung low, faces solemn. Only Camillea still held her chin proud, despite the massive bruise sprouting from her left temple. Brandon tried to keep himself from gaping.

"Your Majesty," he called out with a bow.

"Hello, Captain Lockes," the queen replied, her voice unusually soft. She sighed. "I suppose we had better talk. Come inside."

They gathered in the great hall. Gilliad arrived first, looking disheveled and half asleep, along with a few members of the Honor Guard. Julia slipped in last, positioning herself at Brandon's side. The chamber felt eerie so late at night, with shadows lurking behind each stone pillar. The queen poured herself a glass of red wine before settling onto her throne. She looked tired. Like a bear after a fierce winter.

"The meeting with the Nidarians did not go as planned," Camillea began. She took a long gulp from her glass. "They still refuse to take any part in our fight against Ithirdis. The cowards. Even their passive help would quickly lead to peace."

"The merfolk have never been ones to get their fins dirty," Gilliad grumbled, scratching at his beard. "It's regrettable, but not all that surprising. We will just have to continue this war on our own."

"You don't understand, General. We are so *close*," the queen sighed. She pinched the bridge of her nose. "But I'm afraid that's not the worst of it."

The gathered soldiers exchanged weary glances, and Brandon's own eyes kept drawing back to his queen's battered face.

"What happened, your Majesty? Did you run into bandits on the road?" Brandon asked when no one else seemed able to muster the words.

"No. The Crystal Keep was attacked. Our very first night in Milanthos."

Cries of shock and confusion echoed in the hollow chamber.

"What?"

"Attacked?"

"Why?"

Camillea allowed the uproar to continue for a moment before raising her hand for silence. "One at a time, if you please."

"Who would make a move on Nidaria?" Gilliad questioned, forehead wrinkled.

"Who else? The elves, of course," the queen grumbled bitterly.

"The elves are trading partners with the merfolk," Julia piped up. "Why risk that alliance?"

"Perhaps the Ithirdi are also tired of Nidaria's neutrality. A small force snuck into the castle while we slept. They killed the merfolk that patrolled the hallways. I ran when I found a soldier dead outside my door. Some of the assailants chased me, but the rest of the guard came to my aide. I regret to say, I was entirely useless. " The queen brought a hand to her face.

One of the returning soldiers shook his hand. "With respect, your majesty, there was nothing to be done. The attackers knew their craft. They were in and out with the princess before any of us could respond."

The words sparked a new round of outcries. Brandon looked to the queen with shock. Camillea lowered her head.

"Yes, Princess Koraline was taken. We aided the Nidarians in their search efforts, but the kidnappers were long gone. A ransom note arrived in the Crystal Keep. It ordered Brimhold to surrender the war or risk the princess' life."

"That confirms it then," Brandon growled. "The elves have her."

"The letter was unsigned," Camillea said carefully. "I doubt Ithirdas will take credit for the attack. Just as they deny everything else."

"So, what are we to do, your Majesty?" Gilliad asked.

The queen sighed. Her wine had diminished to a single gulp. "As you said General Norwell, we continue the war."

"So, we're just going to ignore Princess Koraline's kidnapping? Let an innocent girl die?" Brandon demanded. *If Sydney were here, she'd be furious.* Julia lay a calming hand on his arm.

Camillea's frost eyes turned to him. "What would you have me do? Lay down arms? Surrender our people over to those *monsters*? Nidaria's situation is troubling, but I will not concede a twenty year struggle so easily. Besides, the merfolk royalty still refuse to turn against the elves, even after losing their child. We can't help those that won't help themselves."

"Besides," the queen continued, downing the remainder of her drink. "Koraline's abductors will gain nothing from harming her. Our best path to saving her lies in defeating Ithirdas. Once and for all."

"No disrespect, your Majesty," said Gilliad. He passed a weary hand across his face. "But how do we plan on doing that?"

Camillea rose to her feet. Standing on the throne's dais, she towered over everyone in the room. Shoulders back, chin high. A ruler down to her bones. Brandon might not always agree, but the queen always inspired him to follow.

"I think it's time we take the fight to them," Camillea declared, voice and eyes like flaming arrows.

29

Captives

Koraline woke to the sound of a man screaming.

Disoriented, the mermaid pushed herself to a vertical position, her heart hammering in her chest. The princess sat in a small, dimly lit chamber, her back pressed up against a bare wall. Old, iron bars surrounded her on three sides. Her bracelet was gone, lost or taken she didn't know, and her golden fins stretched out before her on the dirt floor. She attempted to move her tail, but only managed to lift it a few inches. A large metal cuff held her fins to the floor with similar chains encircling her wrists. Koraline pulled at the chains, but they were securely fastened to the wall on either side of her.

Koraline grasped at an explanation for her surroundings. Slowly, her last waking moments fluttered back. The attack on the castle. Someone hitting the back of her head. Koraline reached up and touched the base of her skull. Her long hair was matted with dried blood, but the wound itself barely throbbed. She remembered a rocking sensation, a sweet smell, pulling her back into unconsciousness again and again.

Then the worst memory fell into place. Angler, still on the stairs.

Her stomach lurched at the thought.

Another scream snapped Koraline from her musings, and she whipped her head towards the source of the noise. Through the bars to her right was another, much larger cell. The ceiling rose high above the chamber, its apex disappearing into the gloom. Facing each other, in the center of the cell, were two men. The first was dressed plainly in a white cotton shirt. His sleeves were rolled up to his elbows, their edges stained red. The man was of average height, with short, brown hair, a trimmed beard, and a high forehead. He was handsome enough, aside from the jagged, red scar that stretched from his hairline to the bridge of his nose.

The other man was on his knees, and like Koraline, he was bound. Long chains attached the prisoner's wrists to the ceiling, stretching his arms out like a bird mid-flight. The captive was lean and muscular, and he wore no clothes aside from a pair of black trousers. Cuts, bruises, and a thick layer of grime covered the man's torso, and fresh blood ran down his back. The man appeared younger than his captor, with messy black hair that hung over his face.

The man with the scar leaned in so that he was eye level with the prisoner. For the first time, Koraline saw the dagger clasped in his hand.

"I will stop the moment you choose to cooperate." The man spoke softly, but there was an edge to his voice.

"*Lök gondr helgmar*," the captive spat. His voice was gruff, and the harsh words caught in his mouth. The language was not one Koraline recognized.

The scarred man reeled back his arm and punched the prisoner square in the nose. Koraline heard a distinctive crunch, and the man's head flung back before flopping loosely forward. A small groan escaped the man's throat.

"I have warned you about speaking out of turn," the scarred man said politely. "If you have something to say, you may use the common tongue."

The prisoner glared up at his captor. His eyes flashed a startling blue.

"Go to hell."

The scarred man sliced the captive's shoulder with the edge of his knife. The resulting scream sent chills down Koraline's spine.

"Stop it!" Koraline screeched, her voice hoarse.

The torturer fixed his dark eyes on Koraline. The mermaid immediately regretted placing herself at the center of this man's attention.

"Princess." The man stepped away from his captive, wiping the blade of his dagger on his pants. "My apologies, I didn't see you wake up."

He took a few easy strides in Koraline's direction, opening the small door that led to her cell. He crouched down next to her, the tip of his dagger digging into the dirt floor. Koraline shivered as the man gave her a long, scrutinizing look.

"You'll have to forgive the rather drab quarters, but my employer deemed them necessary. Wouldn't want you to try making a run for it, now would we?" The man glanced down at Koraline's tail. "Figuratively speaking, that is."

"Where am I?" Koraline hated the way her voice shook. "Who are you?"

"No need to be frightened, Princess. We're under strict orders to keep you breathing, as long as you cooperate." The warden spoke casually, as if he hadn't been torturing someone a few moments before. "My name is Malcolm. As far as your location, I'm afraid I can't answer that."

"Why am I here? If it's money you want, I promise my family will pay handsomely for my safe return." Koraline tried to sound firm, but her attempt fell flat.

"Oh I'm sure they would," Malcolm replied. "Unfortunately, my employer is not interested in money. But as soon as we get what we want, you'll be on your way, free as a bird."

"And what exactly is your employer after?"

At that moment, two guards entered the room. One of them held a glass vial. The other carried a roll of bandages.

"Perfect timing." Malcolm waved the guards in. As they passed through the adjoining cell, Koraline made eye contact with the chained captive. He gave her a brief, sympathetic glance before turning away.

Malcolm twisted his dagger in the dirt as the two guards squatted down next to Koraline. The glass vial was placed by her arm.

"Hold her down." The order was so quiet that Koraline barely had time to react before four strong arms grabbed hold of her, immobilizing her upper body. A large hand clamped over her mouth.

"Don't struggle dear, this will only take a moment," Malcolm said, as one of the guards held Koraline's forearm over the vial. The warden lifted his knife, and in one swift motion, sliced the mermaid's arm. Koraline let out a muffled scream as pain lanced through her, and she thrashed against her captors. Blood dripped down her arm, finding its way into the open vial.

Koraline's head swam as her blood filled the vial to its top. One of the men capped the container and passed it smoothly to Malcolm. Koraline felt the hands on her arms disappear, and a bandage was wrapped around the fresh wound.

"That wasn't so bad, now was it?" Malcolm murmured, as he gazed at the tube of blood clutched in his hand. "Barely a scratch."

Koraline had nothing to say in response. Maybe she was still dreaming. This was all a new chapter to her ongoing nightmare.

Malcolm and his henchmen left the cell, passing through to give the other prisoner one last kick. Malcolm called back to Koraline as he left the room.

"I'll see you tomorrow, Princess. Thank you for your… cooperation."

A metal door slammed into place, leaving Koraline and her cellmate to themselves. A hushed silence fell, broken only by the pained breath of the chained man, and the occasionally squeak of a rat.

Before Koraline could collect herself, there was movement in the adjoining cell. The chains holding the man's arms slowly loosened, allowing him to move more freely about the cell. He lowered himself against the wall, wincing at the wounds that covered his body.

"So." The man's voice startled Koraline, and she jumped slightly. "What crime have you committed to end up in a place like this?"

Koraline was thrown by the question. It was not one she could answer.

"Existing, I suppose," Koraline replied finally, her voice still wavering.

To the mermaid's surprise, the chained man threw back his head and laughed. A great, booming laugh that shook his body and seemed much too strong for his weakened state.

"Is something amusing?" Koraline demanded.

"My apologies, *allska*." The prisoner flashed a grin. Koraline noticed for the first time that the man spoke with a strange accent, a remnant of the unknown language he was using earlier.

"Well, what are you here for then? Murder? Theft? Did you flirt with the wrong bar maid?"

"Believe it or not, Princess, my sins are not unlike yours. Circumstances of birth and the like." The man spoke casually, running a quick hand through his hair. "We seem to be in a prison that doesn't hold actual criminals."

Koraline was not sure she believed this chained stranger. But then again, she had been kidnapped from her home, held against her will, and drained of her blood. Her captors seemed to lack a certain decency. Maybe her cellmate was also innocent.

"My name is Arkyn," the man said. Once again, the mermaid failed to reply. "Will you tell me your name, or should I make one up for you? Or do you not have a name? Or is it embarrassing? I promise not to mock you unless it's incredibly dreadful…"

"It's Koraline." The princess spoke quickly, mostly to stop Arkyn's monologuing. "Koraline Allantus."

"Princess Koraline," Arkyn mused. "At least Malcolm has found suitable company for me in between our *sessions.*"

"How long have they been holding you here?" Koraline asked. Her eyes tried not to focus on the wounds that covered Arkyn's body.

Arkyn shrugged his shoulders. "Best guess? A few months. But it's hard to keep track of time down here."

Koraline shuddered. Months. She couldn't imagine spending another day in that cell.

"It's not so bad," Arkyn said, guessing her thoughts.

"Not so bad? They're torturing you!"

"Sure, but the porridge is to die for."

A laugh escaped Koraline's lips. She clapped a hand over her mouth to muffle the sound. Arkyn grinned again, clearly pleased with himself.

"They must be doing this for a reason," said Koraline, after she composed herself. "What do they want from you?"

Arkyn's smile slipped away, his expression guarded. It was as if a cloud had passed in front of the sun.

"I don't suppose you're going to tell me," Koraline guessed.

"Can you blame me? We've only just met. For all I know, you're a spy planted here to win my trust by laughing at my jokes." The teasing returned to Arkyn's tone.

"Fair enough," the princess conceded. "May I ask, at least… if you know what our captors need from you, why don't you just give it to them? Maybe they would let you go."

Arkyn was quiet. At last, he said, "I know what they want, but I don't know what they will do once they have it. I doubt they will ever let me go. And if they are willing to kidnap and torture, I'm sure their plans are not for the greater good. I will not cause the suffering of others. Not while there is strength left in me."

"That's very brave," Koraline said softly. The throbbing in her injured arm was suddenly joined by a twinge of regret. *Should I have tried harder to stop them?*

"Or perhaps," Arkyn replied with a smile, "I just love watching that bastard go home empty handed."

30

Unexpected Visitors

Deep in the Wornwood, the air spoke of autumn. Each morning a cool breeze rushed down from the mountains, and the breath of every living creature hung in a cloud of mist. Seemingly overnight, trees shifted to shades of red and yellow and brown, though many stayed a deep evergreen. The calls and cries of animals began to fade as the creatures of the forest started preparations for what promised to be a fierce winter.

With the fall winds and changing leaves came rain. Lots of rain. Some days it was a steady, never-ending drizzle that soaked straight through to the bone. Other days brought downpours so heavy that the elves, and Sydney by default, could barely leave their homes. Those days were spent huddled around crackling fires, eating warm stews, sharing stories, and even playing bait. The elves were terrible baiters, much to Sydney's delight. She built up a nice supply of Ithirdi silver, though she had no idea where she'd spend it.

The days after a storm, when the forest was green and fresh, were Sydney's favorite. The sun would stream through the trees, a welcome friend, and with mountain air in her lungs, Sydney felt unstoppable.

It was one of those perfect autumn days when two visitors rode into Firne.

Sydney walked through the camp with Lukaris and Itari at her side. They were having a lesson in Elvish, and though the day had barely begun, the Brim was already frustrated.

"How can one word mean both hello and goodbye?"

"*Kas!*" Itari barked. She was getting just as irritable as her pupil. "It does not mean hello or goodbye. It is for meeting and parting, but it means more."

"That doesn't make any sense!" Sydney threw up her hands.

Lukaris, the more patient teacher, tried a different approach. "Think about that moment when you part with someone important. You don't always wish to say goodbye. So you say, *silvas.* It is a… connection. A placeholder. Until you see that person again."

"And when next you meet," Itari continued. "Again, you say *silvas.*"

"*Silvas,*" Sydney repeated, turning the word over in her mouth. She let the sound echo for a moment before shaking her head. "Still seems overly complicated."

Before Itari could work herself into a proper rage, Flindir dashed from between two tents, nearly colliding with Lukaris. He seemed more flustered than normal, wide-eyed with a thin sheen of sweat on his forehead.

"Lukaris! I tried to reach you before—" Flindir inhaled deeply. Sydney didn't know if she'd ever seen an elf so out of breath.

"Before what?"

"Novah."

A look of panic fell over Lukaris' face. Itari stiffened. All of the elves shot Sydney an uneasy glance.

"Sydney, I think we'll have to finish our lesson later. There's something I need to attend to. If you wouldn't mind waiting back at your tent…" The leader tried and failed to act casual. Alarms went off in Sydney's head. She shook off Lukaris' guiding hand.

"What's going on?" Sydney fixed her gaze on Flindir, the easiest target. The elf stared pointedly at the ground.

"It's n-nothing, really, we're just um, we just have a meeting. Standard, normal meeting— oh no." Flindir wrung his hands together as two horses trotted into view.

The first horse held a large woman with chestnut hair and deep-set eyes beneath a strong brow. She wore bronze armor and a broadsword at her hip. The stranger looked ready for battle at a moment's notice. And most importantly, the woman was clearly and strikingly human.

Before Sydney could process this realization, her eyes landed on the second rider. A she-elf sat tall upon a gray steed. With cheekbones that could cut glass, a distinct pointed nose, and eyes that darted about like a cat stalking its prey, the elf demanded attention. However, despite these bold features, all eyes were inadvertently drawn to the silk curtain of hair that hung to the elf's waist. The hair was fire. A red so bold it looked unnatural among the soft hues of the forest.

That face. For twenty years, Sydney had seen that face staring out at her from wanted posters across Brimhold. And that hair. The same color as the blood on her hands.

The Red Elf.

Sydney didn't remember where she got the knife. One moment she was unarmed, and the next she was surging towards the elf with a dagger in her hand. If the others tried to stop her, she didn't hear them. Her ears pounded along to the beating of her heart, and she felt the rage of every Brimhold citizen behind her, driving her forward.

If the Red Elf feared for her life, she didn't show it. Her eyes locked with Sydney's. The elf raised a single eyebrow, followed by a single hand.

White light pierced forth, sharp and bright and clear. Sydney tried to close her eyes, but the light bore past her eyelids, blinding her. Her knees struck the earth, and a scream worked its way up her throat. Dropping the knife, she clawed uselessly at her eyes, panic rising.

Gentle hands fell upon Sydney's arms. She lashed out in her pained and sightless state, her elbow smacking something solid. There was a crunch followed by a low moan. The hands departed.

"Novah, enough!" Lukaris' voice cracked like a whip. The light retreated as quickly as it had come. Sydney blinked rapidly, trying to clear the leftover glare from her eyes as the pain faded to a dull ache.

"New pet, *Dynas*?" The Red Elf asked in a low voice, smooth as honey.

A feral shriek slipped through gritted teeth as Sydney scrambled for her abandoned dagger. Strong hands yanked her up and away, just as her fingers brushed the metal.

"It's a long story. What are you doing here, Novah?"

The Red Elf eyed Sydney, as if deciding what she could say in front of the enemy. Finally, she replied, "I've just received word from across the chasm. Knotting has been destroyed. Just like the others."

Sydney's head spun. Another village lost. The same village that Gilliad had fought so hard to save. The village countless soldiers had died defending.

Rage, hot and simmering, grew in Sydney's gut. Lukaris' arms tightened around her.

"I see. Itari, get our guests settled. I'll be along in a moment. Flindir, help me with Sydney," the elf captain said in a tone that left no room for argument.

The elves half led, half dragged Sydney through the camp. She said nothing, eyes closed, heart still racing. She felt them pass into a tent, and four hands pushed her into the closest chair. It was only then that she opened her eyes.

Lukaris stood at the entrance to the tent, arms crossed, a worried crease between his brows. Flindir sat off to the side with his head held back, pinching the bridge of his nose as fresh blood dripped down his face. Sydney felt a small twinge of guilt, but it was quickly drowned by an anger she had rarely known.

"You bastard." Sydney's voice shook. Her entire body shook. "You lying son of a bitch."

Lukaris passed a weary hand across his face. "Sydney—"

"I was beginning to trust you." She wiped furiously at her eyes, tears of frustration forming. "*All* of you. But you were lying from the start."

"I did not lie to you," Lukaris snapped.

"Then explain *her*." Sydney moved threateningly towards Lukaris, jabbing a finger at his chest. Flindir moved to intervene, but his leader raised a hand. The two now stood mere inches apart. "Explain why the woman who murdered a castle full of my people just waltzed into your camp. Why she acted like you were old friends. Why weeks ago you told me Ithirdas never sheltered that *monster*."

"That's not what I said. Novah never attacked Brimhold. You're confused—"

The sound of a fist striking flesh vibrated through the small tent. Sydney stepped back, chest heaving. Lukaris rubbed his jaw. Their eyes locked, and earlier that morning, Sydney might have said the elf seemed sad. Now, every glance felt like a lie.

"Are you done?" Lukaris' voice barely held the weight of a whisper.

As usual, Sydney felt her anger extinguish as quick as it flared. But she preferred the fire to the ash. The emptiness that followed a hard battle, a destroyed town, a perfectly planned betrayal. *How could I have been so stupid?* Sydney slid back into the chair, mouth tasting of dust.

"Yeah, I'm done. I'm done playing this little game of yours. Because that's all it ever was to you, right? You were using me, learning from me, just not in the way I expected. Gods, I really thought you wanted to change things." Sydney held her face, nails digging sharply into her scalp. "Now, another Brim village has been destroyed while I've been humoring my enemies."

"How could you think that of me?" Lukaris asked, voice cracking. "I have made mistakes, Sydney, but I have never, not once, been dishonest with you. I still believe, more than anything, that under-standing between our people is the only way to end this war, and I would not jeopardize that growing trust with lies. Believe me."

Sighing into her hands, Sydney replied, "Why should I?"

"I could have killed you that day in the woods, but I didn't. I could have kept you a prisoner, tortured you as you feared, but I didn't. Do you know why?"

A flicker of hope sparked in Sydney's chest, a light in the darkness. She raised her head.

"Why?"

"Because, I saw something familiar in you. A willingness to travel whatever lengths necessary to do what is right. A desire to find the truth when everyone else accepts what the world wants them to believe. Behind all that stubbornness, all that anger, is a good person. An ambitious smart-mouth, but a good person all the same." Lukaris smiled that now familiar smile, an olive branch, an attempt at peace. And despite herself, Sydney felt it working. How did these elves keep working their way past her armored heart?

Sydney was quiet for a moment. Then, she looked to Flindir. "Sorry about the nose."

"Oh, s'okay," Flindir replied nasally, head still back to stop the flow of blood.

Then, she turned to Lukaris. His face lightened at her tone. With another sigh, she asked, "Why is the Red Elf here, Lukaris?"

"Novah is a member of the Ithirdi forces," the elf began cautiously. When Sydney didn't interrupt, he continued. "I told you that we denied any connection to whoever attacked your castle. That was the truth. Novah did not kill all of those people."

"Ace, there were dozens of witnesses that night," Sydney retorted, skeptically. "Every single one of them placed her there. Queen Camillea describes her in striking detail, and I've seen her face across Brimhold since I was a child. How can you say she didn't do it?"

"Because, that same night, hundreds of leagues away, I saw Novah in Sil Tullian."

"As did I," Flindir added.

"That's not possible," Sydney protested.

"Be that as in may, countless elves will tell you that Novah was no where near Brimhold that night or any of the weeks that followed."

"If that's true, then why didn't you say anything? Why is this the first I'm hearing of this?" Sydney's head swam. She struggled to give up the facts surrounding an event that had shaped her entire life.

"We tried. By the Light, we tried for months. But your young queen, the other leaders of Brimhold, they wouldn't listen. I'm not saying I blame them. After all, who wouldn't believe what they saw with their own eyes? Everyone, of every race, stopped listening to each other. Elves were forced from Brimhold, humans from Ithirdas. And eventually, we stopped trying to calm the rising storm. This war was a long time coming. Tensions between our kingdoms were growing long before the attack on Delm. That was just the breaking point."

"I still don't understand." Sydney rubbed her temples. It was shaping up to be a long day. "If you're telling the truth — and that's a big if — and Novah was in Sil Tullian the night of the attack, then who killed the king and queen? And why frame the Red Elf?"

"Well, that's the question isn't it? Maybe the same person who likes to burn down innocent villages. The same person that set this entire conflict into motion." A light wind whipped through the tent at Lukaris' words.

Sydney sat extremely still, eyes moving from Lukaris to Flindir to the ground, not really seeing. Her stomach churned. A small part of her was glad, glad that the elves might be innocent after all, that she could validate her growing trust in them. But another part of her, a stronger piece, felt ill at the thought. Everything she had done since leaving Briar might have been for nothing. How many innocent people had she hurt? Killed? And all the while, her sight had been set on the wrong enemy. If Lukaris spoke the truth, her family's murderers were farther away than ever.

"Sydney." The word hung between them, soft and pleading. "Please. Believe me."

She looked up at him. His eyes bore into her, like they always did, as if they were seeing straight through to her soul. She couldn't help herself.

"Alright. Okay. I hear you," Sydney sighed. "But no more half-truths, Lukaris. I will finish out the six weeks, as we agreed. But I want the truth, *now*. About Briar, about the Red Elf. All of it."

The *Valen* agreed, nodding eagerly. Flindir opened his mouth, uncertain, but Lukaris stopped him before he could protest. "No, she's right, Flin. She deserves answers. She's put enough trust in us. It's time we return the favor."

Sydney's heart swelled with a mixture of excitement and dread. Would it really be this easy? Was she finally going to find out what happened to her home? And did she truly want to know?

Lukaris offered her a hand.

"Let me gather the others. Then, I'll tell you whatever you wish to know."

31

The Truth

Lukaris and Flindir led Sydney into a large tent at the center of camp. Sydney had never been inside before, but she knew its purpose. A place for council and meetings. For war planning.

Inside, a large oak table dominated the space. There were no chairs, but enough room to form a standing circle. A map of Soarden covered the tabletop, stretching from the furthest reaches of the Viridian Desert all the way to the shore of the Eastern Sea. The tent was rimmed in familiar faces. Ordell, his large arms crossed, and Sarcys, eyes dark and weary. Ettee lurked in a corner. Her small face was unreadable. Itari stood at the table's head, both hands firmly planted on the wood. And then there were the newcomers, the Red Elf and her human companion. Sydney's stomach lurched at the sight of her, but she stayed silent as they filed into the room.

Sarcys straightened up as they entered. "What is *she* doing here, Lukaris?"

Lukaris glared at the black-haired elf. "I'm sorry, Sarcys, am I not still your leader? You will use my title in formal company, or you will keep your mouth shut."

"Apologies, *Valen*," Sarcys muttered, looking away.

"Surprisingly, he brings up a good point, *Dynas*," the Red Elf said in her velvet voice. "Why is an enemy soldier allowed in such a place?"

"I could ask the same of a wanted murderer," Sydney snapped. She gave a smile of sharpened steel as Novah's eyes narrowed.

"Enough," Ordell grumbled. He towered over everyone else in the room. "Let our *Valen* speak."

Lukaris nodded his thanks before stepping up to the table. Sydney followed, never taking her eyes off the Red Elf.

"Captain Krane has been a guest in this camp for weeks now. Per our agreement, we have worked to better understand each other, our kingdoms, and our cultures. In this, we hope to garner trust and perhaps begin down a path to peace. When we first met, I also agreed to tell Sydney everything I know about the destruction of her home, the Brimhold town of Briar. I can no longer withhold this information. She needs to know. She *deserves* to know."

Novah's cat-like eyes flicked from Sydney to Lukaris and back again. Ordell cleared his throat.

"Forgive me, *Valen*. While I'll admit, Captain Krane has proven herself more amiable then I originally expected… this is a heavy secret you mean to reveal. A secret kept from even our own king. Are you prepared for what will happen if she betrays us? If she takes these words back to her queen?"

The elves exchanged glances between them. Even Itari seemed uncertain. Their distrust hurt Sydney more than she expected.

"May I?" Sydney looked to Lukaris for permission to speak. He was the only one without doubt in his eyes. The *Valen* nodded. She addressed the group.

"I understand your hesitation. And I will be honest with you. A month ago, I would have revealed any elvish secret to Queen Camillea, easy as breathing. But I am no longer here as a soldier of Brimhold. I am here as a daughter and a sister, a human and a creature of Light. All I want is justice for the death of my family. I want to know the truth. And if Brimhold is wrong about Ithirdi crimes, tell me. I'm here. I'm listening. If you are innocent, as I hope you to be, I will not betray your trust."

Lukaris had a small smile on his face as he scanned the tent. Her speech seemed to have won them over, if only a little.

"Novah," Lukaris began. "I think it would be best to start with you."

The Red Elf lifted her chin, her neck long and proud. For a split second, she reminded Sydney of Camillea.

"Why should I have to explain myself?" Novah demanded. Her companion placed a comforting arm around her shoulders.

"Because until you do, people will always assume the worst," Lukaris replied evenly.

She hesitated once more, then sighed. "Alright. For you, *Dynas*." Her gaze turned to Sydney, who struggled to meet it.

"I did not attack Delm that night twenty years ago. I did not kill the king and queen of Brimhold. There are a number in this room that can confirm I was in Sil Tullian. Since then, I have served Ithirdis as the *Valen* of my own *tatell*, though I have stayed on this side of the chasm most of the time. Brimhold already believes I am protected by the elves here. There is no point in proving them right." The Red Elf stopped as if finished with her excuses, but Sydney was not ready to believe so easily.

"If you had nothing to do with the attack on Delm, then how did my own people see you there? It's easy enough to get others to lie for you."

Novah snorted. "Believe what you want. Perhaps I was framed, or the citizens of Brimhold can't tell one elf from another. Either way, I never stepped foot in that castle."

"Fine. Say I take you at your word. Would anyone have a reason to frame you?"

The surrounding elves stiffened at the question. Flindir glanced away, wringing his hands. The Red Elf raised her chin even higher, if that was possible.

"Before I held a place in the Ithirdi army, I made a number of enemies. I did things I'm not proud of. I'm sure you know the feeling, Captain Krane."

Sydney ignored the jab. "So what, you were some kind of mercenary? An assassin?"

"You don't have to continue, *Elucetor*." The human at the Red Elf's side spoke for the first time, her voice like gravel under a boot. She guarded Novah protectively.

"No, Darian," she replied, patting her hand. "I have nothing to hide. The past is the past." Novah gave Sydney a hard stare. "I assume you know of the Greyblood Scour?"

Bile rose to Sydney's throat as she nodded. She thought of that burnt out home tucked in the Wornwood. A child's skull buried in the dirt.

"I was... *involved.*"

The unspoken words were clear. The Scour was one thing frowned upon by decent people of all races and all kingdoms. If Novah took part, it meant she killed children. Innocents. Merely because they were greybloods with unexplored magic. In Sydney's mind, it elevated the Red Elf to a whole different breed of monster.

"By the gods, and you let her command soldiers?" Sydney asked the others with disgust. Novah stiffened, eyes flashing, but Lukaris stepped in before she could respond.

"Novah may have a dark past, but she was instrumental in ending the Scour. Without her, things might have gotten much worse."

"So, I'm supposed to trust her because she betrayed her own cause? A murderer and a traitor?" Sydney grumbled.

"*Some* people are capable of change, Captain Krane," Novah hissed. "I was young and foolish when I joined the Scour. I thought the greyblood magic was dangerous. A threat to the Light races. The blood on my hands was the price for protecting our future."

Across the tent, Ordell lowered his head, shoulders tight. A vein bulged on the side of his neck.

"Alright, so what changed your mind?" Sydney demanded.

"Darian," said the Red Elf. She took the other woman's hand, giving it a squeeze. "Near the Scour's end, I was charged with finding a greyblood girl who could cast visions into the minds of others. By the time I tracked her down, her family had hired protection. Darian and a few other warriors. I wasn't expecting them. We fought, and Darian won. She should have killed me. But, she didn't."

Sydney looked to Lukaris. It was a familiar story. Novah continued.

"It wasn't easy to convince me of the error in my ways. But Darian was persistent. She introduced me to the greyblood girl. The girl told me how she used her magic to give sight to those going through their Passing. She had a kind heart. And I almost killed her in cold blood, for what she *might* do." For the first time, something close to remorse wavered in the Red Elf's voice. "Things changed after that. I felt sick. I knew the Scour had to end. So, I went to the king. I turned myself in and offered to help destroy my own organization. When the scourers were cast down, the king pardoned me for my assistance."

The tent fell silent. Sydney stared at Novah, and the elf glared back, unblinking. If it was a lie, it was a good one. The twisting knots in Sydney's stomach grew tighter.

"Alright," she said. She turned once more to Lukaris. "I've heard enough from the Red Elf. I want to know about Briar."

The *Valen* sighed. "It's complicated."

"Then start from the beginning."

"Very well." He moved closer to the table, flattening the map with his fingertips. "I suppose the mess truly began around two years ago. I knew, as Novah knew during the Scour, that something had to change. A darkness grows in the Wornwood, and the eyes of Ithirdis are fixed on Brimhold. On a war with no end. I thought if I spoke with some of the humans, maybe I could slowly start us down the path to peace. I began in Cralin." He stabbed a finger on a tiny village next to the Thorburn Chasm. "I discovered that many Brims weren't happy about the war either. In fact, the fighting was sucking them dry. All their money went to taxes, all their children to battle…" Lukaris' eyes flicked to Sydney. "One day, I brought a human family a deer for their supper. The next, I helped a farmer scare off a bothersome wolf. The people I helped told the rest of the village. Soon, when elves were spotted in the trees, they were smiled upon. A few days and a few good deeds, and I had changed the hearts of an entire town."

"I recruited my *tatell* and Novah's to reach out to more villages. We stayed along the border for the most part. Briar was one of the few so far into Brimhold. We would help the humans as best we could, bringing food and helpful Light talismans, even medicines. Not all of the Brims accepted us, but many did. For a while, it seemed like we were making a difference."

Sydney thought back to the day Gilliad returned from Knotting. *The villagers did not welcome our presence,* he had said. *A few of them were hiding warriors from Ithirdas in their homes.* But now, Knotting lay in a pile of ash. The story was unfinished.

"What happened?" Sydney asked, knowing the answer ended with blood running down the streets of Briar.

"Cralin was the first. We could see the smoke from across the chasm. An entire village and all its people, destroyed." Lukaris shook his head. "We thought the attacks were random. Not every village we helped has burned. But now, with Knotting lost as well… it can't be a coincidence. Someone does not want peace between humans and elves, and what better way to stop it than destroying one side and framing the other?"

"And perhaps the same someone killed Brimhold's king and queen and blamed an elf?" Sydney guessed the *Valen's* thinking. Her head spun. It was too much. A lifetime worth of lies crashing down. Her eyes met Lukaris', and for a moment they steadied her. "What about Briar? I followed your tracks. You were there that day."

"I was afraid. I thought it best to warn the villages we had visited, just in case. We even let some of the humans take refuge in Ithirdis—"

"Refuge?" Sydney interrupted. "Where?"

"Somewhere safe," Lukaris replied, evading the question. Then, he must have seen the expression on her face. "No, I'm sorry, Sydney. Our scout saw riders headed for Briar, and we got there as fast as we could. I didn't even take the time to return Raiden to Firne. But we were too late. The town was already burning and… there was no one left to save."

She'd held the sliver of hope for only a moment, yet it still knocked the wind from her lungs. Sydney leaned forward, her knuckles white against the table. Flindir appeared at her side, healer's hands held ready.

"I'm fine," Sydney insisted. She took a deep breath. The elves were looking to her now, not with distrust, but with sympathy. Somehow it made everything worse.

"And you don't know who they are?" Sydney asked finally. "The riders that are murdering Brimhold's people?"

Lukaris lowered his head, almost ashamed. "We've tried tracking them, but it's hard searching Brimhold without getting caught ourselves. To answer your question… no. We don't know. The only thing I can promise you is that they aren't *us.*"

What a fool she'd been. What had she expected, coming here? All she wanted was justice for her family. She wanted to look their murderers in the eye and make them answer for their crimes. Instead, she'd followed the wrong tracks, involved herself with the wrong enemies. And now? She'd tangled herself in a web of secrets. She knew things about the elves that changed everything, that changed her. Where was she supposed to go from here? Who was she supposed to be?

Run. It was an instinct Sydney had known all her life.

"I need a moment." She raced past Flindir's comforting hands, Lukaris' protests, and out into the mountain air. She wasn't sure where she was headed, but she knew she needed time to think.

Her feet led her, as they often did, to the hillside overlooking Firne. She sat down heavy in the grass, her hands pulling at the blades, weaving them mindlessly into a never-ending braid.

What now? Her mind repeated the question over and over. If she returned to Delm — *when* she returned to Delm — how would she explain all of this to Brandon, to Gilliad, to the queen? How would she tell a kingdom that the war they had fought for twenty years was built on lies? And why should they believe the words of a random elf *tatell*? The Brims would call her mad at best, and a traitor at worst. But if she didn't tell them, didn't try to stop the fighting, then every death, every drop of blood moving forward would be on her hands.

Gods, it was so much easier when she could just fight without thinking about who was on the other end of her swords.

"Sydney," Lukaris said, his voice soft. As usual, she hadn't heard him approach, though she didn't know whether to blame his elvish stealth or her ruminating thoughts. He sat down beside her.

"I'm sorry. I know it's a lot to take in."

"You think?" Sydney responded dryly. She tossed her plait of grass away. "Tell me something, ace. What do you expect me to do with all of this information?"

Lukaris frowned. It didn't suit him. "Nothing."

She snorted. *"Nothing?"*

"At least, nothing you don't want to do. I don't have a secret motive here, Sydney. You asked for the truth, so I gave it to you."

"Did you? Because all I've gained is more questions and exposed lies. Neither of us are any closer to real answers. We don't know who attacked Delm all those years ago, or who is destroying Brimhold's villages now. Who killed my family." She brought her knees up to her chest, hugging them tight. "Maybe it doesn't matter anyway. Maybe the elves and humans were meant to be enemies all along. Our secret enemy just set the wheels in motion."

Lukaris shook his head. "No. I refuse to believe that."

Sydney turned to look at him, cheek resting on her arm. He stared at her the way he always did. Like there was a mystery inside of her that he could solve.

"How do you do that?"

He blinked. "Do what?"

"How do you stay so damn optimistic all the time?"

Lukaris laughed, the breeze ruffling his hair.

"If we don't hold on to hope, the darkness will always win."

"Maybe," Sydney muttered, picking at the grass.

"So, what *are* you planning to do? Now that you know everything?" Lukaris sounded nervous. She realized suddenly how much of a gamble he'd taken, trusting her.

"Well, let's see. If I go back to Brimhold and do nothing with what I know, I'm a monster. I could try to reason with the queen, but I doubt she would believe me without proof. I guess I could look for Briar's murderers on my own." Sydney sighed. "But then, I'm a deserter. Sounds like I don't have a good option."

"You could stay here," the *Valen* said softly.

She looked at him. "Stay here? Then, I'm a traitor."

"You wouldn't be fighting against your people. You'd be fighting to free them from this war."

Sydney shook her head. "I don't think they'd see it that way."

Lukaris let out a rush of breath that turned into a breeze. "Well, you don't have to decide right now. There's still some time before our arrangement is up. Maybe you'll see things more clearly then."

Sydney nodded, doubtful. Each passing day, the conflict inside her only grew. Who would she be when her days with the elves ran out?

32

Tales of Heroes

The first few nights of Koraline's captivity were spent in mourning. The princess sat huddled in the corner of her dank cell, tail bent and pressed to her chest. Unable to cry, dry heaves shook her body, and a tightness clawed at her throat. But the worst was her chest, which felt as if it might tear in two at the thought of Angler or her parents or dying alone in such a terrible place. If Arkyn noticed her grief, he said nothing. The nights were equally hard on him. When he slept, nightmares seized him. Koraline watched night after night as the man thrashed in his chains, muttering and crying out in his strange language. Between her fits of despair, the mermaid found herself puzzling over her cellmate. Was he innocent as he claimed to be? And if so, what could her captors want from him? What did they want from *her*?

Every morning, an older soldier with beady eyes and a balding head brought them bowls of cold porridge, dropping the food sloppily on the floor beside the prisoners. The first day, Koraline tried to make conversation with the guard, hoping she might charm some information from him. The attempt earned her a solid slap across the face. After that, she received her meals in silence. Once they had eaten their measly breakfast, the guard loosened Arkyn's chains and led him into a side chamber, allowing him to stretch his legs and relieve himself. The guard then entered Koraline's cell and scooped her roughly from the floor. Koraline loathed being carried like a child, but with no legs to stand upon, there was nothing to be done. The solider smelled of old tobacco and spoiled meat, and Koraline tried not to gag as he carried her past Arkyn and into the adjoining room. A large metal tub sat at the room's center. The guard dumped the princess unceremoniously into the grimy, gray water. Though the moisture soothed Koraline's dry scales, the water had a sticky quality, with dried blood crusting the edges of the tub. She was happy to return to her cell.

Then, *he* came.

Malcolm spent a good part of the day with Arkyn, poking, cutting, slicing. The warden did unspeakable things, things Koraline saw on the backs of her eyelids, in her dreams. Things she would never unsee. Still, Arkyn persisted, never giving in to the torture and never giving Malcolm what he needed. But the prisoner's spirit could not protect him from the pain, and Koraline listened to his screams until even Malcolm's oily voice seemed a welcome relief.

"All of this will stop when you choose to cooperate," he cooed for what felt like the hundredth time.

Arkyn said nothing, a thin strand of blood dripping from his mouth.

And so, they began again.

Eventually, Malcolm would give up for the day. The warden said little, if anything, to Koraline, for which she was grateful. Her arm still ached where the monster's knife had sliced into her.

Once their leader had gone, the other guards would release the tension in Arkyn's chains, and the bleeding man would return to his spot against the wall. Soon, food would come again, this time a hard bread roll, some variety of charred meat, and a glass of warm water. Then another trip to the tub room. Then night, or what felt like night, came again.

Food. Water. Screams. Food. Water. Nightmares. Over and over the cycle went, an unending wheel.

Conversations with Arkyn became the light in the darkness. After Malcolm left, when the metallic stench of blood still hung in the air, Arkyn would lean against his wall, close his eyes, and ask Koraline for a story. The mermaid was happy to oblige, eager to fill the room with something other than screams. She told him stories from her childhood. Of Tikta Ocell, the first of the merfolk to wear human legs, and her adventures throughout the kingdoms. Of the Siren Uprising, all the lives and history that had been lost. She even recited the greatest story of all. The climax of the Shadow War, in which her ancestor, Asper Allantus, played a vital role. Arkyn smiled at that one, as if he knew something she didn't.

The man shared many legends of his own. A strange story about a winged fox named Uroc. The mythical dragon, Spectar, who was said to have a scale of every color and leave trails of rainbows in his wake. The tragic tale of Blonier and Lerin, two lovers cursed to be invisible to each other by a jealous witch. Arkyn was a good story teller. He gave each character a unique sound, his voice rising and falling as the adventures progressed. Koraline found herself hanging on every word. She relished in forgetting her worries, if only for a moment.

When the myths and epic tales ran dry, Koraline spoke of herself. She told Arkyn about the Crystal Keep, her parents, her few friends, even her rare excursions outside of Milanthos. She knew it might be unwise to reveal so much to a stranger, but the princess found herself trusting him. Despite the daily torment he experienced, the man never lost his laugh. She simply could not imagine him as her enemy. However, despite her openness, Arkyn said nothing about himself in return. Whenever Koraline asked about his past, she was met with a guarded expression and vague responses. It wasn't until a full week after her capture that Koraline finally began to get past the man's mysterious exterior.

"When I was young, I always watched other children playing with their brothers and sisters," Koraline started to say quietly, almost to herself. Malcolm had been particularly cruel that day, and Arkyn had said little since the warden departed. The mermaid did her best to fill the hollow silence. "I wanted that more then anything. Friends that were also your family."

"They're not all they're cracked up to be," Arkyn mused. The princess' head snapped up in surprise. He sat gazing at the dusty floor, blue eyes lost in thought.

"Oh? You have siblings?" Koraline spoke the question carefully, approaching the subject as she would a wild animal.

The man gave a tiny nod.

"You're lucky. I always wanted a brother or sister. But my parents thought they were barren when they had me. It's a miracle I was even born."

Arkyn barked a bitter laugh, so unlike his normal lighthearted chuckle. "I wouldn't call myself lucky. Your family sees you as a blessing. I was a curse. My brother was unbearable, my sister—" He cut off abruptly, leaning his head back against the stone wall. His shaggy hair cast dark shadows across his face.

"I'm sorry, I didn't mean to… Did something happen to them? Your family, I mean." She grasped at the metal bars that separated their cells. "You talk as if they're gone."

"They might as well be. But no. *I* left *them*."

"Why would you leave?" Koraline had always dreamed of traveling to new lands, but she couldn't imagine leaving Milanthos for good.

Never seeing her family again. It was her home, even if she sometimes felt like a prisoner there.

"Let's just say, they wanted me to be someone I wasn't. I ran away." He looked to her, doubt evident on his battered face. "I was a coward."

"A coward?" Koraline blurted, incredulous. "Arkyn, you are the bravest man I've ever met. I don't know a single person who could endure what you have."

"Oh, Malcolm doesn't scare me." He waved off her compliment, but she noticed his smile had returned.

"How old were you when you left home?" she asked.

"Fifteen. Five years ago."

"And you've been on your own all this time?"

Koraline seemed to have finally broken the wall into Arkyn's confidence. While he spoke no more about his family, or why he abandoned them, he talked for hours about the last five years. Koraline listened with fascination as young Arkyn made his way to the Valewood, where all lost and wayward creatures wash up. But the people of the Valewood were strange and lawless, and Arkyn could not find a place there. So he left, making his way into the bogs and moors of northern Nidaria. He took up whatever work he could find. A farm hand, a builder, a messenger.

"I was good at that last one," Arkyn bragged. "Villagers got their news in record time, and I never lost a letter." Still, Arkyn continued to wander. It wasn't until a blacksmith took him on as an apprentice that the young man finally tried to put down roots.

"Cole was his name. A good man. He gave me a chance, taught me his trade. He even let me sleep in his barn and eat supper with his family. I stayed with them for nearly a year."

"What happened?" Koraline asked fearfully.

Chained hands curling into fists, Arkyn glowered at a blood stain on the floor. "Malcolm happened. He rode into town, looking beat up and road sore. He claimed bandits attacked him on the road and stole everything but his horse. I guess Cole and his family had a thing for broken strangers. They invited him to spend the night."

Koraline decided she didn't want to hear the rest. She saw where it ended, here, in this place, with iron bars and blood on the floor. She preferred tales of heroes, where the champions won and the villains lost. But she wasn't living in a fantasy. So, she stayed silent, letting Arkyn finish his story.

"Everything was fine at first. We ate supper together. Malcolm seemed very interested in me and my past. He asked so many questions. How long had I been in town? Where had I come from? I managed to avoid most of them without seeming rude. After that, we all went to bed. Or so I thought. Not an hour after I returned to the barn, I heard a commotion up at the house."

Arkyn sat in silence for a long time. Koraline didn't press him. Her heart hammered in her chest, waiting to be broken. When he finally spoke, his voice cracked.

"I-I found Arri first. Cole's daughter. Her throat was cut. I had never seen so much blood. I screamed and screamed, but no one came to help. They were dead. All of them." Koraline pressed her hand to her mouth. Tears ran in silent tracks down Arkyn's face. "Men in masks came running into the house from all sides. I managed to kill a few, but they overwhelmed me. The last thing I remember is Malcolm pressing a rag to my face. I came in and out of consciousness, but when I finally woke up, I was here."

Koraline closed her eyes and leaned her head against the rough stone, the grooves scratching at her cheek. Was this the world she desired so much? Just a few weeks ago, she would have given anything to see it. But now she would trade it all for safety, for innocence, for ignorance. To return to who she was before.

"I'm so sorry." It was all she could think to say. She knew it wasn't enough.

"It's my fault." Arkyn's voice held the weight of a thousand worlds. "They're dead, because he was looking for me."

"No. Arkyn, no." The mermaid stuck a slender arm through the bars, her shoulder popping as she reached for her friend. "Give me your hand."

Hesitating, head lowered, Arkyn extended a hand. The chains tugged at his wrist, but Koraline managed to lock their fingers, her hand swallowed by his. His skin was like fire.

"Now look at me." The grief in those sapphire eyes almost broke her, but she held his gaze.

"It's not your fault, do you understand? None of it. It's *his*. You are not responsible for his actions." Koraline tried to keep her voice firm as she held his hand. She couldn't save Arkyn, or herself, from Malcolm or this cell. But maybe she could lift the guilt that haunted him.

Arkyn seemed to hear her, some of the anguish leaving his expression. He hesitated again, then nodded, giving her hand a final squeeze before releasing it.

"You're right. *He's* to blame. And when we get out of here, I will make him pay for what he's done."

"When *we* get out of here?" Koraline asked pointedly.

Arkyn blinked, surprise plain on his face. "Of course. You didn't think I would leave without you, did you *allska*?"

The princess found herself smiling. "I've been meaning to ask… what does *allska* mean?"

Arkyn returned her smile with a grin of his own. He lay down in the dirt, using his own arm for a pillow.

"I'll tell you someday. When we're far away from this place, safe and free. That's a promise."

33

Reflections

Dawn had just begun to brush the autumn sky when Camillea came to a halt in front of her floor length mirror. It was one her favorite pieces in the castle. Silver rimmed the edges in intricate swirls, like clouds on a windy day. At the top, an eagle soared with extended wings, feathers brushing the corners of the glass. Ancient and priceless and lovely.

But this morning, the queen's eyes fixed solely on the woman reflected back at her. She had dressed for travel in slim gray trousers and a modest shirt, and she'd already wrapped a violet cloak around her shoulders, necessary for the morning chill that never seemed to work its way from the castle's bones. The royal crown usually sat proudly atop the queen's straw hair, but it was noticeably absent from the reflection. Camillea felt naked without its familiar weight.

Sometimes the queen did not recognize the woman she saw in the mirror. She couldn't find herself in the long neck or the graceful gowns or the careful set of her mouth. She remembered the girl she used to be, and she saw none of her in this pale queen.

Thankfully, the eyes remained the same. Behind the icy blue, somewhere in the depths of her gaze, Camillea saw the child who'd

279

lost her family, who'd started a war at an age when others learned to love and laugh and play. Her eyes always grounded her, even when the rest of the world seemed strange and foreign. The only constant in her life.

"Your Majesty?"

Gilliad Norwell stood in her doorway, looking tired. He always looked tired, gray and sad as morning ash.

"Yes, General?" Camillea asked. She allowed herself a final glance in the mirror.

"Your soldiers are ready to depart," Gilliad grumbled. A frown sat somewhere beneath the man's beard.

"Is something the matter?"

"I still think you should stay here," he admitted. "Let me lead this mission in your place."

Camillea shook her head, strands of hair freeing themselves from their braid. "As I've said, my informant will only work with me. Besides, I need to see this through. For my parents. For all of Brimhold."

"Then at least let me come with you," Gilliad persisted. Camillea crossed the room, boots landing softly on the stone floor, and placed a hand on his shoulder.

"And who will I leave in charge while we're gone? Captain Doren? Lady Elizabeth?" The queen laughed at the general's wince. "You see, I need you here, Gilliad. Please, do this for me."

"Of course, my queen," he relented, giving her the smallest of bows. "I will guard Delm with my life until your safe return."

"Thank you," Camillea said with a smile. "I will meet you at the stables."

The general slipped away. Moving like a wraith, Camillea glided to the end of her bed where an oak chest sat. She pulled at the cold, iron lock and lifted the lid with a tug. Inside, a sword lay in its sheath, swaddled like a baby among folds of fabric. For a moment, the queen merely stared at the blade, her fingers hovering above the grip. When she finally lifted the weapon, it seemed to sigh with relief. It had been an age since she'd held it in her hands. Since its steel had tasted flesh.

It begins now. Not a second longer. My justice is too long coming.

She strapped the sword to her waist and made for the door. The mirror flashed out of the corner of her eye, but she didn't look. She no longer needed to see the person she'd become. She knew who she was. She felt it in the set of her jaw and the blade on her hip.

And so, the queen of Brimhold went to war.

34

Brewing Storms

"At first, we thought it was a sandstorm," Flindir said dramatically. Firelight cast eerie shapes across his expressive face. Outside the safety of their tent, the weather raged in a torrent of rain and wind. Thunder rattled the air. "But as we drew closer, I knew it had to be something else. The shape was too solid, too fast. It grew taller when we approached, big as a tree and three times as wide. When I realized what it was, my stomach dropped to my toes."

"A sand troll," Lukaris continued. Raiden stood on his seat, leaning towards the story. Sydney rolled her eyes. "The color of ground cinnamon with skin like stone. The beast charged across the earth in our direction. None of Flin's magic could aid us so deep in the Sandmarch, and mine beat uselessly against the creature's hide."

"What did you do?" Raiden demanded. Itari gave the boy an amused glance from her place across the table, feet propped up on the wood.

"We tried to fight, at first, but it didn't take us long to realize we were outmatched. The troll swung a great rocky fist and shattered my sword in two," Flindir continued. "When it came to it, we had two choices. Die or flee. So, we ran. We raced towards a fissure in the wastelands, hoping it would slow the beast down. I could feel the troll's pounding steps through my boots as it chased us."

"I reached the cleft first," said Lukaris. "I managed to jump the distance, but when I turned around, the troll was barreling down on Flindir. Sand and rock gave way as their collective weight corroded the cliff's edge. Flin leapt, and I could tell he wasn't going to make it. I only just managed to grab his hand before he plummeted into the fissure."

"And what happened to the troll?" Raiden asked eagerly.

"It crawled back into the storybook it came from," Sydney answered for them. "I hate to be the one to tell you this, kid, but trolls don't exist."

"They do too!" the boy protested, frowning as he teetered on his chair.

"He's right, *scolas*," Itari spoke up. The Viridian tugged on her head scarf. "Sand trolls are very real. I used to see them from a distance at the desert's edge, where the dunes meet the march. However, to think that anyone here has fought one and lived is… laughable."

"You doubt me, my love?" Flindir exclaimed with indignation. He looped an arm around her waist, pulling her close.

"Only your eyesight," Itari laughed, eyes dancing. She pressed a kiss to his lips before he could argue further.

"I doubt a lot more than that," Novah spoke up from the corner. Sydney started. They'd stayed so silent, she'd forgotten the Red Elf and her human companion, Darian, had joined them.

"Well, *I* believe you, Flin," Raiden promised. "You too, Luka."

"I can always count on you, *osan*," Lukaris said with a fond smile. He ruffled the boy's hair. "To answer your question, the troll gave up the chase. It disappeared over the southern march, never to be seen again."

"Now I know you're lying," Sydney teased. "What kind of troll gives up such easy prey?"

A good natured argument broke out, warm and familiar as the dwindling fire.

Thunder cracked, and the tent flap whipped aside, flinging water droplets onto those nearest to the opening. Ordell filled the gap. He stood drenched to the bone, water running in rivulets down his tattooed skull. Smiles fell away at his expression.

"*Valen*. One of my birds carries a message from Nidaria," the elf grunted. Lukaris stood, face tight.

"What is it, *avun?*"

Ordell cleared his throat. "The news might not be fit for all ears." To Sydney's surprise, his gaze flickered to Raiden.

"*Osan*, why don't you go check on Honey? I'm sure she's miserable in this weather," Lukaris said smoothly. Raiden's mouth grew flat with a stubbornness known only to children.

"Luka, I—"

"Please, *osan?*" Lukaris asked, sounding tired. The resistance slipped from Raiden's eyes.

"Fine." He slipped out of the tent, casting one final glance at his uncle's grim face.

"Tell us," the *Valen* said when Raiden was out of earshot.

"The Crystal Keep was attacked. A number of merfolk are dead. The princess..." Ordell shook his head. "The princess was taken."

Color drained from Lukaris' face as he collapsed into Raiden's vacant chair. Shocked silence filled the tent, thick and suffocating. Sydney's head began to throb. Just as things were starting to unravel, a new knot was thrust into their midst.

"Princess Koraline?" Flindir whispered, round eyes brimming. "Who would do this?"

"*Us*, apparently," Ordell said.

Lukaris' eyes flashed. "What do you mean?"

"A ransom note was sent by the kidnappers. It demanded that Brimhold surrender the war. You can guess who the Brims are blaming."

"The merfolk are our allies. Queen Camillea can't really think we'd risk that friendship," Itari reasoned.

Lukaris looked to Sydney. She could feel the unspoken question burning between them in the air.

"Camillea is a reasonable ruler," Sydney began, prefacing her treasonous thoughts. "But she won't consider the elves innocent when there's even a chance they could be guilty. She'll be the first to blame Ithirdas for this attack."

Lukaris leaned back in his chair, the wood groaning. Somehow he looked achingly young and impossibly old all at once.

"And how will your queen respond? Will she give up her war for the sake of an innocent life?"

Sydney knew that answer too.

"No."

No one spoke. Outside, the rain sounded sad. It beat a steady melody against the tent's canvas roof.

"More fuel for the fire," Lukaris murmured, so quietly the words were almost lost to the storm. Sydney leaned forward, pulling at the threads of his thoughts.

"You think this is the work of our mysterious third party? It will certainly stir up fresh hatred between our kingdoms," she said bitterly. "Only now they've dragged Nidaria into the fray. When will it be enough?"

The *Valen* sighed. "I don't know."

Across the tent, Novah got to her feet. Sydney glared. She still couldn't shake the feeling that the Red Elf had started them down this path of blood and death.

"I say we take our *tatells* and search for the princess," Novah said in her velvet voice. She punched an angry fist into her hand. "I'm tired of receiving the blame for crimes we didn't commit."

Ordell scowled, hardly looking in the Red Elf's direction. "We wouldn't even know where to begin. Besides, do you forget that the entirety of Brimhold lies between us and Nidaria? You may think yourself invincible, but we can't help anyone from inside a cell."

Novah's chin lifted, eyes as fiery as her hair, but Lukaris spoke first.

"Ordell's right. It's too dangerous. I won't risk all of your safety on such slim chances."

"So, what *will* we do?" Flindir asked softly. They all looked to the *Valen*. Sydney saw Lukaris falter as the weight of their loyalty fell upon him. She knew the feeling. How were you supposed to lead when you were lost yourself?

"For now, we wait for orders from Sil Tullian. The king will decide how to face this threat," he said at last. His voice carried the same tone as the dying wind and only half its strength.

"*At Valen—*"

"*Dynas—*"

"Are you sure—"

"Enough," Lukaris snapped, silencing the clamor of voices. The elf got to his feet. "That's my decision. Now, if you'll excuse me."

The *Valen* departed, his shoulders hunched against the storm. The remaining elves fell into a tense silence. Novah leaned back in her chair, arms crossed and face tight. Darian said nothing, placing a comforting hand on the Red Elf's shoulder. Ordell only shook his head.

Itari and Flindir exchanged a look, as if deciding which one of them would go after their friend. Sydney sighed and stood.

"I've got this," she told them. Flindir blinked, eyes grateful. She pulled up the hood of her cloak and trudged out into the rain.

By the time she reached Lukaris' tent, Sydney was soaked to the bone. She hovered outside the entrance, shaking the mud from her boots.

"You in there, ace? Can I come in?"

A low grunt echoed from inside. Taking that as a yes, she slipped in beneath the thick, green canvas.

Sydney had never been inside Lukaris' tent before. It was homier than she'd expected. A large, gray hammock dominated half the space, attached to two tall pine trees whose trucks acted as part of the wall. Rimming the room were stacks upon stacks of books and scrolls and maps. Sydney tried to read a few of the titles, but the covers were worn and bare. In the corner, a familiar bundle of items leaned against a tent post. Sydney tried not to stare longingly at her captured belongings as she moved further into the room, her feet stepping on stray arrows that littered the earth.

Lukaris sat across from her at a table, the surface covered in fresh wood shavings. The elf carved at a tiny sculpture, green eyes downcast and focused.

"I was expecting Flindir," the *Valen* noted. He didn't look up from his craft.

Sydney took the seat across from him. Water dripped from her cloak onto the flattened grass. "I thought you could use an impartial ear."

"You are many things, Sydney Krane," Lukaris chuckled. "But impartial isn't one of them."

She shrugged, toying with a few wayward wood shavings. Waiting.

"Are they angry with me?" the elf asked when she made no move to speak. Anxiety lined his tone.

"No. Well, maybe Novah. But who cares what the Red Elf thinks?"

A small smile slipped across his lips. "She's really not that bad once you get to know her."

"I'll take your word for it," Sydney quipped. "Don't try to change the subject."

Lukaris sighed, laying his carving knife gently on the table. He passed a hand through his still damp hair and finally met her eyes.

"Answer something for me, Sydney. Do you ever wish you weren't captain of the Honor Guard? That the responsibility had gone to someone else?"

Sydney didn't have to ponder.

"No."

"Never?" the elf asked, sounding disappointed.

"The truth is, I *asked* to be made captain," Sydney said. "Well, more like demanded."

"Really?" His high forehead furrowed. "Why?"

"Because I deserved it," Sydney admitted, knowing how arrogant it sounded. "Because the duty would've fallen to my friend, Brandon, and I knew he wasn't ready to do it alone. Because I was ready for the challenge."

Sydney smiled. "But mostly, because I knew I would be damn good at it."

Lukaris didn't laugh like she'd expected. Instead, he sighed again.

"You're lucky. Leadership was never something I wanted. And I'm not sure I'm the best person for the job."

"For someone so clever, you sure can be dense, ace," Sydney marveled, shaking her head.

Lukaris blinked. "What do you mean?"

"You think you're a bad *Valen*? Have you talked to your warriors lately?" She waved a frustrated hand in the direction of camp. "Those elves out there would do anything for you. Kill for you, die for you… And even more impressive, they haven't laid a single hand on the enemy captain you dragged into their midst. Not even Sarcys. Because you ordered them not to. That's *loyalty*, feather-brain. And not the kind you earn through fear or obligation. I should know. They believe in you. They trust you."

The elf's lips twitched in the barest hint of a smile.

"I certainly can't doubt their allegiance. I just hope I deserve it."

Sydney moved forward, hoping to shake further sense into him, when something fluttered out of the folds of her damp cloak. Lukaris tracked the weathered sheet of paper as it landed in the grass, bent and soiled. Sydney's eyes caught a single word on the page. *Abigail.*

"What's that?"

"Don't!" Sydney snapped as Lukaris bent down to retrieve the letter. The elf recoiled, eyes wide. She scooped up the paper, desperately smoothing out the wrinkles. Water crept in at the edges, but otherwise the letter was unharmed. Sydney took a deep, shaking breath.

"I'm sorry," she exhaled, panic still hammering at her heart. "I shouldn't have... I didn't mean to yell."

"It's okay," Lukaris replied, cautious. He sat stiffly at the table like Sydney was a wild animal he might spook. Maybe she was.

"It's just..." Sydney swallowed. "This is my sister's final letter. It's the last thing I have of her. Of Briar."

The *Valen* softened. "I see. I'm sorry, Sydney. I wish I could've helped them."

"Me too." Looking up, Sydney saw the elf's forest eyes locked on to the letter, curiosity peaked. She sighed. "You want to read it, don't you?"

"I'm sure it's none of my business," he replied with clearly a great deal of restraint.

"I'll let you read it on one condition," Sydney said. She brandished the letter between them, tempting. His fingers twitched. "This counts as the secret I owe you."

The elf laughed. "It's a deal."

He took the paper gently and spread it out on the table. Sydney paced the tent while he read. She already regretted this. She felt vulnerable. Exposed.

Lukaris leaned back when he finished. He passed a weary hand across his face as he passed the letter back to her.

"I'm sorry," he said again. "Your family should still be here. This shouldn't be your sister's last letter. Maybe I was wrong to try and mend the rift between our kingdoms. If Briar's destroyers are really targeting the villages I helped… then their deaths *are* my fault. All of them."

If some small part of Sydney still clung to the idea that the elves were lying, that Lukaris had manipulated her from the start… it died in that moment. She knew the burden of misplaced guilt. And she saw the weight of it on the *Valen's* face.

"Well, I don't blame you. Not anymore. You were just trying to help," Sydney said.

Lukaris gave her a strange look. Not quite grateful, but something close. She looked down at the paper in her hands. She could still see where her tears had smudged the ink.

"At least you did *something.*"

"I'm sure you did everything you could," the elf assured her. After a pause, he asked. "Your father… how long had he been sick?"

Sydney swallowed a fresh lump in her throat. "I don't know. That letter was the first time I'd heard from my family in nine years."

"I don't understand," Lukaris frowned. "You didn't receive other letters?"

"I got them. I just never read them." Sydney shoved the parchment back into her cloak, suddenly bitter.

Brandon would have goaded her for more. Gilliad would have recycled some advice he stole from an old story and left her alone to her thoughts. But Lukaris just stared at her. Ready and waiting for whatever she decided to share. Maybe that's why she always seemed to spill her secrets around him.

"I was afraid," Sydney finally blurted.

"Afraid of what?"

"I guess… At first, I was afraid reading Abi's letters would send me running back to Briar. Then, I was afraid it had been too long, and I had changed into someone my family wouldn't recognize. And…" Sydney looked down again. "I was even afraid that they were better off without me."

Outside, the rain fell in a chorus of drops, pelting the canvas above them. Meanwhile, Lukaris continued to watch her in that quiet, off-putting way of his.

"I know it's stupid," Sydney snapped when she couldn't take his silence any longer.

"No," the elf said softly. "No, it's not. I think that's an awful lot of fear for a child to carry."

"Yes, well, I'm not afraid any more. Now, I'm just angry."

Lukaris sighed, picking up his whittling once more. The sound of metal against wood was lost to the storm.

"Be careful, Sydney. Fear can unravel you. But fury can destroy you altogether."

35

Dark Waters

All her life, Koraline had valued bravery.

It was so rare, so unheard of, among her people. The merfolk had a tendency to hide, to swim away from trouble until the waters stilled. And if the danger didn't affect them, well, then they ignored it entirely. Koraline wanted to be different. A courageous leader. When other kingdoms looked to Nidaria, they would see strength, not cowardice. She had tried to emphasize that sentiment to her parents, the last night she saw them. The night everything had changed.

But bravery can only come after fear. And as time lost all meaning in the prison that Koraline and Arkyn shared, the mermaid came to realize she had never truly been afraid. Not until this cell, with its screams and blood-stained floor. Now the fear ate away at her, a constant stream of voices whispering horrors into her ear. Dark thoughts about her family, her kingdom, even Arkyn. But more than anything, though she hated to admit it, Koraline feared for herself. *You will die here*, the voices murmured, soft and quiet and constant. *And no one will miss you when you're gone.*

Every day, captivity chipped away at the mermaid's spirit. Slowly, the princess noticed changes, not to her surroundings, but to herself. She had always been thin, but now her bones grew sharp, sticking out beneath her skin as she ate less and less. Her hair hung like straw, and her golden scales turned dull and dry despite daily dips in the tub. And as her body withered, her mind spiraled with it. Late at night, when the torches grew dim, Koraline was sure she saw something, or someone, moving in the shadows. A flash of red out of the corner of her eye. An object moving, there one moment and gone the next. More food appearing, when she was certain she'd eaten it all. Even ghosts seemed a possibility as her nightmare raged on.

The mermaid knew Arkyn worried, so she tried to harness even a piece of her companion's bravery. She continued to laugh at his stories, offer him comfort, give words of encouragement. But as the days bled into weeks, Koraline's act began to slip, and the parts of herself that were strong and hopeful began to fade. Even friendship could not pull her to the surface.

One day, during her allotted time in the rusting tub, Koraline forced her eyes closed. She tried to block out the dim room, the basin, even the beady-eyed man watching her every movement. If she maneuvered just right, she could suspend perfectly in the tepid water. With nothing tying her to the prison, the mermaid could imagine herself somewhere else. Somewhere far away. Perhaps she lay in the shallows near Milanthos, tanning in the afternoon sunlight. Or maybe she floated in a peaceful lagoon, surrounded by fragrant summer blooms and soothing currents. Or perhaps, if she focused hard enough, the princess could even see herself in the Crystal Keep, her parents swimming next to her. And Angler, alive and well with a smile on his face.

The prison door creaked open, snapping Koraline from her daydreams. Cold metal grazed her back, and the smell of blood and dirt came rushing to greet her. The nightmare lived on. With a sigh, the princess opened her eyes.

Malcolm's face hovered next to hers.

The warden's hand clasped over her mouth as Koraline tried to scream. He held a finger to his lips.

"Ssh, ssh, no need for that, Princess," said Malcolm. The point of his dagger appeared at the edge of Koraline's vision, settling sharply on her collar bone. "No screaming today. Understand?"

The mermaid nodded her head as much as she was able, and her captor's hand fell away.

"Very good. Much more cooperative than my *other* guest." The scarred man cast a glare towards the doorway, towards Arkyn. "But then, you're still causing me problems, aren't you? Your capture has not elicited the desired response. And that makes my employer angry. Angry with *me*. And I can't have that, now can I?"

"I don't know what you want from me," Koraline whispered, voice shaking. Her hands knotted into fists beneath the tepid water. *Coward.*

"Unfortunately, there is nothing more you can contribute. You're a puppet, my dear, just a small piece of a grander scheme. Unless…" The dagger dug a little deeper into Koraline's neck. She whimpered, despite herself. Malcolm's breath tickled her ear. "Perhaps no one is taking your capture seriously. Maybe we should send a little present? Something of yours, so my intentions are not misunderstood again."

Malcolm traced the dagger along her jawline, down her chest, along her arm. Koraline shivered, bile rising to her throat as she tried to stay perfectly still. "Maybe a finger?" The blade dragged through the water, coming to rest at the foot of the tub. "Or a fin? Something a little more personal?" Heart pounding, the mermaid tried not to meet the monster's eyes. But Malcolm wouldn't have it. He grasped her chin in one hand, forcing his face next to hers. His scar stared at her, red and ragged, as the warden smiled. "Or maybe an eye.

Such pretty eyes." For a moment, the two stared at each other, the mermaid and the beast. Koraline's chest heaved with fear. The blade hung steady in its master's grip. But eventually, Malcolm sighed, releasing Koraline's face and brushing back a golden lock of hair. Gentle, like a lover instead of a butcher.

"Sadly, my employer still wants you more or less *unharmed.* So for now…" Malcolm reached behind Koraline, and in a single swift motion, cut off a large piece of her hair. "…this will have to do."

Relief crashed over her in a wave, lungs shuddering as they struggled to breath once more.

"As always, Princess." Malcolm waved her severed hair like a flag of victory as he backed from the room. "Thank you for your cooperation."

As quickly as he had entered, the warden was gone.

Koraline wanted to scream. She wanted to shout, to cry, to scrub the feeling of that monster's touch from her skin. But her body refused to move, her limbs stiff with fear. She let the silent soldier carry her limp form back to the main chamber. As they passed through Arkyn's cell, the chained man rose to his feet. Koraline's carrier ground to a halt.

"Sit down," the bald soldier barked, his voice like gravel.

Arkyn looked as if he wished to fight the order, but when he met Koraline's eyes, he slid back to the floor. Koraline's keeper returned her to her cell, shutting the door with unnecessary force before departing.

Arkyn strained against his chains. "*Allska*, are you ok? What happened?"

Koraline didn't answer. She curled her tail towards her chest, wrapping both arms around herself. Golden hair surrounded her face like a veil.

"Princess, please. *Koraline.*"

"He… he…" The mermaid took a deep, shuddering breath. "He didn't hurt me." *Not on the outside, at least.*

When she looked to Arkyn, his eyes were two smoldering blue flames. "What *did* he do?"

"He took some of my hair. He talked about taking… other things." Koraline hugged herself tighter, remembering the kiss of metal as Malcolm's knife traced her body. "He's trying to scare my parents, I think. Whatever ransom he hoped to receive for my kidnapping, he isn't getting it."

Arkyn's hands clawed at the dirt floor, mouth set in a hard line.

"I've never considered myself a violent person." The man spoke softly, but the words were sharp. "But by the gods, I want nothing more than to kill that man."

"I might beat you to it," Koraline mumbled against her fin.

Arkyn laughed that deep, wholesome laugh that echoed within Koraline's own chest. She loved that. That she could still make him laugh while everything else crumbled around her.

"I would gladly allow you the honor, *allska*."

When silence settled over them again, Koraline asked, "Arkyn?"

"Yes?"

"How do you do it?"

He raised his eyebrows. "Do what?"

"How do you stay so strong? Malcolm does awful things to you every day, and you still resist him. He's barely spared me a few sentences. Not that I'm complaining." Koraline traced the thin line on her arm, from that first day in captivity. "But even passing glances from him leave me cowering. I'm terrified *constantly*, Arkyn. I can't stand it. How do you do it?"

"I guess… I guess it helps that part of me feels like I deserve everything that's happened. Oh, don't look at me like that," Arkyn groaned at the mermaid's expression. "I didn't say that for the sympathy, I'm just being honest. But really, enduring Malcolm is easy. Because in the end, bravery isn't about what you fear. It's about what you love."

The words sparked something in Koraline's chest. "What do you mean?"

"I loved my mentor, Cole. I loved his family. They took me in and gave me a place to belong. When Malcolm is tearing into me, and I want to surrender, I think of them. I won't give their murderer the satisfaction of breaking me."

"And that makes you less afraid?" the princess asked.

"No," Arkyn replied with a sad shake of his head. "But it makes it easier to fight back. Who is it that you love?"

Koraline took another calming breath and closed her eyes. "I love… my family. I love my people. Each and every good heart that makes Nidaria what it is."

When she looked up, she noted Arkyn staring at her with a strange expression. He quickly cleared his throat.

"Good. From now on, when this place is too much to bear, you think of them. Try it."

"Now?"

"You have somewhere else to be, *allska*?" Arkyn teased.

Feeling silly, Koraline closed her eyes again. Malcolm's face loomed behind her eyelids the way it always did, haunting her night and day. She felt his breath on her face, heard that sick, oily voice. But then, she saw her mother's eyes. King Triak and Angler stood at her shoulders and, behind her, all of Nidaria. Her kingdom. Her home. All Koraline had ever wanted was to be the ruler her people deserved. What would they ask of her now? Her parents never expected bravery, and some merfolk might say survival itself was enough. But it wasn't, not for her. She needed to prove that strength was not reserved for other kingdoms. Other races. She had to give her people a better version of herself. Even if they never got the chance to see it. Hopeful and determined, a beacon for the future, no matter how short lived.

"Better?" Arkyn asked as her eyes fluttered open.

"Yes," she admitted. The crushing weight that sat on her heart had lifted a little. "But, I'm still afraid."

"I would be worried if you weren't."

"Thank you, Arkyn. I don't know how I'd face all this without you here."

He grinned. "I'll admit, things have been a tad brighter since you came along, *allska*. Though, I'm still not entirely convinced you weren't sent here by the enemy. You still laugh at too many of my jokes."

"Maybe I have a low comedic bar."

"Ouch. Words hurt, you know," Arkyn protested, dramatically clutching his chest as if someone had struck him. They both laughed for a minute, some of the dark knots of the day unraveling.

"You know, sometimes I wish we had met each other some other way," Koraline mused.

"Sometimes?" Arkyn asked, incredulous.

"Oh, you know what I mean. It would have been nice to know you out there, in the world. Maybe I could've met you in a quaint pub in the Valewood or on the road from the marshes to Milanthos. You might've shown me all the places from your stories. I could've taken you to the highest towers of the Crystal Keep, where you feel like you can see every drop of the ocean spread out before you."

Dark hair guarded Arkyn's face, his eyes tinged with red. "You talk as if those things can't happen. We can see all of Soarden together, if that's what you want. We *will* get out of here, *allska*."

"How?" Koraline asked, voice sad.

"I…" Arkyn swallowed. "I don't know."

"And how long until Malcolm decides we're no longer worth the effort?"

Arkyn didn't reply, his shoulders tight. The princess had her answer.

"Well," Koraline spoke softly. She let her eyelids fall closed. For once, no demons lurked behind them. "It was a nice dream, at least."

36

Starflies and Shadows

Sydney had already settled into her tent for the evening when she heard gentle footsteps outside. She swung both legs out of her hammock.

"Who's there?"

A spiky head popped in through the opening.

"*Allon*, Sydney!" Raiden greeted her with a grin. "I thought you could use some fresh air. Want to go on an adventure?"

She couldn't help but smile in response. "Always."

The boy led her outside, practically vibrating with excitement. He started skipping in the direction of the forest. Away from camp. *Out* of camp. Sydney slid to a stop.

"Woah, kid. I don't think I should… I don't think I'm allowed to leave Firne."

Raiden spun around. "Of course you are. Luka said it's okay."

"Did he now?" Sydney replied, crossing her arms at the obvious lie.

"He did." Lukaris materialized at her elbow, quiet as the dead. Sydney prided herself for not jumping out of her skin.

"Let me get this straight," Sydney said, disbelieving. "You're trusting me to go out into the Wornwood at night. Alone. With Raiden?"

"Yes?" the *Valen* answered. His eyebrows lifted. "Is there a reason I shouldn't?"

"Of course not, it's just…"

"Hurry up, Sydney!" Raiden shouted from the edge of the trees. At this point, the young elf was hopping eagerly from foot to foot.

"Have a good evening," Lukaris chuckled. He raised his voice, so Raiden could hear. "And *osan,* no more talking to mountain lions. I mean it!"

"Ah, come on!" came Raiden's distant grumble of protest.

Lukaris held up a hand as Sydney turned to go. "One more thing. Take care of my brother, will you?"

Sydney glanced at Raiden, jumping and waving, barefoot and brazen. When she turned back to Lukaris, her throat was tight.

"You have my word," she promised. Lukaris smiled.

"Off you go, then."

Raiden led Sydney through the trees, bounding and chattering the entire way. The night was bright from a million stars, yet they still had to pick their way carefully through the shadowed undergrowth. They walked for quite a while before Raiden finally turned back to her. He reached up to Sydney's face.

"Close your eyes, close your eyes," the boy demanded.

"I'll run face first into a tree."

"No, you won't. I won't let you."

Sydney sighed but obliged. Raiden's hand found hers, and he led her through the last stretch of forest. He placed her on what she could only assume was a rotting log, before sitting to her left.

"Okay, you can open them," he whispered.

She did. Before her lay nothing but empty forest. She raised an eyebrow at Raiden.

"A bit of a let down, kid, I have to admit."

"Wait, wait!" Raiden cupped his hands around his mouth. *"Eluce!"*

The word echoed through the trees. A pause. Then, the Wornwood erupted to life. A thousand twinkling lights lit up the trunks, the branches, the air itself. The lights swayed, moving in erratic patterns, like sparks from a fire. Sydney sucked in a breath.

"Starflies," she whispered as one of the creatures landed on her arm. Light pulsed from the bulb in its abdomen, on and off, on and off.

"Do you like them?" Raiden asked sheepishly.

"They're incredible," said Sydney. She stepped further into the swarm of glowing bugs. "Can you speak to them?"

The boy cocked his head. "Sort of. Bugs are harder. They don't communicate the way we do. Their minds are small. But they understand me well enough."

Sydney raised her hand, and the creatures parted in the air. "I haven't seen starflies in a long time. Years. When I was little, all the children in Briar used to catch them in glass jars and leave them on their windowsills."

Raiden frowned at that. "Catch them? Why?"

"Because they were beautiful, I suppose. It was like bringing a piece of the night sky inside with you."

"You don't have to own something for it to be beautiful," the boy said, his frown deepening. "Did you keep them prisoner forever?"

"No," she reassured him. "We would release them the next day. They would always stop shining after a while."

"Of course they did. I'm sure they didn't liked being kept in little glass cages."

Sydney could tell he was upset. "I'm sorry, Raiden. We were just kids. We didn't know any better. It's not something I would do now."

Her words seemed to relieve some of his distress. A starfly landed on his small nose. His eyes crossed to focus on the creature better, but it took flight after only a moment. The boy smiled.

"Come and see."

They moved on through the forest. Everywhere they turned, little specks of golden light dotted the sky, blending with the stars. Raiden laughed, dancing and skipping through his private swarm. Sydney held a few of the creatures in her hand, marveling at the orange glow that radiated through her skin. It was a pure and simple magic. Eventually, Sydney and Raiden came to rest on a small outcropping, overlooking the glittering forest.

Raiden was unusually quiet. His soft green eyes held a reflective look that Sydney had only ever seen on his brother.

"Raiden, do you like it here?" Sydney asked on a whim.

"What do you mean?" the boy replied. His eyes were fixed on a starfly that had settled on his knee.

"Do you like it in Firne? With your brother and the *tatell*?"

He still seemed to be giving her only half of his attention. He merely shrugged in response.

Sydney decided to take a different approach. "Ok. If you could be anything, or do anything, what would it be?"

Raiden finally looked up at her. The starfly took flight and joined its brethren in the trees.

"You'll laugh," he said. Sydney gave a quick shake of her head.

"I promise I won't."

"Well…" Raiden lowered his eyes as he spoke. His fingers twisted at the small wooden bear around his neck. "Back home, there was a man that would look after the horses. He would clean their stalls and take them through the streets of *Sil Tullian* when the weather was good. And he always smelled like wind and hay. Sometimes I would visit him and talk to the horses while he gave them new shoes. I always thought that would be a nice job to have."

"You want to be a stable boy?" Sydney tried and failed to keep the smile from her voice.

Raiden frowned. "You promised you wouldn't laugh!"

"I'm not, I'm not," she insisted. "It's not a bad dream. It just seems so… simple."

The boy pulled both knees to his chest, resting his chin. He gave a deep, heaving sigh, too big for his scrawny body. "It doesn't matter. My life will never get to be simple."

Before Sydney could respond, Raiden asked, "What about you? What did you want to be, when you were my age?"

It wasn't an easy question. When Sydney thought back to her childhood, she only remembered looking to the horizon, hosting sword fights in the Lost Wood, and dreaming by the seaside. She had never seen herself running a shop or starting a family, like any sensible young girl would. A life spent doing the same thing, day in and day out.

"Well, let's see. I'm too clumsy to be a blacksmith. Too impatient for cooking. Perhaps a lady in waiting? What do you think, kid, could you see me taking orders from some rich heiress?" Sydney batted her eyelashes innocently. Raiden bent over laughing. "No?"

"Come on, Sydney!" the boy protested when he'd recovered. "I told you mine."

Sydney let out a long breath. "Alright, alright. But it's not as easy to describe. Tell me, do you have a favorite hero from one of those old stories you elves like to tell?"

"Oh, like Uroc the fox?" Raiden asked eagerly.

"Er, sort of. How about Leona Nightslayer?"

His eyes widened. "Oh, she's the best. Itari told me a story where she saved an entire village from an army of Shaédin. With a single dagger. Blindfolded!"

Sydney laughed. "She's a good example then. I always wanted to be like her. Like all the people from those stories. I wanted to see amazing things, and do things others would write songs about."

"Oh. You wanted to be a hero," Raiden stated. He didn't seem to find the notion ridiculous.

Sydney laughed again, this time at herself. "Yeah, I guess so."

"Don't worry. When you and Luka stop the war, you'll be the greatest heroes in all of Soarden," he said, as if it were the easiest thing in the world. Sydney heart squeezed at his confidence.

"And what about after that? Who does the hero become after the world is saved?"

Raiden blinked, his expression making it clear he thought her very dense. "You'll still be Sydney. You don't have to be anything more than that."

*****

Sydney awoke disoriented and confused. Her body stiff from cold, she struggled into a sitting position. Where was she? Her eyes searched through the darkness, finally settling on a small form slumped against a nearby tree. Raiden. The night's activities came rushing back, and Sydney looked around in alarm. How long had they been asleep? Two hours? Three? She suppressed a groan as she imagined Lukaris' disapproval. He would never allow her to leave the camp unsupervised again.

Sydney shivered. It was cold. Very cold. Much too cold for a night in early autumn. The hairs on Sydney's arms began to rise as a prickling unease settled over her. The forest seemed strange and unfamiliar. Everything was too dark, too quiet, too cold. The trees, full of life in the daylight, stood like towering, wooden corpses. Before, the evening had been clear of clouds, but now Sydney couldn't make out a single star in the black sky. And if the darkness was unnerving, the silence was worse. The comforting call of an owl, the light chirping of crickets in the grass, even the whisper of a breeze through the leaves overhead would have been a welcome sound. But as it was, the forest was still. Still and cold and dark as death.

When Sydney's eyes finally fell back upon Raiden, she jumped in alarm. The boy was awake, sitting upright and rigid. His eyes were two round moons in his face as he stared at something through the trees. Sydney had never seen Raiden so afraid. It took all her courage to follow his gaze.

At first, Sydney thought they were wolves. They were shaped like wolves, three beasts on four legs, moving silently through the undergrowth. Their coats were so black that only their movement allowed them to be distinguished from the dark forest around them. But no, they were not wolves. Their muzzles were too long, with many rows of snapping fangs and tiny white pinpricks for eyes. Each step the monsters took seemed strange and gliding. The one closest to Sydney blurred, and its edges came in and out of focus. They were creatures of nightmare, shadows come to life.

"I can't understand them," Raiden whispered fearfully. "I don't know what they're saying. What are they?"

Sydney didn't respond. The boy's voice had pulled her back to the earth, reawakening old instincts. Her hands moved soundlessly across the ground as she searched for some kind of weapon. Her grasping fingers finally settled around a sturdy branch. It would have to do. Sydney locked eyes with Raiden, trying to appear calm. Her heart hammered in her chest.

"Run. Find help," Sydney breathed.

Raiden looked from Sydney to the makeshift weapon across her lap. His mouth settled in a flat line as he shook his head stubbornly. *Not without you.*

"I can't go. They'll see me."

She was right. From Raiden's position, he could easily slip away into the trees back towards the camp. But any movement by Sydney from her hiding place, and she would be quickly spotted by the monsters. Concern replaced the determination on the young elf's face. And were those tears? Sydney stared at the boy in surprise. He continued to baffle her.

"I'll be back," whispered Raiden. Then he was gone, fading into the night as if he had never been there at all. Sydney was alone.

Hardly daring to breath, Sydney rose slowly to her feet. She pressed her back against a tree, thankful for its solid presence. Fear clenched its claws around her heart, and her legs shook as she struggled to grip the branch with clammy hands. What had come over her? She was behaving like a frightened child rather than a high ranking soldier of Brimhold. *Hold yourself together, Sydney,* she thought to herself. *You have faced much worse than a few strange animals in the woods.* But still, the fear remained.

Sydney wasn't sure how long she stood there, shivering in the dark. It felt like a lifetime. She waited so long that, for a moment, she hoped the creatures might have wandered off in another direction. But then, she heard it. A whispering, so slight that at first Sydney was sure she imagined it. But there it was again. The sound felt like ice on the skin, sharp and cold despite its soft shell. It bore into her skull. Were the beasts communicating with each other? Unable to take the anticipation a moment longer, Sydney leapt from her hiding place towards the sound.

The monsters were closer than she expected. Two of them crouched in front of her, shifting smoothly from side to side. Their white eyes bore into her as the whispering grew. Sydney struck out with her branch, but the two creatures stayed just out of reach. But where was the third? No sooner had the thought crossed her mind when Sydney heard a murmur from behind her. Sydney cursed herself. She had let the beasts surround her. Filled with terror,

Sydney swung around blindly, managing to take aim at the third monster as it lunged.

The branch slid through the creature's head as if it was made from smoke instead of flesh and blood. For a moment, the beast blurred into a shapeless black mass. Sydney stared at the shadow, watching the monster reform before her eyes. The branch fell to the ground, useless. Sydney could only watch as the demons surrounded her. Monsters and ghosts. Sydney closed her eyes as the three beasts surged towards her at once. She was shocked to feel real weight knock into her, forcing her to the ground. Cold claws and fangs ripped into her. She heard herself scream, but the sound seemed muted and far away. A pressure settled in her chest. One of the monsters found her throat, its jaw wide and eager. Its sharp teeth brushed against bare skin.

Images danced across Sydney's eyelids. She saw a cave, large and dark and deep. It could fit an entire forest inside. Four shadowy figures outlined in firelight. Blood dripping down stone walls. Swords clashing. And a single set of haunting silver eyes.

A warm light flashed bright and clear through the trees, wiping the visions from Sydney's mind. The light pierced through the creatures, tearing them apart, piece by piece. The whispering became a screeching hiss, and then the shadows were no more, unable to reform under the relentless beam of light. Sydney gasped as the weight lifted from her chest, and air flooded back into her lungs. She lay unmoving in the grass, staring up at the night sky. She could see the stars again.

Three faces appeared above Sydney. The first was small and full of concern. Raiden. The next was pale and beautiful, haloed by a curtain of red hair. Novah. And the last face was angular yet kind, mirroring the anxiety of his brother. Lukaris. Sydney knew the faces were speaking to her, but the words seemed strange. Her splintered mind searched for meaning in the sounds.

"Sydney, can you hear me? Are you hurt?" That was Lukaris' voice. Yes, she was certain. It sounded so afraid.

"She's in shock. We should get her back to Ettee," said Novah grimly. Since when had the Red Elf cared for Sydney's well-being?

Lukaris grunted in agreement, and Sydney felt two arms slide beneath her, lifting her from the ground. The motion stung the wounds left over from the creatures' attack, and Sydney whimpered despite herself. Lukaris looked at her with alarm. Confused, Sydney glanced at her own arms. No cuts. No blood. Nothing. Shaking hands reached for her throat, expecting to find a fresh gaping wound, but the skin was smooth and unmarred. Strange. Sydney could still feel the monster's teeth digging into her.

"Luka," Raiden murmured as the three elves set off through the forest with Sydney in tow. "What were those... things?"

Before Lukaris could reply, Sydney spoke for the first time since her rescue. Her voice sounded odd and hoarse in her own ears. She let out the smallest of whispers, but the sound carried through the trees and into the night.

"Shadow-borne."

37

A New Day

"Lukaris, I said I'm fine," Sydney repeated for the hundredth time. It was the day after the attack. Sydney awoke sore and fatigued, but her mind was clear. The whole scene in the forest seemed like a dream, a lingering nightmare. But Lukaris' presence assured her the ordeal was very real. The elf captain had spent the morning following her around camp, watching her as if she would break at any moment, cracked glass ready to shatter.

"So you keep saying," he responded, dryly.

"Well, it's the truth."

"You know, you don't have to act so damn brave all the time," Lukaris huffed. He grabbed her elbow as they walked, turning her to face him. Sydney stared at him, shocked by his tone. Frustration radiated from the elf, his usual smile gone, his eyes haunted.

"It's not an act." She spoke with confidence, yet Sydney could still feel those cold claws digging into her. See those hollow, pinprick eyes. The memory made her shiver, and Lukaris cast her a knowing look.

"You were attacked by shadow-borne last night. That's enough to shake anyone's nerves. It's nothing to be ashamed of."

"They weren't shadow-borne," Sydney insisted. "Those monsters are gone. Locked away with the Sháedin, if they ever lived at all. They're a story we tell to frighten children. Nothing more."

"That's not what you said last night," Lukaris reminded her.

"Last night, I wasn't… I wasn't myself." *I was terrified. I was helpless. I was broken.* Sydney kept the weak thoughts to herself. Sometimes she still couldn't help but treat Lukaris as an enemy. Even if he kept looking at her with nothing but compassion. Eyes full to the brim with caring.

"That's an understatement. I don't know what you remember, Sydney, but I was there. You would barely speak. You had no wounds to speak of, but every movement caused you pain. You were like an empty shell. And your eyes…" Lukaris rubbed a hand through his unruly hair, shaking his head. "It wasn't *you.* Someone else was looking back at me. I—we didn't know if you would come back."

Sydney remembered. She remembered it all. But she hated the elf's pitying look, so she quipped, "Well, that would have saved you a lot of trouble. Are you sure you didn't send those things just to get rid of me?"

"Don't say that." Lukaris sounded so serious, it took Sydney a moment to gather herself. Sighing, she sat down, right there on the hillside, and started picking at the grass.

"Say you're right. Say they were shadow-borne. Where did they come from? And why now?"

Lukaris didn't reply. He joined her on the ground, looking out across the village. Throughout Firne, the elves were beginning their day. Some went down to the stream, collecting water in clay pots while children threw rocks into the trickling rapids. Others grabbed bows and spears before heading out into the forest to hunt down their next meal. And others still, opening shops, greeting their neighbors, playing and laughing and smiling. Lukaris looked at the village, at the people, with the same concern he showed Sydney, merely amplified. As if it was his sole duty to protect them. To keep them safe. Sydney had seen that look on him once before, and she was surprised how easily she could read it. The way she had always been able to read Brandon.

"Is this the darkness you were afraid of?" Sydney asked quietly. "The *something* that is so much worse than the war?"

"Do you remember those families Itari found a few weeks ago?" Lukaris' voice drifted on the breeze, soft as a breath. "Dead, with no wounds or signs of illness. What if it was the same creatures that attacked you? I don't know what any of this means. But it all feels connected. Something is stirring. Something old and dark. And if these monsters are coming up from the shadows… I hate to see what follows."

They sat there for a while, saying nothing, watching the village come to life before them. Sydney wished she could stay in that moment. Closing her eyes, she listened to the breeze whistle through the branches overhead. She felt the soft grass beneath her fingertips. Breathed in the comforting scent of damp earth. And for a brief instance, her worries ebbed. But eventually she sighed, opened her eyes, and rose to her feet.

"Whatever happens, we'll deal with it," Sydney said, brushing the dirt from her pants. "Ithirdis and Brimhold are strong kingdoms with even stronger people. They can handle a few shadows in the woods."

"Maybe. But can either of our kingdoms fight a war on two fronts?" the elf asked. He stood to meet Sydney's eyes. Green and gray as the forest around them.

Sydney didn't have a response to that. She turned to leave, but Lukaris held up a hand, barring her path.

"Wait. One more thing. I wanted to thank you."

"Thank me? For what?"

"For saving my brother." The air around them stilled, and Lukaris smiled his wry smile for the first time that day. It softened his face, smoothed out some of the angles.

"I promised I would take care of him, and I meant it."

"Still, it is a debt I will never be able to pay."

"Oh, I'm sure we could think of something," Sydney teased. Then, in a serious tone, she asked, "How is he, though? Raiden?"

Lukaris' smile faltered. "He hasn't left his tent. I think he feels guilty for leaving you out there."

Sydney sighed again. She'd been afraid of that. "Don't worry. I'll talk to him."

The elf looked relieved. *"Melánethe." Thank you.* "Again."

Waving off his gratitude, Sydney headed in the direction of Raiden's tent. She spared Lukaris a final glance, watching as he stood sentry on the hillside. His eyes met hers, and she glanced away. The pensive gaze made her uneasy. She wasn't sure what it meant. She wasn't sure what any of it meant.

*****

Sydney made it halfway across the camp when she ran into Novah.

Cursing, she forced herself not to glower. The Red Elf looked beautiful as always, well-rested, scarlet hair shining, as if the previous night had not affected her at all.

"Captain Krane," Novah said evenly. She arched a single eyebrow. "You look… better."

"I am." Sydney stood awkwardly, knowing what needed to be said. But gods, she would fight a hundred shadow-borne not to say it.

"Glad to hear it," Novah replied, waiting.

"I wanted…" Sydney swallowed. Her mouth tasted of ash. "I wanted to thank you. You saved my life. I know you didn't have to. I've done nothing to deserve it. So… thank you."

Novah smiled. A small smile, barely a twist at the corner of her mouth. But still, it was something. "I would have done the same for anyone in this camp. Maybe I'm not such a monster after all?"

With that, the elf departed, and Sydney found herself in need of a strong drink, despite the early hour. Unfortunately, she still had a job to do.

Raiden's tent rested within a giant yew tree, the bottom branches high above Sydney's head. Small grooves dug into the bark, leading to a wooden platform wrapped in brown canvas and covered in sheets of moss. The perfect hideout for Raiden, a small bird perched in his roost. Sydney, however, was not a bird, and she decided to call out to the boy rather than make the climb. Besides, Honey lay wrapped around the base of the tree trunk, and Sydney had no interest in disturbing her.

"Raiden?" Sydney yelled. She cupped her hands around her mouth. "Kid, you there?"

Within seconds, a small, sandy head popped out from the folds of the tent. "Sydney!" Before she could blink, the elf boy shimmied down the tree, agile as a cat, jumping from the trunk to Honey's back to the ground. Skinny arms wrapped around her in a tight embrace.

"Are you alright?" Raiden pulled back his head. His green eyes were wide with worry, and his face spoke of a sleepless night. Sydney hated seeing him so upset.

"Are you kidding? I'm great. You didn't think a few measly shadows would keep me down, did you?" Sydney kept her voice light, ruffling the boy's hair. Despite her efforts, Raiden pulled away, crossing his arms and shooting her a deep frown.

"You're lying," Raiden scolded. "You're not supposed to lie. Not to me."

Sydney sighed. *Sometimes this kid is too clever for his own good.* She dropped to her knees, placing calming hands on Raiden's bony shoulders.

"Look. I know I scared you last night. Gods, the whole thing terrified me too. But what happened wasn't your fault. Okay?" The boy still looked uncertain, so she pressed on. "You saved me. If you hadn't gone to get Lukaris and Novah... well, I don't know what would have happened. You did the right thing. And I'll be okay. I'm already better. I promise."

Her words must have resonated, because most of the tension fell from Raiden's shoulders. The young elf looked down, staring at his feet for a moment. When his eyes returned to Sydney's, they were different. Older. Like his brother's.

"Those things... those creatures." Raiden took a shaking breath. "*Shadow-borne*. What if there's more of them?"

"Whatever happens, we'll deal with it," Sydney said, repeating the words she'd used with Lukaris. "We won't let them hurt us ever again."

In the distance, a bell chimed. The smell of cooked eggs and fresh bread carried on the breeze. On a whim, she took Raiden's hands. A few weeks ago the action would have seemed forced. But now, after the things she'd been through, it felt natural. The elves might still technically be her enemies. But not Raiden. Never this small boy with his grimy hands and wide eyes.

"Come on, let's go get some breakfast." Raiden hesitated, and Sydney realized that it wasn't just guilt that plagued him. The boy saw shadow-borne around every corner. "Lighten up, kid. The sun keeps the shadows at bay, and we have the whole day ahead of us. Besides, those monsters haven't run into Honey, yet. They won't know what hit them."

In response, the golden bear rose from the ground, poking Raiden with her snout. The boy laughed, the sound high and clear.

"Alright, Honey, alright. I'm going."

Raiden let Sydney lead him away, his hand tight around hers. They joined the others who had gathered for a late morning feast. Slowly, the shadows from the previous night began to fade, replaced by food and good company. Sydney watched them all with a strange heaviness in her chest. Flindir, quiet and calm, smiling at Itari beside him. The Viridian, telling stories from her homeland, sparks flying from her hands at all the exciting parts. Next came Ettee, her petite face full of laughter, and for once, not fighting with Flindir. Ordell, tall and broad, taking up half the table, but then it just wouldn't look right without him there. Novah and Darian sat close together, picking food from each other's plates. Then, Raiden, wiping his hands clean in response to his brother's scolding, listening to Itari's stories with rapt attention. Lukaris, watching from the table's head, a perpetual breeze ruffling his hair, his half-smile quick to make an appearance. And among them all, Sydney.

Sydney, who found herself laughing, passing Raiden berries beneath the table, scratching Honey's nearby head, and following along to the bits of Elvish the others tossed around.

Somehow, impossibly and only for moment, Sydney belonged. Here, amongst a group of elves that only a month ago she had sought to kill.

Damn, Sydney cursed, realizing how truly lost she was.

38

Cracks in the Earth

"Raiden, I said no," Lukaris insisted, his amiable face unusually stern.

"But, Luka—"

"*Kas!*"

The young elf crossed his arms in a huff. "It's not fair! I saw the shadow-borne too. I should get to go."

A fresh morning in the Wornwood, Sydney had been searching the camp for Lukaris when she stumbled into the middle of a brothers' quarrel. She hung back, not wanting to interfere.

"That doesn't matter, I'm not risking your safety again. You're not a soldier, and there's no telling what dangers we could face."

"I can help! Maybe I could learn to talk to them or… or…" Raiden grasped for a good excuse, his eyes and voice pleading.

Lukaris just shook his head.

"Father would let me go," the boy grumbled under his breath.

The *Valen* stiffened. Sydney saw a strange emotion pass across those forest eyes, but when he spoke, his tone remained even. "Well, Father isn't here. I am. And I refuse to put my little brother in harms way if I can help it. My decision is final."

Raiden looked around desperately, spotting Sydney just as she tried to duck away. "Sydney!" the boy called, his hope renewed. "You don't think I should be left behind in camp, do you?"

Both brothers looked to her with desperate eyes. So different, yet just the same. With a sigh, Sydney placed a hand on Raiden's shoulder.

"Look, kid, I know you want to help. I get it. But I think you should listen to your brother on this one."

Lukaris blinked at her, eyes screaming, *thank you*. Raiden stepped away from her as if she'd struck him, but he said nothing. With a final scowl, the boy stomped back towards his tent. Lukaris sighed, passing a quick hand through his hair.

"How long do you think it will take him to forgive me?" the elf questioned, eyes sad.

"Not long. I used to fight with my sister all the time. It never lasts. He doesn't love you any less," Sydney assured him. Then, her focus turned. "So… you're going back *there*?"

Lukaris gave her a careful, searching look. "Yes. I need to know where those creatures came from, and if they're truly gone. If shadow-borne are resurfacing in Soarden, we have to be ready."

Sydney nodded, expecting the answer, but her stomach still dropped. "I'm coming with you."

"Sydney—" Lukaris began warily.

She held up a hand. "I know what you're going to say. You don't have to worry. I can handle it."

"No one would think any less of you for staying here."

"That's not what this is about. I need to face the nightmares if I ever plan on waking up," Sydney admitted. She hated sharing her fear, but Lukaris seemed to appreciate it. He cast a teasing smirk.

"Alright, you can come. But I'll warn you, Novah intends to join us."

Lukaris laughed at Sydney's instinctual groan. Secretly, she felt relieved. Light magic might be the only protection from creatures of shadow.

They set out through the dim forest, Novah at the head, with Lukaris, Sydney, Itari, Flindir, and, unfortunately, Sarcys trailing behind. Lukaris called out a farewell to Raiden, but the boy did not respond, his face tight with worry. Sydney made a mental note to seek him out upon their return.

Gray, hungry clouds filled the sky overhead as the team picked their way through the trees. Away, towards the mountains, thunder rattled the heavens, and Itari tensed, as if she could sense the crackle of distant lightening. The air around them swirled damp and heavy, promising rain. No one spoke, their footsteps falling softly on the moss-strewn ground. Silence filled the woods like a slumbering beast, quiet and deadly, ready to wake at the smallest sound. Sydney pulled up the hood of her cloak, the hairs on her neck standing up. Were they being watched? Flindir's round eyes darted from shadow to shadow, and she could feel the same uneasiness radiating from her other companions. The Wornwood felt strange, foreign, even to the elves that called it home.

With every step, Sydney's throat tightened, and she had to force herself to keep moving. What would they find when they reached the site of the shadow-borne attack? Had it been a singular ordeal? Or was the nightmare only just beginning?

At last, the group reached the rise that led to Raiden's overlook. A few nights ago, the area had seemed magical, full of starflies and stories. Now, muted daylight painted the trees in different shades of gray, and the grove could only be described as haunted. Lukaris rounded them up with a wave of his hand.

"Spread out, but stay within earshot," Lukaris ordered. His voice felt too loud for the hushed forest. "We don't know what we're dealing with yet."

"And what exactly are we looking for, *Valen?*" Itari asked, leaning into Flindir's shoulder with a shiver. He wrapped a comforting arm around her. Sydney couldn't remember ever seeing the *Dualin* look afraid.

"I don't know," Lukaris replied softly. He cast Sydney a sympathetic glance. "I think we'll know when we see it."

They wandered slowly in different directions, none eager to leave the safety of the group. Only Novah seemed unperturbed by their surroundings. *Typical,* Sydney thought bitterly. Lukaris kept close to Sydney, some unspoken agreement passing between them. She made her way up the hillside, watching every trunk, every branch, every stone, for some sign of shadow-borne. She stopped at a familiar cluster of trees. *That's where I woke, cold and confused. That's where Raiden sat across from me, eyes filled with fear.* Sydney stepped around the protective pines. *And that's where...* Sydney felt the claws, the teeth, the terror. She closed her eyes, trying to push away the memories, but shadowy wolves danced across her eyelids, pinprick eyes watching her, their teeth stained with her blood.

This was a mistake, Sydney thought, her hands shaking. *I never should have come back here.* She took a step backwards, prepared to leave, to return to Firne and let the elves sort out this mess. But as her foot hit the ground, the dirt crumbled beneath her, a wide hole opening where moments ago there had been solid earth. Before she could jump to safety, or even scream for help, she was falling. But not for long.

The air flew from Sydney's lungs as her back struck packed soil, and black spots coated her vision. From the gaping hole above her, bits of dirt dribbled down into the newly formed pit.

"Son of a bitch," Sydney moaned, rolling over onto her hands and knees. Her head swam, but she managed to find her feet. She stood in a small underground cavern, the walls made of rough stone, the ceiling little more than decaying earth. The only light came from the opening she'd fallen through, just a few small strands of gray sunlight. It did little to illuminate the pit around her.

"Sydney!" Lukaris shouted from above. More dirt landed on her shoulders as a dark silhouette loomed next to the hole. "Are you alright?"

"I'm fine, I'm fine. I just…" Sydney wheezed, words drifting off as her eyes adjusted to the gloom. Across from her, at the far end of the cave, there was a crack in the wall. Tall and narrow, too thin for even a child to slip through. But what the fissure lacked in width, it made up for in depth. Sydney felt as if she were standing at the edge of a cliff, and beneath her, nothing but a black, endless void. The opening emitted a stream of icy air, sending a shiver up her spine. She took a nervous step backwards.

"Lukaris…" Her voice came out as a squeak. Clearing her throat, Sydney repeated, "Lukaris, I think you should see this. And bring the others."

Within moments, the five elves dropped soundlessly into the cavern. Sydney never took her eyes off the fissure. She pointed a shaking finger.

"What in Kon's name is that?"

Novah snapped her fingers, filling the space with white light. The Red Elf's usual controlled demeanor fractured, her eyes wide. Lukaris sucked in a sharp breath. The opening oozed black shadow. It spilled out onto the floor, across the stone walls. Sydney scrambled backwards, Flindir giving a yelp as he followed her lead.

"Dark magic," Itari whispered. She drew a knife, lightening flickering along its edge. "Shadow magic."

Sarcys stood as far from the fissure as possible. He motioned at Novah. "Well, can't you just blast it with light or something?"

Novah glared at the dark-haired elf, before looking to the *Valen*. Lukaris nodded. Raising both hands towards the shadows, the Red Elf closed her eyes, murmuring something in Elvish. Two bright, blinding beams erupted from her outstretched palms. The light poured over the darkness, pushing, ripping, tearing through the shade. Slowly, the shadows retreated, shrinking back into the hole. Sydney breathed a sigh of relief when Novah closed her hands into fists, returning the room to a soft glow.

Everyone relaxed. Sarcys even laughed.

"See? That wasn't so bad."

On cue, shadow billowed from the crack, snaking even farther into the room. Novah scrambled away from the opening, slamming the darkness with small bursts of light. Each time she made contact, the black clouds would recoil away, only to return a moment later.

"You're an idiot," Sydney informed Sarcys as the group huddled out of reach of the darkness.

"She's not wrong," Novah agreed, to everyone's surprise.

"Well, do you have any better ideas?" Sarcys hissed.

Lukaris crouched next to the gloom, eyes watchful. "Flindir, do you... feel anything? Through that fissure, and whatever lies beyond."

Flindir's fearful swallow echoed through the small cavern, but he placed a steady hand on the nearest wall. His head tilted to the side as if he were listening for someone. For something. Goosebumps covered Sydney's arms.

After a moment, Flindir whispered, "I sense... nothing. Not a seed, a root, a sapling. Plant life is usually common at this depth. So, either the earth beyond this pit is dead soil," the elf paused, taking a shaking breath as he removed his hand from the rotting wall, "or that opening goes so deep, no living thing dares grow."

"How ominous," said Novah, dryly.

"If this is the source of the monsters that attacked Sydney and

Raiden… what does it mean?" Flindir asked.

"It means…" As Itari spoke, she sent a small burst of lightning into the invading darkness. The dark mist quivered but did not disperse. "A crack has formed in the shadow-borne's cage. And who's to say the Sháedin won't follow? We must send word to Sil Tullian."

A tightness formed in Lukaris' jaw. "We cannot assume the Sháedin are involved. Not yet. I will not go to the king and queen with mere speculation. For now, this secret stays with us."

"At Valen—"

As the two elves lapsed into fierce debate, Sydney returned her attention to the billowing shadows. Too late, however, to avoid a single tendril of smoke that had wound its way up her foot. With intent, the darkness brushed against bare skin.

Sydney gasped, visions flitting across her eyelids, just as they had that night in the woods. Silver eyes, screams, blood in the air. But this time was different. Deeper. The images ground to a halt, pulling Sydney from her reality and into another.

A cavern opened up in front of her, large and echoing. Bodies covered the floor. Or at least, she thought they were bodies. The presence of death permeated throughout the room, but every time Sydney tried to look at the corpses directly, the shapes crumbled to ash. Still, she caught glimpses, a hand here, a skull there. She stood in the wake of a massacre. In the distance, a fire flickered, casting dancing silhouettes across the stone walls. Seeing no better option, Sydney moved towards the wavering light. She felt strange and disconnected, like a cloud drifting across the sky, playing no part in war or love, life or death. She had been placed here only to observe. So, she did.

Four human-like figures surrounded the fire. Sydney could not see their faces, but she felt power radiating off them in waves. A chanting started low in the their throats, growing until it became a song. The words were foreign, somehow containing every language and none, all at once. In a blink, the figures stood by the cavern wall, hands raised. Together, they dragged their hands down the stone, leaving behind four identical smears of blood. They turned to face her, but where their faces should have been, there was only shadow.

The chanting began again, stronger this time, faster and louder, until Sydney yearned to cover her ears. Amidst the terrible words, the entire cavern shuddered. Something flashed, and for a moment, the cave illuminated in a bright light. She could see every stone, body, bone. When the brightness faded, an archway had opened up in the cavern wall with two of the figures on either side, guardians to the door. In unison, four fingers point at Sydney.

"*Malith,*" the voices droned. "*Your reign upon this world has ended. Surrender, and we will spare your people the same fate.*"

Sydney felt herself laugh, deep and menacing. When she spoke, the voice was not her own.

"*My reign has only just begun.*" Shadow spilled from her fingertips like blood from an open wound. Shadow-borne formed at her feet, the beasts cowering before their master.

The largest of the figures stepped forward. "*So be it,*" a male voice growled.

Light burst forth around the border of the archway. Inside, through the door, Sydney could hear the shouts and screams of living creatures. People. *Her* people. But the knowledge filled her with nothing. No remorse, no regret. Only anger.

The figures resumed their eerie song, and slowly, Sydney felt herself dragged towards the opening. Ancient ruins formed in the silver light, pulsing and growing in time with the music. The shadow-borne slipped through the vortex, their whispered cries filling her ears. She knew, with utter certainty, that the moment the doorway consumed her, all was lost.

Finally, the feeling came rushing back into Sydney's body, and she screamed as the darkness closed in around her.

39

Sealed and Buried

Sydney gasped as a stinging sensation radiated across her cheek. When her gaze came into focus, she found herself back in the pit, kneeling on the ground. Novah towered above her with a raised hand.

"Did you just *slap* me?" Sydney snapped, incredulous.

"Yes," the Red Elf replied without a drop of remorse. She lowered her hand. "You were screaming like a lunatic."

The other elves stared down at her with a mixture of worry and unease. Sydney struggled to her feet with Flindir's help.

"What happened?" Sydney asked. Her mind buzzed, a part of it still back in the vision, in the cave filled with bodies and blood.

"One second you were just standing there, and then you were on your knees, having some sort of fit," Flindir said in a shaky voice. "You wouldn't stop shouting."

Lukaris stepped around his friend to grasp Sydney's shoulder. When their eyes met, she knew he saw a familiar shadow there.

"Tell us what you saw," the *Valen* insisted, voice filled with dread.

"The other night, when the shadow-borne… touched me…" Sydney could not make herself speak above a whisper. "I saw flashes. Images.

I think they were just meant to scare me. But this time was different. It was a nightmare or… maybe even a memory."

"A memory of what?"

She tried to pin down the vision even as it faded. "I stood in a cavern. Bigger than any I've ever seen. I think there was a battle." She rubbed at her temples, trying to remember. "I saw a door with figures on either side. And then I was screaming…"

The elves exchanged wary glances.

"Is that it?" Sarcys demanded.

"I—I don't know. The images are slipping out of my head. It's like waking up from a dream." Sydney's stomach churned.

Uncertainty passed across every face. Itari leaned against a dirt wall, muttering Elvish prayers under her breath.

"The old stories say the shadow-borne could cast unspeakable horrors into the minds of their victims," Flindir muttered, hands crossed behind his neck. "But the shadow-borne were first and foremost, beasts. Monsters, yes, but with no will or intent of their own. But those with Shadow magic… well it's said that some could use the shadow-borne as vessels. To pass on messages or visions."

Sydney stared at the narrow fissure that still bled darkness. She could feel the terror of her companions as if it were her own.

Sarcys snorted, breaking the silence. "Come on. Only one race can wield Shadow magic. And surely you aren't implying the *Sháedin* sent those things?" The elf waved carelessly at the lurking shadows. "Even if they once existed, that was thousands of years ago. Say they could survive that long—underground, cut off from the rest of the world—we still have no reason to believe they've returned. If the legends are right, our ancestors locked every rotten Sháed in an impenetrable prison. Why would that magic fail now?"

Despite Sarcys' patronizing tone, his words helped ease some of the rising tension. Novah breathed a deep sigh, neutral mask back on her face.

"For once, Sarcys is right. Running into a few stray shadow-borne is one thing. Sháedin resurfacing? You said it yourself, *Valen*, this is all just speculation. For all we know, these shadows are fresh monsters from the Mist Lands. We should trust that the Light magic that has held for a millennia is as strong as ever." Novah spoke cool and confident. Flindir and Itari relaxed under the power of her words.

Sydney looked to Lukaris. She could see his mind working, searching for logic amid the uncertainty. They all were. And she knew they would settle on the easy answer, the simple optimism. This was a small invasion by a few shadow-borne that could be squashed with a little Light. Nothing more. But they hadn't seen what Sydney had. They hadn't stood shivering in the woods with the stars blotted out or surrounded by bodies in a shadow-filled cave. The past few days she had felt conflicted. Now, she knew the threat was real. But what good was her fear? Did her words hold power here? Though she had to remind herself daily, the elves were not her people. It wasn't her job to save them. Her duty was to Brimhold, to the humans she'd served since the day that soldier knocked on her father's shop. Maybe if she returned to Delm, she could take action. Warn the queen and her army about the emerging shadows. And if they consumed Ithirdas first, what did that matter to her?

And yet...

She thought of Raiden smiling up at her. Of Flindir's kind voice and Itari's solemn strength. Lukaris...

They may not be her people, Sydney realized, but they were still *people*. Souls that deserved a chance to live, if only long enough to fight another day.

"Lukaris." Sydney cleared her throat. "It may not be my place, but... I don't think this is a threat to be ignored. You've said yourself that something was coming. You've known longer than any of us, since the day I met you. Better to be cautious and wrong then let an enemy rise while your back is turned."

She saw her words stir inside him. The *Valen*'s shoulders slumped.

"I hear you." Lukaris drew in a deep breath. "Very well. We will send a warning to Sil Tullian. At the very least, Ithirdas should know of the shadow-borne in our woods. But we will leave the Sháedin out of it for now."

Sydney and the surrounding elves nodded. It was better than nothing.

"And what about *that*?" Novah asked, motioning towards the rift of shadow.

"I want that abomination sealed and buried," Lukaris replied. His eyes were hard as flint.

Sarcys grinned, cracking his knuckles. "Leave it to me."

Later, the group stood back above the earth, staring down at the sinkhole. Sarcys raised both hands, and the ground shivered beneath them. Dirt and rock collapsed in on itself, filling the hole until it was once again even with the surrounding forest. Flindir placed fingertips against the freshly packed soil, grass and ferns sprouting in arcs away from him. Soon, Sydney couldn't even tell where the pit had been. Some of the weight lifted from her chest at the thought.

The overcast sky grumbled above them as the group picked a quiet path back towards Firne. Raindrops fell sporadically as the sky prepared to burst. Sydney pulled up the hood of her cloak, dreaming of a bright, warm fire and a large distance between her and any shadow-borne that might be lurking in the forest. Her mind buzzed with the things she'd seen over the past few weeks. How she could ever return to her normal life, she didn't know. A mortal war seemed pointless and fleeting with shadowed monsters on their doorstep.

As the elves and Sydney climbed the final hilltop before reaching the village, Lukaris stopped. His eyes were downcast, fixed on something. Sydney moved to stand beside him. A sickly yellow smog hovered a few inches above the ground. It crept silently from over the crest of the hill. From Firne.

"What the shadowed hell is that?" Sarcys wondered aloud. Lukaris and Flindir exchanged a terrified glance. Then, they were running, scrambling up the hill, sprinting through a haze of yellow. The others took up the chase, shouting frantic questions after the friends. Their boots sent up clots of mud where they slammed against the earth. Thunder ripped across the sky above them. As they reached the summit, Sydney's chest tightened with exertion and dread.

It wasn't until Firne melted into view that they heard the screaming.

40

The Battle for Firne

Yellow gas smothered the town below, hovering over grass and stone. Soldiers weaved in and out of the fog. Sydney spotted a violet flag of twin mountains through the trees. Brimhold. Her people. The realization filled her with panic.

From their vantage point, they watched as elves ran from their homes, dragging children as they fled swinging swords. The *tatell* had answered the attack, their lithe, warrior forms easy to distinguish amidst the chaos, but they were hopelessly outnumbered.

"Raiden," Sydney heard Lukaris whisper. Her stomach dropped.

"How did they make it this far into Ithirdis?" Sarcys hissed. He kicked a boot at the oozing smog. "And what *is* this stuff?"

"It's warroot," Flindir answered numbly. His hands were shaking. Itari rested a hand on his arm. "They made it into a gas. A weapon."

"Warroot? What does it do?"

"Our magic." Lukaris was notching an arrow, face strained. He gave Sydney a strange look. "It strips us of our magic."

The color leaked from Novah's face. "Permanently?"

"No, but long enough." The *Valen* started down the hill. "Come on, we have to help them. No, not you, Novah."

The Red Elf already had her sword halfway from its sheath. "Excuse me?"

"The Brims can't see you here. It will only make things worse. Go and get help."

"You can't just expect me to run away—"

"That's exactly what I expect you to do," Lukaris barked. Sydney had never seen his face so sharp, so enraged. "Leave now, or I will pin you to a tree."

Novah lifted her chin, but she didn't argue. "Fine. Be careful. And if you see Darian…" For a moment, her eyes softened, fearful. "Send her after me."

In a blink, she was gone.

"Here." Lukaris passed Sydney a sword without looking. She stared down at the blade in her hands.

"Lukaris, I can't…" Couldn't what? Fight? Kill her own people? Watch either side of this battle lose?

His jaw tightened. "Do what you must." Then, he raced off down the hill.

Flindir, Itari, and Sarcys exchanged a look before chasing after their leader. Sydney had no choice but to follow. As they neared the village, the smog thickened, filling their lungs with each breath. Sydney knew she had no magic to lose, but she still felt poisoned by the air, choked by toxic fumes.

They charged into the village, colliding with a throng of frightened elves. In the confusion, Sydney quickly lost sight of the others. She pushed her way through the crowd, scanning for a familiar face. The forest filled with screams and shouts and slashing metal. Maybe if she could find the leader of the attack, she could stop it. She could explain that the elves were innocent. Nobody had to die today. Surely she could stop this from happening.

She rounded a tree and smashed into something solid. An elf fell away from her, sprawling in the grass as he cast fearful glances over his shoulder. Sydney turned just in time to lift her sword. Weapons clashed as lightning lit up the sky overhead. A Brimhold warrior grimaced, trying to free his weapon. Sydney didn't let him. She sent a quick kick at the man's knees and forced him backwards. With a flick of her hand, his blade landed in the dirt.

"Enough!" Sydney spat. "What are you doing? This elf is clearly a civilian. He's no threat to you."

"We were told to let no elf escape." The soldier was looking at her face for the first time. "Wait… Captain Krane?"

She didn't give the man time to draw any conclusions. The hilt of her sword found his nose, and the warrior collapsed to the earth. She turned, pulling the shaken elf to his feet.

"Get out of here," Sydney ordered. "Escape into the Wornwood. Take as many with you as you can."

The elf had young, bright eyes. He stared at her, placing both hands to his heart with a bow. "As you say, *Advina*."

He disappeared into the mist. *Advina.* She didn't have time to wonder after the word's meaning. Soon enough, the Brim would awaken with a fierce headache and a story of the Honor Guard captain protecting an elf over her own people. She needed to find the head of this attack *now.*

Sydney ran along the stream that split Firne in two. On one bank, elves scrambled past ruined tents and up towards the protection of the trees. On the other, Brimhold's soldiers battled the *tatell.* She dodged two fighters as they pushed past her, weapons locked. Another elf fought two soldiers at once. Her blade swung like an extension of her body, blocking one foe and then the other. Sydney kept running. She passed a body on the ground. An elf, eyes wide and staring. Bile rose to her throat. The dead woman looked familiar, but Sydney couldn't bring herself any closer. She kept running.

She spotted Ettee, her small face set, ducking and weaving from her opponent's blows. The elf lifted a hand, and Sydney's stomach dropped as she realized her intentions. The creek bed sat only a few feet behind her. On a normal day, the water would heed her command, rising from its banks, pushing the enemy warrior away. But the warroot still clung to the air. The water did not move. Ettee looked backwards, astonished. As she hesitated, the Brim slammed into her, hard, and the elf stumbled back, her head striking a rock as she fell. She did not rise again.

The soldier left her, off to seek another fight. Sydney reached Ettee's still form, breathing a sigh of relief when her fingers found a steady pulse. She pulled Ettee's light form out of harms way, tucking her behind a tree. Above her, the sky opened up, and the autumn rain finally came down, growing quickly from a drip to a drizzle to a full downpour. Some of the warroot dispersed with the onslaught, but the damage had already been done.

A sudden roar sent Sydney scrambling for her sword. She glimpsed a moving mass of golden fur between two stone homes. Her heart soared.

Honey battled just as ferociously as the elves around her. Giant claws swatted at soldiers as they passed, throwing them off the ground. She bellowed again, and those closest to her stopped to cover their ears. The sound echoed off the distant mountains.

And on the great beast's back, as always, sat Raiden.

"Raiden!" Sydney shouted. Her voice seemed faint among the shouts and thunder and ringing metal. "Kid!"

The boy turned at her call, and some of the anxiety lifted from his face. "Sydney!"

She had almost reached him when a soldier yanked the boy from his mount. Honey snarled, and something primal welled up in Sydney's own throat. She plowed into the Brim, forcing him to release his hold on Raiden's shirt. The soldier raised his sword, but too late. Sydney struck him so hard, his head whipped backwards.

She turned to Raiden, breathing hard. "Are you alright, kid?"

The boy nodded though his small body shook. "What's happening? I can't talk to Honey. And where's Luka?"

"This fog is blocking your magic," Sydney explained. She hoisted Raiden back onto the bear. "Your brother is here somewhere. You have to find him and get to safety. Do you understand?"

"Yes," Raiden said. His eyes were wide, shining with unshed tears. "What are you going to do?"

"I have to stop the Brims. They don't know the things I do." She took his hand and squeezed. "I'm going to fix this, okay?"

"I trust you." He always had, Sydney realized. This strange, bright elf child.

"Go on," Sydney said, her throat tight.

She watched them go. She sent a silent prayer to any god that would listen. *Protect him.* Then, she ran.

Sydney neared the eastern reaches of Firne. If there was any sense in the world, the soldiers should've attacked from that direction. The thunder rattled her bones, the rain soaking through to her skin, but she kept running. *Where are they, where are they.*

A sword and a shield blocked her path. Without thinking, Sydney surged forward, parrying the weapon. The hood of her cloak fell, and the rain ran into her eyes. She swung blindly. The shield caught her in the chest. She stumbled backwards, ready to fight off another blow, but it never came.

"Syd?"

Sydney's breath caught. She wiped the water from her eyes, and she could finally see the soldier standing before her.

Brandon.

His face. Imprinted in her mind and on her heart, yet different somehow. Same brown hair, square jaw. But his cheeks were rough with stubble, and his eyes held a hollow look. He might have been dragged a hundred miles since last she'd seen him.

They stared at each other for what felt like an eternity. Then, his arms were around her.

"Thank the gods, thank the gods," Brandon muttered over and over. Sydney squeezed him back. She hadn't realized how much she missed him, missed this. Love from the only family she had left.

The scared cries of the elves brought her back down to earth.

"What the hell are you doing here, Lockes?" She pulled away from him. He frowned at her tone.

"What? I'm saving you from your own idiocy, Krane," Brandon snapped back.

Sydney's head spun. Saving *her*. Then all of this, every death, was her fault.

"This attack is because of me?" she choked out. She needed to hear it.

"Well, no," Brandon admitted. "The attack was already planned. But, I got the queen to come sooner."

Well, that was some relief. But wait... "The queen? Camillea is *here*?"

"Yes." He continued to frown at her. "Is that a problem?"

"Damn it, Lockes!" Sydney groaned, rubbing her soaking forehead. "Why couldn't you have just left it alone? I let the elves take me so that you could return to Delm. And now you've turned right back around and made a mess of things."

His eyes widened, incredulous. And there it was, that deep simmering anger he always carried. "You're actually mad at me for coming to rescue you? Unbelievable. I'm sorry I traveled halfway across Soarden to save my best friend's life. You're right, I should've just left you to be tortured and killed by the elves. Honestly, what was I thinking?"

"That's not… you don't…" Sydney threw up her hands, her own anger a spark in dry kindling. "Forget it. I need to talk to the queen. It's urgent. Where is she now?"

"I'll take you," Brandon grumbled. His expression made it clear that this argument was not forgotten. "Here, I'm guessing you'll be wanting these."

From his back, he pulled two worn sheaths. Sydney couldn't suppress her gasp of delight. She took the weapons in her hands, the weight as steady and familiar as her own breath. She had not held her swords since the day she'd fought Lukaris in the Wornwood.

"How did you get these?" she asked. Brandon shrugged.

"They were in the elf leader's tent."

Sydney's heart pounded in her ears. Had Brandon run into Lukaris? And did the elf recognize the "sword for hire" he'd set free?

"Follow me," Brandon said before Sydney could delve deeper into her worries. She let her friend lead the way through the broken village. The noise seemed quieter here. Maybe the Ithirdi had escaped to the shelter of the forest after all.

A fire had broken out in the final row of houses, barring their path, and the onslaught of rain was the only thing keeping the blaze in check. Sydney and Brandon were forced across the stream, now rushing with the surge of fresh water. They hopped from log to stone to root, finally landing safely on the muddy river bank. But when they turned for their destination, a single elf stood in their way.

Brandon attacked before Sydney could protest. His sword swung downwards in a deadly arc, but the elf was faster. Brandon's blade struck empty air. The elf countered, sword slicing at Brandon's chest. Her friend only just managed to raise his shield in time. By then, the dark-haired elf was already surging forward, spinning around the guard, blade poised to slice at Brandon's throat.

"No!" Sydney screamed. Fear squeezed at her chest as she dove between the warriors. She raised her arms, blocking both of their weapons with her own. Black eyes glared down at her.

Sydney thought she had felt the full force of Sarcys' hatred before. She was wrong. The elf took a small step backwards.

"I tried to warn the *Valen* about you," Sarcys spat. He leveled his sword at Sydney's chest, glaring down his long nose. "I always knew you would betray us."

"I haven't betrayed anyone," she retorted. Brandon glanced back and forth between them. Sydney couldn't imagine what he must think.

"Oh really? You found a human ally fast enough. It seems this attack is going just as you planned."

"You don't know what you're talking about," Sydney insisted. They were wasting time. "Now for once in your miserable life, Sarcys, be smart. Run away. Leave me be."

Sarcys tensed as if he were fighting something. His eyes bore into her, dark and brooding. At last, he shook his head. He returned his sword to its sheath.

"I'm giving you one chance, Krane. That's it. If I find you've squandered it, I will be the first volunteer to hunt you down."

Sydney didn't answer. She only watched as the elf disappeared into the trees.

The look Brandon gave her... Sydney realized it was the second time she'd seen it that day. The first was on the hillside with Lukaris. She didn't recognize it then, but now it was unmistakable. Distrust. Betrayal. Hurt.

Sydney swallowed hard. Now wasn't the time to get emotional. She would explain everything later. Right now, she had a job to do. Brandon didn't question her, but Sydney could feel his gaze as they finally reached the edge of the village.

But by then, it was too late. The battle was over.

What elves remained of Firne and the *tatell* knelt on the muddy ground, surrounded by Brimhold's soldiers. They looked thoroughly beaten, their eyes downcast, faces covered in dirt and blood. A child cried out for her mother. Elves supported wounded shoulders and twisted legs. Ettee lay silent in the wet grass, clearly dragged from her hiding place. Sydney's heart sunk at the sight of it all. It didn't look like a battle won. It looked like the end of an invasion.

At the head of it all, was Queen Camillea. She sat like a shining star upon her white stead, chin raised triumphantly, pale eyes sweeping the spoils of her attack. Sydney knew, even before the queen's gaze found her, she wouldn't be able to convince her of the elves' innocence. *What do I do?*

"Captain Krane," the queen called out. Her voice cracked like the thunder overhead. "I am grateful to see you alive and well."

I have to try. Remembering herself, Sydney gave a short bow. "Thank you, your Majesty. I have much to discuss with you. This attack…"

Sydney's words fell away as her eyes finally landed on the front row of Ithirdi prisoners.

Lukaris knelt before her, but his gaze was fixed on something in his lap. He sported a deep cut high on his cheek, the blood trickling down his face as it mixed with the rain. Next to him, Itari rocked back and forth, mouth moving rapidly, though Sydney was too far away to make out the words. And then there was Flindir, eyes wide, hands scrambling frantically. They were covered in blood. Itari shifted, and at last, Sydney was able to see what Lukaris clutched to.

Her breath stopped. Around her, the world seemed to slow. She took a stumbling step forward.

Raiden lay in the grass, wrapped in his brother's arms, an arrow sprouting from his chest.

41

A Parting of Innocence

N^{o.}

Sydney's entire body went numb.

No.

She dragged her feet forward, crossing the invisible line that divided the elves from the humans. She could hear Brandon calling her name, but the sound was a distant echo.

No.

She landed in the mud next to Lukaris, and the world came crashing back. The rain landed in torrents around them, lightning ripping across the sky. Itari's voice accented the storm. Eyes closed, body rocking, her mouth spun Elvish prayers of healing and light, the words spilling out so quickly that Sydney could barely grasp at their meaning. Meanwhile, Flindir and Lukaris were focused on Raiden. Flindir's hands pressed around the protruding arrow. The blood continued to flow, and Sydney's limited knowledge knew there was no easy way to remove the weapon without making matters worse.

Raiden stared up at his brother, green eyes wide. "Luka. It hurts."

"I know, *osan*, I know," Lukaris soothed, pulling Raiden tighter into his chest. His voice cracked. "It will be better soon. We've got you.

340

Flin?"

"I'm trying." Flindir's hands moved impossibly faster. He ripped another piece of cloth from a tattered cloak, pressing the makeshift bandage to the boy's chest.

Raiden's gaze found Sydney where she knelt helplessly in the mud. "Sydney."

"I'm here, kid," she said, her hand finding his. His fingers were like ice.

"I'm sorry." The boy sucked in a wheezing breath. "I tried to find Luka, like you said. I tried."

"Hey." She squeezed his hand. Tears fell down her face to mingle with the rain, but they felt like someone else's. "None of this is your fault, okay? You have nothing to be sorry for."

He nodded a little, then his eyes drifted away, unfocused.

"Luka, you have to find Honey. She's probably—" Raiden coughed, and a bead of blood formed at the corner of his mouth. "—scared. Promise you'll take care of her."

"Of course, you know I will. Don't worry about that now." Lukaris brushed back his brother's wild hair. His hand shook. "We'll find her together when this is all over."

"What can I do? How can I help?" Sydney muttered sideways to Flindir. He looked over at her, face white and stricken.

"I don't know. I don't know what to do. There's nothing I can—" He cut himself off, eyes fixed on his red tinged hands. Itari had stopped praying. Her cheek found Flindir's shoulder.

"Luka," Raiden began again. The word sounded wet.

"Hush, *osan*, save your strength."

But the boy shouldered on. "Do you remember… that rhyme. Mama used to sing. The one about the sky?"

"Yes, I remember," came Lukaris' whispered reply.

"How did it go, again?"

Lukaris' face was tight as a bow string. He pressed his eyes closed. Then, he began to chant, voice quiet and carrying, a gentle lullaby.

Once there was a boy in the sky
Who had comets for lashes
And stars in his eye.

So when trouble came near
He had nothing to fear
For danger knew not how to fly.

Once there was a boy in the sky
Who played with the clouds
Smile flashing and wry.

But when the sun came to play
She brought with her the day
And the boy had to say his goodbye.

Raiden's eyes had fallen shut at the words. Lukaris stirred him, voice panicked.

"*Osan!*"

The boy sighed, eye lids fluttering. "I always… I always liked that one."

"Me too. Stay with me, *osan*, please."

"*Ra valnethe, thair. Ra valnethe,*" came Raiden's tired response. *I love you, brother. I love you.*

"*Ra valnethe,* my *osan.*" *My little bear.* Lukaris choked, pressing his lips to his brother's forehead. Tears fell freely down his cheeks where they landed beside the raindrops in Raiden's hair.

In the distance, past the storm and the soldiers and the broken village, a pack of wolves began to howl. Their voices echoed down through the mountains, intertwining in a sad and hollow song. The ghost of a smile formed on the boy's mouth.

There was a feeling then, deep in Sydney's chest. It was like the release of a breath long held. Like the moment a candle is snuffed out by the wind.

It was the moment Raiden's Light passed from the world.

Sydney could only watch in horror as Lukaris bent over his brother, shoulders heaving. Flindir couldn't seem to stop starring at the blood on his fingers, while Itari muttered new prayers between her sobs. Sydney's own tears stuck in her throat. How had this happened? How had she let this happen?

She was not given time to grieve. Familiar hands yanked her from the ground and pulled her back towards the humans. Only then did she hear Brandon's voice in her ear.

"What are you doing? Syd, do you know what this looks like?" her friend hissed beneath his breath.

She didn't care. Raiden was gone. Brandon's vise-like grip was the only thing keeping her standing.

Camillea's eyes were on her, cold and sharp and brittle. But if she had words for Sydney, she didn't share them. Maybe the queen didn't want to detract from Brimhold's victory by addressing her traitorous captain.

"Citizens and warriors of Ithirdas," Camillea called out. The rain had dissolved to a sprinkle, the thunder a distant rumble, and her voice carried in the solemn quiet. "You have fought and failed against the soldiers of Brimhold. You live now at our mercy and as our prisoners. Should you obey all commands, I swear no further harm will come to you."

The elves glared up at the queen. Their eyes were dozens of daggers in the air. Camillea sniffed.

"Guards, bring me the prince."

Prince? Sydney's sluggish mind puzzled over the word.

Two members of the queen's guard pushed their way through the crowd of elves, stopping before a familiar face.

Sydney stared. It wasn't possible.

She would have known.

He would have told her.

Lukaris gave his brother a final squeeze before passing him to Flindir. The soldiers dragged the prince forward, flinging him carelessly into the mud at Camillea's feet.

"You are Prince Ventir of Sil Tullian, first born heir to the throne of Ithirdas. That boy is your brother, Naherin. Am I correct?" The queen asked.

Lukaris didn't speak, but the set of his jaw was answer enough. Sydney's head spun. How had she missed it? The way he held himself among elves that should be his superiors, the intense devotion from the people of Firne. Sydney had passed it off as due respect given to a *Valen*. But it had always been loyalty to their prince. Their *princes*, she realized.

Elves have many names, Itari had told her. *A few given, many earned. Most elves never use the name they received at birth.*

She had been so blind.

The queen dismounted her horse, moving until she towered above Lukaris. She drew her sword and held it steady at the prisoner's throat.

"I received word that the Red Elf is being sheltered here. Tell me where she is, and things might go easier for you."

In response, the elf put together such an impressive string of profanities, Sydney felt a small twinge of pride. He ended the tirade by spitting directly onto Camillea's boot. A nearby soldier gasped. The watching elves and humans held their collective breath.

The queen's mouth formed a tight, flat line. With the same foot, she gave Lukaris a piercing kick to the gut. The elf doubled over, clutching at his abdomen.

Half of the *tatell* was on its feet in the time it takes to draw a breath. For a moment, there was chaos. Itari tried to push past a soldier, face contorted with rage, while other elf warriors struggled with guards of their own. Sydney took an involuntary step forward.

The rebellion was brief. The elves were too injured and crippled by their lack of magic to form a proper resistance. When order had been restored, Camillea grabbed Lukaris' pointed chin, forcing him to meet her gaze.

The look Lukaris gave her sent shivers down Sydney's spine. His eyes held none of their usual brightness. They were dark and shadowed, rimmed with red.

"I have waited decades to face the monster that killed my parents," the queen hissed. "Now *where is she?*"

"She's long gone from this place," Lukaris spat, voice hoarse. "You're too late. You've failed."

"Failed?" Camillea scoffed. She pushed the prince away. "One Ithirdi prince is dead, and the other is my prisoner. The rest will fall into place soon enough."

All of the anger, all of the defiance, drained from Lukaris' body at the single mention of Raiden. Sydney could hardly bear to look at him.

Camillea seemed satisfied. She remounted her horse and addressed the prisoners. "Your prince will be taken to Delm, where he will face justice for his crimes and those of Ithirdis. The rest of you will remain here, guarded by soldiers of Brimhold. Should any of you resist, I will receive word, and the prince will be executed on the spot."

Sydney sucked in a sharp breath. Brandon glanced at her, that familiar furrow between his brows.

The queen continued. "Likewise, Prince Ventir, should you try and escape, I will send similar orders. My soldiers will kill each and every prisoner in this village, without question."

If the Brims found Camillea's demands extreme, their faces did not show it. *That used to be me,* Sydney realized. A few months ago, she would have stood right there in line with the others. One of Brimhold's loyal swords. She would have murdered any elf the queen ordered. Would she have been the one to kill Raiden? The thought sent her stomach rolling.

Preparations began at once. The elves, including the children, were bound hand and foot. Guards corralled them into a tight, manageable group, dragging those that were too injured to move on their own. A soldier hoisted Lukaris onto a horse, tying him tightly to the saddle. The prince barely seemed to notice.

Sydney watched all of this with a growing dread. She stood to the side, unsure of her place. No one paid her any mind, except Brandon, who kept glancing at her as if she would disappear if his eyes left her for too long.

Eventually, the queen was ready to depart. Only a few dozen soldiers would be joining her, with most remaining behind to guard the prisoners of Firne. The elves watched them all with eyes full of venom. Brandon pulled forward a horse and offered the reigns to Sydney. She took them wordlessly. After all, what choice did she have?

As they turned to leave, Sydney spared a final glance at the beautiful, broken elvish village. In that moment, her eyes met Itari's. The Viridian's lips twitched, and Sydney could almost hear the whispered word in the space between them.

"Silvas."

For meeting and for parting. Until we see each other again.

42

Unburnt

"Have I ever told you about my father?" Malcolm asked, leaning in close to Arkyn's face. "No, of course I haven't. Why would I? But I think, perhaps, you would benefit from the story.

"When I was a boy, my father would take me out on his boat. Every day, I would labor on that ship. I would scrub the deck and manage the sails… whatever my father asked of me. But every day, before we returned to the crumbling shack we called a home, my father would call me onto the deck. He would tie me to the mast and whip me three times. Always three times. He never raised his voice to me. He never explained why I was being punished. But every day, I would struggle to please him, and every day I went home with blood on my back."

Koraline listened to her captor's tale with horror. Arkyn just stared at the man, his expression unreadable.

"One day I broke down and asked the question. 'Why? Father, why do you whip me every day unrelenting?' That day he whipped me five times. As I lay whimpering on the deck, he said a single word to me. 'Control.' My father taught me an important lesson that day.

Pain is the most powerful weapon humanity has at its disposal. It will force a dog to kill for you. It will compel a woman to stay by your side. And it will convince a man to reveal his deepest secrets. When your weapon is pain, no man, woman, or child can stand against you." Malcolm held Arkyn's chin, looking at the prisoner as if he were a riddle to solve.

"Make no mistake. I am a master of agony. It is a craft I have trained in my entire life. Every man has his breaking point if you are clever enough to find it."

A soldier entered the cell behind Malcolm. He held something in his hands, though Koraline could not see what it was from her position on the floor.

"My father taught me a second lesson, the same day I plunged my dagger into the old bastard's heart. A lesson almost as valuable as his first. He gave me this scar." Malcolm ran a finger over the jagged line that decorated his face. "And I learned that not only is pain powerful… it is everlasting. We carry it with us. Forever."

The soldier passed Malcolm a metal pole with a plate at the end. The flat end was glowing bright, red and yellow and white. White hot. Realizing what was happening, Koraline struggled against her chains. She had to help him. But what could she do?

"It is my greatest hope, Arkyn," Malcolm said softly, his mouth by the captive's ear. "That you carry this with you for a very long time."

No, no, no. Malcolm pressed the steaming metal against Arkyn's chest.

Koraline closed her eyes, bracing herself, waiting for Arkyn's now familiar cries. They did not come. For a moment, there was only the sound of sizzling metal. And then, Arkyn began to laugh. A loud, almost crazed laugh that echoed throughout the chamber and chilled Koraline to her core. Her eyes flicked open. Malcolm's soldier stared at Arkyn as if he were the monster from a nightmare. Perhaps he was.

The man fled from the cell, bursting through the doorway at a dead sprint. Malcolm's usual calm, controlled expression had shattered. Shock was plain on his face… along with a hint of fear.

The branding iron clattered to the floor as it fell from Malcolm's grasp. Koraline stared in astonishment. Arkyn's skin lay smooth and unmarred, only a bit red where the steaming iron had touched him. With a powerful tug, the captive pulled loose one of his chains, freeing his arm from its locked position. Malcolm's eyes widened further as Arkyn flung him against the stone wall with alarming strength. Unbent and partially unchained, Arkyn towered over his captor. A hand found the warden's throat.

"You are a fool," Arkyn said, some of the laughter still in his voice. "You speak of pain as if that is all it takes to hold power. Physical pain is nothing. It is used by weak men to make themselves feel strong. And you, Malcolm, you are weak. Spineless, pathetic, cowardly. Clinging to the ghosts of your past and letting them shape you. You can torture and slice and *burn* me all you like. It makes no difference. Because how can you hope to break me when you are broken yourself?"

In the end, it took four guards to pull Arkyn off of Malcolm. The scarred man fell to his knees, gasping for air. When he finally stood, the loathing on his face sent shivers down Koraline's spine. *You will pay,* it promised. Koraline could already hear Arkyn's future screams. Malcolm left the prison in a hurry, without a backwards glance. The remainder of the guards secured Arkyn in new chains before following their master. The prisoners were left alone. The silence was deafening.

Koraline waited for what felt like hours for Arkyn to speak. He didn't. She wasn't sure what there was to say. Who was this man she had shared so much with? Did she really know? She thought they were friends, but he hid so much from her. He still refused to tell her what Malcolm wanted from him. And what secrets lurked behind his disconcerting strength and unburnt skin? She yearned to know, but she also feared losing trust in her only companion. For, despite everything, she did trust him.

"Koraline," Arkyn croaked at last, his accent thick. Koraline turned her face to him, concerned. His voice held a hollowness to it, all of his earlier confidence crumbling like coal to ash.

"I'm sorry. You must think… well, I can't imagine what you must think."

She stared hard at the dirt floor. After a moment, the princess murmured, "When I was very little, my father used to tell me a terrible story about a mermaid and a shark. I hated it. I don't remember the details, but I always remembered the lesson. The girl trusted the shark, despite its nature, and she paid the price." Koraline locked eyes with her friend, blue clashing on gold. "I know you have secrets. I'm not asking you to share them. But please, Arkyn. Don't be the shark in my story."

Her doubt seemed to pain him. The man leaned his head back against the stone, eyes closed tight. After a moment, he whispered, "I have made mistakes. But I would *never* betray you, *allska*."

"I believe you," Koraline assured him. "My father would call me foolish, but it's true all the same."

"I think your father could learn a few things from you. Faith is not a weakness. In fact, I admire it." Arkyn gave her a small smile that she had no choice but to return. If only for a moment.

"Arkyn, I'm glad you stood up to Malcolm today, but I fear the cost. I've never seen him that angry." She glanced at the wounds crisscrossing her companion's chest, trying to fathom, not for the first time, how they were made by a man with a soul.

"What else could he possibly do to me?" Despite the confident words, a shadow crossed Arkyn's face. If not fear, then something close.

"I don't know. But I don't want to be here to find out." The next words hung heavy in the mermaid's throat. Ever present doubt and fear rushed forward, begging to be heard. But Koraline had learned to press past the voices. "We have to try and escape. Tomorrow or the next day, I don't care, but soon. Arkyn, if we stay here any longer that man is going to kill you. Maybe not on purpose, but one day he'll go too far. He'll let his anger cloud his actions. And if I have to watch that happen…" Koraline shuddered. "I think it will kill me too."

Arkyn stared at her. He took a deep breath. "Ok, I hear you. But what hope do we have of escaping?"

Koraline took in their surroundings, the same dirt floor, the same bars, the same chains that she'd stared at for what felt like a lifetime. Her eyes settled on the cuffs that enclosed Arkyn's wrists.

"Can you break out of those again? Like you did before?"

Arkyn looked down, holding up his hands so the metal caught the light. "I worked on the old chains for weeks, and I only managed to break through one. They've got some sort of Blood magic worked into the design." As the prisoner shifted, Koraline noted small ruins etched in the iron. "It's a hopeless pursuit. There's not enough time."

The mermaid tried to hide her disappointment. "Well, that just means we're not getting out with brute force. We'll have to get the keys."

"The keys," Arkyn repeated, skeptical. "Like the ones Malcolm always wears at his belt?"

"Precisely."

"Right. And how do you plan on getting those without him noticing, Princess?"

Koraline shot him a frown. He only called her Princess when he was frustrated with her. "You're giving up before we even try. Aren't you the one who keeps telling me we're going to get out of this place?"

"And we will, but not by making foolish escape attempts. I'm just being realistic. Don't you think I've gone through this before? I was here for months before you were kidnapped. Whatever plan you conceive, I've already tried, failed, and paid for in blood."

"Well, things are different now," Koraline insisted.

"Is that so?"

"Yes, because now you have me."

Arkyn leaned back against his wall, considering her. After a moment, the man shook his head.

"*Niske toth Helgmar,*" he grumbled. Then, he said, "You're right. Malcolm is alone, but we are not. Let's give it a shot. If for no other reason than to get me away from that damn porridge."

"I thought it was to die for?" Koraline laughed.

"Yes, worth dying to escape from."

The friends worked well into the night. At first, it seemed impossible, and ideas died as soon as they were formed. But eventually, working together, Koraline and Arkyn began to piece together a plot, tweaking and revising for hours on end. Finally, as the torchlight fell to a low smolder, they had a plan ready to enact the next day. It relied heavily on Malcolm's predictability. Every day, he opened Arkyn's cell with the set of keys at his belt. But they had realized, after hours of discussion, that the warden never relocked the cell at the end of the day. The task always fell to another soldier. So, if they could take the keys during Malcolm's time in the cell, they should have a window before he realized they were missing. It was simple, but risky. Any number of things could go wrong, and they would be right back where they'd started. If Malcolm allowed them to live, that is.

As Koraline drifted off to sleep, she worried if they were doing the right thing. Maybe they should wait another week, another month.

Give themselves more time to think. But then she remembered the look on their torturer's face. The hatred. No, it was now or never. And if she died as a result? Well, at least she would die fighting for the freedom she had always craved.

43

Guilt and Nightmares

The journey back to Delm was cold and wet and bleak. Rain followed the Brims and their Ithirdi prisoner east through the Wornwood, clouds of mist rolling down from the mountains. Damp air clung to clothes and skin, and few words were spoken through the all encompassing gloom. To Sydney's surprise, they encountered no other elves during their hurried escape. The only other presence was the forest itself, solemn and silent, and if the trees had eyes, they watched on sadly as their prince was stolen away.

When the troop reached the Thorburn Chasm, they crossed the same stone bridge Sydney and Brandon had used all those weeks ago. This time, no guard manned the crossing. Sydney wondered if her fellow soldiers had killed him on their way to attack Firne. Did his body lay somewhere in the chasm's shadowy depths? The thought churned her stomach. Her heart was so sick of death.

They only stopped to rest once they were deep into Brimhold land. Some of the tension dissolved at last, and the warriors lost their stern looks and measured voices. Laughter cropped up. Friends exchanged smiles. They had just won a battle, after all. A great victory in a worthy war. They were warriors of Brimhold, Sydney's friends, not murderers or fierce invaders. Yet, to Sydney, everything was different. She kept herself apart from the revelry, and by extension, Brandon. Her friend watched her with sad, uncertain eyes, saying little. Something between them had fractured. Changed. But whatever the rift, Sydney was too preoccupied to mend it. Every time she closed her eyes, she saw Raiden's face. The blood on Flindir's hands. Lukaris…

The Ithirdi prince rode his horse in silence, hands bound to the saddle in front of him. Sydney tried to bring her steed next to his, but the others wouldn't allow it.

"No talking with the prisoner. Queen's orders." The rule applied to everyone, but Sydney knew it was meant for her. She felt the distrustful stares of her once allies like knives on her skin. They had all seen her cry over an elf. They'd watched her hold his dying hand. What kind of Brim would do such a thing? A captain of the Honor Guard, no less.

When they finally stopped for camp, the soldiers tied Lukaris to a tree for the night, battering him with insults and multiple kicks to the ribs. Still, the elf said nothing. He just watched, forest eyes heavy and hollow. When a guard brought him food, he turned his head, placing slender hands into fists on his lap.

"If the rotten elf won't eat, I'm not going to force him," a soldier growled. "Let him starve for all I care."

"Maybe I should try," Sydney suggested. The warrior gave her an uneasy glance.

"I don't think that's such a good idea."

"What will the queen say if you let her prisoner die before we get to Delm?" Sydney asked, making her voice hard. Some of her old authority bled through. The soldier paled.

"Alright, but make it quick."

Sydney knelt at Lukaris' side, a bowl clutched in her hand like a shield between them. Across the camp, Brandon's gaze followed her every movement.

The *Valen* was different. Aged. His eyes held none of their usual warmth. They were dull, broken things. Even his wild hair seemed lackluster.

"Lukaris," Sydney croaked at last. It was the first word she'd spoken to him since they stood on the hill above Firne, watching the village die below them. "You have to eat."

The elf didn't answer. Didn't even acknowledge her. He shifted, and Sydney glanced the other side of his face. The wound that traced his angled cheekbone had dried into a red gash with a blossoming bruise beneath. No one had bothered to clean off the blood.

"Please," she pleaded. "I'm sorry. I'm so sorry. About everything. I will fix this, I promise, all of this. But not if you die before I get the chance. Please. Raiden would want you to eat."

Lukaris' head snapped up. The wind stirred, and guards glanced over suspiciously. The look he gave Sydney held such venom, such malice, her blood turned to ice.

"How dare you," he hissed in a voice that was the first breath of a hurricane. "How dare you say his name."

Sydney reeled back as if she'd been struck. "I'm sorry, I thought—"

"He's gone. Because of you. Because I trusted you," Lukaris choked. "You got what you wanted. Now leave me to grieve in peace."

Each word hit Sydney in the chest. "You think I wanted this to happen?"

"Enough!" The elf practically shouted. Out of the corner of her eye, she saw Brandon rise to his feet. "No more of your lies. I know you overheard Flindir and I discussing the warroot that day. You led your guard straight to us and handed them the weapon of our destruction. So, keep your false sympathy to yourself."

In many ways, Sydney blamed herself for what happened to Firne. But to think that she planned the whole thing. That she sent the warroot to Brimhold, that she intentionally caused Raiden's death… the idea sent her spinning.

"I had nothing to do with the warroot, and the queen came to Firne all on her own. You have to know that," Sydney said, throat tight from withheld tears.

Lukaris barked a laugh as Brandon arrived at Sydney's shoulder. It was a bitter sound. "Do I? Just like I knew *he* was a sword for hire you met on the road from Delm?" The elf jerked his head in Brandon's direction. Sydney swallowed, trapped in the lie no matter how good her reasons.

"So, you're the one that knocked me out?" Brandon asked darkly. "I owe you for that."

"*Mahil.*" Lukaris leaned against the tree trunk, head back and eyes closed. Sydney winced. The Elvish expression roughly translated to *you are not worthy of my time*. You are less than nothing. Though Brandon did not speak the language, the tone was clear. The captain gritted his teeth, hand finding his sword.

Sydney stepped between them. "Stop. Please. Let's just leave him be."

She managed to pull her friend away before any blood could be shed. She looked back over her shoulder, hoping to send Lukaris a silent message that said they would speak more later. But the elf didn't even open his eyes as they walked away.

She never got her chance. Lukaris was kept well away from her for the remainder of the journey. Even if she'd had the opportunity, Sydney wasn't sure what more she could say. Her only hope in regaining the elf's trust was to talk to the council once they reached Delm. Maybe she could end this conflict once and for all. Maybe.

Time dragged by as they rode through the rugged highlands of

Brimhold, stopping only to sleep and rest the horses. The days were filled with dark clouds and gusts of unrelenting winds. They bowed their heads against the drafts of air, picking their way through canyons, cliffs, and crevices. But as tiresome as the days were, the nights were worse. Wet blankets and rocky earth led to restless sleep.

And for Sydney, nighttime meant nightmares, full of darkness and shadow. Dreams of shadow-borne and fangs and those same piercing silver eyes. She had them every night without fail, waking in a pool of sweat with a scream on her lips.

"Are you alright?" Brandon asked one night as she startled herself awake. His familiar, square face hovered above her in the darkness.

"Fine," Sydney replied, breathless. She glanced over to Lukaris' sleeping form. She wished she could talk to him about the dreams. Because how could Brandon understand? He hadn't been there that night, when the shadow-borne ripped open her mind and left fear behind. He still thought the monsters were trapped between the pages of a fairy tale where they belonged.

Brandon's jaw clenched as he watched her, and a strange emotion passed across his face. Anger? Sadness? Sydney couldn't tell. She used to be able to read him so well.

"Get some sleep. We'll reach Delm tomorrow." He rolled over, back firmly to her face. Sydney pressed both hands to her eyes. How had everything gone so wrong between them?

There was a pulse of excitement in camp the next morning. The rush of being a day's journey from home and the promise of a warm, familiar bed. For Sydney, there was nothing but dread. She didn't know what awaited her when they reached the capital city.

She didn't know if she was strong enough to stop a war.

44

A Final Magic

Flindir couldn't stop staring at the blood on his bound hands. *This can't be real.*

He cradled Raiden in his lap. The boy's tiny frame seemed even smaller now that the Light had left him. Beside them, Itari sat curled in on herself, forehead to her knees. Flindir wanted to comfort her more than anything. To kiss her forehead and tell her everything would be alright. But the words kept catching in his throat.

How did we let this happen?

He remembered so clearly the day Raiden was born. Flindir never had any siblings of his own, and he was almost as excited as Lukaris for the arrival of a new baby. They sat for many long hours in the Sil Tullian palace, side by side, betting on the gender. But somehow, when they were finally called to the royal chambers, they both knew a brother awaited them. Prince Naherin. *Osan.* Raiden. He was so innocent. Perfect. *Theirs.*

And now that same little boy sat still and cold in Flindir's arms.

I couldn't save him, Flindir thought. His hands shook as tried to remove some of the red. *I froze. If only Ettee had been here. Maybe she would've known what to do.*

He looked across the loose huddle of imprisoned elves. His friend and mentor had not moved since the battle's end, when the Brims dragged her from Firne's ruins. Flindir couldn't tell if she was even breathing. Maybe they had lost her too…

No. He could still help her. He wouldn't fail anybody else.

"Love," Flindir whispered to Itari in Elvish, barely a breath. He eyed the human soldiers that paced around them. "Take him."

Itari looked up. Her eyes were swollen, their edges tinged with pink. Tears had formed tracks through the grime on her face. She was still the most beautiful thing Flindir had ever seen.

"What are you doing?" the Viridian croaked back, pulling Raiden into her arms.

"I have to check on Ettee."

"The Brims won't let you treat her."

"I'm not asking for permission."

"You'll never make it over to her unnoticed," Itari urged gently.

"I have to try." He locked eyes with her, begging her to understand. "I have to help if I can."

Itari sighed. She looked down at Raiden, stroking a wayward piece of hair off the boy's forehead. The tender motion sent a fresh stab through Flindir's chest. When she met his gaze again, her eyes were determined.

"I'll create a distraction. But be careful, my love. I need you too."

Before Flindir could choke a reply, Itari leaned to the elf next to her and whispered something in his ear. The elf nodded and, in turn, mumbled a message to the woman behind him. This continued until, on the far end of the huddled elves, one of the Ithirdi warriors called out.

"Guards! Guards, please. Help me. I'm begging you…"

The soldiers moved away, towards the shouting elf. Itari gave Flindir a small wink and shooed him off.

By the Light, he loved her.

He half crawled, half squirmed his way through the captives. They created a subtle path for him, shifting a leg here and a shoulder there, until Ettee lay just a few feet away. He could finally see her face, eyes closed, expression softer than he'd ever seen it while awake. Flindir reached out, fingers brushing his friend's wrist. For a moment, nothing. Then, a steady pulse beneath his thumb. He sucked in a relieved breath.

Then quickly lost it as a boot struck his side.

The force of the kick rolled Flindir out of the mass of elves. He came to a stop with his tied hands trapped beneath him, cheek pressed into the mud. A Brim warrior loomed over him.

"And where do you think you're going?" the soldier snarled, dragging the elf to his knees by a fist full of hair. Flindir gritted his teeth to keep from crying out.

"I was just trying to check on my friend," Flindir wheezed. "She's hurt. Please, just let me help her."

Flindir knew that humans were capable of compassion. He had seen it in the weeks with Sydney and the months helping Brimhold's villages before that. But something in this soldier's eyes looked more animal than human. He barked a laugh at Flindir's plea.

"And why should I care about the life of some she-elf? If it were up to me, you'd all be target practice. Now, get back to your spot, before I get angry."

Flindir looked at Itari. Her shoulders were tight, face twisted with rage. She glared at the back of the Brim's head like her eyes could shoot lightning too.

He had a choice to make. Leave Ettee to suffer alone. Or fight to be by her side.

Flindir thought then of a day, years ago, far away in Sil Tullian. He was just a boy, younger than Raiden, working outside in the family garden. He picked weeds under the afternoon sun while his mother practiced battle stances across the yard. They worked in a silent, peaceful harmony, until Flindir turned to water his favorite daisies. A sad cry split through the air, and his mother was at his side in an instant.

"What's wrong, my sprout?" Calloused fingers wrapped around Flindir's. He pointed to the flowers with his free hand, eyes wet and wide.

"I ruined them!" he sniveled. They stared at the field of wilted petals, a sea of white gone gray.

"Hm, is that so?" His mother squatted among the dead blossoms, cupping Flindir's hands around the nearest flower. "Close your eyes, son. Listen. Feel."

Flindir did as he was told. "I don't hear anything."

"That's because you're listening with *these*." She tugged on his ears. "Instead of *this*," she finished, poking his chest just above the heart.

Flindir huffed and tried again. For a moment, nothing happened. Then he felt it, faintly, a glow between his palms. A Light. He coaxed it, feeding the ember into a flame. When he opened his eyes, the daisy had returned to its former glory. Flindir traced a finger over the ivory petals, awestruck.

"I did it!" Flindir exclaimed, voice filled with wonder. "How did you know they could still be saved?"

His mother wiped a lingering tear from his cheek. "I have learned many things in my time as a warrior, but the most important is this. True strength is knowing when to fight for something and when to let it go."

Back in the Wornwood, knees in the mud and eyes on Ettee's crumpled form, Flindir realized there was really no choice at all.

"I'm not going anywhere until I help my friend," Flindir informed his captor. Surprise flickered across the Brim's face, followed closely by anger.

"Wrong answer."

Flindir's head snapped back as the human punched him squarely in the face. Hard. He collapsed, eyes blurred and ears ringing. Itari shouted something, but he couldn't make out the words. He struggled to rise from the mud, but another blow sent him sprawling. Through a painful haze, Flindir heard the distinct sound of a sword pulling from its sheath. Silver glinted above him.

"Let this be a lesson to any other elf that tries to step out of line," the soldier bellowed. Somewhere, Itari still screamed. Flindir closed his eyes, chest aching. *Stupid, kind-hearted fool.*

"Enough."

The word echoed through the trees, breaking through Flindir's fog and Itari's cries. The human soldier froze, sword still raised, as heads turned in the direction of the order. To the east, two figures stepped from the shadowed forest. One with hair like fire.

Novah. And close behind her, Sarcys. Flindir had never been so happy to see the brooding elf.

"Release these prisoners and return to your own kingdom," Novah demanded, sounding like a true *Valen*. "At once."

The humans froze. Whispers slipped from their tongues. The Red Elf. *Here.*

But their shock only lasted a moment. The Brims erupted with laughter. The taunting sound set a pit in Flindir's stomach.

"You elves really are daft," the soldier above Flindir sneered. "Two of you against a full guard? I'll make you a counter offer. Surrender now, and I *might* let you live to see another sunrise."

Novah looked to the Brim with disdain. "This is not a negotiation. Leave now or face the consequences."

What is she doing? Flindir wondered. Even if their magic had managed to return, the odds were against them. He locked eyes with

Sarcys. The solemn warrior gave him subtle nod.

All around the huddled group of elves, Brims raised their weapons.

"We aren't going anywhere, witch."

Novah smiled.

From the forest behind her, a howl pierced the air. Then another, and another, until the sound was strong enough to make Flindir wince. A few of the humans covered their ears, faces contorted in pain. The head soldier took a slight step backwards as the howls morphed into snarls, and a pack of riphounds paced from the trees. Row after row of sharp, shining fangs and dozens of haunted yellow eyes. Brims cried out in alarm. These were creatures they'd never had the misfortune to face.

With the beasts, came a wind. Slight and soft, slipping through the captured elves like a river over stone. As the breeze brushed against him, tears spiked at the corner of Flindir's eyes. He felt it then, deep in his chest. A Light. Stronger than it'd ever been in life.

It was Raiden. The final touch of his magic, cast out to save them.

Flindir twisted for a glance at Itari. She sat smiling among her tears, tucking Raiden's head against her chest.

"C-call off your pets," the Brim leader stuttered. His eyes were wide and panicked. "If a single one of us comes to harm, our scout will contact Delm. Your precious prince will be executed on the spot."

On cue, a roar joined the chorus of snarls. A great, lumbering shadow rose above Sarcys' shoulder. Honey bellowed in anger, exposing a maw of blood-stained teeth.

"I'm afraid your scout is indisposed," Novah replied with a suggestive pat on Honey's golden side. The humans paled further.

"We don't—" The Brim above Flindir seemed to harden. Resigned. "We will never surrender to the likes of you."

Before Novah could respond, the soldier raised his sword again, swinging it towards Flindir. Itari yelled. The bound elf could only watch as the line of silver sliced towards his neck.

But riphounds were faster than any blade. One of the beasts leapt over Flindir, crashing into the human's chest. A single scream tore from the man's throat before the creature's jaws closed around it. Fresh blood mixed with the mud.

Flindir fell backwards with relief as the creatures surged forward. Brims cried out. Ithirdi cheered.

And Flindir closed his eyes against it all, whispering quietly to himself.

"Melánethe, osan."

45

Prisoners of War

Delm came into view by late afternoon. On the horizon, towers of stone brushed the sky like the fingers of giants. Beside the city, the lake was an expanse of gray, reflecting the melancholy clouds.

Sydney expected to feel at least a spark of joy when her eyes landed on that familiar silhouette. Instead, it was like looking at a memory. Just a reminder that things would never be the way they were.

They rode through the western gates, Brimhold's violet flag flapping in the breeze above as they passed underneath the archway. Trumpets and fanfare welcomed their arrival with the citizens of Delm pouring onto the streets in mobs. At first, there were cheers. Then, hushed and awestruck whispers as they spotted Lukaris, bound and bent on his horse. Last, came the shouts.

"Murderer!"

"Elvish bastard!"

"Lock him up and throw away the key!"

"Set him afire, like he did Briar!"

The Prince of Ithirdas did not waver under the torrent of attacks. He stared straight ahead, sharp jaw clenched. Sydney looked down at the hate-filled faces, wondering if she had ever been that angry and devoid of mercy. She knew the answer.

At the front of the brigade, Queen Camillea rode tall and proud. She redonned her crown, and she looked every bit the returning hero. When the people finished their screams of loathing, they showered their ruler with bouquets of bluebells and dragon's breath. Hundreds of flowers littered the cobblestones, only to be crushed under passing hooves. Camillea flashed her subjects a brilliant smile.

The ride through Delm seemed to take an eternity. Up through the Copper District and Starling Square. Past The Steel Anchor and Gilliad's house with its bright red door. Finally, through the heavy iron gates that secured the castle. Near the stables, General Norwell waited. He looked gruff and gray as ever, but his face brightened when he met Sydney's eyes. She jumped from her horse, throwing both arms around him. His comforting scent wafted over her, all leather and iron. He gave her a tight squeeze.

"I ruined everything, Gilliad," she whispered, his beard scratching her cheek. "I don't know what to do."

"What matters is that you're home now. We'll figure out the rest," he murmured.

Home. Is that what it was?

When they finally broke apart, Brandon was there. Gilliad clapped him heartily on the shoulder.

"Well done, lad. You brought her back in one piece."

Brandon didn't answer. His brow had not released from its furrow in days.

Queen Camillea cleared her throat, bringing everyone to attention. While most of the soldiers had dismounted, she still sat high on her white steed. Her winter eyes swept across the crowd. "Julia, take a few guards and escort our prisoner to the dungeon. Make sure to use Blood rune bindings. I don't want any Light magic surprises."

"Yes, your Majesty," Julia said. She yanked Lukaris from his saddle.

"I'm not finished," Camillea continued. Then, those eyes of ice fixed on Sydney. "You will need to find Captain Krane a cell as well."

Silence. Baited breaths and confused glances.

"What?" Brandon demanded at last, Sydney's own shock mirrored in his voice.

"Your Majesty, I don't understand," Gilliad said at the same time.

The queen regarded them coldly. "Captain Krane has exhibited treasonous behavior since her rescue from the elves. I cannot allow the possibility of a spy in our midst. She will stay in the dungeon until her loyalties can be determined."

"Loyalties?" Brandon exclaimed. He placed himself between Camillea and Sydney. Between Sydney and the world. "She's a captain of your Honor Guard. It's *Sydney*, for gods' sake."

"I've seen the most loyal soldier corrupted by the enemy. If Captain Krane remains dedicated to Brimhold, then she has nothing to fear from a few days in the hold. Now, stand aside, Captain Lockes." Camillea's voice snapped like a whip.

Sydney's mind flashed back to the day, all those years ago, when her father stood between her and the queen's recruiters. The soldier's hand on his weapon. The promise of bloodshed hanging in the air. She felt it now, as Brandon rose to her defense. But unlike her father, Brandon was not a man that backed down from a fight.

"It's okay," Sydney spoke up, trying to keep her voice calm. She tugged at Brandon's wrist, and she could feel his rapid pulse beneath the skin. "I'll go. She's right, Lockes. I'll be fine."

His eyes met hers. Brown and scared and pleading. But, she saw resignation there too.

The other soldiers remained silent as Julia's chosen guards seized Sydney's arms. Brandon and Gilliad stood as two pillars beside her, pale as milk. She tried to give her friends a reassuring smile, but it ended up as more of a grimace. She turned away from them before she could lose her nerve.

Julia led them into the castle and down the stone steps that descended to the dungeon. Down, down, down. Stories said Delm's prison used to be a crypt, and the bones of those long gone still lay beneath the dirt floors. Sydney didn't know if that was true, but her hair stood on end as the torchlight flickered from passing drafts.

They reached Lukaris' cell first. Julia shoved him into the cage, the other soldiers transferring him to new bindings. The elf settled into a corner, head bowed. They gave Sydney a cell just around the corner, a stone wall between her and the prince.

One of the guards held out a hand for Sydney's weapons. She held the boy's gaze as she passed over the swords.

"If anything happens to these, I'll be holding you personally responsible. Got it?"

The boy gave an audible swallow, followed by a hasty nod. Sydney saw a smile flash across Julia's face. It only lasted a moment.

"I'm sorry, Sydney," Julia muttered. Her dark hair cast a shadow across her almond eyes.

"Don't be," Sydney said as the door to her prison creaked closed. "I did this to myself."

Julia and the others departed, and Sydney was left alone. The only sounds came from the steady drip of water onto packed dirt and the squeaking of rats in the gloom. Sydney slid to the floor. *Gods, what am I going to do now?* She picked up a pebble and hurled it at a rat. The animal hissed, racing off down the corridor.

Sydney knew, with utmost certainty, that she would never be able to convince the queen of the elves' innocence. She had seen the hatred in Camillea's face. She would never give Novah the benefit of the doubt. She wouldn't accept that her war had been built on lies. Especially not without a suitable replacement for the blame.

So that left, what? Sydney could appeal to Brandon or Gilliad. But even if they believed her, their words wouldn't be enough to stop the fighting. To set Lukaris free.

Lukaris. Sydney scooted closer to the hall, pressing her body against the iron bars, listening. And there it was, if she strained her ears. The soft cries of grief. There was a sharp jab in her chest, like the cut of a knife.

"Lukaris." Her voice sounded loud in the hollow cell. The sound of muffled tears stopped. She hoped he could hear her. She hoped he would listen.

"I know you think all of this is my fault. And maybe it is. If I had never followed you from Briar, maybe none of this would've happened." She swallowed. "But I want you to know. I *never* meant to hurt you. Well… at first I did. But after I got to know you, after I got to know all of you, I really wanted to make peace. I wanted to help you stop the war. I still want that."

She had always been bad at this. Saying how she felt. No jokes, no jibes. Just her.

"And please, believe me when I say… I would have protected Raiden with my life. I never would have deliberately put him in danger. I loved that kid." Her voice broke. "You know that, right?"

No answer. Just the steady drip of the leaking ceiling. Just rats in the dark. Sydney sighed, head back against the wall.

"I'm sorry," she muttered, half to herself.

Down the corridor, multiple sets of footsteps fell upon the hard ground. Sydney got to her knees, straining to see around the corner. She thought she heard the groan of a cell door.

Then, Lukaris' scream pierced the silence. Sydney was on her feet.

"Hey!" she shouted, hands tight on the iron bars. "What's going on?"

She heard the *Valen* growl something in Elvish. There was a laugh, and then another cry. Sydney gritted her teeth, feeling helpless.

"Hey!" she yelled once more, punching the wall that separated her and Lukaris. *Ow.*

The door squeaked again, and the footsteps retreated. Sydney heard nothing from the neighboring cell.

"Lukaris? Ace, are you alright?"

He didn't answer, but there was a groan and the sound of moving dirt.

Sydney's relieved breath came out in a rush. What was going on? Had a few angry soldiers taken it upon themselves to rough up their prisoner? Or worse. Sydney knew from personal experience that torture was not unheard of among Brimhold's warriors.

Funny, how twisted things became once you were on the other side.

46

Old Friends

Brandon paced back and forth in his tiny room, mind reeling. He had done the impossible. He had saved Sydney from the monster's lair. Yet, it didn't feel like a victory. Not with his friend imprisoned beneath his own feet.

Not when everything was so clearly *wrong*.

Brandon collapsed onto his narrow bed. What was he supposed to *do*? He could fight elves all day, but he couldn't fight orders from his queen. He groaned, head falling to his hands.

Maybe he didn't need to do anything at all. In a few days, the queen would come to her senses and release Sydney. Everything would go back to normal, and they would all laugh about this one day. Right?

A knock on the door shook Brandon from his worrying. He frowned. He never got visitors this late in the evening. He moved to open the door, shoulders tense.

Sydney stood on the threshold.

She looked the same as he'd last seen her. A filthy elvish tunic hidden under the folds of her favorite cloak. A muddy pair of boots. Dark brown hair braided back out of her face, and eyes like hardened steel.

Brandon gaped. "Syd? What are you doing here? *How* are you here?"

Sydney put a finger to her lips and nodded past her shoulder. A guard Brandon hadn't noticed stood off to the side, waiting. She motioned inside his room.

"Right, come in." He stepped aside, and his friend slipped in through the opening. The guard didn't look at them as Brandon pushed the door shut.

"Gods, your room is so barren. It doesn't even look like you live here," Sydney commented, filling the hole Brandon had left on his bed. She was right. Brandon kept only the essentials. Sword, shield, and a few pairs of extra clothes. He'd learned long ago at the orphanage that you should always be ready to pack up your life at a moment's notice.

"Syd, what's going on?" he insisted. "Did you break out of the dungeon?"

Sydney rolled her eyes. "Don't be so dramatic. I bribed the guard out there. He'll take me back once we're done talking."

Well. That was some relief.

"What was so urgent that you needed to see me tonight?" Brandon asked. "I could have come to visit you tomorrow."

"You really think Camillea would have let you?" Sydney said with a snort. "Besides, this gives us more privacy. I don't want anyone overhearing."

"Alright." He leaned against the opposite wall. "I'm listening."

Sydney took a deep breath, like she wasn't sure how to start now that she was here.

"It's about the elves. We can't keep going like this, Brandon."

He frowned. "What do you mean?"

"Fighting for Brimhold is a losing battle. The elves are going to win, it's only a matter of time. But we don't have to be here when everything comes crashing down. We can join the elves. This war doesn't have to be the death of us."

Brandon gaped. He felt like he'd been punched in the gut. "Syd, what are you saying? The elves killed my father. They destroyed Briar. How can you talk about betraying your own people?"

"Ithirdas isn't what we thought it was. The elves aren't the monsters we were trained to see. There's so much you don't know, Brandon. Help me get out of Delm with the prince, and I'll explain everything," she urged.

"The prince?" he hissed in disbelief. "The elf we tracked from Briar? The one who kidnapped you and held you prisoner? *Him?*"

She shook her head. "You don't get it. We reached an understanding. He never hurt me."

"When I woke up in the Wornwood... I found blood on the ground. Are you saying that wasn't yours?"

"Well," Sydney said with a wince. "We had a rough start."

Brandon stared. This wasn't right. What had Camillea said? *I've seen the most loyal soldier corrupted by the enemy.*

Brandon knelt down on the floor in front of his friend. His family. He grasped her arms like he meant to shake some sense into her.

"Syd, please," he whispered, looking up into her familiar face. "What happened to you out there? What did those damn elves do to you?"

The gray in her eyes hardened to stone. "Nothing happened. I'm still the same me."

"No, I refuse to accept that. The Sydney I knew would never turn against her guard. She would have died for Brimhold. For her queen."

Sydney scoffed, brushing off his hands. "The queen? You mean the queen that dragged us from our homes as children and forced us into this bloody war? The queen that did nothing while Briar burned? What loyalty do we owe her?"

Something in her was broken. It had been there for a while now, festering, waiting. Brandon had just been too blind to see it. It started when he found her crying in the woods, bent over her sister's final letter. When he let her pursue the attackers. When he failed to keep her safe.

"Syd, you're not well. Maybe Camillea was right. After a few days in the hold, things might start to look clearer."

Her mouth settled into that stubborn line he knew all too well. "You want to lock me up too. I thought you were my friend. But you won't even listen."

"That's not—"

She stood up, pushing him away. "I should go. Someone might notice if I'm gone much longer."

"Syd," he pleaded, rising after her. She cut him off with the wave of a hand.

"Don't worry. I didn't have much hope of convincing you. You were always weaker than you let on. That's why I had to co-captain the Honor Guard. Someone had to be there to hold your hand." Each sentence hit its mark, sharp and cold and deadly.

The anger that Brandon always carried deep inside began to boil. "You don't mean that."

"Whatever helps you sleep at night," Sydney replied sweetly. She had her hand on the door. "Oh, and Brandon? Remember my offer. When things go south, remember that I wanted you with me."

She seemed almost sad. Then, in a blink, she was gone.

Brandon sank to his knees, all the strength going out of him. Whoever that was, it wasn't the Sydney he loved.

But what was he going to do if it was the only Sydney that was left?

*****

Sydney lay on the dirt floor of her cage, listening to the incessant water drip from the ceiling, when she heard the dungeon door open a second time. She scrambled to her feet. *Gods, please don't put Lukaris through another round of harassment.* But this visitor was for her. Brandon rounded the corner, eyes sad and reserved. He was still dressed in armor and cloak, like the battle was not yet finished. Sydney rushed to the bars that separated them.

"Lockes!"

"Sydney."

She frowned at his tone. "What's wrong? Did something else happen?"

"The queen sent me to speak with you," he said. His face was pinched, as if he'd swallowed something sour.

"Oh." Sydney inhaled the musty air. "Look, I know she thinks I'm a spy or a traitor or something equally awful, but if I could just have a meeting with the council—"

"That won't happen," Brandon cut in. "Ever since we rescued you from Ithirdas, you've been different. Camillea saw it with her own eyes."

"How does she mean to determine my loyalty if she won't even give me the chance to defend myself?" Sydney demanded angrily. After all she'd sacrificed for Brimhold, wasn't she due at least a little trust?

"That's why I'm here," Brandon said. "Tell me what happened when you were with the elves. Give me something I can take back to the queen that might change her mind."

"Or what?" Sydney challenged. "If I say the wrong thing, will I stay in this cell forever?"

Brandon didn't answer, but his expression darkened. His arms knotted across his chest.

"What aren't you telling me?" She gripped the iron bars, trying to catch her friend's gaze.

"I'm— I'm not sure I should say."

Sydney looked at him with disbelief. "You doubt me too."

Brandon huffed, passing a hand through his short hair. "Can you blame me? When I left you, you wanted to kill every elf in the Wornwood. You were willing to do whatever it took to find your family's killers, and I thought I had lost you to that mission. I had to beg the queen to mount a rescue, even though I knew it was a hopeless cause. And then the impossible happened, and I found you alive. And instead of being grateful? Instead of seizing justice for Briar? You acted more concerned for the elves than your own people! You even mourned the death of an enemy prince. If anything, you should be happy there's one less elf in the world."

Bile rose to her throat at the flippant mention of Raiden's death.

"He didn't deserve to die like that," she whispered. "He was just a kid."

"But still an elf. How many Brims would he have killed when he grew up?"

Sydney couldn't imagine Raiden killing a butterfly, let alone a human. She took a steadying breath.

"Look. I know how things must seem, from where you're standing. I thought like you not too long ago. But I've learned that this war was built on lies. The elves never attacked Delm, and they didn't destroy Briar. The Red Elf never killed Camillea's parents. Someone wants this war to continue, and they've been pitting Brimhold and Ithirdas against each other for twenty years. There's no reason to keep fighting the Ithirdi. The real enemy is out there somewhere, hiding. Watching us tear each other apart. If we really want justice, we have to find *them*."

Brandon stared at her. "That's quite the story. What proof do you have?"

It struck her then that she didn't have any. Just words from enemies that had become something close to friends. But, she believed them all the same.

"I don't have proof," Sydney admitted. "Yet. And I know the queen won't believe me. But, maybe she would believe you."

"Those elves really did a number on you. They've brainwashed you against us somehow," Brandon murmured. Sydney saw that she was losing him. With each word, she hammered another nail in her coffin of treason. "I can't tell any of this to the queen. How am I supposed to save you when you say things like this?"

Sydney's ears pricked. "Save me? What do you mean save me?"

Her friend shook his head, and Sydney thought she saw tears forming at the corners of his eyes.

"Sydney…" Brandon swallowed. "If Camillea can't be convinced of your loyalty… she means to execute you alongside the elf."

Execute. The elf.

"What?" Sydney breathed.

"Look, it doesn't have to be like that—"

"When?"

"Sydney—"

"When, Lockes?" she practically shouted. Her knuckles grew white as her hands tightened around the bars.

"Tomorrow."

Only her iron grip kept her from stumbling backwards. "Tomorrow? This is insane. Surely you see that."

"If you were in her place, what would you do?" Brandon asked. "She can't just let betrayal go unpunished."

Sydney couldn't believe she was hearing this. Not from Brandon. Not from the boy who wiped her tears when she missed her family. The boy that held her hand before their first battle and kept her secrets as if they were his own. The man who crossed a continent just to bring her safely home.

Something was wrong. She felt it in her stomach, like the vibration when one sword struck another.

"Brandon." She edged as close as the bars would allow. "Look at me."

He did. They were the eyes she knew from childhood, an autumn brown, set in a square rugged face. But behind the lashes, behind the irises, they were all wrong. They held a different weight, repelling her in a way that sent chills up her arms. Someone stared back at her, certainly, but that someone was not Brandon.

Sydney backed away. Knotted mysteries she'd been struggling with for weeks suddenly unraveled. How could the Red Elf be in two places at once? Because someone else had been wearing her face.

"You're not Brandon," she whispered to the man in front of her. Now that she knew he was a lie, the impostor was a bad imitation of her friend. The way he stood, the small, calculating expressions that flickered across his face. "Who are you?"

The fake Brandon frowned. "Sydney, it's me. It's Brandon. Are you alright?"

Sydney. Brandon rarely used her name. It was always Krane or Syd or liar.

"You won't fool me any longer," Sydney practically snarled. She put all of her fury behind her words. "Tell me who you really are, now. Show yourself!"

The man paused with his head slightly cocked. Then, he smiled, the expression tight and wicked.

"Oh, very well."

The air stirred. Sydney blinked, trying to clear the haze from her eyes. The space around the man twisted and blurred, until it was like looking through a heat mirage on a sizzling summer day. When the world sharpened back into view, Brandon was gone. He'd changed.

Queen Camillea stood in his place, the same twisted smile on her face.

47

The Queen

Every life is filled with a cluster of pivotal moments. For Sydney, they were clear as snow melt. The day the soldiers rode into Briar. The day she made Honor Guard captain. Watching her home burn. Holding Raiden's dying hand. And she could feel this moment, staring at the queen's treacherous face, changing her life forever.

"You." Sydney's head spun. "I don't understand."

"I wouldn't expect you to," Camillea admitted. She held none of her usual royal poise. She looked like a predator eyeing her prey.

"You can change your appearance. What kind of magic…" The pieces clicked together even as Sydney spoke. "You're a greyblood. A half elf. You're not really Camillea. You never were."

"Very good," the queen laughed. The sound was shrill and vicious. "Maybe there's hope for you yet, Captain Krane."

"It was you who attacked Delm all those years ago. You wore the Red Elf's face. You killed the king and queen. Princess Camillea…"

"Dead like her parents, I'm afraid. Really, it was a mercy after all she'd been through that night." The greyblood was clearly enjoying herself. Sydney felt sick. She hoped Lukaris could hear all of this.

He needed to know he was right. Right about everything.

"So, you killed her and took her place. You started a war. But why? And why frame the Red Elf? She doesn't deserve the blame for your crimes."

Camillea's face hardened. Her eyes glimmered like two chips of blue ice. "That vile witch deserves all the blame and worse. And before all of this is over, I will kill her myself."

There was something familiar about Camillea's hatred. The way her voice lusted for justice. For revenge.

"Novah really did kill your family, didn't she? Your real family."

The queen's face contorted. "Did she tell you she was an assassin during the Greyblood Scour? Did she tell you she hunted children because of magic they never asked for?"

Suddenly, all Sydney felt was an aching sadness, deep and old. One death always led to a hundred more. One slaughter bled into another. An endless cycle of bloodshed.

"Yes. She told me," Sydney whispered.

Camillea nodded as if she'd expected this. "Not even ashamed of her past, is she? And why would she be? The Ithirdi royalty gave her a free pass. They made her part of their army. And yet, my parents still lie rotting in their fiery grave."

"I'm sorry," Sydney said, surprised that she meant it. "The Scour was a disgrace. But so is everything you've done since then. You're just as bad as the enemy you claim to hate."

"Is that so, Captain Krane?" the queen sneered. "You think you're so much better than me? I've pointed you at those you might consider innocent for years now. And you killed every elf I asked, without question. You're a murderer, just like everyone else."

The words hit Sydney in her chest. She saw each of them, every death, behind her eyelids. "It's not the same. You lied to me. You lied to all of Brimhold."

Camillea's sinister smile was back. "Oh, not all of them. You'd be surprised how many humans will kill just for the thrill of it. Or the thrill of gold brilleans in their pockets."

Sydney had to draw the line somewhere, and she could not believe that her own people would still fight for the greyblood queen if they knew the truth. "You're lying. You've tricked us all."

"Oh sure, some of you Brims are honorable. Many couldn't be trusted with the reality of things. Others could only handle a bit of the truth. But still, many are loyal to me just as I am." Camillea shrugged, as if not caring whether Sydney believed her or not.

If it were possible, Sydney's spirits sunk even lower. How was she supposed to help her kingdom now, when some of them were in league with the enemy, and always had been?

Sydney swallowed. A question sat on her tongue, but once she knew the answer, she feared her heart might break forever.

"Brandon. Gilliad. Do they know what you are? Tell me the truth."

The queen rolled her eyes, smile slipping away. "Don't fret, Captain Krane, your spineless idiots have been in the dark as much as you."

Sydney closed her eyes. *Thank the gods. Thank the Light. Thank whoever might be listening.*

"So, tell me — whatever your real name is — what's the point of all this? You frame the person that killed your family. I get that. But what about everything else? Why start a war with the elves? The rest of us did nothing to you."

Camillea stepped forward, her own hands wrapping around the prison bars like talons. "You know, I used to think you were smart, Sydney. Clever. You were always able to make the tough choices. I even thought one day I might let you into my inner circle. But now? I realize you're just as pathetic as the rest of them. The elves. The humans. Those cowardly fish in Nidaria, hiding in their crystal towers. This is about so much more than the Red Elf, Captain Krane.

The future belongs to the powerful. The outcasts the rest of Soarden's people rejected. Feared. This world belongs to *me*. And when the rest of you have burned, I will reshape it how I see fit."

She's insane. A monster. Sydney stared at the leader she once held in such high regard. Her whole life had been shaped by this woman, and all of it was crashing down in an instant.

Then, something Camillea said stuck out in her mind. *Burned.* Sydney's mouth tasted of ash. She thought of blood running through familiar streets. The searing smell of burnt hair. She took a step towards the leering queen.

"Did you issue the order—" Sydney swallowed the tears in her throat. "Did your loyalists destroy Briar?"

Camillea barked a laugh. "Of course. I had to take action when entire towns were becoming sympathetic towards the Ithirdi. Besides, it gave me something else to blame on the elves."

There it was. The fire that lived and breathed in Sydney's veins, ready to spark from an ember to a wildfire in a single breath. It sprung to life inside her, the edges of her vision turning red. Before she could think, her hands were through the bars and around Camillea's throat.

"You," Sydney hissed. "Lying, evil, murdering bitch—"

Camillea put her hands over Sydney's, but she didn't struggle. Instead, she laughed again, the sound wheezing.

"Ah, there she is," the queen breathed. "There's the killer I remember."

Sydney had never felt so angry. Her heart pounded with the strength of Allur's waterfall, echoing in her ears, drowning out the world. So many innocent lives gone. Her father. Abigail. Raiden. And all of their deaths were because of Camillea. The justice that Sydney had been searching for, all this time, was right here between her hands. *Kill her,* a voice inside of her screamed. *Watch the life leave her. It's what she deserves.*

Then, another voice spoke. To her surprise, it was Lukaris'.

That sounds more like vengeance to me.

Sydney forced herself to meet Camillea's eyes. She looked deep into whatever twisted soul lay inside. She saw hate. Grief. Endless sorrow caused by the search for revenge. She saw herself, if she took the queen's life, here, now, in this place.

And for what? It wouldn't bring back the ones she'd lost. And it wouldn't stop this war from taking anyone else.

So, with every ounce of strength Sydney could muster, she let them go. She put to rest those she'd lost. She chose a different way.

Tears traced lines down Sydney's cheeks as she released her hold on Camillea. The queen gasped, stepping backwards. She placed a hand to her long neck. Red marks wrapped her throat in the shape of Sydney's fingers.

"I won't be like you," Sydney whispered. She felt fragile, like a strong breeze might sweep her away. "I won't let my hatred for you turn me into something I'm not."

"You're weak," Camillea snapped. "Just like the rest of them. And tomorrow, you will die for it."

Sydney had forgotten about that small detail.

"And how are you going to explain my execution to the other soldiers? A death sentence is a little extreme for a mere sympathizer."

"Oh, I'm sure some of them will protest." The queen shrugged, as if Sydney's defenders were no more than minor irritations. "But after they see how brutally you attacked me, I bet I'll win them over."

"You think a sore neck is enough to convince them?" Sydney scoffed.

Camillea smiled, tucking a delicate blonde strand behind her ear. The air shifted again. Bruises blossomed across the queen's throat. Her lip began to swell. A cut appeared on her left brow. Sydney could only watch in horror.

"That should do it, don't you think?" Camillea asked, looking thoroughly beat to hell.

Sydney could think of nothing to say. The nightmare seemed to keep on giving.

"Oh, and I suppose some witnesses couldn't hurt," the queen mused. She slipped a key from her pocket and unlocked Sydney's cell with a quick turn. Before Sydney could think to take advantage of the opening, the queen collapsed to the ground, shrieking. Sydney took a staggering step forward.

"Guards! Guards! The prisoner is trying to escape! Help!"

Clever witch, was Sydney's only bitter thought before the guards were on her. Strong hands half dragged, half pushed her to the back of the prison. One of them hurled a punch, and Sydney's head flung back into stone. Spots danced across her vision.

"Are you alright, your Majesty?" one of the guards asked as she pulled Queen Camillea to her feet. The other, a beefy young warrior with red knuckles, relocked Sydney's cage.

"I think so," Camillea answered, her voice shaking. "I don't know what happened. I was trying to reason with the captain, and she must have gotten ahold of my key..."

Sydney stopped listening to the queen's performance. She'd already lost whatever battle this was. And gods, her head hurt.

The soldiers began to drift away, insisting Camillea accompany them. She agreed, but paused just before she reached the corridor's bend. Her eyes found Sydney's. She smiled softly.

"Goodbye, Captain Krane. I do wish things had gone differently."

She left. Sydney stared at nothing. A rock found its way into her hand, and she threw it long after her enemy was gone. With a sigh, her head fell into her hands.

Now what?

48

Courage Found

Malcolm did not return to their prison for a long time. Koraline and Arkyn spent the hours racked with anxiety. Their warden never varied from his schedule, and the timing did not bode well. Had Arkyn's outburst truly frightened him, or was he taking time to develop new gruesome tortures? Or worse, had he learned of their plan to escape?

"Maybe we should rethink things," Koraline worried aloud on the second day. But Arkyn just shook his head.

"No, *allska*. The time for thinking is past."

So, they waited. And at last, on the fourth day, Malcolm returned.

"I apologize for my absence," the warden crooned as he entered Arkyn's cell, slowly rolling up his fresh, white sleeves. The terror and rage from his last visit now lay dammed behind a careful mask. "But don't worry, I haven't forgotten about you. And I certainly haven't forgotten the sins you must pay for."

With a dramatic flick of his wrist, Malcolm unraveled a long leather whip. Bile rose in Koraline's throat at the sight of it.

"Now, Arkyn. Are you ready to cooperate?"

As usual, the prisoner said nothing. The fire in his eyes was answer enough.

The whip came slashing down in a wide arc, ripping across Arkyn's chest. Gritting his teeth, the chained man recoiled, a welt already forming on his skin. Koraline pressed a hand to her mouth to keep herself from crying out.

"Really, Malcolm?" Arkyn panted, lifting his chin. "A whip? Are you becoming too much of a coward to bloody your own hands?"

Malcolm dropped the weapon into the dirt, a wicked smile forming like a second scar upon his face. He wound up and punched his victim square in the face. Arkyn grunted and spat blood onto the ground. He returned Malcolm's smile with a grin of his own, teeth stained red.

"That's more like it."

Arkyn dragged himself to his feet, and Koraline readied herself. Malcolm needed to be close for their plan to work, and the two men now stood inches apart.

"On your knees," Malcolm hissed, taking an involuntary step backwards. In the time it took Koraline to blink, Arkyn strained against his chains, knocking into Malcolm. His hand found the ring of keys, and he flung them into the air, towards Koraline's cell, shouting as they struck the earth to muffle the sound.

As the two men grappled, the mermaid's focus narrowed. She saw only the keys, heart hammering until it drowned out all other sound. Stretching an arm through the iron bars, her fingers just brushed the cold metal. She scraped and clawed at the dirt, keys mocking her from the boundaries of her grasp. At last, shoulder ready to pop as it strained, Koraline managed to hook a single finger through the ring. Her heart soared. She carefully dragged the keys towards her cell.

A boot slammed down onto the mermaid's outstretched fingers. She cried out in pain, attempting to recoil away, but the boot held her firm and fast. Malcolm's face loomed between the bars, tight with fury. Behind him, Arkyn lay on his side in the dirt. His hand clutched at his stomach with red seeping between his fingers.

They had failed.

Lost.

Malcolm finally lifted his foot, returned the keys to his belt, and made his way slowly into Koraline's cell. The princess tried to scramble away, but the stone wall lay at her back. He grasped her head, one hand tangled in her hair, the other on her mouth, like a vise around her skull.

"You stupid bitch," Malcolm scolded, voice almost incredulous. "How *dare* you. After all the kindness I've shown you. What, you thought you were going to escape? With no legs and no friends to aide you?" He shook his head. "Oh, Princess. What a foolish move. But then, what else should I have expected from a cowardly, Nidarian fish?"

Every piece of Koraline's mind urged her to cry for mercy. To plead, to quake, to cower. And a week ago, she might have done it. But something else sat in her stomach now. A spark she'd always known was there, but that she'd never given a chance to shine. It spoke of her parents, of Angler, of home. It whispered of Arkyn, the man who bled for the ones he loved. Of every bruise and every pain Malcolm had inflicted throughout the course of his miserable life. And as the spark grew, instead of smothering it, Koraline fanned it into a flame, into a raging fire. Fear retreated against the blaze. It was still there, and perhaps it would always be there. But it no longer controlled her. Malcolm no longer controlled her.

And as the fear fled, rage took its place.

Koraline bit into Malcolm's hand with all her strength, tasting blood and scraping bone. She took a small sort of pleasure in the warden's scream as he reeled back.

"I am Koraline of House Allantus, Princess of Nidaria, heir to the throne, and Cypri of the Eastern Sea. My ancestors have ruled for generations as kings and queens, keepers of the Light." Koraline's voice built in strength, echoing throughout the chamber. Malcolm stared, clutching his hand, while Arkyn looked to her with shining eyes. "You kidnapped me from my home, and you committed war crimes against my people. My escape today would have been a mercy to you. A mercy you will never see. When the merfolk discover what you've done here, there will be no place in Soarden safe from their wrath. If you think us cowards, you have not seen what we do to those that hurt our own. And when the Nidarians are through with you, I will gladly watch the sharks pick the flesh from your bones."

Her speech, though powerful, was exaggerated. Malcolm knew that. Still, Koraline saw a spark of concern in those dark eyes. She used that satisfaction to ready herself.

He slapped her hard across the face. She gasped with shock, but it felt worse watching Arkyn suffer. Maybe she could do this after all. But then he pulled out his dagger, still red with Arkyn's blood. The warden grasped her chin, forcing her to meet his eyes as he gently sliced the edge along her collarbone. She quickly remembered that bravery did not erase pain.

"A bold little speech, Princess. I'm afraid your cellmate's disrespect is rubbing off on you. We will have to cut away at that rebellious spirit. But don't worry, I remember my promise to my employer. I'll make sure to focus on less... visible areas." His gaze raked over her suggestively. She shivered as some of her fire died.

"Keep your hands off of her."

Malcolm and Koraline both turned. Arkyn had pushed himself back onto his knees. He glared at Malcolm, jaw tight.

"Excuse me?" the warden asked.

"I said," something ripped from Arkyn's throat, almost a growl, "take your hands off of her."

Malcolm cocked his head, and the look that crossed his face scared Koraline more than a thousand knives in his hands.

"Interesting." He looked from Arkyn to Koraline and back again, a cold and calculated hunter. "Dear Arkyn, you haven't gone and gotten *attached* to our young princess here, have you?"

Understanding and horror flooded across Arkyn's face as he realized his mistake, too late. Malcolm laughed with the terrible glee of a man who'd won.

"What a fool I've been," Malcolm chuckled to himself. "I should have known, the moment I found you in that blacksmith's house with that dead girl in your arms. What was her name again?"

"Shut up," Arkyn whispered. The color had drained from his face.

"Yes, I don't suppose it matters. The point is, I've been going about this all wrong. Pain is most people's weakness, but not yours, Arkyn. *They* are. *She* is." To emphasize his point, Malcolm yanked Koraline against her chains, forcing her face up against the metal bars. She had no choice but to stare at her friend. Panic reflected back at her in his eyes.

"You're wrong." Arkyn's voice shook, the lies dead as soon as they left his tongue. Malcolm couldn't seem to stop smiling.

"Here's my new offer," the warden cooed. "Give me what I want. *Now.* Or from this moment forward, every punishment I have cooked up for you, Princess Koraline will receive instead."

"Arkyn, don't—" Malcolm backhanded Koraline before she could finish, and she collapsed back into the dirt. Arkyn's hands curled into fists.

"Well? I'm waiting." Malcolm poised his dagger above Koraline's fin. Now that he'd won, he seemed to be in no hurry to collect.

Koraline met Arkyn's eyes. She tried to reach him without using words. *Don't break now. Not after everything. Not for me.*

"I won't... I can't..." Arkyn faltered.

"Very well." Malcolm grinned, happy to toy with his food for a little longer. But just as he raised his hand, there was a commotion on the stairs. A young soldier crashed through the door, panting as if he'd run a great distance. The warden turned in a fury.

"I thought I made myself perfectly clear. *No interruptions,*" Malcolm hissed. The soldier blanched.

"Yes, yes, of course sir, perfectly clear... it's just..." The boy swallowed. "The raiding party just returned, sir, and you did say you wished to be notified the second they arrived..."

"I will be there in a moment," Malcolm replied through gritted teeth.

"Right, of course sir, it's just, you've been summoned, you see. Immediately. And your absence might raise suspicions... sir."

For a moment, Koraline was sure Malcolm would turn his blade on the boy. But after a tense silence, the warden sighed with irritation, reluctantly releasing his hold on her.

"Very well. I'm coming." Malcolm picked his way out of the cell. He eyed both prisoners. "I'll be back shortly. If I were you, I'd use this time to think about what's important. Determine the price you're willing to pay for your resistance."

Koraline's stomach leapt to her throat as the prison door slammed behind the torturer. She released a shuddering breath. In the adjoining cell, Arkyn's chains slackened as usual, but the man did not take up his usual place by the wall. Instead, he remained huddled in the middle of the room, hands clutched to his abdomen, black hair masking his face in shadow. If the merfolk were allowed tears, surely Koraline would have shed them then. *What now?*

"Arkyn," the princess whispered. "Are you okay? Your stomach..."

He lifted a hand for a moment, the palm coated in scarlet, but said nothing. It was too much blood, even for the man's unnatural healing ability.

"Here." Koraline tore two wide strips from the bottom of her human dress, thankful for the garment's length. She passed them through the bars. "Use these."

Arkyn looked up at her. A few tears swam in silent tracks down his cheeks. Each one struck like a knife in Koraline's chest.

"I'm so sorry, *allska*. This is all my fault. I never should have let myself… I should have distanced myself from you. This was always my fight. My burden. And now I've dragged you down with me." Arkyn shook his head.

"Don't be ridiculous. None of this is because of you—"

"*Vök!* You don't understand!" Arkyn snapped. Koraline could only stare, shocked by his tone. He never spoke to her that way. "I'm cursed. I always have been, since the day I was born. Bad things happen because of me. If they hadn't taken me in, Cole and his family would be alive today, and if I had suffered this prison alone, Malcolm wouldn't be using you for his sick games. I knew better, both times. I'm to blame, whatever you might think."

Koraline's internal fire cast out fresh sparks. They'd both endured too much for this to be the end of their struggle.

"I don't care. I don't care if you think you're cursed, and I don't care if Malcolm hurts me because of you. I do not regret knowing you, and I'm sure Cole would've said the same. Bad things have happened to you, Arkyn, terrible things. But victims are not to blame for the actions of their tormentors."

The man's head remained bent. Koraline shook the cloth clutched in her hand, exasperated.

"By the Light! Arkyn, please. Cursed or not, you can't change the past. We have to move forward. Don't make me watch my friend bleed out next to me."

"Alright, *allska*, alright," Arkyn sighed. Crawling towards the bars that separated them, he took the strips from her gently, pressing one into his wound and using the other to tie it into place. "So, what are we going to do now?"

Koraline didn't know. Their only plan had been a complete failure, and now they ran on borrowed time.

"First, we try to get out of these chains. Then, our cells. And if Malcolm comes back before then…" The princess swallowed. Her mouth tasted of sand. "If he comes back, you're not going to give him what he wants. Promise me you won't."

Her words seemed to pain him more than the gash in his stomach. "I can't."

"He won't kill me. His master clearly wants me alive."

"Koraline." The mermaid shivered at his tone. "This isn't up for a debate. If that man raises a hand to you again, I will give him whatever he wants."

She knew he spoke the truth. And she didn't have the time or the strength to change his mind.

"Fine. Do what you must. But until then, we have to keep trying."

And they did try. For hours, Arkyn sawed at his chains, picking, scratching, clawing until his nails bled. Likewise, Koraline tried to pull her small hands out of their bindings. She was close too, so close she even considered breaking her thumb to slip free. But she lacked the strength, and even if she did make it out, what then? Iron bars still barred her freedom, and she couldn't shake the heavy weight of her dried out fins.

Arkyn leaned heavily against the wall.

"It's no use."

Koraline knew he was right, but the words still cut through her. Everything they'd suffered would soon be for nothing. Arkyn would give Malcolm his prize, and shortly after, Arkyn would die. Of that she was certain. And then? Koraline would be left all alone in this place, while the world stumbled along without her. Maybe she would stay imprisoned for the rest of her life, golden hair turned silver, all memory of her passing from existence.

As the dark thoughts gathered, across the prison, the door creaked open. Koraline stiffened. They were out of time.

But Malcolm did not enter the room. No one did. In fact, the door closed so quickly, Koraline thought she might have imagined it. She looked to Arkyn. Her friend stared at the entrance, eyes narrowed.

"Did you see that too?" he asked, voice hushed.

She nodded.

Silence hung heavy in the air. Koraline squinted into the gloom. Then, the sound of a footfall outside Arkyn's cell, a flash of red at the edge of her vision. Arkyn struggled to his feet.

"Who's there?" her friend barked. The princess didn't dare breathe. What fresh horror had this prison brought them? "Show yourself!"

For a moment, nothing happened.

Then, impossibly, the door to Arkyn's cage swung open. A set of keys soared through the air, landing with a clatter at Arkyn's feet. An instant later, the prison door opened and closed once more. Whatever entity had saved them was gone as fast as it arrived.

Koraline and Arkyn stared at the keys together, disbelieving.

"*Niske toth...*"

"How...?"

Arkyn regained himself first. He plucked the keys from the dirt, quick to unlock the chains around his wrists.

"We'll have plenty of time to discuss what just happened later. Right now, we need to move," said Arkyn. He had to fumble through a few different keys, but finally the door to Koraline's cell fell open. Her heart soared as he bent down next to her. She'd never seen him this way before, real and alive, face to face, not through the iron slits of her cell. And in all this time, she hadn't realized how desperately she'd missed the closeness of a friend, the touch of someone she cared for. As Arkyn worked to free her from her chains, she took a moment to grab his hand. He looked at her in surprise, blue eyes even more striking at this distance. They squeezed hands, his like fire, hers an icy sea. He cast her a wild smile as her chains slid off, and a similar weight lifted from her chest.

"May I?" Arkyn asked, holding out his hands dramatically, an offering.

Koraline laughed. "Get us the hell out of here, already."

He lifted her easily from the ground, cradling her in his arms. "I couldn't have said it better myself, *allska*."

And together, they turned their backs on the prison, both silently vowing to face death head-on before relinquishing their freedom again.

49

Saved

You've really mucked things up this time, Krane.

Sydney had spent the better part of an hour berating herself. She missed so many signs. Wasted so much time fighting the wrong enemy. And for what? To be executed a traitor, her loved ones never knowing the truth.

Let the rats take me, she thought sullenly, back flat on the cell floor. She didn't even open her eyes when a door creaked, this time on the other end of the corridor.

"Sydney!" a voice hissed in the silence.

She bolted upright, fast enough to make her head spin. Standing outside her cell, crouched, weapons drawn, were Flindir and Itari.

They were dressed for a fight. Leather armor sat on top of Itari's red linens, and she had covered every spare inch in throwing knives. Lightning rippled up and down her arms. Along with his armor, Flindir wore a matching battle helm that descended to either side of his face. It outlined his jaw, sharpening his normally soft features. Lukaris' bow stuck up over his shoulder. The curly-headed elf had never looked so fierce.

Sydney's heart soared at the sight of them.

"How did you get down here?" she exclaimed, scrambling to her feet.

"There's a delay in the guard by the southern gates," Flindir explained quickly. The Honor Guard part of Sydney cursed. She had told the guards to fix that error months ago. She supposed she should be grateful for their ineptitude.

"Where's the *Valen*?" Itari demanded, wasting no time.

"Just around that corner."

Itari slipped away as Flindir got to work on Sydney's cage. He pulled a ring of keys from his belt.

Sydney stared at the elf's kind face. It took her back to days spent in a disheveled tent, surrounded by the scent of soil and the delighted chirp of Raiden's laugh.

"Flindir, there's something I need to say."

"Hm?" he grunted. His eyes stayed low, testing key after key in the stubborn lock.

"I didn't betray Firne to Brimhold. I never wanted any of this to happen. The queen found out about the warroot on her own somehow," Sydney blurted.

The door swung open with a groan, and Flindir looked up at her. His eyes were the same as ever, a sea of hazel, wide in alarm.

"Oh, I know, Sydney," Flindir assured her.

"I..." She blinked. "You do?"

He smiled, and though small and sad, it was genuine. "Warroot is difficult to grow, even with the help of Light magic. To prepare enough for the attack on Firne, the Brims would've needed the information months ago. Well before you came to us. Besides, I still have faith in you."

Lukaris and Itari rounded the bend before Sydney could stutter a reply. Lukaris looked worse than Sydney remembered, and fresh bruising on his face was enough to make her wince. The prince's eyes flashed to her at Flindir's words, but she couldn't hope to read the guarded expression. For now, Flindir's trust would have to be enough.

The curly-headed elf lit up at the sight of his friend, an exclamation of relief slipping from his lips. He pulled the *Valen* into his arms.

"Thank the Light," Flindir muttered. Lukaris buried his face into Flindir's shoulder, eyes tight.

"Hey, Flin." Lukaris' voice was little more than a croak.

"I'm so sorry," Flindir whispered. "I'm so sorry."

Itari placed a hand on her leader's shoulder and squeezed. Sydney felt out of place, an intruder on their private moment.

"Where is he?" Lukaris asked, voice cracking. He didn't have to elaborate; they all knew who he meant. Raiden.

"Itari ordered a few of the *tatell* to take him to Sil Tullian. He's headed home, I promise." Flindir pulled away and held out a hand. "Here."

A small, wooden bear swung from Flindir's grasp. Eyes brimming, Lukaris fastened Raiden's totem around his neck. For a moment, they all were silent, each trapped in their own bubble of grief. But soon enough, Flindir shattered the quiet with his shocked gasp.

"What happened?" he demanded, grabbing at the prince's arm. At first, Sydney couldn't make out what he meant in the dim torchlight. Then, she saw it. A blood soaked bandage, and beneath it, a long, nauseating gash.

"Just a little welcome present from my human hosts," Lukaris remarked, a flicker of his old humor.

"You're not going anywhere until I wrap that properly," Flindir growled, sounding more like Ettee than himself. He forced Lukaris to the ground and began pulling supplies from his bag.

"I'm glad we have a minute, because there's something you all need to hear, and it can't wait," Sydney said grimly. She told them everything she'd learned. The queen was really a greyblood impostor. She killed the royal family of Brimhold. She started the war. The truth sounded even more insane to Sydney as she repeated it back. Itari and Flindir listened with growing looks of horror. Lukaris merely stared ahead, green eyes full of dread. He already knew then. He'd been able to hear her after all.

When Sydney finished, no one spoke. A rat skittered behind them, casting shadows on the stone walls.

"All of this is…" Itari whispered, stopped, then shook her head.

"It's troll shit crazy," Flindir blurted.

The *Dualin's* lips twitched. "Well, yes."

"It explains everything," Lukaris said as Flindir finished treating his wound. The elf dragged himself to his feet. "And I know there's more that Camillea is hiding. But we can discuss the rest of it later. Right now, we need to get out of here."

"We can try escaping the way we came," Itari said, sounding doubtful. "But we took out a number of guards. They could wake any minute."

"There's a secret exit through the dungeons," Sydney inserted with excitement. "It leads into the woods north of Delm."

She looked to the *Valen* for approval, hoping to redeem herself to him in some small way. But he wouldn't meet her eye, and it was Flindir that answered.

"Sounds like our best shot."

"What in Soarden is taking you so long?" a smooth voice demanded from the darkness.

Novah stepped forth from the shadows, scarlet hair pulled back in a fierce tail. As if that could hide her fire.

"You brought *her*?" Sydney exclaimed. "*Here*? What were you thinking?"

"Nice to see you too, Captain Krane," the Red Elf remarked.

"She insisted on coming," Flindir explained in a way that made it clear he was out voted. "Besides, we could use the help."

Sydney wasn't so sure. Still, there was no use arguing the point now. She just hoped they could escape without everyone in Delm knowing the Red Elf aided the Ithirdi prince.

"Let's go," Itari said, glancing over her shoulder. "I do not care for this place."

The others muttered their agreement. Sydney wished she could join them. But there was something she needed to do first. The thought had planted itself inside her when Flindir mentioned the warroot, and she couldn't let it rest until she knew for sure.

"Go on ahead," Sydney said to the others, backing down the hallway, towards the main part of the castle. "Take the stairs down as far as you can and turn left. The door at the very end will get you out."

The elves paused, eyeing her with varying degrees of concern.

"Where are you going?" Itari asked with a frown.

"If Flindir's right, and warroot is so hard to cultivate, Camillea will have wanted to keep it close. If there's any left, it should be here in the castle. I have to destroy it, if I can." Sydney's throat tightened. "I won't let what happened in Firne happen anywhere else. Not if there's a chance."

The Ithirdi exchanged a look, and Lukaris gave a nod of approval. Itari walked forward, placing a hand to her heart. A sign of respect given to one's equal.

"We're coming with you," the *Dualin* said. She gave Sydney one of her rare smiles. "We all failed Firne, *scolas*. Now we will seek justice together."

Sydney could not say what she felt in that moment. But she was suddenly very thankful for that day Lukaris shot her in the woods.

They found Sydney's weapons in a storage room not far from the cells. She felt better with the blades in her hands. At least now she controlled some small part of her fate.

She led them up from the dungeons into the back half of the castle. This was where, long ago, the royal family of Brimhold had thrived. Stone corridors gave way to gardens and courtyards, libraries and parlors. Only Camillea lived there now. A single pale ghost drifting through ancient rooms. A murderer who had never left the scene of her crime.

Sydney knew of one courtyard the queen seemed to love. She'd had Sydney there for tea once. To congratulate her on making the Honor Guard. Thinking back on it now made her stomach twist into knots of rage.

A deathly silence hung over the castle as the escapees snuck from one pillar to another. Through hollow hallways and empty rooms. Her allies had their elvish stealth to aid them, but this was Sydney's domain. She had spent her youth exploring the fortress and uncovering its secrets. She knew which stones shifted underfoot, which paths led to dead ends. And thanks to the night shifts she'd earned during games of bait, she knew the moment a guard would pass into a blind spot, allowing them to slip by unnoticed.

Against all odds, the five companions reached their destination without alerting the sleeping castle. Barely more than a room exposed to the sky, towering gray walls closed the courtyard in on all sides. They slipped in through a single archway, the only entrance and exit to the lawn. The last time Sydney visited, a table sat at the garden's center, with blossoms looping out in pleasant rings. Now, the space had the feel of farmland. Yellow blooms grew in row after row, packing every inch. Flindir sucked in a sharp breath.

"By the Light, she's got enough to poison all of Sil Tullian," he hissed. His expression darkened. "This should have been used to help Ithirdas. Instead, I've created a weapon against us."

"Not if we destroy every last root here," Lukaris said. His eyes were distant, like he was back on the hillside above Firne, watching the smog suffocate his people. "It's a miracle she got ahold of warroot the first time. We can end this now."

"Well, enough talking then. Get to it," Novah grumbled. For once, Sydney agreed with her. If walls had eyes, Sydney could feel the castle's on her back.

Flindir crouched in the dirt, palms flat against the earth. He closed his eyes, and magic tugged at the air.

Sydney had seen Flindir's magic many times before, always nurturing life. Shoots sprouting from seeds and roots plunging into fertile soil. This was different. Decay dripped from his outstretched hands. Grass withered and bent, green leaves curling in on themselves. The nearest yellow flowers seemed to scream as their petals fell, one by one, drifting softly to the ground. Death took the warroot one row at a time.

"Well done," Itari said to Sydney, coming up beside her. "I was focused only on the *Valen*'s rescue. Without you, we might have left this weapon in the enemy's hands. I am glad to have you with us."

Sydney didn't want praise. "It won't change what's happened."

"No," the elf answered softly. "But you are not to blame for that."

She looked over to where Lukaris leaned against the castle wall, head bowed. "Not everyone agrees with you."

Itari followed her gaze. She sighed, wrapping slender arms around herself.

"Grief is a dangerous thing," she said, voice low. "We often say things we regret. My *Valen* has always had a heart prone to breaking. Have patience, Sydney. He will come back to us when he can."

"I hope you're right," Sydney murmured. She still remembered the way Lukaris looked at her on the road back to Delm. She wasn't sure they could heal from that.

Flindir had almost finished his task. The once flourishing garden now looked like a graveyard, full of dried out blooms. Maybe they would pull this off after all. Then, Sydney heard a footfall behind her. Across the quad, Lukaris straightened, his eyes wide. He lifted a finger.

"Stop him!"

The others whirled, weapons half from their sheaths. In the archway, a single Brim soldier blinked, clearly in a state of shock. For a second, he just stood there. His mouth opened. Then, he ran.

"After him!" someone hissed. Itari and Sydney stood closest to the entryway, and they dove after the guard, flying back into the castle. The soldier fled down the corridor in front of them, boots like clopping hooves on the floor. Itari aimed a knife as he neared a corner while Sydney held her breath. The blade flew from the Viridian's grip, tumbling end over end through the air. It missed the Brim by a breath, striking off a wall as he rounded the bend. Electricity flickered along the steel where it lay on the stones.

"Damn it!" Sydney growled. A second later, a bell tolled, piercing the quiet night. A second bell followed the first, and then another and another, until the entire castle rolled with the chimes. Soldiers called out somewhere in the distance.

They raced back to the courtyard, arriving just as the last warroot blossom shriveled into a gray husk. Flindir stood and dusted his hands across his trousers. He wore a look of grim satisfaction.

"Time to go," Sydney urged from the archway.

"I'm guessing those bells are for us?" Lukaris asked, arrow already nocked.

"Good guess. I don't think we're going to make it back to the dungeons without a fight."

Novah shouldered her sword. "Lead the way."

Exiting the garden, Sydney turned away from the approaching cries of angry soldiers. The elves kept close on her heals as she sprinted down narrow hallways, secret stairs, and rooms so underused they sat under a permanent film of dust.

"The door we need is in the next hall," Sydney passed along in a hushed voice. Itari nodded behind her. They skidded into the final corridor.

And crashed into a full squadron of Delm's warriors.

50

Dungeons and Duels

How quickly a night can turn bloody.

Sydney dodged the swing of a sword, back parallel to the floor. The soldier rotated his heal in an attempt to bring the weapon back around, but she didn't give him the chance. Straightening, Sydney sliced at his hands just as her foot struck his pivoting knee. It was a cheap shot. Her opponent staggered, crying out as blood dripped down the grip of his sword. Bile rose in Sydney's throat at the sight. She pushed the wounded man aside and kept moving.

The castle was in chaos. Shouts and screams and clashing metal pressed in from all sides. The elves came in and out of Sydney's view as they fought their way towards the dungeon stairs. A knife struck a guard beside her, and his back arched as lightning seared its way through his armor. He fell to the ground, steaming. Wind howled through the hallway, and arrows made impossible turns into necks and shoulders. Through a gap in the fighting, Sydney spotted Flindir and Novah, back to back, their weapons slashing out in deadly arcs.

All the while, Sydney wanted to scream. *Stop. Gods, please stop.* Behind every silver helmet, she saw Brandon or Gilliad or

Julia. Innocents falling at her hand. Friends she had known since childhood. And yet, if she stopped fighting, the blood pooling on the stones would be her own.

A shield came out of no where, striking Sydney in the chest. The air flew from her lungs as she staggered backwards, boots slipping on the wet floor. She fell to her knees and raised twin blades in a cross above her head. Her opponent's weapon met hers, and for a moment they struggled, steel on steel, caught in a dead lock. Her arms shook with the strain. She could feel the guard's hot breath.

An elf crashed in the Brim, sending him flying against a wall. A quick strike to the head, and the soldier slid to the ground, chin to chest. Lukaris pulled Sydney to her feet. A fresh cut on his forehead sent blood running down his sharp nose. His eyes met hers, and Sydney thought she saw a hint of concern in the green depths. But, in a blink, the reserved mask fell back into place.

"We need to get out of here," he yelled, parrying with his bow.

"You don't say?" Sydney shouted back.

They inched forward, bit by bit, but it wasn't enough. Brimhold's reinforcements poured in from other parts of the castle, and with every defeated soldier, two more took their place. Only the hallway's chokehold kept the escapees from being overrun. The elves and Sydney stumbled together, forming a tight fighting knot. Then, down the corridor, a cry broke through the noise.

"You!"

Camillea stood in the passage ahead of them, face tight with rage. She was dressed plainly in a velvet dress cinched at the waist, blonde hair tied back in half a dozen braids. She might be a lady in waiting or a rich lord's daughter. But the clench in her jaw and the sword in her hand said otherwise. She was a fighter in her own right. A warrior queen. And her dagger eyes were fixed on Novah.

"The murderer shows her face at last," Camillea snarled as she picked her way through the battle. The Red Elf turned to face her, expression blank and unconcerned. Sydney realized, too late, that they'd failed to tell Novah the truth about Brimhold's queen.

"I do not claim your dead," Novah announced. The queen reached her, sword swinging. Their blades met. "The killing of your family was not my doing."

"Liar!" Camillea hissed between furious flicks of her weapon. The Red Elf struggled to dodge the blows. Sydney had never seen the queen fight, but she was starting to see how the greyblood managed to wipe out an entire castle on her own.

"You killed them in their home. They were simple people. They were *kind*. And you watched them burn, because they would not give up their child." The queen's voice wavered. Sydney glanced around while she dodged a flying dagger, but none of the Brims were listening to the exchange. She wondered how many of them already knew about the greyblood queen and fought anyway.

Novah's steady demeanor slipped, replaced with confusion. Before she could respond, Itari shouted something in Elvish. Sydney couldn't make out the words among the mayhem. Beside her, Lukaris raised a hand. Wind sliced the air in front of them, encircling their group. The harsh current cut between Camillea and Novah, pushing them away from each other. Itari snapped, and lightning joined the tempest. White and blue ripples of static formed a protective barrier. They stood in the middle of their own personal storm.

Sydney lowered her arms, grateful for the reprieve. The soldiers paced outside the bubble of sparking wind, probing for an opening. Meanwhile, Camillea stood across from Novah, face contorted. So close to her vengeance and unable to reach it.

A sheen of sweat stood out on Lukaris' high forehead. His hands shook.

"I can't hold this for long," the *Valen* panted. Itari grunted her agreement, eyes fixed on the magical hurricane.

"We need a distraction if we want to make a break for it," said Sydney.

"I can give us a few seconds," Novah suggested. Her focus remained on Camillea. "But the rest of you will have to close your eyes and stay with me."

The elves looked to Lukaris for approval. Sydney was still getting used to seeing him as their prince. He gave a weary nod.

"Tell us when, Novah."

"You want the second door past the queen," Sydney added quickly.

The Red Elf nodded. "On three, hands on each others shoulders and close your eyes. Don't open them until I say."

Sydney sheathed one of her blades, edging closer to Flindir.

"One."

Behind the mass of wind and lightning, the queen's eyes narrowed. Could she guess their plan?

"Two."

The storm grew tighter, and the hairs on Sydney's arms rose from the static. She took a deep breath, ready to blindly follow the ex-assassin turned ally.

"Three."

Sydney slammed her eyes shut and searing light erupted behind her eyelids. She latched on to Flindir's shoulder, and she felt another hand grab her own. The storm fell like a hammer. All around, the soldiers yelled in panic and pain. Among the confusion, they weaved through the enemy as a single chain. Sydney crashed into someone but kept moving. Somewhere behind them, Camillea shouted orders, the sound fading with each step. At last, Sydney's feet hit stone steps, and she stumbled down into the dark.

"We're clear for now," Novah whispered. Sydney opened her eyes, blinking frantically to adjust to the dim torchlight. They stood in a narrow stairway, the sounds of battle a distant memory.

"Keep moving," she urged. She pushed Flindir gently. "They'll discover where we went any moment."

They rushed down the steps. Itari seemed to be limping, but she didn't stop, fierce determination locked on her face. A never ending spiral of stairs. Corridors branched off on different landings, but Sydney ignored them. Their escape hid in the deepest passageways, where the ancient dead of Delm were said to sleep in buried tombs. Just when Sydney thought they might never reach the bottom, the steps ended, opening up to a wide dirt passage.

"Left," Sydney whispered, and Novah led them on. They passed rows of empty cells, some so large the ceiling disappeared into shadow. Dried blood stains splattered the walls, rats picking at piles of old rags. Sydney wasn't sure what Camillea used these prisons for. She didn't want to know.

At the end of the passage, a single door stood wide open. The moonlight seemed bright as sunshine where it streamed across the dungeon floor. Sydney slowed to a walk, uneasy.

"That's our exit," she said. "But why is it open?"

"No time to question it," Lukaris panted. He was right. Far away, at the other end of the corridor, they could hear the growing sounds of boots and shifting armor.

One by one, they rushed out into the night air, sliding down a steep embankment. Sydney brought up the rear. She glanced over her shoulder, eyes searching for enemies on their tail. Then, from a side passageway, a flash of movement. Something barreled into her, flinging her against the stone wall.

Typical. Sydney groaned as she backed away from her new adversary. He stood between her and escape, a black silhouette against the starlit exit. The elves picked their way down the hillside, unaware of her absence. Behind her, Brimhold's soldiers grew ever closer. The warning bells seemed to pound at the base of her skull. She clenched her teeth, drew her swords, and attacked.

The warrior grunted as he parried her blows, shifting to stay in front of the doorway. She aimed a swipe at his legs, but a shield blocked her, steel on wood. She tried again, both blades swinging down towards the soldier's neck. He raised a broadsword in response, and with their weapons locked, he pushed her back into the corridor. Sydney snarled as she lost ground. Her arms shook. Then, her foot twisted. She collapsed, back striking the packed earth.

Her opponent stepped into the torchlight, and she saw his face for the first time.

Brandon. The real Brandon.

A multitude of emotions flickered across his face. Surprise. Anger. Settling on sadness. He lowered his sword. Sydney scrambled quickly to her feet, never taking her eyes off him.

"I told you I'd best you one day, Krane," he said, voice hollow.

Grief stung in her throat. How had she ever mistaken Camillea for him? *This* was her friend. Her brother.

"Lockes," she choked. She had so much to tell him. So much she needed to say. She wanted more than anything for him to come with her. But there wasn't time to explain. If she let the Brims catch up with her, she didn't stand a chance. And she couldn't stop Camillea from inside a cell. Or worse, from the end of a noose.

Brandon watched her like he could read her thoughts. Maybe he could. His shoulders stiffened. What would she do if he tried to stop her again? She couldn't bring herself to hurt him.

"Brandon, please." She put all her sorrow into the words. She hoped he understood. "Let me pass."

For a moment, his dark eyes searched her face. Like he was searching for the person she used to be.

He sighed and stepped aside.

Thank the gods. Sydney sheathed her swords and stepped closer. The look on his face almost broke her. She'd still managed to hurt him. But what other choice did she have?

She reached into her cloak, fingers gripping cold metal. She pressed an object into Brandon's hand. With a frown, he looked down. The Honor Guard emblem, crossed silver swords, looked tiny in his grip. He closed his eyes for a moment, as if in pain, fingers closing around the pin.

"I'm sorry," Sydney whispered. She took in every angle of his face. The square jaw, the chestnut hair. The way his brow furrowed in the middle. She wasn't sure when she would see him again. Or if she ever would.

A sad ghost of a smile played on his lips. "Liar."

Sydney swallowed. Then, she turned and fled, following her allies into the night. She reached the shelter of the trees before she had the strength to look back, hoping for one last glance of her friend. But when her eyes found the dark hole in the castle wall, Brandon was gone.

*****

"Are you alright?" Itari asked as Sydney finally caught up with the elves.

"Fine," Sydney lied. She didn't want to discuss her encounter with Brandon. "Just ran into a little trouble. Let's keep moving."

Above them, the towering castle continued to chime, alerting the entire city to their escape. They sprinted through the dark forest, picking their way over boulders and streams, silent except for the occasional whispered instruction or gasping breath. Larimar Lake, a steady presence to the west, reflected moonlight like glass. Eventually, the steepening landscape forced them farther inland, as hills rose and fell in great grassy basins.

"Do you think… we're safe?" Flindir panted as they clambered down into one of the hollows.

As if on cue, a crossbow bolt flew from above, piercing a tree trunk. The arrow thrummed inches from Itari's head.

"I see them!" a woman's voice shouted.

The elves scattered. Sydney dove behind a boulder, her back to the rock. "Does that answer your question?"

"Make for the other side of the clearing!" Lukaris ordered from his hiding place. Sydney looked to the expanse of exposed forest.

"We'll never make it," she argued. "*Look.*"

A dozen Brims poured from the northern trees. The enemy had circled ahead. Behind them, more soldiers climbed down the ravine, silver armor glittering in the shadows. They were surrounded. Trapped.

Novah drew her sword. "Any bright ideas?"

No one answered. They backed away from the approaching warriors, forming a loose circle at the clearing's center. Somewhere in the woods, Sydney heard the mechanical sound of a crossbow reloading. Her eyes darted from one Brim to the next. They continued to rush from the trees like gleaming silver beetles.

"I don't know about the rest of you," Sydney spoke at last, hands sweaty where they gripped her swords. "But I don't plan on returning to that dungeon."

"Nor I," Lukaris growled. Everything about him looked sharp and deadly.

Itari and Flindir nodded their agreement. Novah raised a perfect eyebrow.

"Glad we understand one another."

The Brims surged forward. The basin erupted.

Itari's daggers cut down the first line of fighters, lightning jumping from one blade to the next. Novah and Flindir leapt forward. Their swords struck flesh, and blood fell to the grass like rain. Meanwhile, Lukaris hung back, releasing arrow after arrow. A soldier fell from high up the ravine, his body landing with a thud to the earth.

Sydney rolled, barely dodging a flying bolt. She settled in a crouch and swung at the closest soldier. One sword met his axe, the other his chest. He staggered backwards, and with a spin, her elbow cracked against his nose. The Brim fell in a crumpled heap of armor.

Three more warriors advanced. One died before he reached her, a dagger sticking from his back. The other two circled like vultures. Sydney extended a sword to each of them, watchful, waiting.

The Brims brought down their weapons in unison. Sydney's blades caught both in the air, and she dodged to the left, pushing them aside. But as she stepped, her foot slipped into a hole. Her ankle twisted. She staggered. The nearest soldier sliced at her arm, and she barely manage to block the blow in time. The sword slipped from her hand. She could see the soldier's grin beneath his helm. *Damn it.* Sydney thought frantically as she braced herself. Steel whistled through the air.

But the hit never came. Wind knocked her enemy backwards, giving her enough time to swing her other blade. The weapon sunk into his knee until Sydney could feel the scrape of bone. He screamed, collapsing to the ground. Lukaris helped Sydney find her footing as the other warrior backed away, face white.

"Thanks," Sydney muttered. He always seemed to be there when she needed him. The *Valen* nodded, expression unreadable.

Despite their victories, they remained outnumbered. More Brims hurried from the trees. Lukaris wiped a weary hand across his forehead, blood streaking the skin.

"No!" Flindir's scream echoed across the clearing. Sydney and Lukaris spun in alarm. At the forest's edge, a soldier had thrown

Itari up against a boulder. She squirmed against the stone, holding off her attacker with bare hands. Her cry sunk into Sydney's chest as the soldier's weapon cut into her hands. Flindir ran to her, knocking over anyone that stood in his path. Itari's attacker pulled back his sword, and she barely dodged as he tried to plunge the blade into her stomach. Even from a distance, Sydney could see the anger on the elf's face. With a scream, lightning erupted all over her body, rippling up and down her arms. The soldier convulsed and fell, just as Flindir arrived. Itari slumped into his arms.

"We can't keep this up," Sydney told Lukaris. She parried a sword, knocking its owner backwards. An arrow flew past her cheek.

"I know," the elf snapped. He drew a dagger as enemies paced closer. "I'm open to suggestions."

"Any chance you could do that storm… thing again?"

Exhaustion swept over his face. "Not likely."

They backed up together. Behind them, Novah fought like a storm of her own. Scarlet hair spun in circles as she sliced down one soldier after another. One Brim made a dive for her, and she took a single deliberate step to the side. Her hand slapped across the soldier's eyes, light bursting from every fingertip. The warrior buckled with a scream, and the Red Elf dispatched him with a single slice across the throat. The calculated killing sent chills up Sydney's spine.

Still, it wasn't enough. For all their skill, all their magic, they were seconds from being overrun. Sydney looked around desperately. There had to be an opening. There had to be *something* she could do. It couldn't end like this.

Then, everything stopped. Sydney froze. The trees themselves seemed to quiver.

And an ear-splintering, earth-shattering roar ripped through the forest.

51

A Prison Break

Arkyn eased open the door to their prison while Koraline tensed, preparing for trouble. Beyond, the corridor was empty. Torches cast long shadows on the walls, and the tunnel faded away into the distance. Not a soul stirred. Not a guard, not Malcolm, not a wayward servant come to bring dinner or sweep the floors. They were alone. Koraline and Arkyn shared a look of unease. Where was everyone?

Koraline held her breath as Arkyn took a few hesitant steps into the passage. His bare feet made no sound on the dirt floor. To their left, an opening revealed a set of winding steps, leading up into the dark. Arkyn continued past them.

"I was blindfolded when they brought me here," Arkyn whispered in Koraline's ear. "They didn't know I was awake. We didn't go up or down any stairs, so there must be another way out."

He moved quicker down the hallway. The silence hung heavy as they passed empty cells, a lonely table with a single mug, and rows of locked doors. At last they stumbled upon a small storage alcove. Pieces of guard uniforms cluttered the space, boots and helms and trousers. Koraline's heart squeezed as light flickered off of something on a high shelf.

"Arkyn," she breathed. She motioned to the object. "What's that?"

He set her gently on the ground, then reached up to the shelf. Silver scales glimmered in his hand.

"My cufflet!" Koraline took the band gently, placing it on her wrist. She shivered as the familiar ripping sensation washed over her fin. When she looked down, two pale legs had replaced her golden tail.

If Arkyn was surprised by the transformation, he didn't show it. He helped her to unsteady feet.

"Well, that will certainly make our escape attempt easier," he noted. "As will these."

Arkyn passed her a pair of small boots. She stared at them, dumbfounded, as he slipped a worn jacket over his bare chest and donned shoes of his own. When he turned back to her, she still held the boots in her outstretched hands.

"What's wrong?" Arkyn asked. "Are they too small?"

"Are these really necessary?"

"They are unless you want to tear your feet on every rock and thorn from here to Milanthos. What's the problem?"

"Well, it's just… I've never worn them before," Koraline sniffed.

"Boots?"

"*Shoes.*"

Arkyn blinked at her. Once. Twice. Then, he passed a hand through his hair.

"*Av skeid,*" he muttered with a small chuckle.

Koraline did not understand the language, but she knew when she was being mocked.

"I'm so sorry that the merfolk are not well versed in traveling over *land,*" the mermaid huffed. "Perhaps I should toss you into the Eastern Sea and see how well you fair?"

"My apologies, *allska.*" Arkyn cast up his hands in a remorseful gesture, though he fought to hide his smile. "Let me help."

He placed the boots on the floor, guiding her feet into one and then the other. Koraline took a few tentative steps. Her feet felt large and bulky, weighed down.

"How do humans do this?" the princess marveled.

"You grow used to it," Arkyn said, mouth still quirked up at the corner. "Believe me, you'll be grateful for them soon enough."

They continued their escape down the main passage, though the going was slow with Koraline's newfound legs. Silence filtered in from side hallways, broken only by the squeak of an occasional mouse. The lack of resistance filled Koraline's stomach with dread. What trouble could have caused their captors to abandon them?

At last, the friends reached the dungeon's end. A large door blocked their path, sealed by bars and iron locks. Arkyn ripped the bars free with little trouble, but the locks proved more difficult.

"Wait!" Koraline whispered, remembering. She pulled the ring of keys from their forgotten place in Arkyn's pocket.

They were lucky. The third key fit tight and true, and the locks sprung open with ease. As Koraline cast them into the dirt, Arkyn leaned into the door.

Fresh air washed over them. Koraline gulped in the smell of open sky, and Arkyn turned his face towards the breeze. It was nighttime, but the glow of the stars and beams of silver moonlight seemed blinding after months in torchlight. They stood on a steep hillside, the slope leading down into a tight grove of trees. Above them loomed walls of gray stone. A castle? Koraline squinted and saw to her left, beyond the forest, the flat glimmer of water. And beyond the lake… mountains?

"I think we're in Brimhold," said Arkyn. "Is this Delm?"

Koraline's mind reeled. "The night Milanthos was attacked, guests from Brimhold had come to visit. Queen Camillea herself was there.

You don't think she could have had something to do with this?"

"There's no time to speculate," Arkyn said as he began to guide them down the cliff. "Right now, we need to worry about getting as far away from here as possible."

As he spoke, a bell chimed high in the castle above them. No, not a bell. *Bells.* They exchanged a look.

"Run," Arkyn hissed. He took Koraline's hand, and together they raced down the hillside. Koraline tripped over her boots time and time again, but Arkyn kept her on her feet. They reached the shelter of the trees, the shadows swallowing them whole as they weaved between closely packed trunks. Bushes and briars snagged at their clothes, but they didn't stop. Not until Koraline's lungs ached, and her breathing came in shallow gasps.

"I have to… to rest," Koraline wheezed, at last.

Arkyn's face was covered in sweat and dirt. His hands clutched at the wound on his stomach. "Alright…but only for… a moment."

The pair found a small hollow carved into the earth; when sitting, undergrowth and boulders shielded them from view. There, they huddled together. They didn't speak. In the distance, the sound of tolling bells filled the evening air.

"We should keep going," Arkyn spoke reluctantly after a while, just as Koraline's heart had finally diminished into a gentle hammer.

"Wait!" Koraline whispered. She yanked at Arkyn's arm, dragging him back to the ground. "Someone's coming."

Sure enough, a handful of hushed voices drew closer, hanging between them and the castle. Footsteps fell in quick succession. The group raced past Arkyn and Koraline's hiding place. The princess held her breath. Then, they were gone as quick as they'd come.

"Soldiers?" Koraline asked.

Arkyn shrugged. "Either way, let's go this way." They continued away from the castle, but parallel to the mysterious footsteps. Farther east.

They jogged until Koraline's feet barely lifted from the earth. The warning bells had faded into the distance. Arkyn was quiet. Occasionally, she'd see him wince, hand to his stomach. But he was always quick to wash the pain from his face. Huffing and puffing, they made their way up a large hill. Koraline took a moment to glance back. The great city of Delm loomed up at the edge of its neighboring lake, lights twinkling in the dark. It was beautiful. The princess had always dreamed of visiting Brimhold's capital. How had she come to be a prisoner within its walls, fleeing in the dead of night?

When they reached the hill's summit, Arkyn and Koraline heard shouts from the other side of the embankment. Curiosity won out over logic, and the friends inched towards the noise, peeking out over the cliff.

Koraline sucked in a sharp breath. They had stumbled onto a battle. Below them, in a small clearing, Brimhold soldiers fought against a ragged band of elves. The mermaid wormed closer, trying to make out their features. The elf closest to her… well, no, it wasn't an elf after all. It was a human woman. She had dark hair that swung like a whip as she fought. Dual swords flashed in her hands as she battled off two soldiers at once. Koraline shivered at the ferocity in her face.

As the princess watched, the woman lost her footing. One of the soldiers seized at the opening. He dashed passed her guard, knocking a sword from her grip. But just as he raised his own weapon, a strong wind pushed him back on his heals. An elf appeared at the woman's side. He had sharp features and light hair that burst from his head in unruly strands.

"Lukaris?" Koraline gasped. And there, the curly-haired elf darting through the trees. Across the clearing, a Viridian with lightning flashing down the length of her arms. What were the Ithirdi doing

so far from their kingdom? Arkyn stared at her.

"You know them?" He kept his voice hushed.

Koraline knew her mouth must be gaping like a fish. "Yes. That's the eldest Ithirdi prince and his warriors. They've visited Milanthos a dozen times since I was a child. They're my *friends*." She winced as Itari was thrown back against a boulder, barely missing a sword to the gut. "I don't understand. Why are they here?"

"I don't think those warning bells were for us," Arkyn noted. "They were for *them*."

"We have to help." Koraline half stood out of her crouch, but Arkyn quickly pulled her back down to the earth.

"Help? Are you so keen to be captured again? There are dozens of armed soldiers down there. The elves can take care of themselves." Arkyn's eyes were unusually dark. "Besides, I promised I would get you to safety, and I mean to."

Koraline shook her head. "I can't leave knowing my friends are in trouble. If you won't help, then I'll just go down there alone."

"*Allska*," he snapped. "Be reasonable. You're not a warrior. All you'll do is get yourself killed alongside them."

The mermaid stiffened under his grip. She knew he was right. She *hated* that he was right. But the fire still burned in her stomach. Cowards ran when things got hard. Cowards chose safety over doing what was right. She couldn't live with herself if she became that person. Even if it meant doing something incredibly, undeniably stupid.

"I'm going down there." She spoke with a clear certainty. The voice of a princess, a future queen. "I know I'm not a fighter, and there's likely nothing I can do. But I'm going to try. Leave me if you must. But if you're the man I've grown to know, and the friend I've grown to care for, I ask that you help me now. Maybe I can't save the elves. But I know *you* can."

His unspoken secret hung between them like a shadow. The one thing he refused to share with her. A myriad of emotions flickered over Arkyn's face, dominated by uncertainty and fear. Eventually, he settled on acceptance.

"After that plea, how can I resist, *allska?*" Arkyn sighed softly. He pinched at the bridge of his nose. "Ok. I'll do what I can. But you have to promise me something."

"Anything," she agreed.

"Whatever happens tonight, whatever you see…" He swallowed hard, unable to meet her gaze. "Just please… don't think any different of me."

Koraline felt a sharp tug in her chest. She took his hands in her own.

"Arkyn," she said his name like a vow. "Whatever lies ahead or behind us doesn't matter. You're my friend. Always."

The man closed his eyes and nodded, as if absorbing the words. Then he rose to his feet.

"Stay safe." His smile was a startling white in the darkness. Koraline's whispered reply, "You too," was lost as he raced off down the hill.

Then, a familiar sound echoed across the small valley.

A shifting. A change.

Before Koraline's eyes, Arkyn began to grow. Bent and dark, the size of a boulder, the size of a tree. One second he ran on two legs, the next on four. His hands morphed to talons, his skin a million black scales. From his back, two wings unfurled, reaching upwards towards the sky. Behind him, a long tail thrashed in the undergrowth like a giant snake. A roar echoed through the trees, and Koraline fell back on her heals.

The princess blinked once, twice, sure she had to be mistaken.

Arkyn was a dragon.

52

Of Fire and Friends

A dragon. A damn *dragon.*

Sydney and Lukaris dove behind a tree trunk as the beast swooped across the clearing. Sydney could still feel its roar rattling in her chest. Fire erupted in great tongues of red and orange, sweeping across the grass, feeding on human and vegetation alike. Brimhold's soldiers screamed as their helms melted from the heat.

"Please tell me you see the giant winged lizard too," Sydney shouted over the commotion. Lukaris only nodded, his eyes wide and dazed.

"Let's get to the others."

They rounded the glen, slipping from tree to boulder to brush. A flaming branch crashed to the earth behind them, sending sparks dancing into the air. A soldier ran past, screeching in terror.

"Demon! Save yourselves!"

Finally, they reached the spot where the other elves cowered behind any shelter they could find. Even Novah looked shaken. Flindir still held Itari in his arms, wrapping her injured hands in spare bits of cloth. Battered, but alive.

"*Valen*, what in Alur's name is going on?" Novah hissed. Sydney peeked out from behind a boulder. The dragon had landed in the clearing's center. Its dark scales glinted in the moonlight as it roared again, sweeping its great tail through a line of Brims. She winced at the sound of crushing armor and choked cries.

"How should I know?" Lukaris snapped, flustered. Sydney couldn't blame him. The first dragon seen in an age. A black-scaled dragon, no less. As if they needed another sign of disaster.

"What should we do? Attack it?" Flindir's voice made it clear that was the last thing he wanted to do.

Bolts and arrows bounced harmlessly off the creature's armored hide, falling useless to the charred ground. Still, a few of Brimhold's warriors were holding their ground. They dodged beneath the dragon's gnashing fangs, their blades finding gaps between the scales. Another roar shook the earth, this time a cry of pain.

"You have to help him!" a new voice exclaimed from the undergrowth behind them. Sydney spun, swords up, slashing blindly.

A girl dodged the swinging weapons with a yelp. No, not a girl. A young woman. She stood just a pinch taller than Ettee, a long mane of stunning golden hair shrouding her face. She wore a grungy silver dress, ripped above her skinny knees, and a pair of soldiers' boots that looked bigger than she was. The newcomer stumbled backwards, hands in the air.

"Kori?" came Lukaris' stunned voice. Sydney looked to him with surprise, her blade still hovering.

"You *know* her?"

"Hi, Luka," the golden girl said with a small smile. "I'm so glad to see you."

"Princess," Itari said, a slight bow in her head. Sydney finally lowered her sword.

"Princess?" Sydney paused, the pieces finally clicking into place. Her eyes landed on the cufflet the girl wore around her wrist. "Princess *Koraline?* Gods, how many royals are running around in these woods tonight?"

"How did you get here?" Lukaris asked, ignoring Sydney.

"And how do you know the *dragon*?" Novah added.

"I was being held captive," Koraline explained quickly. She made a motion south, towards Delm. "Arkyn and I escaped together. He was… well I didn't know he was a dragon until a few minutes ago. But don't worry, he's on your side."

"What a relief," Sydney said dryly, just as the dragon swept a soldier off his feet with a single swipe of his claws. The warrior went flying, crashing into a nearby tree.

"You have to help him," Princess Koraline insisted again.

"The dragon?" Novah scoffed. "I'm sure he can handle himself."

But that seemed only partially true. Arkyn was wearing down, the slash of his talons growing weaker with each pass. The Brims pressed the dragon back, and spears searched for holes in the creature's armor.

Koraline's eyes locked onto Sydney's, gold and pleading.

"I can't believe I'm going to say this," Sydney grumbled at last, throwing up her hands. "But, let's go help the damn dragon."

"Stay with the princess," Lukaris ordered, motioning to Flindir and Itari. They gave twin weary nods. "Sydney, Novah… Let's finish this."

They charged from the undergrowth. Fire ate at the grass, singeing Sydney's face as she raced across the clearing and dove back into the fray. A soldier fell as she plunged a sword into his gut. Another raised his shield against her, but she pushed forward, spinning around his guard. Their weapons clashed for a moment, just long enough for Sydney to catch the fear in her opponent's eyes. Then, her second blade swung upwards, catching him on the chin. The warrior staggered backwards into a fresh swath of flame. Sydney turned away as he caught like dry tinder.

Another Brim surged to meet her, but he ground to a halt as an arrow sprouted from his neck. Sydney sent a silent thanks to Lukaris as she leapt over the body and kept moving. She'd almost made it to the dragon.

He loomed above her, dark and imposing, eyes as blue as the Midsummer Ocean. Teeth flashed as another roar shook the forest. Sydney staggered backwards, gritting her teeth. *Gods, it was even louder up close.*

A soldier ran past her, slamming into her shoulder. Sydney raised a sword, but the Brim wasn't focused on her. He held a spear by his shoulder, eyes determined. And he was headed straight for the dragon's wing.

Sydney didn't know much about dragons, but she imagined that would hurt.

She raced after the warrior, but two more soldiers closed ranks in front of her. *Damn it. I don't have time for this.* A few more steps and the spear wielder would be in range. If the dragon fell, they were all doomed. They would execute the elves. Brand Sydney a traitor. And Camillea would get away with all of it. No one would ever see her brought to justice.

Sydney could not let that happen.

"Move. *Now!*" Sydney snarled, spinning her bloodstained weapons. Her vision went red.

And to her surprise, they did. The soldiers stumbled aside, looking stricken. Lukaris locked into battle with one, Novah the other. Sydney's path was clear.

She dove for the spear wielder. Her body crashed into his, hard, and they both tumbled into the grass beneath the dragon's wing. Unfortunately, the Brim recovered first. Sydney scrambled for her swords, but the soldier was on top of her, knee pressed to her chest. The tip of the spear came stabbing downwards.

Sydney caught the soldier's hands just in time. The spear head hovered above her face, edging closer. The dragon's wing coated the sky in ink.

"Sydney!" She heard Lukaris shout from far away. Too far. Sydney lost another inch against the spear.

Come on, Krane.

She managed to move her head to the side just as the spear plunged lower, the point digging slowly into the old wound on her shoulder. She hissed in pain. The soldier smiled down at her.

The sky shifted. For a moment, Sydney saw nothing but startling blue.

Jaws closed over the Brim, ripping him from the ground. The spear fell to the grass. Sydney gasped as the weight lifted off her chest. The soldier's scream sounded high above her as the dragon flung him across the clearing.

With that, the tide of the battle turned. Too few Brims remained, and they knew it. Certainly too few to face a dragon. And so, with the loss of their advantage, the rest of the soldiers exchanged fearful looks, turned, and fled.

Sydney sat up and watched her old allies disappear in the direction of Delm. By morning, half the city would be abuzz with the news. A dragon in Soarden. What did this mean for the war? For the world?

Lukaris materialized nearby, yanking her from her thoughts.

"Sydney?" The word was careful. He extended a hand down, pulling her to her feet. Blood dripped down her arm, but she'd had worse.

"I'm okay," she replied, tone just as measured. The elf nodded and turned away. Sydney smothered a sigh. So much left unsaid.

Princess Koraline and the others hurried from the shelter of the trees. The dragon paced at the clearing's edge, crouched, eyes darting suspiciously from one elf to another. At Koraline's appearance, the tension seemed to fall from the dragon's spiked shoulders. He lowered his head until it was eye level.

"Arkyn!" Koraline chirped. She pushed past Sydney, unafraid.

The air rippled with magic. A strange tearing sound echoed across the grass. Sydney blinked, incredulous, as the dragon began to shrink. To change. Before she could take another breath, a man stood in the dragon's place.

Sydney eyed the dragon turned human. He stood a good head higher than her with an average build, his hair a mop of pure midnight. Younger than she'd expected. Beneath the shadowed strands, his eyes were the same striking blue they'd been in his true form. He wore loose black clothing with pants stuffed into a pair of dark boots, almost reminiscent of Itari's Viridian attire.

Koraline reached the dragon just as his transformation solidified. Tanned face stretched tight with exhaustion, he gave the princess a weary smile.

"Hey, *allska*."

"By the Light, Arkyn. Are you alright?" Koraline demanded. Her hands looked tiny where they gripped his arms.

"Just a little tired," the dragon replied unconvincingly. He swayed on his feet, dark shirt growing wet where it clung to his skin.

"This is Lukaris, Prince of Ithirdas, and his warriors." Sydney felt strange being lumped in with the rest, but she didn't argue. "They're friends. We can trust them."

Arkyn gave the elves a curt nod. Lukaris stepped forward.

"You're a dragon," the *Valen* blurted, eyes wide with awe.

"There's that elvish wit you hear so much about," Arkyn said dryly, deep voice slurring over the words. Then, his eyes fluttered shut, and the dragon collapsed.

"Arkyn!" Koraline cried as her friend landed hard in the grass. She fell to her knees, pillowing his head onto her lap. Flindir rushed to join them while the others huddled around in an uncertain circle.

Flindir lifted the edge of Arkyn's shirt, and they all sucked in a collective breath. Wounds crisscrossed his abdomen, some fresh with blood, others old and bruised. Sydney winced. She knew enough to spot torture when she saw it.

"Who did this to him?" Flindir demanded.

Koraline's eyes became two angry flecks of gold. "Malcolm."

"Malcolm? Malcolm Moor? Angry fellow, giant scar?" Sydney traced an imaginary line with her finger.

The princess' hold on the dragon tightened. "That's him."

Sydney turned to the elves. "Brimhold's new training commander. Looks like Camillea gave him a side project."

"Surely Queen Camillea wasn't involved in our imprisonment," Koraline insisted. She sounded like she was trying to convince herself. "She's always been so kind to me."

Sydney sighed and looked to Lukaris. His face held all the exhaustion she was feeling.

"We'll explain later, Kori, I promise. But right now, we all need to get out of here. Even a dragon won't scare the Brims off for long."

"What about Arkyn? Will he be alright?" Koraline asked desperately. Flindir's hands moved with a determined precision, working to bind the worst of Arkyn's injuries.

"Nothing looks fatal, but I'm no dragon expert. Staying in human form for so long, plus not eating enough and added blood loss..." Flindir muttered to himself. "Then shifting twice in a short period. I don't know. I just don't know. I'm sorry."

Koraline closed her eyes and nodded.

"Not to interrupt," Novah interjected. "But what's he *doing*?"

"By the Light," Itari whispered. Sydney stared.

Arkyn had begun to glow. A faint white light, starting at his chest, radiating outwards. It grew until it encompassed his entire body, hovering like a second skin.

Gods, Sydney thought dumbly. *We're all in over our heads.*

"Incredible," Flindir breathed.

"What is it?" the princess asked. Her hand brushed Arkyn's forehead and passed harmlessly through the aura.

"Light magic. Dragon magic," Lukaris said, some of his old spark returning. Sydney could see his mind turning with questions.

Questions they didn't have time for. Sydney felt Delm's looming presence to the south, the sound of warning bells still ringing in her ears. Her feet itched with the need to run.

While the others talked in hushed voices, Sydney took in the strange band of fugitives. Flindir, Novah, and Koraline seemed relatively uninjured aside from a few cuts and bruises. Itari's hands were wrapped in layers of bandages, and she still favored one of her legs. Lukaris looked half-dead, like a strong wind might split him in two. Meanwhile, Sydney's re-injured shoulder ached where the spear had pierced it, blood crusting on its way down her arm. Finally, their unconscious dragon. Arkyn showed no signs of movement, and he was far too large to carry across Brimhold.

Sydney's eyes met Novah's, and something unspoken passed between them. A resolve. Maybe it was the decision to take charge. Maybe it was a determination to stay strong for the others.

"I sent word to my *tatell* before leaving Ithirdas. They're supposed to meet us at the base of the Western Horn with horses and supplies," the Red Elf spoke up. She said this to the group, but Sydney knew the words were meant for her.

"Right." Sydney gathered her scattered thoughts. *Focus, Krane. Lead.* "Novah, come with me, and we'll work on building a litter to pull the dra— er, Arkyn. The rest of you, get him under the trees. We're too visible here. Rest and get ready to move when we come back."

No one argued or even looked to Lukaris for approval. The threat of death has a way of altering one's priorities.

*****

A good deal of cursing later, Sydney and Novah returned with a makeshift litter of branches and cloaks. Together, they lugged the limp dragon onto the device, securing him as best they could.

After that, there was nothing left to do but continue their desperate flight through the forest.

The night grew chill beneath the trees as Sydney led them further north and west, the ground morphing into waves the closer they got to the mountains. Flindir and Novah huffed with the effort of dragging Arkyn across the wild terrain, but they didn't complain. All the while, Princess Koraline stayed at the dragon's side, her face illuminated by the soft glow on his skin.

To fill the time, and keep themselves awake, the group shared the stories that brought them to each other. Koraline told them of dark days spent in Delm's dungeon, Arkyn's firm resistance, and their strange, inexplicable escape. Sydney's throat tightened at the mermaid's words. What could Camillea want so badly from a dragon? And what had she meant to gain from Koraline's kidnapping?

Meanwhile, Itari explained how the elves managed to escape Firne and mount a rescue for their prince. How they'd fought free of their bonds when their allies appeared. How Raiden's final breath had saved them all. Koraline face went white when she learned of the boy's fate.

"I can still remember him running through the corridors back home," the princess whispered, words thick. "He kept asking to talk to a shark. He was so full of Light. I can't believe he's gone."

Lukaris trudged in silence at the back of their brigade, his angled face lost to the darkness. Still, Sydney felt his anguish in her chest. The breeze stirred the leaves in a sad melody.

Finally, Sydney shared her encounter with Camillea. Her discovery of the impostor queen.

"She's a greyblood?" Novah snapped angrily. "You didn't think to tell me this before?"

"We were a little busy fleeing for our lives," Sydney hissed right back.

"She's been manipulating us all this time," Koraline said. "She attacked Milanthos. My *home*. By the Light, I thought she was my friend."

Sydney didn't have the words to comfort her. She was holding on to her own sanity by a single thread.

They traveled on through the night. After a while, words faded into silence, and the only sound came from wind whispering through the dark branches overhead. Sydney focused on putting one foot in front of the other, mind and body clouded with exhaustion. A hand brushed her shoulder when the first streaks of orange began to coat the sky.

"Sydney," Flindir murmured. "We have to rest. If Camillea catches up to us like this, we're as good as dead anyway."

She turned back and looked at the others. They looked as ragged as she felt.

"Alright," she agreed, though the closeness of Delm still set her on edge. "Let's find a safe spot to camp."

They managed to find a hollowed out crevice between two cliff faces, opening up towards the south. At the very least, they should have fair warning of approaching Brims. The group heaved a collective sigh of relief as they got off their aching feet.

Gods, what a night, Sydney thought to herself, just as a new dawn broke over Soarden.

53

The Savior

P*lease, wake up.*

Koraline had repeated the words over and over in her mind for hours. A prayer or a spell, she didn't know which. Still, Arkyn's eyes remained closed. The strange light still enveloped his body like a shroud.

All of this was Koraline's fault. She'd pressured Arkyn into helping the elves. He'd known he was too weak, but he'd fought the soldiers anyway. For her.

Please, wake up. The princess brushed a strand of midnight hair away from her friend's forehead. Morning rays of sunlight crept across his face. She'd never seen him so peaceful.

"You should get some sleep." Lukaris materialized at her shoulder. He had a way of doing that, like he was a part of the wind instead of merely its master. Behind him, the others were sprawled out in the grass, Flindir's light snores already echoing across their makeshift camp.

"You're one to talk," Koraline replied softly.

"I offered to take first watch," the prince said as he settled down next to her. Koraline watched him closely. Something had changed in him, and it wasn't just his battered appearance. This wasn't the elf that had visited her in the Crystal Keep all her life, bringing her presents and making her laugh. His forest eyes, usually full of joy and life, were hollow. Distant.

"Luka…" The mermaid swallowed. "I'm so sorry. About Raiden. I know what he meant to you."

Lukaris' face tightened with pain. "*Melánethe.* I— I would rather not talk about it."

Koraline took his hand in hers and squeezed. "I understand."

"I'm sorry too, Kori," the *Valen* said. "When you were kidnapped, I should have looked for you. I should have at least tried."

The princess blinked. "Don't be ridiculous. There was nothing you could've done. Besides, I found my own way in the end."

Lukaris glanced at Arkyn's sleeping form. "You certainly did. Still, I'm glad you're safe, *niél.*"

Koraline couldn't help but smile at the old nickname. *Little sister.*

The elf went to release their knotted hands when he froze. The grip on Koraline's fingers tightened.

"How did this happen?" Lukaris demanded. His thumb traced over the long scar on her forearm.

"The first day I woke up in Delm, Malcolm he… he came into my cell. He cut my arm. Took my blood." Koraline shivered at the memory. "It was awful. But not compared to what he did to Arkyn."

Lukaris' face went white as she spoke. Slowly, he drew up his sleeve, fingers grazing a bloodstained bandage. The elf's expression filled her veins with ice.

"What is it? What's wrong?"

"I thought the Brims were just taking some kind of sick trophy," he murmured. He unraveled the cloth, revealing a fresh slice down his arm. Almost a twin of Koraline's old wound.

"They took your blood too?" Koraline whispered. "Why? For what purpose?"

"I don't know," the elf replied. He looked so tired. "But if Camillea is behind it, it can't be good. Blood magic is rare, but I wouldn't put it past her."

Koraline's stomach knotted. She remembered the last time she'd seen Camillea. The anger on her face.

"What should we do?"

Lukaris sighed. "Unfortunately, there's nothing we *can* do at the moment. We'll have to figure this out once we're safe."

Once we're safe. Arkyn had made similar promises. She wasn't sure safety existed for her any longer. That ship sailed when she found Angler on the steps of the Crystal Keep. The night everything changed.

"Try to rest, Kori," Lukaris urged in the silence. He moved away, leaving her alone with her thoughts.

With a sigh, Koraline settled down beside Arkyn. She tried to calm her racing mind, focusing on the forest around her. It was strange, after a lifetime spent in the ocean, to lay beneath the swaying tree branches. The cries of strange birds, the steady creak of the woods. Every sound was foreign.

It's why Koraline almost didn't notice the snap of a twig just outside their camp.

Across from her, Lukaris sat up straight, face tight. Their eyes locked.

"Wake the others," the elf muttered, so quiet it must have been sent on the wind.

Koraline glanced anxiously at the undergrowth as she shook Itari awake. The human warrior, Sydney, already stood near Lukaris, eyes like two shining daggers as they swept the treeline.

"What's going—" Flindir groaned as someone kicked him with a boot. Novah hushed him.

"Maybe it was a squirrel," Sydney mumbled as her hand tightened on a sword hilt.

High in the trees, a bird chirped. Then, closer, a rustle in the bushes. Much too big for a squirrel.

Lukaris nocked an arrow. "Should we run?"

"Run *where?*" Novah hissed. "We're blocked in."

Koraline shuffled behind her friends, throat tight. She imagined soldiers dragging her away. Back to a dark cell with blood-stained dirt. She couldn't. She *wouldn't*.

Next to her, Sydney must have had a similar thought. The former captain stepped forward, face set in stone.

"Enough of this! Show yourself!" Sydney bellowed. Her voice sliced through the morning calm.

"*What are you doing?*" Novah whispered angrily.

Then, as if from nothing, a girl appeared in the middle of camp.

Flindir shrieked. Itari stumbled away, lightning flashing. The others merely froze, jaws to the earth.

The girl hovered above Arkyn, half crouched on bare feet caked in mud. She was small, perched on that strange edge between child and teen, with a mane of frizzy, strawberry hair. Her eyes were dark and feral, face dotted with an array of dirt and freckles.

And she held a dagger that swayed over Arkyn in a way that made Koraline's chest clench.

"Who are you?" Sydney demanded, clearly taken aback.

The girl didn't answer. She shifted from one foot to the other, eyes darting like a caged beast.

"We aren't going to hurt you," Lukaris said softly. His eyes, like Koraline's, were on the knife. "Why don't you put that down?"

The girl's grip tightened around the weapon. The motion sent Koraline stumbling forward. Close enough to see the fear in the girl's eyes. Close enough to see the details of the dagger.

She sucked in a sharp breath.

The blade was as familiar as Arkyn's screams. And Koraline had hoped to never see it again.

"Where did you get that?" Koraline whispered.

The girl's jaw clenched as she lifted a pointed chin. At last, she spoke.

"I took it." Her voice was low and rasping, strained from disuse.

"Took it?" Sydney asked. "From who?"

The girl scowled.

"From the bad man."

Koraline shivered. The blade looked bigger in the girl's hand, but she could never forget it's shape. She could still feel the echo of metal piercing her flesh.

"How did you steal Malcolm's dagger?" Koraline asked around the lump in her throat. The others blinked in varying degrees of shock and confusion.

"Hiding," the girl replied, as if the answer was obvious.

"Hiding? I don't understand. Where were you—" The mermaid froze. A breeze had caught a stray strand of the girl's hair, spinning it up into the sunlight. The strawberry color blazed like fire in the morning light. And with it, pieces began clicking in Koraline's head.

She remembered dark days in a cell when her mind seemed to spiral. Flashes of red at the corner of her vision, like streaks of fire. Objects moving when her eyes shifted. Food appearing when before there had been an empty plate.

A door opening on its own.

Keys tossed in the dirt.

An invisible, impossible savior.

"It was you," Koraline breathed, incredulous. She realized now that the girl's stance over Arkyn wasn't threatening at all. It was protective. "You saved us from the dungeon. I was there with Arkyn, remember?"

The girl relaxed ever so slightly. "Yes."

Koraline bent before the girl, eye level. "We owe you our lives. You don't have to be afraid. No one here will harm you."

She glanced pointedly at her friends. They slowly eased from their stances, confused, but nodding their agreement. Novah was the last to release her hold on her sword hilt. Her face carried a strange expression Koraline couldn't read.

The mysterious girl's eyes flickered suspiciously around the camp, lingering on Koraline. After a moment, she reluctantly lowered Malcolm's dagger, but remained close to Arkyn.

Koraline took a tentative step forward. The girl flinched, but didn't run.

"I'm Koraline. What's your name?"

The girl sniffed. "Wren."

"Wren. What a beautiful name. Did your parents like song birds?"

The girl flinched again. "No parents."

"Oh. I'm sorry. Wren, can you tell me what happened last night? How did you come to be in Delm's dungeon? Why did you rescue us?"

Koraline could feel her companions leaning forward around her, hungry for answers. But she kept her eyes fixed on the small girl.

"The bad man... took me. Made me... hide. Listen." Wren's words came in short bursts, as if she wasn't used to speaking for so long. "I listened to... him. To Arkyn."

Wren paused, glancing down at the still dragon. She said his name with reverence.

"The bad man said... he knew if I lied. Would know if I tried to leave." Wren tapped her temple as she spoke. "But last night... he was going to kill him. Arkyn. He always said he would but..."

The girl's breath caught. Koraline placed a soft hand on Wren's shoulder.

"It's okay. He's not here. He can't hurt you."

Wren closed her eyes, continuing. "I had to try and stop him. I hid… from the bad man. Took the keys. His knife. He didn't even notice. Gave you the keys. But I couldn't stay. If he came back and saw you gone…"

"So, you followed us," Lukaris marveled. The girl nodded.

"That was very brave of you, Wren," Koraline said, squeezing her shoulder. "Thank you."

And in a blink, the girl vanished. Koraline gasped.

"What in the shadowed hell?" Sydney spluttered, spinning.

A second later, Wren appeared on the other side of the princess, crouched, as if trying to hide in Koraline's shadow. Lukaris took in a sharp breath, his gaze going to Novah.

"Was that… magic?" Flindir whispered.

"Not Light magic," Novah replied grimly. Her face held a deep dread. "She's a greyblood."

Koraline looked to the small girl in wonder. She thought greybloods were all but extinct, and now she had learned of two in a single day. Her head spun at what this could mean. For them and for Soarden.

"Greyblood?" Wren muttered. A lump caught in Koraline's throat. The poor girl didn't even know what she was. "Bad man said… demon. Monster. Do I… have to leave?"

Koraline wrapped both arms around her, brushing back a strand of orange hair. She looked to Lukaris pleadingly.

"Of course not, Wren," Lukaris said softly. He gave the girl a comforting smile. "You will come with us."

Novah's mouth sat in a flat line. Sydney glared at the Red Elf as if daring her to speak.

Koraline didn't care about whatever silent battle raged between her companions. Her only concern was for the girl in her arms and the sleeping dragon at her feet. Her eyes caught on the menacing glint of Malcolm's dagger. She pulled Wren closer.

"You're safe now. We're never going back to that place."

54

Beginnings and Endings

Sydney knew she was dreaming, but she couldn't seem to wake up.

She stood in a dark forest. All around, the trees ached and moaned like restless ghosts. Bark drifted off the trunks in thin, black flakes, and the grass charred to ash beneath her boots. Somewhere, behind the decaying oaks and the starless sky, something watched her. Stalking her.

Sydney tried to run, but her body felt heavy as lead. She couldn't move her feet anymore than she could open her mouth to scream.

Wake up, wake up, wake up.

Shadow-borne drifted from cracks in the wood, each taking the shape of some great beast. Wolves and bears, riphounds and trolls. Black as ink, with the same hollow, pinprick eyes. Sydney shuddered. Their whispered snarls echoed in the air.

But something was wrong. The shadow-borne seemed… unsettled. Their misty outlines shivered. The shadow-borne's fear sent goosebumps across her skin. What could frighten monsters? The thing that watched Sydney from the trees grew closer.

Then, a voice like breaking bones, like dripping blood. The last breath before death.

"*Escaped?*" the voice snarled. It was both a shout and a whisper. "*We were so close, and you let them escape?*"

Sydney didn't know who the voice was talking to, but there was no reply that she could hear. The shadow-borne cowered under the entity's weight.

"*I have waited for a millennia. Do not speak to me of patience!*" the voice bellowed to Sydney's right. She finally managed to drag herself behind the feeble shelter of a broken tree. There was a pause, and a howling wind whipped cinders into the sky. She smothered a cough behind shaking hands.

"*I don't want apologies. I want Soarden on its knees.*" Another pause. "*Very well. Another chance. But, do not fail me again.*"

The ashen air swirled even tighter, a threat and a promise. Sydney wheezed, unable to hold back the noise any longer. *Damn.*

"*What was that?*" the voice murmured. Sydney held her breath.

"Captain Krane?"

Silver eyes hovered among the trees, set at a human height. But there was nothing human about them. Shining irises swam in a sea of black.

"Captain Krane, wake up."

"Who…?"

"Captain Krane!"

Sydney jerked awake. Morning sunlight filtered in through the leaves. Golden eyes replaced the silver.

"Are you alright, Captain?" Princess Koraline asked. The mermaid knelt next to Sydney, hands raised helplessly.

Sydney struggled to a sitting position, eyes blinking away the remains of her dream. She shivered in the autumn air.

"Fine. And I'm not a captain anymore, Princess."

"Oh." Koraline winced. She brushed a nervous hand through her bright hair. "I'm sorry. Lady Krane?"

"I'm no lady either," Sydney replied, amusement coloring her tone. For a royal, the mermaid had a gentle air about her. "Sydney is fine."

"Right," Koraline replied with an embarrassed smile. She rocked back onto her heals.

Sydney rubbed her eyes and took in the rest of their camp. Lukaris sat across the way, speaking to Wren in a soft voice. Arkyn remained unmoving amid his Light cocoon, while Flindir paced the perimeter of their hollow.

The group of fugitives had made their way to the base of the Western Horn, a towering mountain that loomed to the north of Delm. They'd managed to find a hidden indent in the hills, closed off and isolated. Flindir spent days adding vines and leaves to further shelter them from prying eyes.

Three days. That's how long they'd been waiting for Ithirdis to send help. That's how long they'd waited for Camillea to track them down and finish what she started.

For Sydney, the wait was worse than the fight.

Sighing, she began to weave her tangled hair into a loose plait. "Where are Novah and Itari?"

"Hunting and scouting," Koraline answered. "They left just after dawn."

Sydney looked to the sky. Based on the sun, they were still several hours from midday. She stifled a groan. If nightfall came again without any news, she might just make the hike to Ithirdas herself.

Lukaris looked up then, as if reading her thoughts, and their eyes locked. For a moment, Sydney thought she saw some of the old, familiar Lukaris looking back at her. The one that had taken her deep into the Wornwood on a summer day, just to see something new. The one that treated her like a guest instead of an enemy, even when he had no reason to.

But the moment passed like a breeze, and Lukaris glanced away, his green gaze cast downwards and sullen. The hope that sprung up in Sydney's chest dropped to her stomach. The exchange verified what she had already feared.

No matter what happened next, there was no going back to the way things were.

*****

The day passed slowly. Achingly slow. Sydney paced and paced until she'd worn a dirt path through the brittle mountain grass.

"Please sit down," Flindir begged. "You're making my feet hurt."

"They should've been back by now."

She was right. Evening crept in at the forest's edge, firelight growing stronger as the sky turned a dull and deepening gray. Novah and Itari were long past their normal scouting time.

Flindir frowned. "Should we go look for them?"

Lukaris rose to his feet. "I'll go. Flin, you and Sydney guard the camp."

"You are *not* going off on your own."

"And I'm not leaving an unconscious dragon and two civilians any less defended than I have to," Lukaris argued.

"I can come," Koraline volunteered.

"I can hide," Wren offered. She vanished between blinks.

"Absolutely not."

The princess scowled. "I'm not useless, you know."

"That's not what I meant…"

"By the gods!" Sydney exclaimed. This was getting them no where. "*I'll go.*"

She turned on her heels before anyone could protest. She'd almost made it to the wall of undergrowth before a hand caught at her elbow.

Temper flaring, Sydney spun to face a grim-faced Lukaris.

"Look, I'm perfectly capable of—"

Lukaris put a finger to his lips.

"Did you hear that?" He slowly released her arm. Behind him, the others stood like statues, alert and uneasy.

Sydney strained her ears. Sure enough, something large made its way towards their hideout. *Straight* for the hideout. As if it knew exactly where they were. A chill ran up Sydney's spine. Had Novah and Itari been captured? Were they being forced to lead their enemies back to camp?

Lukaris whipped towards Koraline. "Hide. And if things go south, run."

Wren and the princess formed a wall in front of Arkyn, Koraline's face turning rigid and stubborn.

"We're not going anywhere. We're in this together."

Brave, Sydney thought. *Stupid, but brave.*

Before Lukaris could respond, the noise stopped. Several agonizing seconds passed.

Then, from the woods, a bird call.

A signal. Not as natural as Raiden's all those weeks ago, but just as lovely.

Novah surged through the undergrowth and woven vines, her scarlet hair the strongest color among the darkening trees. She led a horse by its reins with an uncharacteristically wide smile on her face. Atop the mare, sat Darian. The woman's eyes kept flicking to Novah. The relief on her face was palpable.

More came, a line of horses. Some without a rider, others carrying elves and humans alike. A few Sydney recognized, Yunara and Rovin from Firne's *tatell*, but others were new and foreign. From the way the humans blended with the Ithirdi, Sydney could only guess they were the refugees from Brimhold's burnt villages. The ones she now knew were destroyed at Camillea's command.

Itari brought up the rear, and at the sight of her, the tension broke. Flindir ran up to the Viridian, lifting and spinning her in his arms, laughing with joy. Koraline wrapped an arm around Wren's bony shoulders, looking unsure but excited, while Wren's eyes darted from one newcomer to the next. Lukaris clapped Darian on the back as she dismounted her horse. He looked happier than Sydney had seen him since Raiden's death.

"You came," Lukaris said with an exhale. Darian raised an eyebrow. "You doubted?"

"It couldn't have been easy," Lukaris replied. "And the path home will be even worse."

They fell into discussion, debating the best route back across Brimhold to safety. Sydney turned away to find Itari staring at her. The elf's expression was unreadable.

"*Scolas*," Itari began. Her tone made Sydney's throat tighten.

"What? What is it?"

Itari opened her mouth to speak, hesitated, and then stepped aside to reveal the line of horses behind her.

A woman stood next to a gray horse, separated from the others. Waves of dark hair hung past her shoulders, and brown eyes shimmered from a heart-shaped face. She was thin, exceptionally so. A much too large linen dress hung from her limbs like drying laundry. Her hand clutched the horse's mane beside her. It seemed to be rooting her in place.

Sydney's breath caught. Somewhere, Itari was saying her name, but it sounded like a distant echo.

The woman looked up.

Their eyes met.

And Sydney fell.

Back in time. Days spent in a loft above a shop. Golden sunsets on the beach. Adventures in the Lost Wood.

All of it burned to ash. Or so she thought.

"Sydney." The woman took a small step forward. Her voice was impossibly the same. Like the world had aged around it.

Sydney mirrored the step, backwards, away. Her head spun.

"Abi?"

Some part of Sydney noticed that the conversation around her had dimmed. Elves and humans watched the two women. Wondering. Waiting.

Twin tears spilled out of Abigail's eyes. As they ran down her cheeks, the final dam inside Sydney burst. She surged forward, pushing past anyone in her path, not stopping until her arms were wrapped around Abi's shoulders.

Sydney hugged her sister as the last rays of daylight slipped from the sky.

Acknowledgments

You never realize how many people have impacted your life and work until you try and put it on paper. Thank you—

To my parents, for being my rocks, my support, my heart. I wouldn't be me without you, and I wouldn't have the strength to follow my dreams without your hands in mine.

To my sister. I love you even though you slapped me that one time.

To my grandparents, for encouraging my love of reading from a young age.

To Sam. I miss you every single day. You will always be my hero, my guardian angel.

To my incredible beta readers and friends: Grace, Anna, Mario, Lisa.

To Grace, for being my first reader and cheerleader. My life is better every day you're in it. Thank you for your endless support and love.

To Anna, for getting this book over the finish line. Without you, I may never have gained the courage to follow my dreams. You inspire me constantly, and you are the best self-publishing buddy a girl could ask for.

To Mario, for your kindness and encouragement. The way you show up for your friends is a beautiful thing. I'm so glad you're in my life.

To Lisa, for your undying strength and amazing heart. Thank you for creating a safe space for me to be myself.

To Kelly, for an incredible book cover, and your patience as I learned how to do this publishing thing.

To Mandi. For the hours spent in coffee shops, and the late night brainstorming sessions where these characters were born. Thank you for your renewed passion for this project, all these years later. For a beautiful map and logo. For continued friendship.

To all the other friends and family that have celebrated this accomplishment and shared my story. There are too many of you to name, but I love and thank you all.

About the Author

E.M. Downey is the creator of Spellcast Books and the author of YA Fantasy novel, *Blood of Briar.* Born and raised in Kerrville, TX, she's spent her life in local coffee shops, writing stories and building worlds. When she's not writing, she enjoys hanging with her dog, Suki, playing video games, and visiting America's national parks.

You can connect with me on:

🌐 https://www.spellcastbooks.com